How
I Found America

Anzia Yezierska

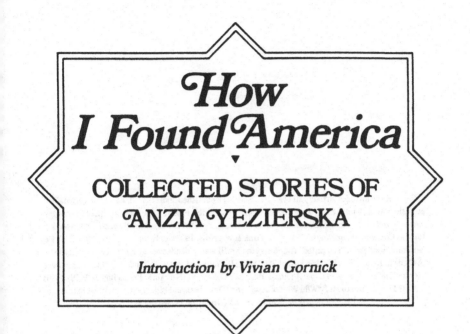

How I Found America

COLLECTED STORIES OF ANZIA YEZIERSKA

Introduction by Vivian Gornick

A Karen & Michael Braziller Book

PERSEA BOOKS / NEW YORK

Acknowledgments

This volume includes virtually all of Anzia Yezierska's published short fiction. Part I was originally published in book form as *Hungry Hearts* (Boston: Houghton Mifflin, 1920) and reprinted in *Hungry Hearts and Other Stories* (New York: Persea Books, 1985). Part II was originally published in book form as *Children of Loneliness* (New York: Funk & Wagnalls, 1923); only the interview, "You Can't Be an Immigrant Twice" is omitted. The stories in Part III were uncollected during Yezierska's lifetime. "A Chair in Heaven," "A Window Full of Sky," "Take Up Your Bed and Walk," and "The Open Cage" were later included in *The Open Cage: An Anzia Yezierska Collection* (New York: Persea Books, 1979). "This Is What $10,000 Did to Me," "Wild Winter Love," and "One Thousand Pages of Research" were collected in *Hungry Hearts and Other Stories* (New York: Persea Books, 1985).

For information, write the publisher:
Persea Books
90 Broad Street, Suite 2100
New York, NY 10004

Library of Congress Cataloging-in-Publication Data

Yezierska, Anzia, 1880?–1970.
How I found America : collected stories of Anzia Yezierska / introduction by Vivian Gornick.
    p.   cm.
1. Jews—New York (N.Y.)—Fiction.   2. Lower East Side (New York, N.Y.)—Fiction.
3. New York (N.Y.)—Fiction.   I. Title.
        PS3547.E95A6   1991
813'.52—dc20   90-23771

ISBN 0-89255-211-5

Designed by REM Studio, Inc.
Typeset in Clearface Regular by Keystrokes, Lenox, Massachusetts.
Manufactured in the United States of America

Contents

Introduction

She was a misfit all her life. Throughout the years she saw herself standing on the street with her nose pressed against the bakery window: hungry and shut out. No matter what happened, she felt marginal. Not belonging became her identity, and then her subject. After she began to write, it was her necessity. In *Red Ribbon on a White Horse* the relief she feels at finding herself poor again in the Thirties is palpable. She had this in common with other talented neurotics—Jack Kerouac, George Gissing, Jean Rhys—who also managed to keep themselves poverty-stricken and socially outcast, for very much the same reason.

Anzia Yezierska was born in the 1880s in a village in the Russian part of Poland into a family of seven children. The father was religious, the mother passive, and the children wild to survive. Sometime around 1890 the family emigrated to America. They got off the boat in New York and the oldest brother, who'd preceded them by a year or two, brought them home to a tenement flat on the Lower East Side. Their life as poor immigrant Jews had begun.

The brothers managed to get themselves educated. The girls worked in sweatshops, married early and repeated their mother's life. Anzia was the youngest: intense and explosive, loudmouthed, impassioned. Where it had come from—this extraordinary rebelliousness of spirit—no one knew. But there it was. Her life as a misfit had begun. The men in the family recoiled from her, the women were beguiled but didn't know what to do with her. She seemed possessed of a fever nothing could reduce, a restlessness no one could satisfy, some hunger for experience that had begun growing the minute she learned to read. Anger and frustration sent her flying daily. She seemed literally, in the incomparable Yiddish phrase, to "throw herself from the walls."

Then, somehow, she got out. It was an age of anxious reformers, guilty liberals. Her passionate intelligence engaged everyone whose path she crossed. The night school teacher sent her on. She took a class at Columbia, found her way to John Dewey's seminar. Stirred and excited, she walked into the famous educator's office. She leaned across his desk, burning-eyed and red-haired. "I want to make from myself a person!" Dewey was enchanted. Middle-aged, idealistic, WASP, he never knew what hit him. Of course, he said, and took her on, gave her a place in his seminar and in his projects.

They were exotics to one another and, very soon, objects of romantic fantasy. But they were both sexual innocents. When Dewey made his move, Anzia was horrified. In less than a minute she lost him, completely and irrevocably. Next day in his office he was stiff, cold, unreachable: literally, as well as emotionally. From then on Dewey blazed in her psyche as the genteel America forever beyond her grasp.

During all this tumult Anzia had (in confusion and chaos) married and discarded two husbands, borne and half-discarded a child, *and* been writing down her experiences in her "I want to make from myself a person!" voice, the one that made the page jump with violent life. These pieces began to get published. In 1919 one of the stories was chosen for Edward J. O'Brien's *The Best Short Stories,* and in 1920 a collection of them was published under the title *Hungry Hearts.* As if this weren't extraordinary enough, Hollywood bought the book, paid Yezierska $10,000 for it, and brought her out to California to write the screenplay. She spent some months there, made a lot of money, remained as lost and angry and forlorn out of the ghetto as she had been, gasping for breath, in it. What could she do but return to New York and write it all down? The words continued to flood the page. Five novels were published, and another story collection as well.

By the Thirties she was broke, working on the WPA Writers Project, unable to get her stories published. The slightly hallucinated cry of Yezierska's immigrant anguish did not mesh readily with Depression realism. The words continued to pour from her pen, this time for the drawer alone. Now began her true exile.

Sometime during these years she must have understood that she was doomed, was never going to know one easy minute inside her own skin. Now, and for the rest of her life, she was between worlds, unable to go forward, unable to go back, wandering in a purgatory from which none could release her. Inevitably, people between worlds alienate those who occupy the territory in which they themselves have only one foot. She was staring into unabating loneliness.

For years nothing she wrote saw the light of day. In 1950 her memoir, *Red Ribbon on a White Horse*, was published, but the book went unresponded to. She lived on in obscurity and semi-poverty until 1970, a vivid presence on New York's Upper West Side, intense and voluble, announcing daily her passion and her necessity.

In the story "My Own People," Yezierska, speaking in the third person, writes: "Would she ever become articulate enough to express beautifully what she saw and felt? What had she, after all, but a stifling, sweatshop experience, a meager night-school education and this wild, blind hunger to release the dumbness that choked her?"

In "How I Found America," speaking in the first person, she says to the night-school teacher, "Do you think like the others that I'm all wrapped up in self?"

The teacher tells her, "No—no—but too intense."

Yezierska cries, "I hate to be so all the time intense. But how can I help it? Everything always drives me back in myself."

The intelligent teacher replies, "Some of us...have a sort of divine fire which if it does not find expression turns into smoke. This egoism and self-centeredness which troubles you is only the smoke of repression."

Inevitably, in Yezierska's work, whether the narrator speaks in the first person or in the third, the story is divided between the time the character announces her "wild, blind hunger" for her own life, and the time she realizes she is trapped in a "repression" from which hope of release is dim. The strength of this simple repetition is such that it achieves metaphoric status. Yezierska the immigrant, Yezierska the woman, Yezierska the permanently bereft child are all trapped in that "I want to make from myself a person!" voice. They galvanize one another. With each cry, the words cut deeper, the situation feels more urgent. The character begins to sound as though she were born to speak her piece in this place at this time, and in no other.

In the 1920s the cry of the immigrant locked out of mainstream life was heard as something startling, painful, significant. The First World War had left the century up for grabs. The idea of the democracy glimmered with new anger and new hope. It echoed the cry of middle-class women conscious enough to claim they were being locked out of their lives. After sixty years of terrible struggle, suffrage had just been won. The idea of the New Woman was still an open wound in American life. Many novels of the time reflect national disturbance over the question of independence for women. Yezierska's immigrant girl, spilling over with her "wild, blind hunger" to live her life, spoke eloquently—on every score—to the moment.

In Yezierska, the writer, the time, and the experience seem profoundly well-met. This, of course, is why we still read her. Her character remains compelling in exactly the same way that Jack Kerouac's adolescent traveler is compelling, or George Gissing's unhappy writer, or Jean Rhys' seduced-and-abandoned heroine: they all speak so well to the moment in which they were born. Each of these writers, working out of an extraordinary sense of bereftness—personal and neurotic—created a character and a world that mirrored the times and haunted the reader. Kerouac on the road was Huckleberry Finn come again, at a moment in American social history when the need to break out was paramount; Gissing's hopelessly impoverished man of letters speaks directly to the spiritual straitjacket of late Victorian England; Rhys' woman adrift, repeatedly left "all smashed up" in a nameless hotel in a foreign city, is an essence of urban Depression life. Yezierska's immigrant girl, frantic with social repression, takes her place beside these fictional creatures made memorable by virtue of their timeliness.

The immigrant experience is Yezierska's idiom, but the subject is original loss. The bakery against whose window her nose is pressed is not America, it is her own unfrightened self. At the end of *Red Ribbon on a White Horse* Yezierska writes, "With a sudden sense of clarity I realized the battle I thought I was waging against the world had been against myself, against the Jew in me." By which, of course, she means the shamed and fearful self of which she will never be free.

This insight was Yezierska's real wisdom, and her obsession as well. She saw the thing clearly and unrestrainedly, in one headlong rush: without shape, form, or development. Pent-up, reckless, overwhelming, it poured out again and again, at the beginning of her life and at the end. It's not that the subject is explored better, or less better, in this story or that novel. There is no subject, really. The subject is the thing itself: the sound of that unleashed voice announcing, in turbulence and tumult, its hunger and its necessity.

In this sense Yezierska resembles Thomas Wolfe more than any other American writer: language used like a river bursting its floodgates, language by the rushing mile, language the writer stops up, cuts off at one length or another, calls a story or a novel, but really it's the extraordinary ongoingness of that voice—that hungry, demanding, ruthless, clear-sighted voice—that is memorable.

She is like Wolfe also in that she is her only character, the longing for her own life the thing that seizes her repeatedly by the throat, drives her to find release in the writing. Like the impassioned southerner, Yezierska too stands inside her own need, fierce, compelled, stripped of shame, amazed by its awfulness and its power.

Repeatedly, she exhausts the reader—here again like Wolfe—and repeatedly, she seduces the reader anew. Again and again, in the most unexpected places, out of a rush of hurricane-force prose, suddenly the page is calm, radiant with clarity, shrewdness, detachment. Yezierska sees herself as she is seen. She knows how she looks in the eyes of the world. We feel the electric power of her intelligence and we are startled into experiencing her again, as though for the first time:

On Hester Street she overhears a man describing her to another man as the one with "the starved-dog look in her eyes."

In a crucial conversation with Zalmon the fish peddler—a man of unexpected dimension—she is told she "belongs to the company of cripples."

In another conversation, the Dewey character—variously called John Barnes or John Morrow—tells her, "You don't love me. You only dramatize your want of love." She hears him and thinks, "Was it possible? Could it be true? . . . . that my suffering was only acting? [my] pain unreal?"

In Hollywood she lets Will Rogers say to her, "Sad sad sad little sister. You got success on a tearjerker the hard way. Must you fiddle the same tune forever? Suppose you give us another number?"

At which point she observes, "My obsession with my murderous ego, which had driven people from me on Hester Street, was now catching up with me in Hollywood."

We see the helplessness of her circumstance, and our feeling for her plight deepens. She is an essence of the alienated immigrant, and of the alienating, independent woman. Her situation is so real, so human, so crucial. She is destined to eat herself alive forever. We all see that. And we see also that—she refuses.

That's the thing finally about Yezierska. She is one of the great refuseniks of the world. She refuses to accept life's meanness and littleness. She refuses to accommodate herself to loneliness of the spirit. She refuses to curb emotional ambition. She's an immigrant? She's a woman? Her hunger is voracious? intrusive? exhausting? *Still* she refuses. And on a big scale. We cannot turn away from her. Obsessing as grandly as the Ancient Mariner, her words continue, even now seventy years after they were written, to grab us by the collar. They shake and demand, compel, and remind. Attention must be paid. "I want to make from myself a person!"

The performance is astonishing.

VIVIAN GORNICK
NEW YORK CITY, 1991

I.
HUNGRY
HEARTS

Wings

"**M**y heart chokes in me like in a prison! I'm dying for a little love and I got nobody—nobody!" wailed Shenah Pessah, as she looked out of the dismal basement window.

It was a bright Sunday afternoon in May, and into the gray, cheerless, janitor's basement a timid ray of sunlight announced the day of spring.

"Oi weh! Light!" breathed Shenah Pessah, excitedly, throwing open the sash. "A little light in the room for the first time!" And she stretched out her hands hungrily for the warming bit of sun.

The happy laughter of the shopgirls standing on the stoop with their beaux and the sight of the young mothers with their husbands and babies fanned anew the consuming fire in her breast.

"I'm not jealous!" she gasped, chokingly. "My heart hurts too deep to want to tear from them their luck to happiness. But why should they live and enjoy life and why must I only *look on* how they are happy?"

She clutched at her throat like one stifled for want of air. "What is the matter with you? Are you going out of your head? For what is your crying? Who will listen to you? Who gives a care what's going to become from you?"

Crushed by her loneliness, she sank into a chair. For a long time she sat motionless, finding drear fascination in the mocking faces traced in the patches of the torn plaster. Gradually, she became aware of a tingling warmth playing upon her cheeks. And with a revived breath, she drank in the miracle of the sunlit wall.

"Ach!" she sighed. "Once a year the sun comes to light up even this dark cellar, so why shouldn't the High One send on me too a little brightness?"

This new wave of hope swept aside the fact that she was the "greenhorn" janitress, that she was twenty-two and dowryless, and, according to the traditions of her people, condemned to be shelved aside as an unmated thing—a creature of pity and ridicule.

"I can't help it how old I am or how poor I am!" she burst out to the deaf and dumb air. "I want a little life! I want a little joy!"

The bell rang sharply, and as she turned to answer the call, she saw a young man at the doorway—a framed picture of her innermost dreams.

The stranger spoke.

Shenah Pessah did not hear the words, she heard only the music of his voice. She gazed fascinated at his clothes—the loose Scotch tweeds, the pongee shirt, a bit open at the neck, but she did not see him or the things he wore. She only felt an irresistible presence seize her soul. It was as though the god of her innermost longings had suddenly taken shape in human form and lifted her in mid-air.

"Does the janitor live here?" the stranger repeated.

Shenah Pessah nodded.

"Can you show me the room to let?"

"Yes, right away, but wait only a minute," stammered Shenah Pessah, fumbling for the key on the shelf.

"Don't fly into the air!" She tried to reason with her wild, throbbing heart, as she walked upstairs with him. In an effort to down the chaos of emotion that shook her she began to talk nervously: "Mrs. Stein who rents out the room ain't going to be back till the evening, but I can tell you the price and anything you want to know. She's a grand cook and you can eat by her your breakfast and dinner—" She did not have the slightest notion of what she was saying, but talked on in a breathless stream lest he should hear the loud beating of her heart.

"Could I have a drop-light put in here?" the man asked, as he looked about the room.

Shenah Pessah stole a quick, shy glance at him. "Are you maybe a teacher or a writing man?"

"Yes, sometimes I teach," he said, studying her, drawn by the struggling soul of her that cried aloud to him out of her eyes.

"I could tell right away that you must be some kind of a somebody," she said, looking up with wistful worship in her eyes. "Ach, how grand it must be to live only for learning and thinking."

"Is this your home?"

"I never had a home since I was eight years old. I was living by strangers even in Russia."

"Russia?" he repeated with quickened attention. So he was in their midst, the people he had come to study. The girl with her hungry eyes and intense eagerness now held a new interest for him.

John Barnes, the youngest instructor of sociology in his university, congratulated himself at his good fortune in encountering such a splendid type for his research. He was preparing his thesis on the "Educational Problems of the Russian Jews," and in order to get into closer touch with his subject, he had determined to live on the East Side during his spring and summer vacation.

He went on questioning her, unconsciously using all the compelling power that made people open their hearts to him. "And how long have you been here?"

"Two years already."

"You seem to be fond of study. I suppose you go to night-school?"

"I never yet stepped into a night-school since I came to America. From where could I get the time? My uncle is such an old man he can't do much and he got already used to leave the whole house on me."

"You stay with your uncle, then?"

"Yes, my uncle sent for me the ticket for America when my aunt was yet living. She got herself sick. And what could an old man like him do with only two hands?"

"Was that sufficient reason for you to leave your homeland?"

"What did I have out there in Savel that I should be afraid to lose? The cows that I used to milk had it better than me. They got at least enough to eat and me slaving from morning till night went around hungry."

"You poor child!" broke from the heart of the man, the scientific inquisition of the sociologist momentarily swept away by his human sympathy.

Who had ever said "poor child" to her—and in such a voice? Tears gathered in Shenah Pessah's eyes. For the first time she mustered the courage to look straight at him. The man's face, his voice, his bearing, so different from any one she had ever known, and yet what was there about him that made her so strangely at ease with him? She went on talking, led irresistibly by the friendly glow in his eyes.

"I got yet a lot of luck. I learned myself English from a Jewish English reader, and one of the boarders left me a grand book. When I only begin to read, I forget I'm on this world. It lifts me on wings with high thoughts." Her whole face and figure lit up with animation as she poured herself out to him.

"So even in the midst of these sordid surroundings were 'wings' and 'high thoughts,'" he mused. Again the gleam of the visionary—the eternal desire to reach out and up, which was the predominant racial trait of the Russian immigrant.

"What is the name of your book?" he continued, taking advantage of this providential encounter.

"The book is 'Dreams,' by Olive Schreiner."

"H—m," he reflected. "So these are the 'wings' and 'high thoughts.' No wonder the blushes—the tremulousness. What an opportunity for a psychological test-case, and at the same time I could help her by pointing the way out of her nebulous emotionalism and place her feet firmly on earth." He made a quick, mental note of certain books that he would place in her hands and wondered how she would respond to them.

"Do you belong to a library?"

"Library? How? Where?"

Her lack of contact with Americanizing agencies appalled him.

"I'll have to introduce you to the library when I come to live here," he said.

"Ci-i! You really like it, the room?" Shenah Pessah clapped her hands in a burst of uncontrollable delight.

"I like the room very much, and I shall be glad to take it if you can get it ready for me by next week."

Shenah Pessah looked up at the man. "Do you mean it? You really want to come and live here, in this place? The sky is falling to the earth!"

"Live here?" Most decidedly he would live here. He became suddenly enthusiastic. But it was the enthusiasm of the scientist for the specimen of his experimentation—of the sculptor for the clay that would take form under his touch.

"I'm coming here to live—" He was surprised at the eager note in his voice, the sudden leaven of joy that surged through his veins. "And I'm going to teach you to read sensible books, the kind that will help you more than your dream book."

Shenah Pessah drank in his words with a joy that struck back as fear lest this man—the visible sign of her answered prayer—would any moment be snatched up and disappear in the heavens where he belonged. With a quick leap toward him she seized his hand in both her own. "Oi, mister! Would you like to learn me English lessons too? I'll wash for you your shirts for it. If you would even only talk to me, it would be more to me than all the books in the world."

He instinctively recoiled at this outburst of demonstrativeness. His eyes narrowed and his answer was deliberate. "Yes, you ought to learn English," he said, resuming his professional tone, but the girl was too overwrought to notice the change in his manner.

"There it is," he thought to himself on his way out. "The whole gamut of the Russian Jew—the pendulum swinging from abject servility to boldest aggressiveness."

Shenah Pessah remained standing and smiling to herself after Mr. Barnes left. She did not remember a thing she had said. She only felt herself whirling in space, millions of miles beyond the earth. The god of dreams had arrived and nothing on earth could any longer hold her down.

Then she hurried back to the basement and took up the broken piece of mirror that stood on the shelf over the sink and gazed at her face trying to see herself through his eyes. "Was it only pity that made him stop to talk to me? Or can it be that he saw what's inside me?"

Her eyes looked inward as she continued to talk to herself in the mirror. "God from the world!" she prayed. "I'm nothing and nobody now, but ach! How beautiful I would become if only the light from his eyes would fall on me!"

Covering her flushed face with her hands as if to push back the tumult of desire that surged within her, she leaned against the wall. "Who are you to want such a man?" she sobbed.

"But no one is too low to love God, the Highest One. There is no high in love and there is no low in love. Then why am I too low to love him?"

"Shenah Pessah!" called her uncle angrily. "What are you standing there like a yok, dreaming in the air? Don't you hear the tenants knocking on the pipes? They are hollering for the hot water. You let the fire go out."

At the sound of her uncle's voice all her "high thoughts" fled. The mere reminder of the furnace with its ashes and cinders smothered her buoyant spirits and again she was weighed down by the strangling yoke of her hateful, daily round.

It was evening when she got through with her work. To her surprise she did not feel any of the old weariness. It was as if her feet danced under her. Then from the open doorway of their kitchen she overheard Mrs. Melker, the matchmaker, talking to her uncle.

"Motkeh, the fish-peddler, is looking for a wife to cook him his eating and take care on his children," she was saying in her shrill, grating voice.

"So I thought to myself this is a golden chance for Shenah Pessah to grab. You know a girl in her years and without money, a single man wouldn't give a look on her."

Shenah Pessah shuddered. She wanted to run away from the branding torture of their low talk, but an unreasoning curiosity drew her to listen.

"Living is so high," went on Mrs. Melker, "that single men don't want to marry themselves even to *young* girls, except if they can get themselves into a family with money to start them up in business. It is Shenah Pessah's luck yet that Motkeh likes good eating and he can't stand it any more the meals in a restaurant. He heard from people what a good cook and housekeeper Shenah Pessah is, so he sent me around to tell you he would take her as she stands without a cent."

Mrs. Melker dramatically beat her breast. "I swear I shouldn't live to go away from here alive, I shouldn't live to see my own children married if I'm talking this match for the few dollars that Motkeh will pay me for it, but because I want to do something good for a poor orphan. I'm a mother, and it weeps in me my heart to see a girl in her years and not married."

"And who'll cook for me my eating, if I'll let her go?" broke out her uncle angrily. "And who'll do me my work? Didn't I spend out fifty dollars to send for her the ticket to America? Oughtn't I have a little use from her for so many dollars I laid out on her?"

"Think on God!" remonstrated Mrs. Melker. "The girl is an orphan and time is pushing itself on her. Do you want her to sit till her braids grow gray, before you'll let her get herself a man? It stands in the Talmud that a man should take the last bite away from his mouth to help an orphan get married. You'd beg yourself out a place in heaven in the next world—"

"In America a person can't live on hopes for the next world. In America everybody got to look out for himself. I'd have to give up the janitor's work to let her go, and then where would I be?"

"You lived already your life. Give her also a chance to lift up her head in the world. Couldn't you get yourself in an old man's home?"

"These times you got to have money even in an old man's home. You know how they say, if you oil the wheels you can ride. With dry hands you can't get nothing in America."

"So you got no pity on an orphan and your own relation? All her young years she choked herself in darkness and now comes already a little light for her, a man that can make a good living wants her—"

"And who'll have pity on me if I'll let her out from my hands? Who is this Motkeh, anyway? Is he good off? Would I also have a place where to lay my old head? Where stands he out with his pushcart?"

"On Essex Street near Delancey."

"Oi-i! You mean Motkeh Pelz? Why, I know him yet from years ago. They say his wife died him from hunger. She had to chew the earth before she could beg herself out a cent from him. By me Shenah Pessah has at least enough to eat and shoes on her feet. I ask you only is it worth already to grab a man if you got to die from hunger for it?"

Shenah Pessah could listen no longer.

"Don't you worry yourself for me," she commanded, charging into the room. "Don't take pity on my years. I'm living in America, not in Russia. I'm not hanging on anybody's neck to support me. In America, if a girl earns her living, she can be fifty years old and without a man, and nobody pities her."

Seizing her shawl, she ran out into the street. She did not know where her feet carried her. She had only one desire—to get away. A fierce rebellion against everything and everybody raged within her and goaded her on until she felt herself choked with hate.

All at once she visioned a face and heard a voice. The blacker, the more stifling the ugliness of her prison, the more luminous became the light of the miraculous stranger who had stopped for a moment to talk to her. It was as though inside a pit of darkness the heavens opened and hidden hopes began to sing.

Her uncle was asleep when she returned. In the dim gaslight she looked at his yellow, care-crushed face with new compassion in her heart. "Poor old man!" she thought, as she turned to her room. "Nothing beautiful never happened to him. What did he have in life outside the worry for bread and rent? Who knows, maybe if such a god of men would have shined on him—" She fell asleep and she awoke with visions opening upon visions of new, gleaming worlds of joy and hope. She leaped out of bed singing a song she had not heard since she was a little child in her mother's home.

Several times during the day, she found herself at the broken mirror, arranging and rearranging her dark mass of unkempt hair with fumbling fingers. She was all atremble with breathless excitement to imitate the fluffy style of the much-courted landlady's daughter.

For the first time she realized how shabby and impossible her clothes were. "Oi weh!" she wrung her hands. "I'd give away everything in the world only to have something pretty to wear for him. My whole life hangs on how I'll look in his eyes. I got to have a hat and a new dress. I can't no more wear my 'greenhorn' shawl going out with an American.

"But from where can I get the money for new clothes? Oi weh! How bitter it is not to have the dollar! Woe is me! No mother, no friend, nobody to help me lift myself out of my greenhorn rags."

"Why not pawn the feather bed your mother left you?" She jumped at the thought.

"What? Have you no heart? No feelings? Pawn the only one thing left from your dead mother?

"Why not? Nothing is too dear for him. If your mother could stand up from her grave, she'd cut herself in pieces, she'd tear the sun and stars out from the sky to make you beautiful for him."

Late one evening Zaretsky sat in his pawnshop, absorbed in counting the money of his day's sales, when Shenah Pessah, with a shawl over her head and a huge bundle over her shoulder, edged her way hesitantly into the store. Laying her sacrifice down on the counter, she stood dumbly and nervously fingered the fringes of her shawl.

The pawnbroker lifted his miserly face from the cash-box and shot a quick glance at the girl's trembling figure.

"Nu?" said Zaretsky, in his cracked voice, cutting the twine from the bundle and unfolding a feather bed. His appraising hand felt that it was of the finest down. "How much ask you for it?"

The fiendish gleam of his shrewd eyes paralyzed her with terror. A lump came in her throat and she wavered speechless.

"I'll give you five dollars," said Zaretsky.

"Five dollars?" gasped Shenah Pessah. Her hands rushed back anxiously to the feather bed and her fingers clung to it as if it were a living thing. She gazed panic-stricken at the gloomy interior of the pawnshop with its tawdry jewels in the cases; the stacks of second-hand clothing hanging overhead, back to the grisly face of the pawnbroker. The weird tickings that came from the cheap clocks on the shelves behind Zaretsky, seemed to her like the smothered heart-beats of people who like herself had been driven to barter their last precious belongings for a few dollars.

"Is it for yourself that you come?" he asked, strangely stirred by the mute anguish in the girl's eyes. This morgue of dead belongings had taken its toll of many a pitiful victim of want. But never before had Zaretsky been so affected. People bargained and rebelled and struggled with him on his own plane. But the dumb helplessness of this girl and her coming to him at such a late hour touched the man's heart.

"Is it for yourself?" he repeated, in a softened tone.

The new note of feeling in his voice made her look up. The hard, crafty expression on his face had given place to a look of sympathy.

"Yes, it's mine, from my mother," she stammered, brokenly. "The last memory from Russia. How many winters it took my mother to pick together the feathers. She began it when I was yet a little baby in the cradle—and—" She covered her face with her shawl and sobbed.

"Any one sick? Why do you got to pawn it?"

She raised her tear-stained face and mutely looked at him. How could she explain and how could he possibly understand her sudden savage desire for clothes?

Zaretsky, feeling that he had been clumsy and tactless, hastened to add, "Nu—I'll give you—a—a—a—ten dollars," he finished with a motion of his hand, as if driving from him the onrush of generosity that seized him.

"Oi, mister!" cried Shenah Pessah, as the man handed her the bill. "You're saving me my life! God will pay you for this goodness." And crumpling the money in her hand, she hurried back home elated.

The following evening, as soon as her work was over, Shenah Pessah scurried through the ghetto streets, seeking in the myriad-colored shop windows the one hat and the one dress that would voice the desire of her innermost self. At last she espied a shining straw with cherries so red, so luscious, that they cried out to her, "Bite me!" That was the hat she bought.

The magic of those cherries on her hat brought back to her the green fields and orchards of her native Russia. Yes, a green dress was what she craved. And she picked out the greenest, crispest organdie.

That night, as she put on her beloved colors, she vainly tried to see herself from head to foot, but the broken bit of a mirror that she owned could only show her glorious parts of her. Her clothes seemed to enfold her in flames of desire leaping upon desire. "Only to be beautiful! Only to be beautiful!" she murmured breathlessly. "Not for myself, but only for him."

Time stood still for Shenah Pessah as she counted the days, the hours, and the minutes for the arrival of John Barnes. At last, through her basement window, she saw him walk up the front steps. She longed to go over to him and fling herself at his feet and cry out to him with what hunger of heart she awaited his coming. But the very intensity of her longing left her faint and dumb.

He passed to his room. Later, she saw him walk out without even stopping to look at her. The next day and the day after, she watched him from her hidden corner pass in and out of the house, but still he did not come to her.

Oh, how sweet it was to suffer the very hurt of his oblivion of her! She gloried in his great height that made him so utterly unaware of her existence. It was enough for her worshiping eyes just to glimpse him from afar. What was she to him? Could she expect him to greet the stairs on which he stepped? Or take notice of the door that swung open for him? After all, she was nothing but part of the house. So why should he take notice of her? She was the steps on which he walked. She was the door that swung open for him. And he did not know it.

For four evenings in succession, ever since John Barnes had come to live in the house, Shenah Pessah arrayed herself in her new things and waited. Was it not a miracle that he came the first time when she did not even dream that he was on earth? So why shouldn't the miracle happen again? This evening, however, she was so spent with the hopelessness of her longing that she had no energy left to put on her adornments.

All at once she was startled out of her apathy by a quick tap on her window-pane. "How about going to the library, to-morrow evening?" asked John Barnes.

"Oi-i-i! Yes! Thanks—" she stammered in confusion.

"Well, to-morrow night, then, at seven. Thank you." He hurried out embarrassed by the grateful look that shone to him out of her eyes. The gaze haunted him and hurt him. It was the beseeching look of a homeless dog, begging to be noticed. "Poor little immigrant," he thought, "how lonely she must be!"

"So he didn't forget," rejoiced Shenah Pessah. "How only the sound from his voice opens the sky in my heart! How the deadness and emptiness in me flames up into life! Ach! The sun is again beginning to shine!"

An hour before the appointed time, Shenah Pessah dressed herself in all her finery for John Barnes. She swung open the door and stood in readiness watching the little clock on the mantel-shelf. The ticking thing seemed to throb with the unutterable hopes compressed in her heart, all the mute years of her stifled life. Each little thud of time sang a wild song of released joy—the joy of his coming nearer.

For the tenth time Shenah Pessah went over in her mind what she would say to him when he'd come.

"It was so kind from you to take from your dear time—to—"

"No—that sounds not good. I'll begin like this—Mr. Barnes! I can't give it out in words your kindness, to stop from your high thoughts to—to—"

"No—no! Oi weh! God from the world! Why should it be so hard for me to say to him what I mean? Why shouldn't I be able to say to him plain out—Mr. Barnes! You are an angel from the sky! You are saving me my life to let me only give a look on you! I'm happier than a bird in the air when I think only that such goodness like you—"

The sudden ring of the bell shattered all her carefully rehearsed phrases and she met his greeting in a flutter of confusion.

"My! Haven't you blossomed out since last night!" exclaimed Mr. Barnes, startled by Shenah Pessah's sudden display of color.

"Yes," she flushed, raising to him her radiant face. "I'm through for always with old women's shawls. This is my first American dress-up."

"Splendid! So you want to be an American! The next step will be to take up some work that will bring you in touch with American people."

"Yes. You'll help me? Yes?" Her eyes sought his with an appeal of unquestioning reliance.

"Have you ever thought what kind of work you would like to take up?" he asked, when they got out into the street.

"No—I want only to get away from the basement. I'm crazy for people."

"Would you like to learn a trade in a factory?"

"Anything—anything! I'm burning to learn. Give me only an advice. What?"

"What can you do best with your hands?"

"With the hands the best? It's all the same what I do with the hands. Think you not maybe now, I could begin already something with the head? Yes?"

"We'll soon talk this over together, after you have read a book that will tell you how to find out what you are best fitted for."

When they entered the library, Shenah Pessah halted in awe. "What a stillness full from thinking! So beautiful, it comes on me like music!"

"Yes. This is quite a place," he acquiesced, seeing again the public library in a new light through her eyes. "Some of the best minds have worked to give us just this."

"How the book-ladies look so quiet like the things."

"Yes," he replied, with a tell-tale glance at her. "I too like to see a woman's face above her clothes."

The approach of the librarian cut off further comment. As Mr. Barnes filled out the application card, Shenah Pessah noted the librarian's simple attire. "What means he a woman's face above her clothes?" she wondered. And the first shadow of a doubt crossed her mind as to whether her dearly bought apparel was pleasing to his eyes. In the few brief words that passed between Mr. Barnes and the librarian, Shenah Pessah sensed that these two were of the same world and that she was different. Her first contact with him in a well-lighted room made her aware that "there were other things to the person besides the dress-up." She had noticed their well-kept hands on the desk and she became aware that her own were calloused and rough. That is why she felt her dirty finger-nails curl in awkwardly to hide themselves as she held the pen to sign her name.

When they were out in the street again, he turned to her and said, "If you don't mind, I'd prefer to walk back. The night is so fine and I've been in the stuffy office all day."

"I don't mind"—the words echoed within her. If he only knew how above all else she wanted this walk.

"It was grand in there, but the electric lights are like so many eyes looking you over. In the street it is easier for me. The dark covers you up so good."

He laughed, refreshed by her unconscious self-revelation.

"As long as you feel in your element let's walk on to the pier."

"Like for a holiday, it feels itself in me," she bubbled, as he took her arm in crossing the street. "Now see I America for the first time!"

It was all so wonderful to Barnes that in the dirt and noise of the overcrowded ghetto, this erstwhile drudge could be transfigured into such a vibrant creature of joy. Even her clothes that had seemed so bold and garish awhile ago, were now inexplicably in keeping with the carnival spirit that he felt steal over him.

As they neared the pier, he reflected strangely upon the fact that out of the thousands of needy, immigrant girls whom he might have befriended, this eager young being at his side was ordained by some peculiar providence to come under his personal protection.

"How long did you say you have been in this country, Shenah Pessah?"

"How long?" She echoed his words as though waking from a dream. "It's two years already. But that didn't count life. From now on I live."

"And you mean to tell me that in all this time, no one has taken you by the hand and shown you the ways of our country? The pity of it!"

"I never had nothing, nor nobody. But now—it dances under me the whole earth! It feels in me grander than dreams!"

He drank in the pure joy out of her eyes. For the moment, the girl beside him was the living flame of incarnate Spring.

"He feels for me," she rejoiced, as they walked on in silence. The tenderness of his sympathy enfolded her like some blessed warmth.

When they reached the end of the pier, they paused and watched the moonlight playing on the water. In the shelter of a truck they felt benignly screened from any stray glances of the loiterers near by.

How big seemed his strength as he stood silhouetted against the blue night! For the first time Shenah Pessah noticed the splendid straightness of his shoulders. The clean glowing youth of him drew her like a spell.

"Ach! Only to keep always inside my heart the kindness, the gentlemanness that shines from his face," thought Shenah Pessah, instinctively nestling closer.

"Poor little immigrant!" murmured John Barnes. "How lonely, how barren your life must have been till—" In an impulse of compassion, his arms opened and Shenah Pessah felt her soul swoon in ecstasy as he drew her toward him.

It was three days since the eventful evening on the pier and Shenah Pessah had not seen John Barnes since. He had vanished like a dream, and yet he was not a dream. He was the only thing real in the unreal emptiness of her unlived life. She closed her eyes and she saw again his face with its joy-giving smile. She heard again his voice and felt again his arms around her as he kissed her lips. Then in the midst of her sweetest visioning a gnawing emptiness seized her and the cruel ache of withheld love sucked dry all those beautiful feelings his presence inspired. Sometimes there flashed across her fevered senses the memory of his compassionate endearments: "Poor lonely little immigrant!" And she felt his sweet words smite her flesh with their cruel mockery.

She went about her work with restlessness. At each step, at each sound, she started, "Maybe it's him! Maybe!" She could not fall asleep at night, but sat up in bed writing and tearing up letters to him. The only lull to the storm that uprooted her being was in trying to tell him how every throb within her clamored for him, but the most heart-piercing cry that she could utter only stabbed her heart with the futility of words.

In the course of the week it was Shenah Pessah's duty to clean Mrs. Stein's floor. This brought her to Mr. Barnes's den in his absence. She gazed about her, calling up his presence at the sight of his belongings.

"How fine to the touch is the feel from everything his," she sighed, tenderly resting her cheek on his dressing-gown. With a timid hand she picked up a slipper that stood beside his bed and she pressed it to her heart reverently. "I wish I was this leather thing only to hold his feet!" Then she turned to his dresser and passed her hands caressingly over the ivory things on it. "Ach! You lucky brush—smoothing his hair every day!"

All at once she heard footsteps, and before she could collect her thoughts, he entered. Her whole being lit up with the joy of his coming. But one glance at him revealed to her the changed expression that darkened his face. His arms hung limply at his side—the arms she expected to stretch out to her and enfold her. As if struck in the face by his heartless rebuff, she rushed out blindly.

"Just a minute, please," he managed to detain her. "As a gentleman, I owe you an apology. That night—it was a passing moment of forgetfulness. It's not to happen again—"

Before he had finished, she had run out scorched with shame by his words.

"Good Lord!" he ejaculated, when he found he was alone. "Who'd ever think that she would take it so? I suppose there is no use trying to explain to her."

For some time he sat on his bed, staring ruefully. Then, springing to his feet, he threw his things together in a valise. "You'd be a cad if you did not clear out of here at once," he muttered to himself. "No matter how valuable the scientific inquiry might prove to be, you can't let the girl run away with herself."

Shenah Pessah was at the window when she saw John Barnes go out with his suitcases.

"In God's name, don't leave me!" she longed to cry out. "You are the only bit of light that I ever had, and now it will be darker and emptier for my eyes than ever before!" But no voice could rise out of her parched lips. She felt a faintness stunning her senses as though someone had cut open the arteries of her wrists and all the blood rushed out of her body.

"Oi weh!" she moaned. "Then it was all nothing to him. Why did he make bitter to me the little sweetness that was dearer to me than my life? What means he a gentleman?

"Why did he make me to shame telling me he didn't mean nothing? Is it because I'm not a lady alike to him? Is a gentleman only a make-believe man?"

With a defiant resolve she seized hold of herself and rose to her feet. "Show him what's in you. If it takes a year, or a million years, you got to show him you're a person. From now on, you got why to live. You got to work not with the strength of one body and one brain, but with the strength of a million bodies and a million brains. By day and by night, you got to push, push yourself up till you get to him and can look him in his face eye to eye."

Spent by the fervor of this new exaltation, she sat with her head in her hands in a dull stupor. Little by little the darkness cleared from her soul and a wistful serenity crept over her. She raised her face toward the solitary ray of sunlight that stole into her basement room.

"After all, he done for you more than you could do for him. You owe it to him the deepest, the highest he waked up in you. He opened the wings of your soul."

Hunger

Shenah Pessah paused in the midst of scrubbing the stairs of the tenement. "Ach!" she sighed. "How can his face still burn so in me when he is so long gone? How the deadness in me flames up with life at the thought of him!"

The dark hallway seemed flooded with white radiance. She closed her eyes that she might see more vividly the beloved features. The glowing smile that healed all ills of life and changed her from the weary drudge into the vibrant creature of joy.

It was all a miracle—his coming, this young professor from one of the big colleges. He had rented a room in the very house where she was janitress so as to be near the people he was writing about. But more wonderful than all was the way he stopped to talk to her, to question her about herself as though she were his equal. What warm friendliness had prompted him to take her out of her dark basement to the library where there were books to read!

And then—that unforgettable night on the way home, when the air was poignant with spring! Only a moment—a kiss—a pressure of hands! And the world shone with light—the empty, unlived years filled with love!

She was lost in dreams of her one hour of romance when a woman elbowed her way through the dim passage, leaving behind her the smell of herring and onions.

Shenah Pessah gripped the scrubbing-brush with suppressed fury. "Meshugeneh! Did you not swear to yourself that you would tear his memory out from your heart? If he would have been only a man I could have forgotten him. But he was not a man! He was God Himself! On whatever I look shines his face!"

The white radiance again suffused her. The brush dropped from her hand. "He—he is the beating in my heart! He is the life in me—the hope in me—the breath of prayer in me! If not for him in me, then what am I? Deadness—emptiness—nothingness! You are going out of your head. You are living only on rainbows. He is no more real—

"What is real? These rags I wear? This pail? This black hole? Or him and the dreams of him?" She flung her challenge to the murky darkness.

"Shenah Pessah! A black year on you!" came the answer from the cellar below. It was the voice of her uncle, Moisheh Rifkin.

"Oi weh!" she shrugged young shoulders, wearied by joyless toil. "He's beginning with his hollering already." And she hurried down.

"You piece of earth! Worms should eat you! How long does it take you to wash up the stairs?" he stormed. "Yesterday, the eating was burned to coal; and to-day you forget the salt."

"What a fuss over a little less salt!"

"In the Talmud it stands a man has a right to divorce his wife for only forgetting him the salt in his soup."

"Maybe that's why Aunt Gittel went to the grave before her time— worrying how to please your taste in the mouth."

The old man's yellow, shriveled face stared up at her out of the gloom. "What has he from life? Only his pleasure in eating and going to the synagogue. How long will he live yet?" And moved by a surge of pity, "Why can't I be a little kind to him?"

"Did you chop me some herring and onions?" he interrupted harshly.

She flushed with conscious guilt. Again she wondered why ugly things and ugly smells so sickened her.

"What don't you forget?" His voice hammered upon her ears. "No care lays in your head. You're only dreaming in the air."

Her compassion was swept away in a wave of revolt that left her trembling. "I can't no more stand it from you! Get yourself somebody else!" She was surprised at her sudden spirit.

"You big mouth, you! That's your thanks for saving you from hunger."

"Two years already I'm working the nails off my fingers and you didn't give me a cent."

"Beggerin! Money yet, you want? The minute you get enough to eat you turn up your head with freshness. Are you used to anything from home? What were you out there in Savel? The dirt under people's feet. You're already forgetting how you came off from the ship—a bundle of rags full of holes. If you lived in Russia a hundred years would you have lived to wear a pair of new shoes on your feet?"

"Other girls come naked and with nothing to America and they work themselves up. Everybody gets wages in America—"

"Americanerin! Didn't I spend out enough money on your ship-ticket to have a little use from you? A thunder should strike you!"

Shenah Pessah's eyes flamed. Her broken finger-nails pierced the callous flesh of her hands. So this was the end—the awakening of her dreams of America! Her memory went back to the time her ship-ticket came. In her simple faith she had really believed that they wanted her—her father's brother and his wife who had come to the new world before ever she was born. She thought they wanted to give her a chance for happiness, for life and love. And then she came—to find the paralytic aunt—housework—janitor's drudgery. Even after her aunt's death, she had gone on uncomplainingly, till her uncle's nagging had worn down her last shred of self-control.

"It's the last time you'll holler on me!" she cried. "You'll never see my face again if I got to go begging in the street." Seizing her shawl, she rushed out. "Woe is me! Bitter is me! For what is my life? Why didn't the ship go under and drown me before I came to America?"

Through the streets, like a maddened thing, she raced, not knowing where she was going, not caring. "For what should I keep on suffering? Who needs me? Who wants me? I got nobody—nobody!"

And then the vision of the face she worshiped flashed before her. His beautiful kindness that had once warmed her into new life breathed over her again. "Why did he ever come but to lift me out of my darkness into his light?"

Instinctively her eyes sought the rift of blue above the tenement roofs and were caught by a boldly printed placard: "HANDS WANTED." It was as though the sign swung open on its hinges like a door and arms stretched out inviting her to enter. From the sign she looked to her own hands—vigorous, young hands—made strong through toil.

Hope leaped within her. "Maybe I got yet luck to have it good in this world. Ach! God from the sky! I'm so burning to live—to work myself up for a somebody! And why not?" With clenched fist she smote her bosom.

"Ain't everything possible in the new world? Why is America but to give me the chance to lift up my head with everybody alike?"

Her feet scarcely touched the steps as she ran up. But when she reached the huge, iron door of Cohen Brothers, a terror seized her. "Oi weh! They'll give a look on my greenhorn rags, and down I go—For what are you afraid, you fool?" she commanded herself. "You come not to beg. They need hands. Don't the sign say so? And you got good, strong hands that can turn over the earth with their strength. America is before you. You'll begin to earn money. You'll dress yourself up like a person and men will fall on their knees to make love to you—even him—himself!"

All fear had left her. She flung open the door and beheld the wonder of a factory—people—people—seas of bent heads and busy hands of people—the whirr of machinery—flying belts—the clicking clatter of whirling wheels—all seemed to blend and fuse into one surging song of hope—of new life—a new world—America!

A man, his arms heaped with a bundle of shirts, paused at sight of the radiant face. Her ruddy cheeks, the film of innocence shining out of eyes that knew no guile, carried him back to the green fields and open plains of his native Russia.

"Her mother's milk is still fresh on her lips," he murmured, as his gaze enveloped her.

The bundle slipped and fell to her feet. Their eyes met in spontaneous recognition of common race. With an embarrassed laugh they stooped to gather up the shirts.

"I seen downstairs hands wanted," came in a faltering voice.

"Then you're looking for work?" he questioned with keen interest. She was so different from the others he had known in his five years in this country. He was seized with curiosity to know more.

"You ain't been long in America?" His tone was an unconscious caress.

"Two years already," she confessed. "But I ain't so green like I look," she added quickly, overcome by the old anxiety.

"Trust yourself on me," Sam Arkin assured her. "I'm a feller that knows himself on a person first off. I'll take you to the office myself. Wait only till I put away these things."

Grinning with eagerness, he returned and together they sought the foreman.

"Good luck to you! I hope you'll be pushed up soon to my floor," Sam Arkin encouraged, as he hurried back to his machine.

Because of the rush of work and the scarcity of help, Shenah Pessah was hired without delay. Atremble with excitement, she tiptoed after the foreman as he led the way into the workroom.

"Here, Sadie Kranz, is another learner for you." He addressed a big-bosomed girl, the most skillful worker in the place.

"Another greenhorn with a wooden head!" she whispered to her neighbor as Shenah Pessah removed her shawl. "Gevalt! All these greenhorn hands tear the bread from our mouths by begging to work so cheap."

But the dumb appeal of the immigrant stirred vague memories in Sadie Kranz. As she watched her run her first seam, she marveled at her speed. "I got to give it to you, you have a quick head." There was conscious condescension in her praise.

Shenah Pessah lifted a beaming face. "How kind it was from you to learn me! You good heart!"

No one had ever before called Sadie Kranz "good heart." The words lingered pleasantly.

"Ut! I like to help anybody, so long it don't cost me nothing. I get paid by the week anyhow," she half apologized.

Shenah Pessah was so thrilled with the novelty of the work, the excitement of mastering the intricacies of her machine, that she did not realize that the day was passed until the bell rang, the machines came to a halt, and the "hands" made a wild rush for the cloak-room.

"Oi weh! Is it a fire?" Shenah Pessah blanched with dread.

Loud laughter quelled her fears. "Greenie! It's six o'clock. Time to go home," chorused the voices.

"Home?" The cry broke from her. "Where will I go? I got no home." She stood bewildered, in the fast-dwindling crowd of workers. Each jostling by her had a place to go. Of them all, she alone was friendless, shelterless!

"Help me find a place to sleep!" she implored, seizing Sadie Kranz by the sleeve of her velvet coat. "I got no people. I ran away."

Sadie Kranz narrowed her eyes at the girl. A feeling of pity crept over her at sight of the out-stretched, hungry hands.

"I'll fix you by me for the while." And taking the shawl off the shelf, she tossed it to the forlorn bundle of rags. "Come along. You must be starved for some eating."

As Shenah Pessah entered the dingy hallroom which Sadie Kranz called home, its chill and squalor carried her back to the janitor's basement she had left that morning. In silence she watched her companion prepare the hot dogs and potatoes on the oil-stove atop the trunk. Such pressing sadness weighed upon her that she turned from even the smell of food.

"My heart pulls me so to go back to my uncle." She swallowed hard her crust of black bread. "He's so used to have me help him. What'll he do—alone?"

"You got to look out for yourself in this world." Sadie Kranz gesticulated with a hot potato. "With your quickness, you got a chance to make money and buy clothes. You can go to shows—dances. And who knows—maybe meet a man to get married."

"Married? You know how it burns in every girl to get herself married—that's how it burns in me to work myself up for a person."

"Ut! For what need you to work yourself up. Better marry yourself up to a rich feller and you're fixed for life."

"But him I want—he ain't just a man. He is—" She paused seeking for words and a mist of longing softened the heavy peasant features. "He is the golden hills on the sky. I'm as far from him as the earth is from the stars."

"Yok! Why wills itself in you the stars?" her companion ridiculed between swallows.

Shenah Pessah flung out her hands with Jewish fervor. "Can I help it what's in my heart? It always longs in me for the higher. Maybe he has long ago forgotten me, but only one hope drives in me like madness—to make myself alike to him."

"I'll tell you the truth," laughed Sadie Kranz, fishing in the pot for the last frankfurter. "You are a little out of your head—plain meshugeh."

"Meshugeh?" Shenah Pessah rose to her feet vibrant with new resolve. "Meshugeh?" she challenged, her peasant youth afire with ambition. "I'll yet show the world what's in me. I'll not go back to my uncle—till it rings with my name in America."

She entered the factory, the next day, with a light in her face, a sureness in her step that made all pause in wonder. "Look only! How high she holds herself her head! Has the matchmaker promised her a man?"

Then came her first real triumph. Shenah Pessah was raised above old hands who had been in the shop for years and made assistant to Sam Arkin, the man who had welcomed her that first day in the factory. As she was shown to the bench beside him, she waited expectantly for a word of welcome. None came. Instead, he bent the closer to his machine and the hand that held the shirt trembled as though he were cold, though the hot color flooded his face.

Resolutely, she turned to her work. She would show him how skillful she had become in those few weeks. The seams sped under her lightning touch when a sudden clatter startled her. She jumped up terror-stricken.

"The belt! The belt slipped! But it's nothing, little bird," Sam Arkin hastened to assure her. "I'll fix it." And then the quick warning, "Sh-h! The foreman is coming!"

Accustomed to her uncle's harsh bickering, this man's gentleness overwhelmed her. There was something she longed to say that trembled on her lips, but her voice refused to come.

Sam Arkin, too, was inarticulate. He felt he must talk to her, must know more of her. Timidly he touched her sleeve. "Lunch-time—here—wait for me," he whispered, as the foreman approached.

A shrill whistle—the switch thrown—the slowing-down of the machines, then the deafening hush proclaiming noon. Followed the scraping of chairs, raucous voices, laughter, and the rush on the line to reach the steaming cauldron. One by one, as their cups of tea were filled, the hungry workers dispersed into groups. Seated on window-sills, table-tops, machines, and bales of shirts, they munched black bread and herring and sipped tea from saucers. And over all rioted the acrid odor of garlic and onions.

Rebecca Feist, the belle of the shop, pulled up the sleeve of her Georgette waist and glanced down at her fifty-nine-cent silk stocking. "A lot it pays for a girl to kill herself to dress stylish. Give only a look on Sam Arkin, how stuck he is on that new hand."

There followed a chorus of voices. "Such freshness! We been in the shop so long and she just gives a come-in and grabs the cream as if it's coming to her."

"It's her innocent-looking baby eyes that fools him in—"

"Innocent! Pfui! These make-believe innocent girls! Leave it to them! They know how to shine themselves up to a feller!"

Bleemah Levine, a stoop-shouldered, old hand, grown gray with the grayness of unrelieved drudgery, cast a furtive look in the direction of the couple. "Ach! The little bit of luck! Not looks, not smartness, but only luck, and the world falls to your feet." Her lips tightened with envy. "It's her greenhorn, red cheeks—"

Rebecca Feist glanced at herself in the mirror of her vanity bag. It was a pretty, young face, but pale and thin from undernourishment. Adroitly applying a lip-stick, she cried indignantly: "I wish I could be such a false thing like her. But only, I'm too natural—the hypocrite!"

Sadie Kranz rose to her friend's defense. "What are you falling on her like a pack of wild dogs, just because Sam Arkin gives a smile on her? He ain't marrying her yet, is he?"

"We don't say nothing against her," retorted Rebecca Feist, tapping her diamond-buckled foot, "only, she pushes herself too much. Give her a finger and she'll grab your whole hand. Is there a limit to the pushings of such a green animal? Only a while ago, she was a learner, a nobody, and soon she'll jump over all our heads and make herself for a forelady."

Sam Arkin, seated beside Shenah Pessah on the window-sill, had forgotten that it was lunch-hour and that he was savagely hungry. "It shines so from your eyes," he beamed. "What happy thoughts lay in your head?"

"Ach! When I give myself a look around on all the people laughing and talking, it makes me so happy I'm one of them."

"Ut! These Americanerins! Their heads is only on ice-cream soda and style."

"But it makes me feel so grand to be with all these hands alike. It's as if I just got out from the choking prison into the open air of my own people."

She paused for breath—a host of memories overpowering her. "I can't give it out in words," she went on. "But just as there ain't no bottom to being poor, there ain't no bottom to being lonely. Before, everything I done was alone, by myself. My heart hurt so with hunger for people. But here, in the factory, I feel I'm with everybody together. Just the sight of people lifts me on wings in the air."

Opening her bag of lunch which had lain unheeded in her lap, she turned to him with a queer, little laugh, "I don't know why I'm so talking myself out to you—"

"Only talk more. I want to know everything about yourself." An aching tenderness rushed out of his heart to her, and in his grave simplicity he told her how he had overheard one of the girls say that she, Shenah Pessah, looked like a "greeneh yenteh," just landed from the ship, so that he cried out, "Gottuniu! If only the doves from the sky were as beautiful!"

They looked at each other solemnly—the girl's lips parted, her eyes wide and serious.

"That first day I came to the shop, the minute I gave a look on you, I felt right away, here's somebody from home. I used to tremble so to talk to a man, but you—you—I could talk myself out to you like thinking in myself."

"You're all soft silk and fine velvet," he breathed reverently. "In this hard world, how could such fineness be?"

An embarrassed silence fell between them as she knotted and unknotted her colored kerchief.

"I'll take you home? Yes?" he found voice at last.

Under lowered lashes she smiled her consent.

"I'll wait for you downstairs, closing time." And he was gone.

The noon hour was not yet over, but Shenah Pessah returned to her machine. "Shall I tell him?" she mused. "Sam Arkin understands so much, shall I tell him of this man that burns in me? If I could only give out to someone about him in my heart—it would make me a little clear in the head." She glanced at Sam Arkin furtively. "He's kind, but could he understand? I only made a fool from myself trying to tell Sadie Kranz." All at once she began to sob without reason. She ran to the cloak-room and hid from prying eyes, behind the shawls and wraps. The emptiness of all for which she struggled pressed upon her like a dead weight, dragging her down, down—the reaction of her ecstasy.

As the gong sounded, she made a desperate effort to pull herself together and returned to her work.

The six o'clock whistles still reverberated when Sam Arkin hurried down the factory stairs and out to the corner where he was to meet Shenah Pessah. He cleared his throat to greet her as she came, but all he managed was a bashful grin. She was so near, so real, and he had so much to say—if he only knew how to begin.

He cracked his knuckles and bit his fingertips, but no words came. "Ach! You yok! Why ain't you saying something?" He wrestled with his shyness in vain. The tense silence remained unbroken till they reached her house.

"I'm sorry"—Shenah Pessah colored apologetically—"But I got no place to invite you. My room is hardly big enough for a push-in of one person."

"What say you to a bite of eating with me?" he blurted.

She thought of her scant supper upstairs and would have responded eagerly, but glancing down at her clothes, she hesitated. "Could I go dressed like this in a restaurant?"

"You look grander plain, like you are, than those twisted up with style. I'll take you to the swellest restaurant on Grand Street and be proud with you!"

She flushed with pleasure. "Nu, come on, then. It's good to have a friend that knows himself on what's in you and not what's on you, but still, when I go to a place, I like to be dressed like a person so I can feel like a person."

"You'll yet live to wear diamonds that will shine up the street when you pass!" he cried.

Through streets growing black with swarming crowds of toil-released workers they made their way. Sam Arkin's thick hand rested with a lightness new to him upon the little arm tucked under his. The haggling pushcart peddlers, the newsboys screaming, "Tageblatt, Abendblatt, Herold," the roaring noises of the elevated trains resounded the pæan of joy swelling his heart.

"America was good to me, but I never guessed how good till now." The words were out before he knew it. "Tell me only, what pulled you to this country?"

"What pulls anybody here? The hope for the better. People who got it good in the old world don't hunger for the new."

A mist filled her eyes at memory of her native village. "How I suffered in Savel. I never had enough to eat. I never had shoes on my feet. I had to go barefoot even in the freezing winter. But still I love it. I was born there. I love the houses and the straw roofs, the mud streets, the cows, the chickens and the goats. My heart always hurts me for what is no more."

The brilliant lights of Levy's Café brought her back to Grand Street.

"Here is it." He led her in and over to a corner table. "Chopped herring and onions for two," he ordered with a flourish.

"Ain't there some American eating on the card?" interposed Shenah Pessah.

He laughed indulgently. "If I lived in America for a hundred years I couldn't get used to the American eating. What can make the mouth so water like the taste and the smell from herring and onions?"

"There's something in me—I can't help—that so quickly takes on to the American taste. It's as if my outside skin only was Russian; the heart in me is for everything of the new world—even the eating."

"Nu, I got nothing to complain against America. I don't like the American eating, but I like the American dollar. Look only on me!" He expanded his chest. "I came to America a ragged nothing—and—see—" He exhibited a bank-book in four figures, gesticulating grandly, "And I learned in America how to sign my name!"

"Did it come hard to learn?" she asked under her breath.

"Hard?" His face purpled with excitement. "It would be easier for me to lift up this whole house on my shoulders than to make one little dot of a letter. When I took my pencil—Oi weh! The sweat would break out on my face! 'I can't, I can't!' I cried, but something in me jumped up. 'You can—you yok—you must!'—Six months, night after night, I stuck to it—and I learned to twist around the little black hooks till it means—me—Sam Arkin."

He had the rough-hewn features of the common people, but he lifted his head with the pride of a king. "Since I can write out my name, I feel I can do anything. I can sign checks, put money in the bank, or take it out without nobody to help me."

As Shenah Pessah listened, unconsciously she compared Sam Arkin, glowing with the frank conceit of the self-made man, his neglected teeth, thick, red lips, with that of the Other One—made ever more beautiful with longings and dreams.

"But in all these black years, I was always hoping to get to the golden country," Sam Arkin's voice went on, but she heard it as from afar. "Before my eyes was always the shine of the high wages and the easy money and I kept pushing myself from one city to another, and saving and saving till I saved up enough for my ship-ticket to the new world. And then when I landed here, I fell into the hands of a cockroach boss."

"A cockroach boss?" she questioned absently and reproached herself for her inattention.

"A black year on him! He was a landsman, that's how he fooled me in. He used to come to the ship with a smiling face of welcome to all the greenhorns what had nobody to go to. And then he'd put them to work in his sweatshop and sweat them into their grave."

"Don't I know it?" she cried with quickened understanding. "Just like my uncle, Moisheh Rifkin."

"The blood-sucker!" he gasped. "When I think how I slaved for him sixteen hours a day—for what? Nothing!"

She gently stroked his hand as one might a child in pain. He looked up and smiled gratefully.

"I want to forget what's already over. I got enough money now to start for myself—maybe a tailor-shop—and soon—I—I want to marry myself— but none of those crazy chickens for me." And he seemed to draw her unto himself by the intensity of his gaze.

Growing bolder, he exclaimed: "I got a grand idea. It's Monday and the bank is open yet till nine o'clock. I'll write over my bank-book on your name? Yes?"

"My name?" She fell back, dumbstruck.

"Yes—you—everything I only got—you—" he mumbled. "I'll give you dove's milk to drink—silks and diamonds to wear—you'll hold all my money."

She was shaken by this supreme proof of his devotion.

"But I—I can't—I got to work myself up for a person. I got a head. I got ideas. I can catch on to the Americans quicker'n lightning."

"My money can buy you everything. I'll buy you teachers. I'll buy you a piano. I'll make you for a lady. Right away you can stop from work." He leaned toward her, his eyes welling with tears of earnestness.

"Take your hard-earned money? Could I be such a beggerin?"

"God from the world! You are dearer to me than the eyes from my head! I'd give the blood from under my nails for you! I want only to work for you—to live for you—to die for you—" He was spent with the surge of his emotion.

Ach! To be loved as Sam Arkin loved! She covered her eyes, but it only pressed upon her the more. Home, husband, babies, a bread-giver for life!

And the Other—a dream—a madness that burns you up alive. "You might as well want to marry yourself to the President of America as to want him. But I can't help it. *Him and him only* I want."

She looked up again. "No—no!" she cried, cruel in the self-absorption of youth and ambition. "You can't make me for a person. It's not only that I got to go up higher, but I got to push myself up by myself, by my own strength—"

"Nu, nu," he sobbed. "I'll not bother you with me—only give you my everything. My bank-book is more than my flesh and blood—only take it, to do what you want with it."

Her eyes deepened with humility. "I know your goodness—but there's something like a wall around me—him in my heart."

"Him?" The word hurled itself at him like a bomb-shell. He went white with pain. And even she, immersed in her own thoughts, lowered her head before the dumb suffering on his face. She felt she owed it to him to tell him.

"I wanted to talk myself out to you about him yet before.—He ain't just a man. He is all that I want to be and am not yet. He is the hunger of me for the life that ain't just eating and sleeping and slaving for bread."

She pushed back her chair and rose abruptly. "I can't be inside walls when I talk of him. I need the earth, the whole free sky to breathe when I think of him. Come out in the air."

They walked for a time before either spoke. Sam Arkin followed where she led through the crooked labyrinth of streets. The sight of the young mothers with their nursing infants pressed to their bared bosoms stabbed anew his hurt.

Shenah Pessah, blind to all but the vision that obsessed her, talked on. "All that my mother and father and my mother's mother and father ever wanted to be is in him. This fire in me, it's not just the hunger of a woman for a man—it's the hunger of all my people back of me, from all ages, for light, for the life higher!"

A veil of silence fell between them. She felt almost as if it were a sacrilege to have spoken of that which was so deeply centered within her.

Sam Arkin's face became lifeless as clay. Bowed like an old man, he dragged his leaden feet after him. The world was dead—cold—meaningless. Bank-book, money—of what use were they now? All his years of savings couldn't win her. He was suffocated in emptiness.

On they walked till they reached a deserted spot in the park. So spent was he by his sorrow that he lost the sense of time or place or that she was near.

Leaning against a tree, he stood, dumb, motionless, unutterable bewilderment in his sunken eyes.

"I lived over the hunger for bread—but this—" He clutched at his aching bosom. "Highest One, help me!" With his face to the ground he sank, prostrate.

"Sam Arkin!" She bent over him tenderly. "I feel the emptiness of words—but I got to get it out. All that you suffer I have suffered, and must yet go on suffering. I see no end. But only—there is a something—a hope—a help out—it lifts me on top of my hungry body—the hunger to make from myself a person that can't be crushed by nothing nor nobody—the life higher!"

Slowly, he rose to his feet, drawn from his weakness by the spell of her. "With one hand you throw me down and with the other you lift me up to life again. Say to me only again, your words," he pleaded, helplessly.

"Sam Arkin! Give yourself your own strength!" She shook him roughly. "I got no pity on you, no more than I got pity on me."

He saw her eyes fill with light as though she were seeing something far beyond them both. "This," she breathed, "is only the beginning of the hunger that will make from you a person who'll yet ring in America."

The Lost "Beautifulness"

"**O**i weh! How it shines the beautifulness!" exulted Hanneh Hayyeh over her newly painted kitchen. She cast a glance full of worship and adoration at the picture of her son in uniform; eyes like her own, shining with eagerness, with joy of life, looked back at her.

"Aby will not have to shame himself to come back to his old home," she rejoiced, clapping her hands—hands blistered from the paintbrush and calloused from rough toil. "Now he'll be able to invite all the grandest friends he made in the army."

The smell of the paint was suffocating, but she inhaled in it huge draughts of hidden beauty. For weeks she had dreamed of it and felt in each tin of paint she was able to buy, in each stroke of the brush, the ecstasy of loving service for the son she idolized.

Ever since she first began to wash the fine silks and linens for Mrs. Preston, years ago, it had been Hanneh Hayyeh's ambition to have a white-painted kitchen exactly like that in the old Stuyvesant Square mansion. Now her own kitchen was a dream come true.

Hanneh Hayyeh ran in to her husband, a stoop-shouldered, care-crushed man who was leaning against the bed, his swollen feet outstretched, counting the pennies that totaled his day's earnings.

"Jake Safransky!" she cried excitedly, "you got to come in and give a look on my painting before you go to sleep."

"Oi, let me alone. Give me only a rest."

Too intoxicated with the joy of achievement to take no for an answer, she dragged him into the doorway. "Nu? How do you like it? Do I know what beautiful is?"

"But how much money did you spend out on that paint?"

"It was my own money," she said, wiping the perspiration off her face with a corner of her apron. "Every penny I earned myself from the extra washing."

"But you had ought save it up for the bad times. What'll you do when the cold weather starts in and the pushcart will not wheel itself out?"

"I save and pinch enough for myself. This I done in honor for my son. I want my Aby to lift up his head in the world. I want him to be able to invite even the President from America to his home and not shame himself."

"You'd pull the bananas off a blind man's pushcart to bring to your Aby. You know nothing from holding tight to a dollar and saving a penny to a penny like poor people should."

"What do I got from living if I can't have a little beautifulness in my life? I don't allow for myself the ten cents to go to a moving picture that I'm crazy to see. I never yet treated myself to an ice-cream soda even for a holiday. Shining up the house for Aby is my only pleasure."

"Yah, but it ain't your house. It's the landlord's."

"Don't I live in it? I soak in pleasure from every inch of my kitchen. Why, I could kiss the grand white color on the walls. It lights up my eyes like sunshine in the room."

Her glance traveled from the newly painted walls to the geranium on the window-sill, and back to her husband's face.

"Jake!" she cried, shaking him, "ain't you got eyes? How can you look on the way it dances the beautifulness from every corner and not jump in the air from happiness?"

"I'm only thinking on the money you spent out on the landlord's house. Look only on me! I'm black from worry, but no care lays on your head. It only dreams itself in you how to make yourself for an American and lay in every penny you got on fixing out the house like the rich."

"I'm sick of living like a pig with my nose to the earth, all the time only pinching and scraping for bread and rent. So long my Aby is with America, I want to make myself for an American. I could tear the stars out from heaven for my Aby's wish."

Her sunken cheeks were flushed and her eyes glowed with light as she gazed about her.

"When I see myself around the house how I fixed it up with my own hands, I forget I'm only a nobody. It makes me feel I'm also a person like Mrs. Preston. It lifts me with high thoughts."

"Why didn't you marry yourself to a millionaire? You always want to make yourself like Mrs. Preston who got millions laying in the bank."

"But Mrs. Preston does make me feel that I'm alike with her," returned Hanneh Hayyeh, proudly. "Don't she talk herself out to me like I was her friend? Mrs. Preston says this war is to give everybody a chance to lift up his head like a person. It is to bring together the people on top who got everything and the people on the bottom who got nothing. She's been telling me about a new word—democracy. It got me on fire. Democracy means that everybody in America is going to be with everybody alike."

"Och! Stop your dreaming out of your head. Close up your mouth from your foolishness. Women got long hair and small brains," he finished, muttering as he went to bed.

At the busy gossiping hour of the following morning when the butcher-shop was crowded with women in dressing-sacks and wrappers covered over with shawls, Hanneh Hayyeh elbowed her way into the clamorous babel of her neighbors.

"What are you so burning? What are you so flaming?"

"She's always on fire with the wonders of her son."

"The whole world must stop still to listen to what news her son writes to her."

"She thinks her son is the only one soldier by the American army."

"My Benny is also one great wonder from smartness, but I ain't such a crazy mother like she."

The voices of her neighbors rose from every corner, but Hanneh Hayyeh, deaf to all, projected herself forward.

"What are you pushing yourself so wild? You ain't going to get your meat first. Ain't it, Mr. Sopkin, all got to wait their turn?"

Mr. Sopkin glanced up in the midst of cutting apart a quarter of meat. He wiped his knife on his greasy apron and leaned across the counter.

"Nu? Hanneh Hayyeh?" his ruddy face beamed. "Have you another letter from little Aby in France? What good news have you got to tell us?"

"No—it's not a letter," she retorted, with a gesture of impatience. "The good news is that I got done with the painting of my kitchen—and you all got to come and give a look how it shines in my house like in a palace."

Mr. Sopkin resumed cutting the meat.

"Oi weh!" clamored Hanneh Hayyeh, with feverish breathlessness. "Stop with your meat already and quick come. The store ain't going to run away from you! It will take only a minute. With one step you are upstairs in my house." She flung out her hands. "And everybody got to come along."

"Do you think I can make a living from looking on the wonders you turn over in your house?" remonstrated the butcher, with a twinkle in his eye.

"Making money ain't everything in life. My new-painted kitchen will light up your heart with joy."

Seeing that Mr. Sopkin still made no move, she began to coax and wheedle, woman-fashion. "Oi weh! Mr. Sopkin! Don't be so mean. Come only. Your customers ain't going to run away from you. If they do, they only got to come back, because you ain't a skinner. You weigh the meat honest."

How could Mr. Sopkin resist such seductive flattery?

"Hanneh Hayyeh!" he laughed. "You're crazy up in the air, but nobody can say no to anything you take into your head."

He tossed his knife down on the counter. "Everybody!" he called; "let us do her the pleasure and give a look on what she got to show us."

"Oi weh! I ain't got no time," protested one. "I left my baby alone in the house locked in."

"And I left a pot of eating on the stove boiling. It must be all burned away by this time."

"But you all got time to stand around here and chatter like a box of monkeys, for hours," admonished Mr. Sopkin. "This will only take a minute. You know Hanneh Hayyeh. We can't tear ourselves away from her till we do what wills itself in her mind."

Protesting and gesticulating, they all followed Mr. Sopkin as Hanneh Hayyeh led the way. Through the hallway of a dark, ill-smelling tenement, up two flights of crooked, rickety stairs, they filed. When Henneh Hayyeh opened the door there were exclamations of wonder and joy: "Oi! Oi!" and "Ay! Ay! Takeh! Takeh!"

"Gold is shining from every corner!"

"Like for a holiday!"

"You don't need to light up the gas, so it shines!"

"I wish I could only have it so grand!"

"You ain't got worries on your head, so it lays in your mind to make it so fancy."

Mr. Sopkin stood with mouth open, stunned with wonder at the transformation.

Hanneh Hayyeh shook him by the sleeve exultantly. "Nu? Why ain't you saying something?"

"Grand ain't the word for it! What a whiteness! And what a cleanliness! It tears out the eyes from the head! Such a tenant the landlord ought to give out a medal or let down the rent free. I saw the rooms before and I see them now. What a difference from one house to another."

"Ain't you coming in?" Hanneh Hayyeh besought her neighbors.

"God from the world! To step with our feet on this new painted floor?"

"Shah!" said the butcher, taking off his apron and spreading it on the floor. "You can all give a step on my apron. It's dirty, anyhow."

They crowded in on the outspread apron and vied with one another in their words of praise.

"May you live to see your son married from this kitchen, and may we all be invited to the wedding!"

"May you live to eat here cake and wine on the feasts of your grandchildren!"

"May you have the luck to get rich and move from here into your own bought house!"

"Amen!" breathed Hanneh Hayyeh. "May we all forget from our worries for rent!"

Mrs. Preston followed with keen delight Hanneh Hayyeh's every movement as she lifted the wash from the basket and spread it on the bed. Hanneh Hayyeh's rough, toil-worn hands lingered lovingly, caressingly over each garment. It was as though the fabrics held something subtly animate in their texture that penetrated to her very fingertips.

"Hanneh Hayyeh! You're an artist!" There was reverence in Mrs. Preston's low voice that pierced the other woman's inmost being. "You do my laces and batistes as no one else ever has. It's as if you breathed part of your soul into it."

The hungry-eyed, ghetto woman drank in thirstily the beauty and goodness that radiated from Mrs. Preston's person. None of the cultured elegance of her adored friend escaped Hanneh Hayyeh. Her glance traveled from the exquisite shoes to the flawless hair of the well-poised head.

"Your things got so much fineness. I'm crazy for the feel from them. I do them up so light in my hands like it was thin air I was handling."

Hanneh Hayyeh pantomimed as she spoke and Mrs. Preston, roused from her habitual reserve, put her fine, white hand affectionately over Hanneh Hayyeh's gnarled, roughened ones.

"Oi-i-i-i! Mrs. Preston! You always make me feel so grand!" said Hanneh Hayyeh, a mist of tears in her wistful eyes. "When I go away from you I could just sit down and cry. I can't give it out in words what it is. It chokes me so—how good you are to me—You ain't at all like a rich lady. You're so plain from the heart. You make the lowest nobody feel he's somebody."

"You are not a 'nobody,' Hanneh Hayyeh. You are an artist—an artist laundress."

"What mean you an artist?"

"An artist is so filled with love for the beautiful that he has to express it in some way. You express it in your washing just as a painter paints it in a picture."

"Paint?" exclaimed Hanneh Hayyeh. "If you could only give a look how I painted up my kitchen! It lights up the whole tenement house for blocks around. The grocer and the butcher and all the neighbors were jumping in the air from wonder and joy when they seen how I shined up my house."

"And all in honor of Aby's home-coming?" Mrs. Preston smiled, her thoughts for a moment on her own son, the youngest captain in his regiment whose home-coming had been delayed from week to week.

"Everything I do is done for my Aby," breathed Hanneh Hayyeh, her hands clasping her bosom as if feeling again the throb of his babyhood at her heart. "But this painting was already dreaming itself in my head for years. You remember the time the hot iron fell on my foot and you came to see me and brought me a red flower-pot wrapped around with green crêpe paper? That flower-pot opened up the sky in my kitchen." The words surged from the seething soul of her. "Right away I saw before my eyes how I could shine up my kitchen like a parlor by painting the walls and sewing up new curtains for the window. It was like seeing before me your face every time I looked on your flowers. I used to talk to it like it could hear and feel and see. And I said to it: 'I'll show you what's in me. I'll show you that I know what beautiful is.'"

Her face was aglow with an enthusiasm that made it seem young, like a young girl's face.

"I begged myself by the landlord to paint up my kitchen, but he wouldn't listen to me. So I seen that if I ever hoped to fix up my house, I'd have to spend out my own money. And I began to save a penny to a penny to have for the paint. And when I seen the painters, I always stopped them to ask where and how to buy it so that it should come out the cheapest. By day and by night it burned in me the picture—my kitchen shining all white like yours, till I couldn't rest till I done it."

With all her breeding, with all the restraint of her Anglo-Saxon for-bears, Mrs. Preston was strangely shaken by Hanneh Hayyeh's consuming passion for beauty. She looked deep into the eyes of the Russian Jewess as if drinking in the secret of their hidden glow.

"I am eager to see that wonderful kitchen of yours," she said, as Hanneh Hayyeh bade her good-bye.

Hanneh Hayyeh walked home, her thoughts in a whirl with the glad anticipation of Mrs. Preston's promised visit. She wondered how she might share the joy of Mrs. Preston's presence with the butcher and all the neighbors. "I'll bake up a shtrudel cake," she thought to herself. "They will all want to come to get a taste of the cake and then they'll give a look on Mrs. Preston."

Thus smiling and talking to herself she went about her work. As she bent over the wash-tub rubbing the clothes, she visualized the hot, steaming shtrudel just out of the oven and the exclamations of pleasure as Mrs. Preston and the neighbors tasted it. All at once there was a knock at the door. Wiping her soapy hands on the corner of her apron, she hastened to open it.

"Oi! Mr. Landlord! Come only inside," she urged. "I got the rent for you, but I want you to give a look around how I shined up my flat."

The Prince Albert that bound the protruding stomach of Mr. Benjamin Rosenblatt was no tighter than the skin that encased the smooth-shaven face. His mouth was tight. Even the small, popping eyes held a tight gleam.

"I got no time. The minutes is money," he said, extending a claw-like hand for the rent.

"But I only want you for a half a minute." And Hanneh Hayyeh dragged the owner of her palace across the threshold. "Nu? Ain't I a good painter? And all this I done while other people were sleeping themselves, after I'd come home from my day's work."

"Very nice," condescended Mr. Benjamin Rosenblatt, with a hasty glance around the room. "You certainly done a good job. But I got to go. Here's your receipt." And the fingers that seized Hanneh Hayyeh's rent-money seemed like pincers for grasping molars.

Two weeks later Jake Safransky and his wife Hanneh Hayyeh sat eating their dinner, when the janitor came in with a note.

"From the landlord," he said, handing it to Hanneh Hayyeh, and walked out.

"The landlord?" she cried, excitedly. "What for can it be?" With trembling fingers she tore open the note. The slip dropped from her hand. Her face grew livid, her eyes bulged with terror. "Oi weh!" she exclaimed, as she fell back against the wall.

"Gewalt!" cried her husband, seizing her limp hand, "you look like struck dead."

"Oi-i-i! The murderer! He raised me the rent five dollars a month."

"Good for you! I told you to listen to me. Maybe he thinks we got money laying in the bank when you got so many dollars to give out on paint."

She turned savagely on her husband. "What are you tearing yet my flesh? Such a money-grabber! How could I imagine for myself that so he would thank me for laying in my money to painting up his house?"

She seized her shawl, threw it over her head, and rushed to the landlord's office.

"Oi weh! Mr. Landlord! Where is your heart? How could you raise me my rent when you know my son is yet in France? And even with the extra washing I take in I don't get enough when the eating is so dear?"

"The flat is worth five dollars more," answered Mr. Rosenblatt, impatiently. "I can get another tenant any minute."

"Have pity on me! I beg you! From where I can squeeze out the five dollars more for you?"

"That don't concern me. If you can't pay, somebody else will. I got to look out for myself. In America everybody looks out for himself."

"Is it nothing by you how I painted up your house with my own blood-money?"

"You didn't do it for me. You done it for yourself," he sneered. "It's nothing to me how the house looks, so long as I get my rent in time. You wanted to have a swell house, so you painted it. That's all."

With a wave of his hand he dismissed her.

"I beg by your conscience! Think on God!" Hanneh Hayyeh wrung her hands. "Ain't your house worth more to you to have a tenant clean it out and paint it out so beautiful like I done?"

"Certainly," snarled the landlord. "Because the flat is painted new, I can get more money for it. I got no more time for you."

He turned to his stenographer and resumed the dictation of his letters.

Dazedly Hanneh Hayyeh left the office. A choking dryness contracted her throat as she staggered blindly, gesticulating and talking to herself.

"Oi weh! The sweat, the money I laid into my flat and it should all go to the devil. And I should be turned out and leave all my beautifulness. And from where will I get the money for moving? When I begin to break myself up to move, I got to pay out money for the moving man, money for putting up new lines, money for new shelves and new hooks besides money for the rent. I got to remain where I am. But from where can I get together the five dollars for the robber? Should I go to Moisheh Itzek, the pawnbroker, or should I maybe ask Mrs. Preston? No—She shouldn't think I got her for a friend only to help me. Oi weh! Where should I turn with my bitter heart?"

Mechanically she halted at the butcher-shop. Throwing herself on the vacant bench, she buried her face in her shawl and burst out in a loud, heart-piercing wail: "Woe is me! Bitter is me!"

"Hanneh Hayyeh! What to you happened?" cried Mr. Sopkin in alarm.

His sympathy unlocked the bottom depths of her misery.

"Oi-i-i! Black is my luck! Dark is for my eyes!"

The butcher and the neighbors pressed close in upon her.

"Gewalt! What is it? Bad news from Aby in France?"

"Oi-i-i! The murderer! The thief! His gall should burst as mine is bursting! His heart should break as mine is breaking! It remains for me nothing but to be thrown out in the gutter. The landlord raised me five dollars a month rent. And he ripped yet my wounds by telling me he raised me the rent because my painted-up flat is so much more worth."

"The dogs! The blood-sucking landlords! They are the new czars from America!"

"What are you going to do?"

"What should I do? Aby is coming from France any day, and he's got to have a home to come to. I will have to take out from my eating the meat and the milk to save together the extra five dollars. People! Give me an advice! What else can I do? If a wild wolf falls on you in the black night, will crying help you?"

With a gesture of abject despair, she fell prone upon the bench. "Gottuniu! If there is any justice and mercy on this earth, then may the landlord be tortured like he is torturing me! May the fires burn him and the waters drown him! May his flesh be torn from him in pieces and his bones be ground in the teeth of wild dogs!"

Two months later, a wasted, haggard Hanneh Hayyeh stood in the kitchen, folding Mrs. Preston's wash in her basket, when the janitor—the servant of her oppressor—handed her another note.

"From the landlord," he said in his toneless voice.

Hanneh Hayyeh paled. She could tell from his smirking sneer that it was a second notice of increased rental.

It grew black before her eyes. She was too stunned to think. Her first instinct was to run to her husband; but she needed sympathy—not nagging. And then in her darkness she saw a light—the face of her friend, Mrs. Preston. She hurried to her.

"Oi—friend! The landlord raised me my rent again," she gasped, dashing into the room like a thing hounded by wild beasts.

Mrs. Preston was shocked by Hanneh Hayyeh's distraught appearance. For the first time she noticed the ravages of worry and hunger.

"Hanneh Hayyeh! Try to calm yourself. It is really quite inexcusable the way the landlords are taking advantage of the situation. There must be a way out. We'll fix it up somehow."

"How fix it up?" Hanneh Hayyeh flared.

"We'll see that you get the rent you need." There was reassurance and confidence in Mrs. Preston's tone.

Hanneh Hayyeh's eyes flamed. Too choked for utterance, her breath ceased for a moment.

"I want no charity! You think maybe I came to beg? No—I want justice!"

She shrank in upon herself, as though to ward off the raised whip of her persecutor. "You know how I feel?" Her voice came from the terrified depths of her. "It's as if the landlord pushed me in a corner and said to me: 'I want money, or I'll squeeze from you your life!' I have no money, so he takes my life.

"Last time, when he raised me my rent, I done without meat and without milk. What more can I do without?"

The piercing cry stirred Mrs. Preston as no mere words had done.

"Sometimes I get so weak for a piece of meat, I could tear the world to pieces. Hunger and bitterness are making a wild animal out of me. I ain't no more the same Hanneh Hayyeh I used to be."

The shudder that shook Hanneh Hayyeh communicated itself to Mrs. Preston. "I know the prices are hard to bear," she stammered, appalled.

"There used to be a time when poor people could eat cheap things," the toneless voice went on. "But now there ain't no more cheap things. Potatoes—rice—fish—even dry bread is dear. Look on my shoes! And I who used to be so neat with myself. I can't no more have my torn shoes fixed up. A pair of shoes or a little patch is only for millionaires."

"Something must be done," broke in Mrs. Preston, distraught for the first time in her life. "But in the meantime, Hanneh Hayyeh, you must accept this to tide you over." She spoke with finality as she handed her a bill.

Hanneh Hayyeh thrust back the money. "Ain't I hurt enough without you having to hurt me yet with charity? You want to give me hush money to swallow down an unrightness that burns my flesh? I want justice."

The woman's words were like bullets that shot through the static security of Mrs. Preston's life. She realized with a guilty pang that while strawberries and cream were being served at her table in January, Hanneh Hayyeh had doubtless gone without a square meal in months.

"We can't change the order of things overnight," faltered Mrs. Preston, baffled and bewildered by Hanneh Hayyeh's defiance of her proffered aid.

"Change things? There's got to be a change!" cried Hanneh Hayyeh with renewed intensity. "The world as it is is not to live in any longer. If only my Aby would get back quick. But until he comes, I'll fight till all America will have to stop and listen to me. You was always telling me that the lowest nobody got something to give to America. And that's what I got to give to America—the last breath in my body for justice. I'll wake up America from its sleep. I'll go myself to the President with my Aby's soldier picture and ask him was all this war to let loose a bunch of blood-suckers to suck the marrow out from the people?"

"Hanneh Hayyeh," said Mrs. Preston, with feeling, "these laws are far from just, but they are all we have so far. Give us time. We are young. We are still learning. We're doing our best."

Numb with suffering the woman of the ghetto looked straight into the eyes of Mrs. Preston. "And you too—you too hold by the landlord's side?—Oi—I see! Perhaps you too got property out by agents."

A sigh that had in it the resignation of utter hopelessness escaped from her. "Nothing can hurt me no more—And you always stood out to me in my dreams as the angel from love and beautifulness. You always made-believe to me that you're only for democracy."

Tears came to Mrs. Preston's eyes. But she made no move to defend herself or reply and Hanneh Hayyeh walked out in silence.

A few days later the whole block was astir with the news that Hanneh Hayyeh had gone to court to answer her dispossess summons.

From the windows, the stoop, from the hallway, and the doorway of the butcher-shop the neighbors were talking and gesticulating while waiting for Hanneh Hayyeh's return.

Hopeless and dead, Hanneh Hayyeh dragged herself to the butcher-shop. All made way for her to sit on the bench. She collapsed in a heap, not uttering a single sound, nor making a single move.

The butcher produced a bottle of brandy and, hastily filling a small glass, brought it to Hanneh Hayyeh.

"Quick, take it to your lips," he commanded. Weak from lack of food and exhausted by the ordeal of the court-room, Hanneh Hayyeh obeyed like a child.

Soon one neighbor came in with a cup of hot coffee; another brought bread and herring with onion over it.

Tense, breathless, with suppressed curiosity quivering on their lips, they waited till Hanneh Hayyeh swallowed the coffee and ate enough to regain a little strength.

"Nu? What became in the court?"

"What said the judge?"

"Did they let you talk yourself out like you said you would?"

"Was the murderer there to say something?"

Hanneh Hayyeh wagged her head and began talking to herself in a low, toneless voice as if continuing her inward thought. "The judge said the same as Mrs. Preston said: the landlord has the right to raise our rent or put us out."

"Oi weh! If Hanneh Hayyeh with her fire in her mouth couldn't get her rights, then where are we?"

"To whom should we go? Who more will talk for us now?"

"Our life lays in their hands."

"They can choke us so much as they like!"

"Nobody cares. Nobody hears our cry!"

Out of this babel of voices there flashed across Hanneh Hayyeh's deadened senses the chimera that to her was the one reality of her aspiring soul—"Oi-i-i-i! My beautiful kitchen!" she sighed as in a dream.

The butcher's face grew red with wrath. His eyes gleamed like sharp, darting steel. "I wouldn't give that robber the satisfaction to leave your grand painted house," he said, turning to Hanneh Hayyeh. "I'd smash down everything for spite. You got nothing to lose. Such a murderer! I would learn him a lesson! 'An eye for an eye and a tooth for a tooth.'"

Hanneh Hayyeh, hair disheveled, clothes awry, the nails of her fingers dug in her scalp, stared with the glazed, impotent stare of a mad-woman. With unseeing eyes she rose and blindly made her way to her house.

As she entered her kitchen she encountered her husband hurrying in.

"Oi weh! Oi weh!" he whined. "I was always telling you your bad end. Everybody is already pointing their fingers on me! and all because you, a meshugeneh yideneh, a starved beggerin, talked it into your head that you got to have for yourself a white-painted kitchen alike to Mrs. Preston. Now you'll remember to listen to your husband. Now, when you'll be laying in the street to shame and to laughter for the whole world."

"Out! Out from my sight! Out from my house!" shrieked Hanneh Hayyeh. In her rage she seized a flat-iron and Jake heard her hurl it at the slammed door as he fled downstairs.

It was the last night before the eviction. Hanneh Hayyeh gazed about her kitchen with tear-glazed eyes. "Someone who got nothing but only money will come in here and get the pleasure from all this beautifulness that cost me the blood from my heart. Is this already America? What for was my Aby fighting? Was it then only a dream—all these millions people from all lands and from all times, wishing and hoping and praying that America is? Did I wake myself from my dreaming to see myself back in the black times of Russia under the czar?"

Her eager, beauty-loving face became distorted with hate. "No—the landlord ain't going to get the best from me! I'll learn him a lesson. 'An eye for an eye'—"

With savage fury, she seized the chopping-axe and began to scratch down the paint, breaking the plaster on the walls. She tore up the floor-boards. She unscrewed the gas-jets, turned on the gas full force so as to blacken the white-painted ceiling. The night through she raged with the frenzy of destruction.

Utterly spent she flung herself on the lounge, but she could not close her eyes. Her nerves quivered. Her body ached, and she felt her soul ache there—inside her—like a thing killed that could not die.

The first grayness of dawn filtered through the air-shaft window of the kitchen. The room was faintly lighted, and as the rays of dawn got stronger and reached farther, one by one the things she had mutilated in the night started, as it were, into consciousness. She looked at her dish-closet, once precious, that she had scratched and defaced; the uprooted geranium-box on the window-sill; the marred walls. It was unbearable all this waste and desolation that stared at her. "Can it be I who done all this?" she asked herself. "What devil got boiling in me?"

What had she gained by her rage for vengeance? She had thought to spite the landlord, but it was her own soul she had killed. These walls that stared at her in their ruin were not just walls. They were animate—they throbbed with the pulse of her own flesh. For every inch of the broken plaster there was a scar on her heart. She had destroyed that which had taken her so many years of prayer and longing to build up. But this demolished beauty like her own soul, though killed, still quivered and ached with the unstilled pain of life. "Oi weh!" she moaned, swaying to and fro. "So much lost beautifulness—"

Private Abraham Safransky, with the look in his eyes and the swing of his shoulders of all the boys who come back from overseas, edged his way through the wet Delancey Street crowds with the skill of one born to these streets and the assurance of the United States Army. Fresh from the ship, with a twenty-four-hour leave stowed safely in his pocket, he hastened to see his people after nearly two years' separation.

On Private Safransky's left shoulder was the insignia of the Statue of Liberty. The three gold service stripes on his left arm and the two wound stripes of his right were supplemented by the Distinguished Service Medal on his left breast bestowed by the United States Government.

As he pictured his mother's joy when he would surprise her in her spotless kitchen, the soldier broke into the double-quick.

All at once he stopped; on the sidewalk before their house was a heap of household things that seemed familiar and there on the curbstone a woman huddled, cowering, broken.—Good God—his mother! His own mother—and all their worldly belongings dumped there in the rain.

The Free Vacation House

How came it that I went to the free vacation house was like this:

One day the visiting teacher from the school comes to find out for why don't I get the children ready for school in time; for why are they so often late.

I let out on her my whole bitter heart. I told her my head was on wheels from worrying. When I get up in the morning, I don't know on what to turn first: should I nurse the baby, or make Sam's breakfast, or attend on the older children. I only got two hands.

"My dear woman," she says, "you are about to have a nervous breakdown. You need to get away to the country for a rest and vacation."

"Gott im Himmel!" says I. "Don't I know I need a rest? But how? On what money can I go to the country?"

"I know of a nice country place for mothers and children that will not cost you anything. It is free."

"Free! I never heard from it."

"Some kind people have made arrangements so no one need pay," she explains.

Later, in a few days, I just finished up with Masha and Mendel and Frieda and Sonya to send them to school, and I was getting Aby ready for kindergarten, when I hear a knock on the door, and a lady comes in. She had a white starched dress like a nurse and carried a black satchel in her hand.

"I am from the Social Betterment Society," she tells me. "You want to go to the country?"

Before I could say something, she goes over to the baby and pulls out the rubber nipple from her mouth, and to me, she says, "You must not get the child used to sucking this; it is very unsanitary."

"Gott im Himmel!" I beg the lady. "Please don't begin with that child, or she'll holler my head off. She must have the nipple. I'm too nervous to hear her scream like that."

When I put the nipple back again in the baby's mouth, the lady takes herself a seat, and then takes out a big black book from her satchel. Then she begins to question me. What is my first name? How old I am? From where come I? How long I'm already in this country? Do I keep any boarders? What is my husband's first name? How old he is? How long he is in this country? By what trade he works? How much wages he gets for a week? How much money do I spend out for rent? How old are the children, and everything about them.

"My goodness!" I cry out. "For why is it necessary all this to know? For why must I tell you all my business? What difference does it make already if I keep boarders, or I don't keep boarders? If Masha had the whooping-cough or Sonya had the measles? Or whether I spend out for my rent ten dollars or twenty? Or whether I come from Schnipishock or Kovner Gubernie?"

"We must make a record of all the applicants, and investigate each case," she tells me. "There are so many who apply to the charities, we can help only those who are most worthy."

"Charities!" I scream out. "Ain't the charities those who help the beggars out? I ain't no beggar. I'm not asking for no charity. My husband, he works."

"Miss Holcomb, the visiting teacher, said that you wanted to go to the country, and I had to make out this report before investigating your case."

"Oh! Oh!" I choke and bit my lips. "Is the free country from which Miss Holcomb told me, is it from the charities? She was telling me some kind people made arrangements for any mother what needs to go there."

"If your application is approved, you will be notified," she says to me, and out she goes.

When she is gone I think to myself, I'd better knock out from my head this idea about the country. For so long I lived, I didn't know nothing about the charities. For why should I come down among the beggars now?

Then I looked around me in the kitchen. On one side was the big wash-tub with clothes, waiting for me to wash. On the table was a pile of breakfast dishes yet. In the sink was the potatoes, waiting to be peeled. The baby was beginning to cry for the bottle. Aby was hollering and pulling me to take him to kindergarten. I felt if I didn't get away from here for a little while, I would land in a crazy house, or from the window jump down. Which was worser, to land in a crazy house, jump from the window down, or go to the country from the charities?

In about two weeks later around comes the same lady with the satchel again in my house.

"You can go to the country to-morrow," she tells me. "And you must come to the charity building to-morrow at nine o'clock sharp. Here is a card with the address. Don't lose it, because you must hand it to the lady in the office."

I look on the card, and there I see my name wrote; and by it, in big printed letters, that word "CHARITY."

"Must I go to the charity office?" I ask, feeling my heart to sink. "For why must I come there?"

"It is the rule that everybody comes to the office first, and from there they are taken to the country."

I shivered to think how I would feel, suppose somebody from my friends should see me walking into the charity office with my children. They wouldn't know that it is only for the country I go there. They might think I go to beg. Have I come down so low as to be seen by the charities? But what's the use? Should I knock my head on the walls? I had to go.

When I come to the office, I already found a crowd of women and children sitting on long benches and waiting. I took myself a seat with them, and we were sitting and sitting and looking on one another, sideways and crosswise, and with lowered eyes, like guilty criminals. Each one felt like hiding herself from all the rest. Each one felt black with shame in the face.

We may have been sitting and waiting for an hour or more. But every second was seeming years to me. The children began to get restless. Mendel wanted water. The baby on my arms was falling asleep. Aby was crying for something to eat.

"For why are we sittin' here like fat cats?" says the woman next to me. "Ain't we going to the country to-day yet?"

At last a lady comes to the desk and begins calling us our names, one by one. I nearly dropped to the floor when over she begins to ask: Do you keep boarders? How much do you spend out for rent? How much wages does your man get for a week?

Didn't the nurse tell them all about us already? It was bitter enough to have to tell the nurse everything, but in my own house nobody was hearing my troubles, only the nurse. But in the office there was so many strangers all around me. For why should everybody have to know my business? At every question I wanted to holler out: "Stop! Stop! I don't want no vacations! I'll better run home with my children." At every question I felt like she was stabbing a knife into my heart. And she kept on stabbing me more and more, but I could not help it, and they were all looking at me. I couldn't move from her. I had to answer everything.

When she got through with me, my face was red like fire. I was burning with hurts and wounds. I felt like everything was bleeding in me.

When all the names was already called, a man doctor with a nurse comes in, and tells us to form a line, to be examined. I wish I could ease out my heart a little, and tell in words how that doctor looked on us, just because we were poor and had no money to pay. He only used the ends from his finger-tips to examine us with. From the way he was afraid to touch us or come near us, he made us feel like we had some catching sickness that he was trying not to get on him.

The doctor got finished with us in about five minutes, so quick he worked. Then we was told to walk after the nurse, who was leading the way for us through the street to the car. Everybody what passed us in the street turned around to look on us. I kept down my eyes and held down my head and I felt like sinking into the sidewalk. All the time I was trembling for fear somebody what knows me might yet pass and see me. For why did they make us walk through the street, after the nurse, like stupid cows? Weren't all of us smart enough to find our way without the nurse? Why should the whole world have to see that we are from the charities?

When we got into the train, I opened my eyes, and lifted up my head, and straightened out my chest, and again began to breathe. It was a beautiful, sunshiny day. I knocked open the window from the train, and the fresh-smelling country air rushed upon my face and made me feel so fine! I looked out from the window and instead of seeing the iron fire-escapes with garbage-cans and bedclothes, that I always seen when from my flat I looked—instead of seeing only walls and wash-lines between walls, I saw the blue sky, and green grass and trees and flowers.

Ah, how grand I felt, just on the sky to look! Ah, how grand I felt just to see the green grass—and the free space—and no houses!

"Get away from me, my troubles!" I said. "Leave me rest a minute. Leave me breathe and straighten out my bones. Forget the unpaid butcher's bill. Forget the rent. Forget the wash-tub and the cook-stove and the pots and pans. Forget the charities!"

"Tickets, please," calls the train conductor.

I felt knocked out from heaven all at once. I had to point to the nurse what held our tickets, and I was feeling the conductor looking on me as if to say, "Oh, you are only from the charities."

By the time we came to the vacation house I already forgot all about my knock-down. I was again filled with the beauty of the country. I never in all my life yet seen such a swell house like that vacation house. Like the grandest palace it looked. All round the front, flowers from all colors was smelling out the sweetest perfume. Here and there was shady trees with comfortable chairs under them to sit down on.

When I only came inside, my mouth opened wide and my breathing stopped still from wonder. I never yet seen such an order and such a cleanliness. From all the corners from the room, the cleanliness was shining like a looking-glass. The floor was so white scrubbed you could eat on it. You couldn't find a speck of dust on nothing, if you was looking for it with eyeglasses on.

I was beginning to feel happy and glad that I come, when, Gott im Himmel! again a lady begins to ask us out the same questions what the nurse already asked me in my home and what was asked over again in the charity office. How much wages my husband makes out for a week? How much money I spend out for rent? Do I keep boarders?

We were hungry enough to faint. So worn out was I from excitement, and from the long ride, that my knees were bending under me ready to break from tiredness. The children were pulling me to pieces, nagging me for a drink, for something to eat and such like. But still we had to stand out the whole list of questionings. When she already got through asking us out everything, she gave to each of us a tag with our name written on it. She told us to tie the tag on our hand. Then like tagged horses at a horse sale in the street, they marched us into the dining-room.

There was rows of long tables, covered with pure-white oilcloth. A vase with bought flowers was standing on the middle from each table. Each person got a clean napkin for himself. Laid out by the side from each person's plate was a silver knife and fork and spoon and teaspoon. When we only sat ourselves down, girls with white starched aprons was passing around the eatings.

I soon forgot again all my troubles. For the first time in ten years I sat down to a meal what I did not have to cook or worry about. For the first time in ten years I sat down to the table like a somebody. Ah, how grand it feels, to have handed you over the eatings and everything you need. Just as I was beginning to like it and let myself feel good, in comes a fat lady all in white, with a teacher's look on her face. I could tell already, right away by the way she looked on us, that she was the boss from this place.

"I want to read you the rules from this house, before you leave this room," says she to us.

Then she began like this: We dassen't stand on the front grass where the flowers are. We dassen't stay on the front porch. We dassen't sit on the chairs under the shady trees. We must stay always in the back and sit on those long wooden benches there. We dassen't come in the front sitting-room or walk on the front steps what have carpet on it—we must walk on the back iron steps. Everything on the front from the house must be kept perfect for the show for visitors. We dassen't lay down on the beds in the daytime, the beds must always be made up perfect for the show for visitors.

"Gott im Himmel!" thinks I to myself; "ain't there going to be no end to the things we dassen't do in this place?"

But still she went on. The children over two years dassen't stay around by the mothers. They must stay by the nurse in the play-room. By the meal-times, they can see their mothers. The children dassen't run around the house or tear up flowers or do anything. They dassen't holler or play rough in the play-room. They must always behave and obey the nurse.

We must always listen to the bells. Bell one was for getting up. Bell two, for getting babies' bottles. Bell three, for coming to breakfast. Bell four, for bathing the babies. If we come later, after the ring from the bell, then we'll not get what we need. If the bottle bell rings and we don't come right away for the bottle, then the baby don't get no bottle. If the breakfast bell rings, and we don't come right away down to the breakfast, then there won't be no breakfast for us.

When she got through with reading the rules, I was wondering which side of the house I was to walk on. At every step was some rule what said don't move here, and don't go there, don't stand there, and don't sit there. If I tried to remember the endless rules, it would only make me dizzy in the head. I was thinking for why, with so many rules, didn't they also have already another rule, about how much air in our lungs to breathe.

On every few days there came to the house swell ladies in automobiles. It was for them that the front from the house had to be always perfect. For them was all the beautiful smelling flowers. For them the front porch, the front sitting-room, and the easy stairs with the carpet on it.

Always when the rich ladies came the fat lady, what was the boss from the vacation house, showed off to them the front. Then she took them over to the back to look on us, where we was sitting together, on long wooden benches, like prisoners. I was always feeling cheap like dirt, and mad that I had to be there, when they smiled down on us.

"How nice for these poor creatures to have a restful place like this," I heard one lady say.

The next day I already felt like going back. The children what had to stay by the nurse in the play-room didn't like it neither.

"Mamma," says Mendel to me, "I wisht I was home and out in the street. They don't let us do nothing here. It's worser than school."

"Ain't it a play-room?" asks I. "Don't they let you play?"

"Gee wiss! play-room, they call it! The nurse hollers on us all the time. She don't let us do nothing."

The reason why I stayed out the whole two weeks is this: I think to myself, so much shame in the face I suffered to come here, let me at least make the best from it already. Let me at least save up for two weeks what I got to spend out for grocery and butcher for my back bills to pay out. And then also think I to myself, if I go back on Monday, I got to do the big washing; on Tuesday waits for me the ironing; on Wednesday, the scrubbing and cleaning, and so goes it on. How bad it is already in this place, it's a change from the very same sameness of what I'm having day in and day out at home. And so I stayed out this vacation to the bitter end.

But at last the day for going out from this prison came. On the way riding back, I kept thinking to myself: "This is such a beautiful vacation house. For why do they make it so hard for us? When a mother needs a vacation, why must they tear the insides out from her first, by making her come down to the charity office? Why drag us from the charity office through the streets? And when we live through the shame of the charities and when we come already to the vacation house, for why do they boss the life out of us with so many rules and bells? For why don't they let us lay down our heads on the bed when we are tired? For why must we always stick in the back, like dogs what have got to be chained in one spot? If they would let us walk around free, would we bite off something from the front part of the house?

"If the best part of the house what is comfortable is made up for a show for visitors, why ain't they keeping the whole business for a show for visitors? For why do they have to fool in worn-out mothers, to make them think they'll give them a rest? Do they need the worn-out mothers as part of the show? I guess that is it, already."

When I got back in my home, so happy and thankful I was I could cry from thankfulness. How good it was feeling for me to be able to move around my own house, like I pleased. I was always kicking that my rooms was small and narrow, but now my small rooms seemed to grow so big like the park. I looked out from my window on the fire-escapes, full with bedding and garbage-cans, and on the wash-lines full with the clothes. All these ugly things was grand in my eyes. Even the high brick walls all around made me feel like a bird what just jumped out from a cage. And I cried out, "Gott sei dank! Gott sei dank!"

The Miracle

*L*ike all people who have nothing, I lived on dreams. With nothing but my longing for love, I burned my way through stone walls till I got to America. And what happened to me when I became an American is more than I can picture before my eyes, even in a dream.

I was a poor Melamid's daughter in Savel, Poland. In my village, a girl without a dowry was a dead one. The only kind of a man that would give a look on a girl without money was a widower with a dozen children, or someone with a hump or on crutches.

There was the village water-carrier with red, teary eyes, and warts on his cracked lip. There was the janitor of the bath-house, with a squash nose, and long, black nails with all the dirt of the world under them. Maybe one of these uglinesses might yet take pity on me and do me the favor to marry me. I shivered and grew cold through all my bones at the thought of them.

Like the hunger for bread was my hunger for love. My life was nothing to me. My heart was empty. Nothing I did was real without love. I used to spend nights crying on my pillow, praying to God: "I want love! I want love! I can't live—I can't breathe without love!"

And all day long I'd ask myself: "Why was I born? What is the use of dragging on day after day, wasting myself eating, sleeping, dressing? What is the meaning of anything without love?" And my heart was so hungry I couldn't help feeling and dreaming that somehow, somewhere, there must be a lover waiting for me. But how and where could I find my lover was the one longing that burned in my heart by day and by night.

Then came the letter from Hanneh Hayyeh, Zlata's daughter, that fired me up to go to America for my lover.

"America is a lover's land," said Hanneh Hayyeh's letter. "In America millionaires fall in love with poorest girls. Matchmakers are out of style, and a girl can get herself married to a man without the worries for a dowry."

"God from the world!" began knocking my heart. "How grand to live where the kind of a man you get don't depend on how much money your father can put down! If I could only go to America! There—there waits my lover for me."

That letter made a holiday all over Savel. The butcher, the grocer, the shoemaker, everybody stopped his work and rushed to our house to hear my father read the news from the Golden Country.

"Stand out your ears to hear my great happiness," began Hanneh Hayyeh's letter. "I, Hanneh Hayyeh, will marry myself to Solomon Cohen, the boss from the shirtwaist factory, where all day I was working sewing on buttons. If you could only see how the man is melting away his heart for me! He kisses me after each step I walk. The only wish from his heart is to make me for a lady. Think only, he is buying me a piano! I should learn piano lessons as if I were from millionaires."

Fire and lightning burst through the crowd. "Hanneh Hayyeh a lady!" They nudged and winked one to the other as they looked on the loose fatness of Zlata, her mother, and saw before their eyes Hanneh Hayyeh, with her thick, red lips, and her shape so fat like a puffed-out barrel of yeast.

"In America is a law called 'ladies first,'" the letter went on. "In the cars the men must get up to give their seats to the women. The men hold the babies on their hands and carry the bundles for the women, and even help with the dishes. There are not enough women to go around in America. And the men run after the women, and not like in Poland, the women running after the men."

Gewalt! What an excitement began to burn through the whole village when they heard of Hanneh Hayyeh's luck!

The ticket agents from the ship companies seeing how Hanneh Hayyeh's letter was working like yeast in the air for America, posted up big signs by all the market fairs: "Go to America, the New World. Fifty rubles a ticket."

"Fifty rubles! Only fifty rubles! And there waits your lover!" cried my heart.

Oi weh! How I was hungering to go to America after that! By day and by night I was tearing and turning over the earth, how to get to my lover on the other side of the world.

"Nu, Zalmon?" said my mother, twisting my father around to what I wanted. "It's not so far from sense what Sara Reisel is saying. In Savel, without a dowry, she had no chance to get a man, and if we got to wait much longer she will be too old to get one anywhere."

"But from where can we get together the fifty rubles?" asked my father. "Why don't it will itself in you to give your daughter the moon?"

I could no more think on how to get the money than they. But I was so dying to go, I felt I could draw the money out from the sky.

One night I could not fall asleep. I lay in the darkness and stillness, my wild, beating heart on fire with dreams of my lover. I put out my hungry hands and prayed to my lover through the darkness: "Oh, love, love! How can I get the fifty rubles to come to you?"

In the morning I got up like one choking for air. We were sitting down to eat breakfast, but I couldn't taste nothing. I felt my head drop into my hands from weakness.

"Why don't you try to eat something?" begged my mother, going over to me.

"Eat?" I cried, jumping up like one mad. "How can I eat? How can I sleep? How can I breathe in this deadness? I want to go to America. I *must* go, and I *will* go!"

My mother began wringing her hands. "Oi weh! Mine heart! The knife is on our neck. The landlord is hollering for the unpaid rent, and it wills itself in you America?"

"Are you out of your head?" cried my father.

"What are you dreaming of golden hills on the sky? How can we get together the fifty rubles for a ticket?"

I stole a look at Yosef, my younger brother. Nothing that was sensible ever laid in his head to do; but if there was anything wild, up in the air that willed itself in him, he could break through stone walls to get it. Yosef gave a look around the house. Everything was old and poor, and not a thing to get money on—nothing except father's Saifer Torah—the Holy Scrolls—and mother's silver candlesticks, her wedding present from our grandmother.

"Why not sell the Saifer Torah and the candlesticks?" said Yosef.

Nobody but my brother would have dared to breathe such a thing.

"What? A Jew sell the Saifer Torah or the Sabbath candlesticks?" My father fixed on us his burning eyes like flaming wells. His hands tightened over his heart. He couldn't speak. He just looked on the Saifer Torah, and then on us with a look that burned like live coals on our naked bodies. "What?" he gasped. "Should I sell my life, my soul from generation and generation? Sell my Saifer Torah? Not if the world goes under!"

There was a stillness of thunder about to break. Everybody heard everybody's heart beating.

"Did I live to see this black day?" moaned my father, choking from quick breathing. "Mine own son, mine Kadish—mine Kadish tells me to sell the Holy Book that our forefathers shed rivers of blood to hand down to us."

"What are you taking it so terrible?" said my brother. "Doesn't it stand in the Talmud that to help marry his daughter a man may sell the holiest thing—even the Holy Book?"

"*Are there miracles in America?* Can she yet get there a man at her age and without a dowry?"

"If Hanneh Hayyeh, who is older than Sara Reisel and not half as good-looking," said my brother, "could get a boss from a factory, then whom cannot Sara Reisel pick out? And with her luck all of us will be lifted over to America."

My father did not answer. I waited, but still he did not answer.

At last I burst out with all the tears choking in me for years: "Is your old Saifer Torah that hangs on the wall dearer to you than that I should marry? The Talmud tells you to sell the holiest thing to help marry your daughter, but you—you love yourself more than your own child!"

Then I turned to my mother. I hit my hands on the table and cried in a voice that made her tremble and grow frightened: "Maybe you love your silver candlesticks more than your daughter's happiness? To whom can I marry myself here, I ask you, only—to the bath janitor, to the water-carrier? I tell you I'll kill myself if you don't help me get away! I can't stand no more this deadness here. I must get away. And you must give up everything to help me get away. All I need is a chance. I can do a million times better than Hanneh Hayyeh. I got a head. I got brains. I feel I can marry myself to the greatest man in America."

My mother stopped crying, took up the candlesticks from the mantelpiece and passed her hands over them. "It's like a piece from my flesh," she said. "We grew up with this, you children and I, and my mother and my mother's mother. This and the Saifer Torah are the only things that shine up the house for the Sabbath."

She couldn't go on, her words choked in her so. I am seeing yet how she looked, holding the candlesticks in her hands, and her eyes that she turned on us. But then I didn't see anything but to go to America.

She walked over to my father, who sat with his head in his hands, stoned with sadness. "Zalmon!" she sobbed. "The blood from under my nails I'll give away, only my child should have a chance to marry herself well. I'll give away my candlesticks—"

Even my brother Yosef's eyes filled with tears, so he quick jumped up and began to whistle and move around. "You don't have to sell them," he cried, trying to make it light in the air. "You can pawn them by Moisheh Itzek, the usurer, and as soon as Sara Reisel will get herself married, she'll send us the money to get them out again, and we'll yet live to take them over with us to America."

I never saw my father look so sad. He looked like a man from whom the life is bleeding away. "I'll not stand myself against your happiness," he said, in a still voice. "I only hope this will be to your luck and that you'll get married quick, so we could take out the Saifer Torah from the pawn."

In less than a week the Saifer Torah and the candlesticks were pawned and the ticket bought. The whole village was ringing with the news that I am going to America. when I walked in the street people pointed on me with their fingers as if I were no more the same Sara Reisel.

Everybody asked me different questions.

"Tell me how it feels to go to America? Can you yet sleep nights like other people?"

"When you'll marry yourself in America, will you yet remember us?"

God from the world! That last Friday night before I went to America! Maybe it is the last time we are together was in everybody's eyes. Everything that happened seemed so different from all other times. I felt I was getting ready to tear my life out from my body.

Without the Saifer Torah the house was dark and empty. The sun, the sky, the whole heaven shined from that Holy Book on the wall, and when it was taken out it left an aching emptiness on the heart, as if something beautiful passed out of our lives.

I yet see before me my father in the Rabbi's cap, with eyes that look far away into things; the way he sang the prayer over the wine when he passed around the glass for every one to give a sip. The tears rolled out from my little sister's eyes down her cheeks and fell into the wine. On that my mother, who was all the time wiping her tears, burst out crying. "Shah! Shah!" commanded my father, rising up from his chair and beginning to walk around the room. "It's Sabbath night, when every Jew should be happy. Is this the way you give honor to God on His one day that He set aside for you?"

On the next day, that was Sabbath, father as if held us up in his hands, and everybody behaved himself. A stranger coming in couldn't see anything that was going on, except that we walked so still and each one by himself, as if somebody dying was in the air over us.

On the going-away morning, everybody was around our house waiting to take me to the station. Everybody wanted to give a help with the bundles. The moving along to the station was like a funeral. Nobody could hold in their feelings any longer. Everybody fell on my neck to kiss me, as if it was my last day on earth.

"Remember you come from Jews. Remember to pray every day," said my father, putting his hands over my head, like in blessing on the day of Atonement.

"Only try that we should be together soon again," were the last words from my mother as she wiped her eyes with the corner of her shawl.

"Only don't forget that I want to study, and send for me as quick as you marry yourself," said Yosef, smiling good-bye with tears in his eyes.

As I saw the train coming, what wouldn't I have given to stay back with the people in Savel forever! I wanted to cry out: "Take only away my ticket! I don't want any more America! I don't want any more my lover!"

But as soon as I got into the train, although my eyes were still looking back to the left-behind faces, and my ears were yet hearing the good-byes and the partings, the thoughts of America began stealing into my heart. I was thinking how soon I'd have my lover and be rich like Hanneh Hayyeh. And with my luck, everybody was going to be happy in Savel. The dead people will stop dying and all the sorrows and troubles of the world will be wiped away with my happiness.

I didn't see the day. I didn't see the night. I didn't see the ocean. I didn't see the sky. I only saw my lover in America, coming nearer and nearer to me, till I could feel his eyes bending on me so near that I got frightened and began to tremble. My heart ached so with the joy of his nearness that I quick drew back and turned away, and began to talk to the people that were pushing and crowding themselves on the deck.

Nu, I got to America.

Ten hours I pushed a machine in a shirtwaist factory, when I was yet lucky to get work. And always my head was drying up with saving and pinching and worrying to send home a little from the little I earned. All that my face saw all day long was girls and machines—and nothing else. And even when I came already home from work, I could only talk to the girls in the working-girls' boarding-house, or shut myself up in my dark, lonesome bedroom. No family, no friends, nobody to get me acquainted with nobody! The only men I saw were what passed me by in the street and in cars.

"Is this 'lovers' land'?" was calling in my heart. "Where are my dreams that were so real to me in the old country?"

Often in the middle of the work I felt like stopping all the machines and crying out to the world the heaviness that pressed on my heart. Sometimes when I walked in the street I felt like going over to the first man I met and cry out to him: "Oh, I'm so lonely! I'm so lonely!"

One day I read in the Jewish "Tageblatt" the advertisement from Zaretzky, the matchmaker. "What harm is it if I try my luck?" I said to myself. "I can't die away an old maid. Too much love burns in my heart to stand back like a stone and only see how other people are happy. I want to tear myself out from my deadness. I'm in a living grave. I've got to lift myself up. I have nobody to try for me, and maybe the matchmaker will help."

As I walked up Delancey Street to Mr. Zaretzky, the street was turning with me. I didn't see the crowds. I didn't see the pushcart peddlers with their bargains. I didn't hear the noises or anything. My eyes were on the sky, praying: "Gottuniu! Send me only the little bit of luck!"

"Nu? Nu? What need you?" asked Mr. Zaretzky when I entered.

I got red with shame in the face the way he looked at me. I turned up my head. I was too proud to tell him for what I came. Before I walked in I thought to tell him everything. But when I looked on his face and saw his hard eyes, I couldn't say a word. I stood like a yok unable to move my tongue. I went to the matchmaker with my heart, and I saw before me a stone. The stone was talking to me—but—but—he was a stone!

"Are you looking for a shidduch?" he asked.

"Yes," I said, proud, but crushed.

"You know I charge five dollars for the stepping in," he bargained.

It got cold by my heart. It wasn't only to give him the five dollars, nearly a whole week's wages, but his thick-skinness for being only after the money. But I couldn't help myself—I was like in his fists hypnotized. And I gave him the five dollars.

I let myself go to the door, but he called me back.

"Wait, wait. Come in and sit down. I didn't question you yet."

"About what?"

"I got to know how much money you got saved before I can introduce you to anybody."

"Oh—h—h! Is it only depending on the *money?*"

"Certainly. No move in this world without money," he said, taking a pinch of snuff in his black, hairy fingers and sniffing it up in his nose.

I glanced on his thick neck and greasy, red face. "And to him people come looking for love," I said to myself, shuddering. Oh, how it burned in my heart, but still I went on, "Can't I get a man in America without money?"

He gave a look on me with his sharp eyes. Gottuniu! What a look! I thought I was sinking into the floor.

"There are plenty of *young* girls with money that are begging themselves the men to take them. So what can you expect? *Not young, not lively, and without money, too?* But, anyhow, I'll see what I can do for you."

He took out a little book from his vest-pocket and looked through the names.

"What trade do you go on your hands?" he asked, turning to me. "Sometimes a dressmaker or a hairdresser that can help make a living for a man, maybe—"

I couldn't hear any more. It got black before my eyes, my voice stopped inside of me.

"If you want to listen to sense from a friend, so I have a good match for you," he said, following me to the door. "I have on my list a widower with not more than five or six children. He has a grand business, a herring-stand on Hester Street. He don't ask for no money, and he don't make an objection if the girl is in years, so long as she knows how to cook well for him."

How I got myself back to my room I don't know. But for two days and for two nights I lay still on my bed, unable to move. I looked around on my empty walls, thinking, thinking, "Where am I? Is this the world? Is this America?"

Suddenly I sprang up from bed. "What can come from pitying yourself?" I cried. "If the world kicks you down and makes nothing of you, you bounce yourself up and make something of yourself." A fire blazed up in me to rise over the world because I was downed by the world.

"Make a person of yourself," I said. "Begin to learn English. Make yourself for an American if you want to live in America. American girls don't go to matchmakers. American girls don't run after a man: if they don't get a husband they don't think the world is over; they turn their mind to something else.

"Wake up!" I said to myself. "You want love to come to you? Why don't you give it out to other people? Love the women and children, everybody in the street and the shop. Love the rag-picker and the drunkard, the bad and the ugly. All those whom the world kicks down you pick up and press to your heart with love."

As I said this I felt wells of love that choked in me all my life flowing out of me and over me. A strange, wonderful light like a lover's smile melted over me, and the sweetness of lover's arms stole around me.

The first night I went to school I felt like falling on everybody's neck and kissing them. I felt like kissing the books and the benches. It was such great happiness to learn to read and write the English words.

Because I started a few weeks after the beginning of the term, my teacher said I might stay after the class to help me catch up with my back lessons. The minute I looked on him I felt that grand feeling: "Here is a person! Here is America!" His face just shined with high thoughts. There was such a beautiful light in his eyes that it warmed my heart to steal a look on him.

At first, when it came my turn to say something in the class, I got so excited the words stuck and twisted in my mouth and I couldn't give out my thoughts. But the teacher didn't see my nervousness. He only saw that I had something to say, and he helped me say it. How or what he did I don't know. I only felt his look of understanding flowing into me like draughts of air to one who is choking.

Long after I already felt free and easy to talk to him alone after the class, I looked at all the books on his desk. "Oi weh!" I said to him, "if I only knew half of what is in your books, I couldn't any more sit still in the chair like you. I'd fly in the air with the joy of so much knowledge."

"Why are you so eager for learning?" he asked me.

"Because I want to make a person of myself," I answered. "Since I got to work for low wages and I can't be young any more, I'm burning to get among people where it's not against a girl if she is in years and without money."

His hand went out to me. "I'll help you," he said. "But you must first learn to get hold of yourself."

Such a beautiful kindness went out of his heart to me with his words! His voice, and the goodness that shone from his eyes, made me want to burst out crying, but I choked back my tears till I got home. And all night long I wept on my pillow: "Fool! What is the matter with you? Why are you crying?" But I said, "I can't help it. He is so beautiful!"

My teacher was so much above me that he wasn't a man to me at all. He was a god. His face lighted up the shop for me, and his voice sang itself in me everywhere I went. It was like healing medicine to the flaming fever within me to listen to his voice. And then I'd repeat to myself his words and live in them as if they were religion.

Often as I sat at the machine sewing the waists I'd forget what I was doing. I'd find myself dreaming in the air. "Ach!" I asked myself, "what was that beautifulness in his eyes that made the lowest nobody feel like a somebody? What was that about him that when his smile fell on me I felt lifted up to the sky away from all the coldness and the ugliness of the world? Gottunui!" I prayed, "if I could only always hold on to the light of high thoughts that shined from him. If I could only always hear in my heart the sound of his voice I would need nothing more in life. I would be happier than a bird in the air.

"Friend," I said to him once, "if you could but teach me how to get cold in the heart and clear in the head like you are!"

He only smiled at me and looked far away. His calmness was like the sureness of money in the bank. Then he turned and looked on me, and said: "I am not so cold in the heart and clear in the head as I make-believe. I am bound. I am a prisoner of convention."

"You make-believe—you bound?" I burst out. "You who do not have foreladies or bosses—you who do not have to sell yourself for wages—you who only work for love and truth—you a prisoner?"

"True, I do not have bosses just as you do," he said. "But still I am not free. I am bound by formal education and conventional traditions. Though you work in a shop, you are really freer than I. You are not repressed as I am by the fear and shame of feeling. You could teach me more than I could teach you. You could teach me how to be natural."

"I'm not so natural like you think," I said. "I'm afraid."

He smiled at me out of his eyes. "What are you afraid of?"

"I'm afraid of my heart," I said, trying to hold back the blood rushing to my face. "I'm burning to get calm and sensible like the born Americans. But how can I help it? My heart flies away from me like a wild bird. How can I learn to keep myself down on earth like the born Americans?"

"But I don't want you to get down on earth like the Americans. That is just the beauty and the wonder of you. We Americans are too much on earth; we need more of your power to fly. If you would only know how much you can teach us Americans. You are the promise of the centuries to come. You are the heart, the creative pulse of America to be."

I walked home on wings. My teacher said that I could help him; that I had something to give to Americans. "But how could I teach him?" I wondered; "I who had never had a chance to learn anything except what he taught me. And what had I to give to the Americans, I who am nothing but dreams and longings and hunger for love?"

When school closed down for vacation, it seemed to me all life stopped in the world. I had no more class to look forward to, no more chance of seeing my teacher. As I faced the emptiness of my long vacation, all the light went out of my eyes, and all the strength out of my arms and fingers.

For nearly a week I was like without air. There was no school. One night I came home from the shop and threw myself down on the bed. I wanted to cry, to let out the heavy weight that pressed on my heart, but I couldn't cry. My tears felt like hot, burning sand in my eyes.

"Oi-i-i! I can't stand it no more, this emptiness," I groaned. "Why don't I kill myself? Why don't something happen to me? No consumption, no fever, no plague or death ever comes to save me from this terrible world. I have to go on suffering and choking inside myself till I grow mad."

I jumped up from the bed, threw open the window, and began fighting with the deaf-and-dumb air in the air-shaft.

"What is the matter with you?" I cried. "You are going out of your head. You are sinking back into the old ways from which you dragged yourself out with your studies. Studies! What did I get from all my studies? Nothing. Nothing. I am still in the same shop with the same shirtwaists. A lot my teacher cares for me once the class is over."

A fire burned up in me that he was already forgetting me. And I shot out a letter to him:

"You call yourself a teacher? A friend? How can you go off in the country and drop me out of your heart and out of your head like a read-over book you left on the shelf of your shut-down classroom? How can you enjoy your vacation in the country while I'm in the sweatshop? You learned me nothing. You only broke my heart. What good are all the books you ever gave me? They don't tell me how to be happy in a factory. They don't tell me how to keep alive in emptiness, or how to find something beautiful in the dirt and ugliness in which I got to waste away. I want life. I want people. I can't live inside my head as you do."

I sent the letter off in the madness in which I wrote it, without stopping to think; but the minute after I dropped it in the mail-box my reason came again to my head. I went back tearing my hair. "What have I done? Meshugeneh!"

Walking up the stairs I saw my door open. I went in. The sky is falling to the earth! Am I dreaming? There was my teacher sitting on my trunk? My teacher come to see me? Me, in my dingy room? For a minute it got blind before my eyes, and I didn't know where I was any more.

"I had to come," he said, the light of heaven shining on me out of his eyes. "I was so desolate without you. I tried to say something to you before I left for my vacation, but the words wouldn't come. Since I have been away I have written you many letters, but I did not mail them, for they were like my old self from which I want to break away."

He put his cool, strong hand into mine. "You can save me," he said. "You can free me from the bondage of age-long repressions. You can lift me out of the dead grooves of sterile intellectuality. Without you I am the dry dust of hopes unrealized. You are fire and sunshine and desire. You make life changeable and beautiful and full of daily wonder."

I couldn't speak. I was so on fire with his words. Then, like whirlwinds in my brain, rushed out the burning words of the matchmaker: "Not young, not lively, and without money, too!"

"You are younger than youth," he said, kissing my hands. "Every day of your unlived youth shall be relived with love, but such a love as youth could never know."

And then how it happened I don't know; but his arms were around me. "Sara Reisel, tell me, do you love me," he said, kissing me on my hair and on my eyes and on my lips.

I could only weep and tremble with joy at his touch. "The miracle!" cried my heart; "the miracle of America come true!"

Where Lovers Dream

For years I was saying to myself—Just so you will act when you meet him. Just so you will stand. So will you look on him. These words you will say to him.

I wanted to show him that what he had done to me could not down me; that his leaving me the way he left me, that his breaking my heart the way he broke it, didn't crush me; that his grand life and my pinched-in life, his having learning and my not having learning—that the difference didn't count so much like it seemed; that on the bottom I was the same like him.

But he came upon me so sudden, all my plannings for years smashed to the wall. The sight of him was like an earthquake shaking me to pieces.

I can't yet see nothing in front of me and can't get my head together to anything, so torn up I am from the shock.

It was at Yetta Solomon's wedding I met him again. She was after me for weeks I should only come.

"How can I come to such a swell hall?" I told her. "You know I ain't got nothing decent to wear."

"Like you are without no dressing-up, I want you to come. You are the kind what people look in your eyes and not on what you got on. Ain't you yourself the one what helped me with my love troubles? And now, when everything is turning out happy, you mean to tell me that you ain't going to be there?"

She gave me a grab over and kissed me in a way that I couldn't say "No" to her.

So I shined myself up in the best I had and went to the wedding.

I was in the middle from giving my congratulations to Yetta and her new husband, when—Gott! Gott im Himmel! The sky is falling to the earth! I see him—him, and his wife leaning on his arm, coming over.

I gave a fall back, like something sharp hit me. My head got dizzy, and my eyes got blind.

I wanted to run away from him, but, ach! everything in me rushed to him.

I was feeling like struck deaf, dumb, and blind all in one.

He must have said something to me, and I must have answered back something to him, but how? What? I only remember like in a dream my getting to the cloakroom. Such a tearing, grinding pain was dragging me down to the floor that I had to hold on to the wall not to fall.

All of a sudden I feel a pull on my arm. It was the janitor with the broom in his hand.

"Lady, are you sick? The wedding people is all gone, and I swept up already."

But I couldn't wake up from myself.

"Lady, the lights is going out," he says, looking on me queer.

"I think I ain't well," I said. And I went out.

Ach, I see again the time when we was lovers! How beautiful the world was then!

"Maybe there never was such love like ours, and never will be," we was always telling one another.

When we was together there was like a light shining around us, the light from his heart on mine, and from my heart on his. People began to look happy just looking on us.

When we was walking we didn't feel we was touching the earth but flying high up through the air. We looked on the rest of the people with pity, because it was seeming to us that we was the only two persons awake, and all the rest was hurrying and pushing and slaving and crowding one on the other without the splendidness of feeling for what it was all for, like we was feeling it.

David was learning for a doctor. Daytimes he went to college, and nights he was in a drugstore. I was working in a factory on shirtwaists. We was poor. But we didn't feel poor. The waists I was sewing flyed like white birds through my fingers, because his face was shining out of everything I touched.

David was always trying to learn me how to make myself over for an American. Sometimes he would spend out fifteen cents to buy me the "Ladies' Home Journal" to read about American life, and my whole head was put away on how to look neat and be up-to-date like the American girls. Till long hours in the night I used to stay up brushing and pressing my plain blue suit with the white collar what David liked, and washing my waists, and fixing up my hat like the pattern magazines show you.

On holidays he took me out for a dinner by a restaurant, to learn me how the Americans eat, with napkins, and use up so many plates—the butter by itself, and the bread by itself, and the meat by itself, and the potatoes by itself.

Always when the six o'clock whistle blowed, he was waiting for me on the corner from the shop to take me home.

"Ut, there waits Sara's doctor feller," the girls were nudging one to the other, as we went out from the shop. "Ain't she the lucky one!"

All the way as we walked along he was learning me how to throw off my greenhorn talk, and say out the words in the American.

He used to stop me in the middle of the pavement and laugh from me, shaking me: "No t'ink or t'ank or t'ought, now. You're an American," he would say to me. And then he would fix my tongue and teeth together and make me say after him: "th-think, th-thank, th-thought; this, that, there." And if I said the words right, he kissed me in the hall when we got home. And if I said them wrong, he kissed me anyhow.

He moved next door to us, so we shouldn't lose the sweetness from one little minute that we could be together. There was only the thin wall between our kitchen and his room, and the first thing in the morning, we would knock in one to the other to begin the day together.

"See what I got for you, Hertzele," he said to me one day, holding up a grand printed card.

I gave a read. It was the ticket invitation for his graduation from college. I gave it a touch, with pride melting over in my heart.

"Only one week more, and you'll be a doctor for the world!"

"And then, heart of mine," he said, drawing me over to him and kissing me on the lips, "when I get my office fixed up, you will marry me?"

"Ach, such a happiness," I answered, "to be together all the time, and wait on you and cook for you, and do everything for you, like if I was your mother!"

"Uncle Rosenberg is coming special from Boston for my graduation."

"The one what helped out your chance for college?" I asked.

"Yes, and he's going to start me up the doctor's office, he says. Like his son he looks on me, because he only got daughters in his family."

"Ach, the good heart! He'll yet have joy and good luck from us! What is he saying about me?" I ask.

"I want him to see you first, darling. You can't help going to his heart, when he'll only give a look on you."

"Think only, Mammele—David is graduating for a doctor in a week!" I gave a hurry in to my mother that night. "And his Uncle Rosenberg is coming special from Boston and says he'll start him up in his doctor's office."

"Oi weh, the uncle is going to give a come, you say? Look how the house looks! And the children in rags and no shoes on their feet!"

The whole week before the uncle came, my mother and I was busy nights buying and fixing up, and painting the chairs, and nailing together solid the table, and hanging up calendar pictures to cover up the broken plaster on the wall, and fixing the springs from the sleeping lounge so it didn't sink in, and scrubbing up everything, and even washing the windows, like before Passover.

I stopped away from the shop, on the day David was graduating. Everything in the house was like for a holiday. The children shined up like rich people's children, with their faces washed clean and their hair brushed and new shoes on their feet. I made my father put away his black shirt and dress up in an American white shirt and starched collar. I fixed out my mother in a new white waist and a blue checked apron, and I blowed myself to dress up the baby in everything new, like a doll in a window. Her round, laughing face lighted up the house, so beautiful she was.

By the time we got finished the rush to fix ourselves out, the children's cheeks was red with excitement and our eyes was bulging bright, like ready to start for a picnic.

When David came in with his uncle, my father and mother and all the children gave a stand up.

But the "Boruch Chabo" and the hot words of welcome, what was rushing from us to say, froze up on our lips by the stiff look the uncle throwed on us.

David's uncle didn't look like David. He had a thick neck and a red face and the breathing of a man what eats plenty.—But his eyes looked smart like David's.

He wouldn't take no seat and didn't seem to want to let go from the door.

David laughed and talked fast, and moved around nervous, trying to cover up the ice. But he didn't get no answers from nobody. And he didn't look in my eyes, and I was feeling myself ashamed, like I did something wrong which I didn't understand.

My father started up to say something to the uncle—"Our David—" But I quick pulled him by the sleeve to stop. And nobody after that could say nothing, nobody except David.

I couldn't get up the heart to ask them to give a taste from the cake and the wine what we made ready special for them on the table.

The baby started crying for a cake, and I quick went over to take her up, because I wanted to hide myself with being busy with her. But only the crying and nothing else happening made my heart give a shiver, like bad luck was in the air.

And right away the uncle and him said good-bye and walked out.

When the door was shut the children gave a rush for the cakes, and then burst out in the street.

"Come, Schmuel," said my mother, "I got to say something with you." And she gave my father a pull in the other room and closed the door.

I felt they was trying not to look on me, and was shrinking away from the shame that was throwed on me.

"Och, what's the matter with me! Nothing can come between David and me. His uncle ain't everything," I said, trying to pull up my head.

I sat myself down by the table to cool down my nervousness. "Brace yourself up," I said to myself, jumping up from the chair and beginning to walk around again. "Nothing has happened. Stop off nagging yourself."

Just then I hear loud voices through the wall. I go nearer. Ut, it's his uncle!

The plaster from the wall was broken on our side by the door. "Lay your ear in this crack, and you can hear plain the words," I say to myself.

"What's getting over you? You ain't that kind to do such a thing," I say. But still I do it.

Oi weh, I hear the uncle plainly! "What's all this mean, these neighbors? Who's the pretty girl what made such eyes on you?"

"Ain't she beautiful? Do you like her?" I hear David.

"What? What's that matter to you?"

"I'll marry myself to her," says David.

"Marry! Marry yourself into that beggar house! Are you crazy?"

"A man could get to anywhere with such a beautiful girl."

"Koosh! Pretty faces is cheap like dirt. What has she got to bring you in for your future? An empty pocketbook? A starving family to hang over your neck?"

"You don't know nothing about her. You don't know what you're saying. She comes from fine people in Russia. You can see her father is a learned man."

"Ach! You make me a disgust with your calf talk! Poverty winking from every corner of the house! Hunger hollering from all their starved faces! I got too much sense to waste my love on beggars. And all the time I was planning for you an American family, people which are somebodies in this world, which could help you work up a practice! For why did I waste my good dollars on you?"

"Gott! Ain't David answering?" my heart cries out. "Why don't he throw him out of the house?"

"Perhaps I can't hear him," I think, and with my finger-nails I pick thinner the broken plaster.

I push myself back to get away and not to do it. But it did itself with my hands. "Don't let me hear nothing," I pray, and yet I strain more to hear.

The uncle was still hollering. And David wasn't saying nothing for me.

"Gazlen! You want to sink your life in a family of beggars?"

"But I love her. We're so happy together. Don't that count for something? I can't live without her."

"Koosh! Love her! Do you want to plan your future with your heart or with your head? Take for your wife an ignorant shopgirl without a cent! Can two dead people start up a dance together?"

"So you mean not to help me with the office?"

"Yah-yah-yah! I'll run on all fours to do it! The impudence from such penniless nobodies wanting to pull in a young man with a future for a doctor! Nobody but such a yok like you would be such an easy mark."

"Well, I got to live my own life, and I love her."

"That's all I got to say.—Where's my hat? Throw yourself away on the pretty face, make yourself to shame and to laughter with a ragged Melamid for a father-in-law, and I wash my hands from you for the rest of your life."

A change came over David from that day. For the first time we was no more one person together. We couldn't no more laugh and talk like we used to. When I tried to look him in the eyes, he gave them a turn away from me.

I used to lie awake nights turning over in my head David's looks, David's words, and it made me frightened like something black rising over me and pushing me out from David's heart. I could feel he was blaming me for something I couldn't understand.

Once David asked me, "Don't you love me no more?"

I tried to tell him that there wasn't no change in my love, but I couldn't no more talk out to him what was in my mind, like I used.

"I didn't want to worry you before with my worries," he said to me at last.

"Worry me, David! What am I here for?"

"My uncle is acting like a stingy grouch," he answered me, "and I can't stand no more his bossing me."

"Why didn't you speak yourself out to me what was on your mind, David?" I asked him.

"You don't know how my plans is smashed to pieces," he said, with a worried look on his face. "I don't see how I'll ever be able to open my doctor's office. And how can we get married with your people hanging on for your wages?"

"Ah, David, don't you no longer feel that love can find a way out?"

He looked on me, down and up, and up and down, till I drawed myself back, frightened.

But he grabbed me back to him. "I love you. I love you, heart of mine," he said, kissing me on the neck, on my hair and my eyes. "And nothing else matters, does it, does it?" and he kissed me again and again, as if he wanted to swallow me up.

Next day I go out from the shop and down the steps to meet him, like on every day.

I give a look around.

"Gott! Where is he? He wasn't never late before," gave a knock my heart.

I waited out till all the girls was gone, and the streets was getting empty, but David didn't come yet.

"Maybe an accident happened to him, and I standing round here like a dummy," and I gave a quick hurry home.

But nobody had heard nothing.

"He's coming! He *must* come!" I fighted back my fear. But by evening he hadn't come yet.

I sent in my brother next door to see if he could find him.

"He moved to-day," comes in my brother to tell me.

"My God! David left me? It ain't possible!"

I walk around the house, waiting and listening. "Don't let nobody see your nervousness. Don't let yourself out. Don't break down."

It got late and everybody was gone to bed.

I couldn't take my clothes off. Any minute he'll come up the steps or knock on the wall. Any minute a telegram will come.

It's twelve o'clock. It's one. Two!

Every time I hear footsteps in the empty street, I am by the window— "Maybe it's him."

It's beginning the day.

The sun is rising. Oi weh, how can the sun rise and he not here? Mein Gott! He ain't coming!

I sit myself down on the floor by the window with my head on the sill. Everybody is sleeping. I can't sleep. And I'm so tired.

Next day I go, like pushed on, to the shop, glad to be swallowed up by my work.

The noise of the knocking machines is like a sleeping-medicine to the cryings inside of me. All day I watched my hands push the waists up and down the machine. I wasn't with my hands. It was like my breathing stopped and I was sitting inside of myself, waiting for David.

The six o'clock whistle blowed. I go out from the shop.

I can't help it—I look for him.

"Oi, Gott! Do something for me once! Send him only!"

I hold on to the iron fence of the shop, because I feel my heart bleeding away.

I can't go away. The girls all come out from the shops, and the streets get empty and still. But at the end of the block once in a while somebody crosses and goes out from sight.

I watch them. I begin counting, "One, two, three—"

Underneath my mind is saying, "Maybe it's him. Maybe the next one!"

My eyes shut themselves. I feel the end from everything.

"Ah, David! David! Gott! Mein Gott!"

I fall on the steps and clinch the stones with the twistings of my body. A terrible cry breaks out from me—"David! David!" My soul is tearing itself out from my body. It is gone.

Next day I got news—David opened a doctor's office uptown.

Nothing could hurt me no more. I didn't hope for nothing. Even if he wanted me back, I couldn't go to him no more. I was like something dying what wants to be left alone in darkness.

But still something inside of me wanted to see for itself how all is dead between us, and I write him:

"David Novak: You killed me. You killed my love. Why did you leave me yet living? Why must I yet drag on the deadness from me?"

I don't know why I wrote him. I just wanted to give a look on him. I wanted to fill up my eyes with him before I turned them away forever.

I was sitting by the table in the kitchen, wanting to sew, but my hands was lying dead on the table, when the door back of me burst open.

"O God! What have I done? Your face is like ashes! You look like you are dying!" David gave a rush in.

His hair wasn't combed, his face wasn't shaved, his clothes was all wrinkled. My letter he was holding crushed in his hand.

"I killed you! I left you! But I didn't rest a minute since I went away! Heart of mine, forgive me!"

He gave a take my hand, and fell down kneeling by me.

"Sarale, speak to me!"

"False dog! Coward!" cried my father, breaking in on us. "Get up! Get out! Don't dare touch my child again! May your name and memory be blotted out!"

David covered up his head with his arm and fell back to the wall like my father had hit him.

"You yet listen to him?" cried my father, grabbing me by the arm and shaking me. "Didn't I tell you he's a Meshumid, a denier of God?"

"Have pity! Speak to me! Give me only a word!" David begged me.

I wanted to speak to him, to stretch out my hands to him and call him over, but I couldn't move my body. No voice came from my lips no more than if I was locked in my grave.

I was dead, and the David I loved was dead.

I married Sam because he came along and wanted me, and I didn't care about nothing no more.

But for long after, even when the children began coming, my head was still far away in the dream of the time when love was. Before my eyes was always his face, drawing me on. In my ears was always his voice, but thin, like from far away.

I was like a person following after something in the dark.

For years when I went out into the street or got into a car, it gave a knock my heart—"Maybe I'll see him yet to-day."

When I heard he got himself engaged, I hunted up where she lived, and with Sammy in the carriage and the three other children hanging on to my skirts, I stayed around for hours to look up at the grand stone house where she lived, just to take a minute's look on her.

When I seen her go by, it stabbed awake in me the old days.

It ain't that I still love him, but nothing don't seem real to me no more. For the little while when we was lovers I breathed the air from the high places where love comes from, and I can't no more come down.

Soap and Water

What I so greatly feared, happened! Miss Whiteside, the dean of our college, withheld my diploma. When I came to her office, and asked her why she did not pass me, she said that she could not recommend me as a teacher because of my personal appearance.

She told me that my skin looked oily, my hair unkempt, and my finger-nails sadly neglected. She told me that I was utterly unmindful of the little niceties of the well-groomed lady. She pointed out that my collar did not set evenly, my belt was awry, and there was a lack of freshness in my dress. And she ended with: "Soap and water are cheap. Anyone can be clean."

In those four years while I was under her supervision, I was always timid and diffident. I shrank and trembled when I had to come near her. When I had to say something to her, I mumbled and stuttered, and grew red and white in the face with fear.

Every time I had to come to the dean's office for a private conference,

I prepared for the ordeal of her cold scrutiny, as a patient prepares for a surgical operation. I watched her gimlet eyes searching for a stray pin, for a spot on my dress, for my unpolished shoes, for my uncared-for finger-nails, as one strapped on the operating table watches the surgeon approaching with his tray of sterilized knives.

She never looked into my eyes. She never perceived that I had a soul. She did not see how I longed for beauty and cleanliness. How I strained and struggled to lift myself from the dead toil and exhaustion that weighed me down. She could see nothing in people like me, except the dirt and the stains on the outside.

But this last time when she threatened to withhold my diploma, because of my appearance, this last time when she reminded me that "Soap and water are cheap. Anyone can be clean," this last time, something burst within me.

I felt the suppressed wrath of all the unwashed of the earth break loose within me. My eyes blazed fire. I didn't care for myself, nor the dean, nor the whole laundered world. I had suffered the cruelty of their cleanliness and the tyranny of their culture to the breaking point. I was too frenzied to know what I said or did. But I saw clean, immaculate, spotless Miss Whiteside shrivel and tremble and cower before me, as I had shriveled and trembled and cowered before her for so many years.

Why did she give me my diploma? Was it pity? Or can it be that in my outburst of fury, at the climax of indignities that I had suffered, the barriers broke, and she saw into the world below from where I came?

Miss Whiteside had no particular reason for hounding and persecuting me. Personally, she didn't give a hang if I was clean or dirty. She was merely one of the agents of clean society, delegated to judge who is fit and who is unfit to teach.

While they condemned me as unfit to be a teacher, because of my appearance, I was slaving to keep them clean. I was slaving in a laundry from five to eight in the morning, before going to college, and from six to eleven at night, after coming from college. Eight hours of work a day, outside my studies. Where was the time and the strength for the "little niceties of the well-groomed lady"?

At the time when they rose and took their morning bath, and put on their fresh-laundered linen that somebody had made ready for them, when they were being served with their breakfast, I had already toiled for three hours in a laundry.

When the college hours were over, they went for a walk in the fresh air. They had time to rest, and bathe again, and put on fresh clothes for dinner. But I, after college hours, had only time to bolt a soggy meal, and rush back to the grind of the laundry till eleven at night.

At the hour when they came from the theater or musicale, I came from the laundry. But I was so bathed in the sweat of exhaustion that I could not think of a bath of soap and water. I had only strength to drag myself home, and fall down on the bed and sleep. Even if I had had the desire and the energy to take a bath, there were no such things as bathtubs in the house where I lived.

Often as I stood at my board at the laundry, I thought of Miss Whiteside, and her clean world, clothed in the snowy shirtwaists I had ironed. I was thinking—I, soaking in the foul vapors of the steaming laundry, I, with my dirty, tired hands, I am ironing the clean, immaculate shirtwaists of clean, immaculate society. I, the unclean one, am actually fashioning the pedestal of their cleanliness, from which they reach down, hoping to lift me to the height that I have created for them.

I look back at my sweatshop childhood. One day, when I was about sixteen, someone gave me Rosenfeld's poem "The Machine," to read. Like a spark thrown among oil rags, it set my whole being aflame with longing for self-expression. But I was dumb. I had nothing but blind, aching feeling. For days I went about with agonies of feeling, yet utterly at sea how to fathom and voice those feelings—birth-throes of infinite worlds, and yet dumb.

Suddenly, there came upon me this inspiration. I can go to college! There I shall learn to express myself, to voice my thoughts. But I was not prepared to go to college. The girl in the cigar factory, in the next block, had gone first to a preparatory school. Why shouldn't I find a way, too?

Going to college seemed as impossible for me, at that time, as for an ignorant Russian shop-girl to attempt to write poetry in English. But I was sixteen then, and the impossible was a magnet to draw the dreams that had no outlet. Besides, the actual was so barren, so narrow, so strangling, that the dream of the unattainable was the only air in which the soul could survive.

The ideal of going to college was like the birth of a new religion in my soul. It put new fire in my eyes, and new strength in my tired arms and fingers.

For six years I worked daytimes and went at night to a preparatory school. For six years I went about nursing the illusion that college was a place where I should find self-expression, and vague, pent-up feelings could live as thoughts and grow as ideas.

At last I came to college. I rushed for it with the outstretched arms of youth's aching hunger to give and take of life's deepest and highest, and I came against the solid wall of the well-fed, well-dressed world—the frigid whitewashed wall of cleanliness.

Until I came to college I had been unconscious of my clothes. Suddenly

I felt people looking at me at arm's length, as if I were crooked or crippled, as if I had come to a place where I didn't belong, and would never be taken in.

How I pinched, and scraped, and starved myself, to save enough to come to college! Every cent of the tuition fee I paid was drops of sweat and blood from underpaid laundry work. And what did I get for it? A crushed spirit, a broken heart, a stinging sense of poverty that I never felt before.

The courses of study I had to swallow to get my diploma were utterly barren of interest to me. I didn't come to college to get dull learning from dead books. I didn't come for that dry, inanimate stuff that can be hammered out in lectures. I came because I longed for the larger life, for the stimulus of intellectual associations. I came because my whole being clamored for more vision, more light. But everywhere I went I saw big fences put up against me, with the brutal signs: "No trespassing. Get off the grass."

I experienced at college the same feeling of years ago when I came to this country, when after months of shut-in-ness, in dark tenements and stifling sweatshops, I had come to Central Park for the first time. Like a bird just out from a cage, I stretched out my arms, and then flung myself in ecstatic abandon on the grass. Just as I began to breathe in the fresh-smelling earth, and lift up my eyes to the sky, a big, fat policeman with a club in his hand, seized me, with: "Can't you read the sign? Get off the grass!" Miss Whiteside, the dean of the college, the representative of the clean, the educated world, for all her external refinement, was to me like that big, brutal policeman, with the club in his hand, that drove me off the grass.

The death-blows to all aspiration began when I graduated from college and tried to get a start at the work for which I had struggled so hard to fit myself. I soon found other agents of clean society, who had the power of giving or withholding the positions I sought, judging me as Miss Whiteside judged me. One glance at my shabby clothes, the desperate anguish that glazed and dulled my eyes and I felt myself condemned by them before I opened my lips to speak.

Starvation forced me to accept the lowest-paid substitute position. And because my wages were so low and so unsteady, I could never get the money for the clothes to make an appearance to secure a position with better pay. I was tricked and foiled. I was considered unfit to get decent pay for my work because of my appearance, and it was to the advantage of those who used me that my appearance should damn me, so as to get me to work for the low wages I was forced to accept. It seemed to me the whole vicious circle of society's injustices was thrust like a noose around my neck to strangle me.

The insults and injuries I had suffered at college had so eaten into my flesh that I could not bear to get near it. I shuddered with horror whenever I had to pass the place blocks away. The hate which I felt for Miss Whiteside spread like poison inside my soul, into hate for all clean society. The whole clean world was massed against me. Whenever I met a well-dressed person, I felt the secret stab of a hidden enemy.

I was so obsessed and consumed with my grievances that I could not get away from myself and think things out in the light. I was in the grip of that blinding, destructive, terrible thing—righteous indignation. I could not rest. I wanted the whole world to know that the college was against democracy in education, that clothes form the basis of class distinctions, that after graduation the opportunities for the best positions are passed out to those who are best-dressed, and the students too poor to put up a front are pigeon-holed and marked unfit and abandoned to the mercy of the wind.

A wild desire raged in the corner of my brain. I knew that the dean gave dinners to the faculty at regular intervals. I longed to burst in at one of those feasts, in the midst of their grand speech-making, and tear down the fine clothes from these well-groomed ladies and gentlemen, and trample them under my feet, and scream like a lunatic: "Soap and water are cheap! Soap and water are cheap! Look at me! See how cheap it is!"

There seemed but three avenues of escape to the torments of my wasted life, madness, suicide, or a heart-to-heart confession to someone who understood. I had not energy enough for suicide. Besides, in my darkest moments of despair, hope clamored loudest. Oh, I longed so to live, to dream my way up on the heights, above the unreal realities that ground me and dragged me down to earth.

Inside the ruin of my thwarted life, the *unlived* visionary immigrant hungered and thirsted for America. I had come a refugee from the Russian pogroms, aflame with dreams of America. I did not find America in the sweatshops, much less in the schools and colleges. But for hundreds of years the persecuted races all over the world were nurtured on hopes of America. When a little baby in my mother's arms, before I was old enough to speak, I saw all around me weary faces light up with thrilling tales of the far-off "golden country." And so, though my faith in this so-called America was shattered, yet underneath, in the sap and roots of my soul, burned the deathless faith that America is, must be, somehow, somewhere. In the midst of my bitterest hates and rebellions, visions of America rose over me, like songs of freedom of an oppressed people.

My body was worn to the bone from overwork, my footsteps dragged with exhaustion, but my eyes still sought the sky, praying, ceaselessly praying, the dumb, inarticulate prayer of the lost immigrant: "America! Ach, America! Where is America?"

It seemed to me if I could only find some human being to whom I could unburden my heart, I would have new strength to begin again my insatiable search for America.

But to whom could I speak? The people in the laundry? They never understood me. They had a grudge against me because I left them when I tried to work myself up. Could I speak to the college people? What did these icebergs of convention know about the vital things of the heart?

And yet, I remembered, in the freshman year, in one of the courses in chemistry, there was an instructor, a woman, who drew me strangely. I felt she was the only real teacher among all the teachers and professors I met. I didn't care for the chemistry, but I liked to look at her. She gave me life, air, the unconscious emanation of her beautiful spirit. I had not spoken a word to her, outside the experiments in chemistry, but I knew her more than the people around her who were of her own class. I felt in the throb of her voice, in the subtle shading around the corner of her eyes, the color and texture of her dreams.

Often in the midst of our work in chemistry I felt like crying out to her: "Oh, please be my friend. I'm so lonely." But something choked me. I couldn't speak. The very intensity of my longing for her friendship made me run away from her in confusion the minute she approached me. I was so conscious of my shabbiness that I was afraid maybe she was only trying to be kind. I couldn't bear kindness. I wanted from her love, understanding, or nothing.

About ten years after I left college, as I walked the streets bowed and beaten with the shame of having to go around begging for work, I met Miss Van Ness. She not only recognized me, but stopped to ask how I was, and what I was doing.

I had begun to think that my only comrades in this world were the homeless and abandoned cats and dogs of the street, whom everybody gives another kick, as they slam the door on them. And here was one from the clean world human enough to be friendly. Here was one of the well-dressed, with a look in her eyes and a sound in her voice that was like healing oil over the bruises of my soul. The mere touch of that woman's hand in mine so overwhelmed me, that I burst out crying in the street.

The next morning I came to Miss Van Ness at her office. In those ten years she had risen to a professorship. But I was not in the least intimidated by her high office. I felt as natural in her presence as if she were my own sister. I heard myself telling her the whole story of my life, but I felt that even if I had not said a word she would have understood all I had to say as if I had spoken. It was all so unutterable, to find one from the other side of the world who was so simply and naturally that miraculous thing—a friend. Just as contact with Miss Whiteside had tied and bound all my thinking processes, so Miss Van Ness unbound and freed me and suffused me with light.

I felt the joy of one breathing on the mountain-tops for the first time. I looked down at the world below. I was changed and the world was changed. My past was the forgotten night. Sunrise was all around me.

I went out from Miss Van Ness's office, singing a song of new life: "America! I found America."

"The Fat of the Land"

In an air-shaft so narrow that you could touch the next wall with your bare hands, Hanneh Breineh leaned out and knocked on her neighbor's window.

"Can you loan me your wash-boiler for the clothes?" she called.

Mrs. Pelz threw up the sash.

"The boiler? What's the matter with yours again? Didn't you tell me you had it fixed already last week?"

"A black year on him, the robber, the way he fixed it! If you have no luck in this world, then it's better not to live. There I spent out fifteen cents to stop up one hole, and it runs out another. How I ate out my gall bargaining with him he should let it down to fifteen cents! He wanted yet a quarter, the swindler. Gottuniu! My bitter heart on him for every penny he took from me for nothing!"

"You got to watch all those swindlers, or they'll steal the whites out of your eyes," admonished Mrs. Pelz. "You should have tried out your boiler before you paid him. Wait a minute till I empty out my dirty clothes in a pillow-case; then I'll hand it to you."

Mrs. Pelz returned with the boiler and tried to hand it across to Hanneh Breineh, but the soap-box refrigerator on the window-sill was in the way.

"You got to come in for the boiler yourself," said Mrs. Pelz.

"Wait only till I tie my Sammy on to the high-chair he shouldn't fall on me again. He's so wild that ropes won't hold him."

Hanneh Breineh tied the child in the chair, stuck a pacifier in his mouth, and went in to her neighbor. As she took the boiler Mrs. Pelz said:

"Do you know Mrs. Melker ordered fifty pounds of chicken for her daughter's wedding? And such grand chickens! Shining like gold! My heart melted in me just looking at the flowing fatness of those chickens."

Hanneh Breineh smacked her thin, dry lips, a hungry gleam in her sunken eyes.

"Fifty pounds!" she gasped. "It ain't possible. How do you know?"

"I heard her with my own ears. I saw them with my own eyes. And she said she will chop up the chicken livers with onions and eggs for an appetizer, and then she will buy twenty-five pounds of fish, and cook it sweet and sour with raisins, and she said she will bake all her shtrudels on pure chicken fat."

"Some people work themselves up in the world," sighed Hanneh Breineh. "For them is America flowing with milk and honey. In Savel Mrs. Melker used to get shriveled up from hunger. She and her children used to live on potato-peelings and crusts of dry bread picked out from the barrels; and in America she lives to eat chicken, and apple shtrudels soaking in fat."

"The world is a wheel always turning," philosophized Mrs. Pelz. "Those who were high go down low, and those who've been low go up higher. Who will believe me here in America that in Poland I was a cook in a banker's house? I handled ducks and geese every day. I used to bake coffee-cake with cream so thick you could cut it with a knife."

"And do you think I was a nobody in Poland?" broke in Hanneh Breineh, tears welling in her eyes as the memories of her past rushed over her. "But what's the use of talking? In America money is everything. Who cares who my father or grandfather was in Poland? Without money I'm a living dead one. My head dries out worrying how to get for the children the eating a penny cheaper."

Mrs. Pelz wagged her head, a gnawing envy contracting her features.

"Mrs. Melker had it good from the day she came," she said, begrudgingly. "Right away she sent all her children to the factory, and she began to cook meat for dinner every day. She and her children have eggs and buttered rolls for breakfast each morning like millionaires."

A sudden fall and a baby's scream, and the boiler dropped from Hanneh Breineh's hands as she rushed into her kitchen, Mrs. Pelz after her. They found the high-chair turned on top of the baby.

"Gewalt! Save me! Run for a doctor!" cried Hanneh Breineh, as she dragged the child from under the high-chair. "He's killed! He's killed! My only child! My precious lamb!" she shrieked as she ran back and forth with the screaming infant.

Mrs. Pelz snatched little Sammy from the mother's hands.

"Meshugeneh! What are you running around like a crazy, frightening the child? Let me see. Let me tend to him. He ain't killed yet." She hastened to the sink to wash the child's face, and discovered a swelling lump on his forehead. "Have you a quarter in your house?" she asked.

"Yes I got one," replied Hanneh Breineh, climbing on a chair. "I got to keep it on a high shelf where the children can't get it."

Mrs. Pelz seized the quarter Hanneh Breineh handed down to her.

"Now pull your left eyelid three times while I'm pressing the quarter, and you'll see the swelling go down."

Hanneh Breineh took the child again in her arms, shaking and cooing over it and caressing it.

"Ah-ah-ah, Sammy! Ah-ah-ah-ah, little lamb! Ah-ah-ah, little bird! Ah-ah-ah-ah, precious heart! Oh, you saved my life; I thought he was killed," gasped Hanneh Breineh, turning to Mrs. Pelz. "Oi-i!" she sighed, "a mother's heart! Always in fear over her children. The minute anything happens to them all life goes out of me. I lose my head and I don't know where I am any more."

"No wonder the child fell," admonished Mrs. Pelz. "You should have a red ribbon or red beads on his neck to keep away the evil eye. Wait. I got something in my machine-drawer."

Mrs. Pelz returned, bringing the boiler and a red string, which she tied about the child's neck while the mother proceeded to fill the boiler.

A little later Hanneh Breineh again came into Mrs. Pelz's kitchen, holding Sammy in one arm and in the other an apronful of potatoes. Putting the child down on the floor, she seated herself on the unmade kitchen-bed and began to peel the potatoes in her apron.

"Woe to me!" sobbed Hanneh Breineh. "To my bitter luck there ain't no end. With all my other troubles, the stove got broke. I lighted the fire to boil the clothes, and it's to get choked with smoke. I paid rent only a week ago, and the agent don't want to fix it. A thunder should strike him! He only comes for the rent, and if anything has to be fixed, then he don't want to hear nothing.

"Why comes it to me so hard?" went on Hanneh Breineh, the tears streaming down her cheeks. "I can't stand it no more. I came into you for a minute to run away from my troubles. It's only when I sit myself down to peel potatoes or nurse the baby that I take time to draw a breath, and beg only for death."

Mrs. Pelz, accustomed to Hanneh Breineh's bitter outbursts, continued her scrubbing.

"Ut!" exclaimed Hanneh Breineh, irritated at her neighbor's silence, "what are you tearing up the world with your cleaning? What's the use to clean up when everything only gets dirty again?"

"I got to shine up my house for the holidays."

"You've got it so good nothing lays on your mind but to clean your house. Look on this little blood-sucker," said Hanneh Breineh, pointing to the wizened child, made prematurely solemn from starvation and neglect. "Could anybody keep that brat clean? I wash him one minute, and he is dirty the minute after." Little Sammy grew frightened and began to cry. "Shut up!" ordered the mother, picking up the child to nurse it again. "Can't you see me take a rest for a minute?"

The hungry child began to cry at the top of its weakened lungs.

"Na, na, you glutton." Hanneh Breineh took out a dirty pacifier from her pocket and stuffed it into the baby's mouth. The grave, pasty-faced infant shrank into a panic of fear, and chewed the nipple nervously, clinging to it with both his thin little hands.

"For what did I need yet the sixth one?" groaned Hanneh Breineh, turning to Mrs. Pelz. "Wasn't it enough five mouths to feed? If I didn't have this child on my neck, I could turn myself around and earn a few cents." She wrung her hands in a passion of despair. "Gottuniu! The earth should only take it before it grows up!"

"Shah! Shah!" reproved Mrs. Pelz. "Pity yourself on the child. Let it grow up already so long as it is here. See how frightened it looks on you." Mrs. Pelz took the child in her arms and petted it. "The poor little lamb! What did it done you should hate it so?"

Hanneh Breineh pushed Mrs. Pelz away from her.

"To whom can I open the wounds of my heart?" she moaned. "Nobody has pity on me. You don't believe me, nobody believes me until I'll fall down like a horse in the middle of the street. Oi weh! Mine life is so black for my eyes! Some mothers got luck. A child gets run over by a car, some fall from a window, some burn themselves up with a match, some get choked with diphtheria; but no death takes mine away."

"God from the world, stop cursing!" admonished Mrs. Pelz. "What do you want from the poor children? Is it their fault that their father makes small wages? Why do you let it all out on them?" Mrs. Pelz sat down beside Hanneh Breineh. "Wait only till your children get old enough to go to the shop and earn money," she consoled. "Push only through those few years while they are yet small; your sun will begin to shine; you will live on the fat of the land, when they begin to bring you in the wages each week."

Hanneh Breineh refused to be comforted.

"Till they are old enough to go to the shop and earn money they'll eat the head off my bones," she wailed. "If you only knew the fights I got by each meal. Maybe I gave Abe a bigger piece of bread than Fanny. Maybe Fanny got a little more soup in her plate than Jake. Eating is dearer than diamonds. Potatoes went up a cent on a pound, and milk is only for millionaires. And once a week, when I buy a little meat for the Sabbath, the butcher weighs it for me like gold, with all the bones in it. When I come to lay the meat out on a plate and divide it up, there ain't nothing to it but bones. Before, he used to throw me in a piece of fat extra or a piece of lung, but now you got to pay for everything, even for a bone to the soup."

"Never mind; you'll yet come out from all your troubles. Just as soon as your children get old enough to get their working papers the more children you got, the more money you'll have."

"Why should I fool myself with the false shine of hope? Don't I know it's already my black luck not to have it good in this world? Do you think American children will right away give everything they earn to their mother?"

"I know what is with you the matter," said Mrs. Pelz. "You didn't eat yet to-day. When it is empty in the stomach, the whole world looks black. Come, only let me give you something good to taste in the mouth; that will freshen you up." Mrs. Pelz went to the cupboard and brought out the saucepan of gefüllte fisch that she had cooked for dinner and placed it on the table in front of Hanneh Breineh. "Give a taste my fish," she said, taking one slice on a spoon, and handing it to Hanneh Breineh with a piece of bread. "I wouldn't give it to you on a plate because I just cleaned up my house, and I don't want to dirty up more dishes."

"What, am I a stranger you should have to serve me on a plate yet!" cried Hanneh Breineh, snatching the fish in her trembling fingers.

"Oi weh! How it melts through all the bones!" she exclaimed, brightening as she ate. "May it be for good luck to us all!" she exulted, waving aloft the last precious bite.

Mrs. Pelz was so flattered that she even ladled up a spoonful of gravy.

"There is a bit of onion and carrot in it," she said, as she handed it to her neighbor.

Hanneh Breineh sipped the gravy drop by drop, like a connoisseur sipping wine.

"Ah-h-h! A taste of that gravy lifts me up to heaven!" As she disposed leisurely of the slice of onion and carrot she relaxed and expanded and even grew jovial. "Let us wish all our troubles on the Russian Czar! Let him burst with our worries for rent! Let him get shriveled with our hunger for bread! Let his eyes dry out of his head looking for work!

"Shah! I'm forgetting from everything," she exclaimed, jumping up. "It must be eleven or soon twelve, and my children will be right away out of school and fall on me like a pack of wild wolves. I better quick run to the market and see what cheaper I can get for a quarter."

Because of the lateness of her coming, the stale bread at the nearest bakeshop was sold out, and Hanneh Breineh had to trudge from shop to shop in search of the usual bargain, and spent nearly an hour to save two cents.

In the meantime the children returned from school, and, finding the door locked, climbed through the fire-escape, and entered the house through the window. Seeing nothing on the table, they rushed to the stove. Abe pulled a steaming potato out of the boiling pot, and so scalded his fingers that the potato fell to the floor; where upon the three others pounced on it.

"It was my potato," cried Abe, blowing his burned fingers, while with the other hand and his foot he cuffed and kicked the three who were struggling on the floor. A wild fight ensued, and the potato was smashed under Abe's foot amid shouts and screams. Hanneh Breineh, on the stairs, heard the noise of her famished brood, and topped their cries and curses and invectives.

"They are here already, the savages! They are here already to shorten my life! They heard you all over the hall, in all the houses around!"

The children, disregarding her words, pounced on her market-basket, shouting ravenously: "Mamma, I'm hungry! What more do you got to eat?"

They tore the bread and herring out of Hanneh Breineh's basket and devoured it in starved savagery, clamoring for more.

"Murderers!" screamed Hanneh Breineh, goaded beyond endurance. "What are you tearing from me my flesh? From where should I steal to give you more? Here I had already a pot of potatoes and a whole loaf of bread and two herrings, and you swallowed it down in the wink of an eye. I have to have Rockefeller's millions to fill your stomachs."

All at once Hanneh Breineh became aware that Benny was missing. "Oi weh!" she burst out, wringing her hands in a new wave of woe, "where is Benny? Didn't he come home yet from school?"

She ran out into the hall, opened the grime-coated window, and looked up and down the street; but Benny was nowhere in sight.

"Abe, Jake, Fanny, quick, find Benny!" entreated Hanneh Breineh, as she rushed back into the kitchen. But the children, anxious to snatch a few minutes' play before the school-call, dodged past her and hurried out.

With the baby on her arm, Hanneh Breineh hastened to the kindergarten.

"Why are you keeping Benny here so long?" she shouted at the teacher as she flung open the door. "If you had my bitter heart, you would send him home long ago and not wait till I got to come for him."

The teacher turned calmly and consulted her record-cards.

"Benny Safron? He wasn't present this morning."

"Not here?" shrieked Hanneh Breineh. "I pushed him out myself he should go. The children didn't want to take him, and I had no time. Woe is me! Where is my child?" She began pulling her hair and beating her breast as she ran into the street.

Mrs. Pelz was busy at a pushcart, picking over some spotted apples, when she heard the clamor of an approaching crowd. A block off she recognized Hanneh Breineh, her hair disheveled, her clothes awry, running toward her with her yelling baby in her arms, the crowd following.

"Friend mine," cried Hanneh Breineh, falling on Mrs. Pelz's neck, "I lost my Benny, the best child of all my children." Tears streamed down her red, swollen eyes as she sobbed. "Benny! mine heart, mine life! Oi-i-i!"

Mrs. Pelz took the frightened baby out of the mother's arms.

"Still yourself a little! See how you're frightening your child."

"Woe to me! Where is my Benny? Maybe he's killed already by a car. Maybe he fainted away from hunger. He didn't eat nothing all day long. Gottuniu! Pity yourself on me!"

She lifted her hands full of tragic entreaty.

"People, my child! Get me my child! I'll go crazy out of my head! Get me my child, or I'll take poison before your eyes!"

"Still yourself a little!" pleaded Mrs. Pelz.

"Talk not to me!" cried Hanneh Breineh, wringing her hands. "You're having all your children. I lost mine. Every good luck comes to other people. But I didn't live yet to see a good day in my life. Mine only joy, mine Benny, is lost away from me."

The crowd followed Hanneh Breineh as she wailed through the streets, leaning on Mrs. Pelz. By the time she returned to her house the children were back from school; but seeing that Benny was not there, she chased them out in the street, crying:

"Out of here, you robbers, gluttons! Go find Benny!" Hanneh Breineh crumpled into a chair in utter prostration. "Oi weh! He's lost! Mine life; my little bird; mine only joy! How many nights I spent nursing him when he had the measles! And all that I suffered for weeks and months when he had the whooping-cough! How the eyes went out of my head till I learned him how to walk, till I learned him how to talk! And such a smart child! If I lost all the others, it wouldn't tear me so by the heart."

She worked herself up into such a hysteria, crying, and tearing her hair, and hitting her head with her knuckles, that at last she fell into a faint. It took some time before Mrs. Pelz, with the aid of neighbors, revived her.

"Benny, mine angel!" she moaned as she opened her eyes.

Just then a policeman came in with the lost Benny.

"Na, na, here you got him already!" said Mrs. Pelz. "Why did you carry on so for nothing? Why did you tear up the world like a crazy?"

The child's face was streaked with tears as he cowered, frightened and forlorn. Hanneh Breineh sprang toward him, slapping his cheeks, boxing his ears, before the neighbors could rescue him from her.

"Woe on your head!" cried the mother. "Where did you lost yourself? Ain't I got enough worries on my head than to go around looking for you? I didn't have yet a minute's peace from that child since he was born!"

"See a crazy mother!" remonstrated Mrs. Pelz, rescuing Benny from another beating. "Such a mouth! With one breath she blesses him when he is lost, and with the other breath she curses him when he is found."

Hanneh Breineh took from the window-sill a piece of herring covered with swarming flies, and putting it on a slice of dry bread, she filled a cup of tea that had been stewing all day, and dragged Benny over to the table to eat.

But the child, choking with tears, was unable to touch the food.

"Go eat!" commanded Hanneh Breineh. "Eat and choke yourself eating!"

"Maybe she won't remember me no more. Maybe the servant won't let me in," thought Mrs. Pelz, as she walked by the brownstone house on Eighty-Fourth Street where she had been told Hanneh Breineh now lived. At last she summoned up enough courage to climb the steps. She was all out of breath as she rang the bell with trembling fingers. "Oi weh! even the outside smells riches and plenty! Such curtains! And shades on all windows like by millionaires! Twenty years ago she used to eat from the pot to the hand, and now she lives in such a palace."

A whiff of steam-heated warmth swept over Mrs. Pelz as the door opened, and she saw her old friend of the tenements dressed in silk and diamonds like a being from another world.

"Mrs. Pelz, is it you!" cried Hanneh Breineh, overjoyed at the sight of her former neighbor. "Come right in. Since when are you back in New York?"

"We came last week," mumbled Mrs. Pelz, as she was led into a richly carpeted reception-room.

"Make yourself comfortable. Take off your shawl," urged Hanneh Breineh.

But Mrs. Pelz only drew her shawl more tightly around her, a keen sense of her poverty gripping her as she gazed, abashed by the luxurious wealth that shone from every corner.

"This shawl covers up my rags," she said, trying to hide her shabby sweater.

"I'll tell you what; come right into the kitchen," suggested Hanneh Breineh. "The servant is away for this afternoon, and we can feel more comfortable there. I can breathe like a free person in my kitchen when the girl has her day out."

Mrs. Pelz glanced about her in an excited daze. Never in her life had she seen anything so wonderful as a white-tiled kitchen, with its glistening porcelain sink and the aluminum pots and pans that shone like silver.

"Where are you staying now?" asked Hanneh Breineh, as she pinned an apron over her silk dress.

"I moved back to Delancey Street, where we used to live," replied Mrs. Pelz, as she seated herself cautiously in a white enameled chair.

"Oi weh! What grand times we had in that old house when we were neighbors!" sighed Hanneh Breineh, looking at her old friend with misty eyes.

"You still think on Delancey Street? Haven't you more high-class neighbors uptown here?"

"A good neighbor is not to be found every day," deplored Hanneh Breineh. "Uptown here, where each lives in his own house, nobody cares if the person next door is dying or going crazy from loneliness. It ain't anything like we used to have it in Delancey Street, when we could walk into one another's rooms without knocking, and borrow a pinch of salt or a pot to cook in."

Hanneh Breineh went over to the pantry-shelf.

"We are going to have a bite right here on the kitchen-table like on Delancey Street. So long there's no servant to watch us we can eat what we please."

"Oi! How it waters my mouth with appetite, the smell of the herring and onion!" chuckled Mrs. Pelz, sniffing the welcome odors with greedy pleasure.

Hanneh Breineh pulled a dish-towel from the rack and threw one end of it to Mrs. Pelz.

"So long there's no servant around, we can use it together for a napkin. It's dirty, anyhow. How it freshens up my heart to see you!" she rejoiced as she poured out her tea into a saucer. "If you would only know how I used to beg my daughter to write for me a letter to you; but these American children, what is to them a mother's feelings?"

"What are you talking!" cried Mrs. Pelz. "The whole world rings with you and your children. Everybody is envying you. Tell me how began your luck?"

"You heard how my husband died with consumption," replied Hanneh Breineh. "The five hundred dollars lodge money gave me the first lift in life, and I opened a little grocery store. Then my son Abe married himself to a girl with a thousand dollars. That started him in business, and now he has the biggest shirtwaist factory on West Twenty-Ninth Street."

"Yes, I heard your son had a factory." Mrs. Pelz hesitated and stammered; "I'll tell you the truth. What I came to ask you—I thought maybe you would beg your son Abe if he would give my husband a job."

"Why not?" said Hanneh Breineh. "He keeps more than five hundred hands. I'll ask him if he should take in Mr. Pelz."

"Long years on you, Hanneh Breineh! You'll save my life if you could only help my husband get work."

"Of course my son will help him. All my children like to do good. My daughter Fanny is a milliner on Fifth Avenue, and she takes in the poorest girls in her shop and even pays them sometimes while they learn the trade." Hanneh Breineh's face lit up, and her chest filled with pride as she enumerated the successes of her children. "And my son Benny he wrote a play on Broadway and he gave away more than a hundred free tickets for the first night."

"Benny? The one who used to get lost from home all the time? You always did love that child more than all the rest. And what is Sammy your baby doing?"

"He ain't a baby no longer. He goes to college and quarterbacks the football team. They can't get along without him.

"And my son Jake, I nearly forgot him. He began collecting rent in Delancey Street, and now he is boss of renting the swellest apartment-houses on Riverside Drive."

"What did I tell you? In America children are like money in the bank," purred Mrs. Pelz, as she pinched and patted Hanneh Breineh's silk sleeve. "Oi weh! How it shines from you! You ought to kiss the air and dance for joy and happiness. It is such a bitter frost outside; a pail of coal is so dear, and you got it so warm with steam heat. I had to pawn my feather bed to have enough for the rent, and you are rolling in money."

"Yes, I got it good in some ways, but money ain't everything," sighed Hanneh Breineh.

"You ain't yet satisfied?"

"But here I got no friends," complained Hanneh Breineh.

"Friends?" queried Mrs. Pelz. "What greater friend is there on earth than the dollar?"

"Oi! Mrs. Pelz; if you could only look into my heart! I'm so choked up! You know they say a cow has a long tongue, but can't talk." Hanneh Breineh shook her head wistfully, and her eyes filmed with inward brooding. "My children give me everything from the best. When I was sick, they got me a nurse by day and one by night. They bought me the best wine. If I asked for dove's milk, they would buy it for me; but—but—I can't talk myself out in their language. They want to make me over for an American lady, and I'm different." Tears cut their way under her eyelids with a pricking pain as she went on: "When I was poor, I was free, and could holler and do what I like in my own house. Here I got to lie still like a mouse under a broom. Between living up to my Fifth-Avenue daughter and keeping up with the servants, I am like a sinner in the next world that is thrown from one hell to another." The doorbell rang, and Hanneh Breineh jumped up with a start.

"Oi weh! It must be the servant back already!" she exclaimed, as she tore off her apron. "Oi weh! Let's quickly put the dishes together in a dish-pan. If she sees I eat on the kitchen table, she will look on me like the dirt under her feet."

Mrs. Pelz seized her shawl in haste.

"I better run home quick in my rags before your servant sees me."

"I'll speak to Abe about the job," said Hanneh Breineh, as she pushed a bill into the hand of Mrs. Pelz, who edged out as the servant entered.

"I'm having fried potato lotkes special for you, Benny," said Hanneh Breineh, as the children gathered about the table for the family dinner given in honor of Benny's success with his new play. "Do you remember how you used to lick the fingers from them?"

"Oh, mother!" reproved Fanny. "Anyone hearing you would think we were still in the pushcart district."

"Stop your nagging, sis, and let ma alone," commanded Benny, patting his mother's arm affectionately. "I'm home only once a month. Let her feed me what she pleases. My stomach is bomb-proof."

"Do I hear that the President is coming to your play?" said Abe, as he stuffed a napkin over his diamond-studded shirt-front.

"Why shouldn't he come?" returned Benny. "The critics say it's the greatest antidote for the race hatred created by the war. If you want to know, he is coming to-night; and what's more, our box is next to the President's."

"Nu, mammeh," sallied Jake, "did you ever dream in Delancey Street that we should rub sleeves with the President?"

"I always said that Benny had more head than the rest of you," replied the mother.

As the laughter died away, Jake went on:

"Honor you are getting plenty; but how much mezummen does this play bring you? Can I invest any of it in real estate for you?"

"I'm getting ten per cent royalties of the gross receipts," replied the youthful playwright.

"How much is that?" queried Hanneh Breineh.

"Enough to buy up all your fish-markets in Delancey Street," laughed Abe in good-natured raillery at his mother.

Her son's jest cut like a knife-thrust in her heart. She felt her heart ache with the pain that she was shut out from their successes. Each added triumph only widened the gulf. And when she tried to bridge this gulf by asking questions, they only thrust her back upon herself.

"Your fame has even helped me get my hat trade solid with the Four Hundred," put in Fanny. "You bet I let Mrs. Van Suyden know that our box is next to the President's. She said she would drop in to meet you. Of course she let on to me that she hadn't seen the play yet, though my designer said she saw her there on the opening night."

"Oh, gosh, the toadies!" sneered Benny. "Nothing so sickens you with success as the way people who once shoved you off the sidewalk come crawling to you on their stomachs begging you to dine with them."

"Say, that leading man of yours, he's some class!" cried Fanny. "That's the man I'm looking for. Will you invite him to supper after the theater?"

The playwright turned to his mother.

"Say, ma," he said, laughingly, "how would you like a real actor for a son-in-law?"

"She should worry," mocked Sam. "She'll be discussing with him the future of the Greek drama. Too bad it doesn't happen to be Warfield, or mother could give him tips on the 'Auctioneer.'"

Jake turned to his mother with a covert grin.

"I guess you'd have no objection if Fanny got next to Benny's leading man. He makes at least fifteen hundred a week. That wouldn't be such a bad addition to the family, would it?"

Again the bantering tone stabbed Hanneh Breineh. Everything in her began to tremble and break loose.

"Why do you ask me?" she cried, throwing her napkin into her plate. "Do I count for a person in this house? If I'll say something, will you even listen to me? What is to me the grandest man that my daughter could pick out? Another enemy in my house! Another person to shame himself from me!" She swept in her children in one glance of despairing anguish as she rose from the table. "What worth is an old mother to American children? The President is coming to-night to the theater, and none of you asked me to go." Unable to check the rising tears, she fled toward the kitchen and banged the door.

They all looked at one another guiltily.

"Say, sis," Benny called out sharply, "what sort of frame-up is this? Haven't you told mother that she was to go with us to-night?"

"Yes—I—" Fanny bit her lips as she fumbled evasively for words. "I asked her if she wouldn't mind my taking her some other time."

"Now you have made a mess of it!" fumed Benny. "Mother'll be too hurt to go now."

"Well, I don't care," snapped Fanny. "I can't appear with mother in a box at the theater. Can I introduce her to Mrs. Van Suyden? And suppose your leading man should ask to meet me?"

"Take your time, sis. He hasn't asked yet," scoffed Benny.

"The more reason I shouldn't spoil my chances. You know mother. She'll spill the beans that we come from Delancey Street the minute we introduce her anywhere. Must I always have the black shadow of my past trailing after me?"

"But you have no feelings for mother?" admonished Abe.

"I've tried harder than all of you to do my duty. I've *lived* with her." She turned angrily upon them. "I've borne the shame of mother while you bought her off with a present and a treat here and there. God knows how hard I tried to civilize her so as not to have to blush with shame when I take her anywhere. I dressed her in the most stylish Paris models, but Delancey Street sticks out from every inch of her. Whenever she opens her mouth, I'm done for. You fellows had your chance to rise in the world because a man is free to go up as high as he can reach up to; but I, with all my style and pep, can't get a man my equal because a girl is always judged by her mother."

They were silenced by her vehemence, and unconsciously turned to Benny.

"I guess we all tried to do our best for mother," said Benny, thoughtfully. "But wherever there is growth, there is pain and heartbreak. The trouble with us is that the ghetto of the Middle Ages and the children of the twentieth century have to live under one roof, and—"

A sound of crashing dishes came from the kitchen, and the voice of Hanneh Breineh resounded through the dining-room as she wreaked her pent-up fury on the helpless servant.

"Oh, my nerves! I can't stand it any more! There will be no girl again for another week!" cried Fanny.

"Oh, let up on the old lady," protested Abe. "Since she can't take it out on us any more, what harm is it if she cusses the servants?"

"If you fellows had to chase around employment agencies, you wouldn't see anything funny about it. Why can't we move into a hotel that will do away with the need of servants altogether?"

"I got it better," said Jake, consulting a notebook from his pocket. "I have on my list an apartment on Riverside Drive where there's only a small kitchenette; but we can do away with the cooking, for there is a dining service in the building."

The new Riverside apartment to which Hanneh Breineh was removed by her socially ambitious children was for the habitually active mother an empty desert of enforced idleness. Deprived of her kitchen, Hanneh Breineh felt robbed of the last reason for her existence. Cooking and marketing and puttering busily with pots and pans gave her an excuse for living and struggling and bearing up with her children. The lonely idleness of Riverside Drive stunned all her senses and arrested all her thoughts. It gave her that choked sense of being cut off from air, from life, from everything warm and human. The cold indifference, the each-for-himself look in the eyes of the people about her were like stinging slaps in the face. Even the children had nothing real or human in them. They were starched and stiff miniatures of their elders.

But the most unendurable part of the stifling life on Riverside Drive was being forced to eat in the public dining-room. No matter how hard she tried to learn polite table manners, she always found people staring at her, and her daughter rebuking her for eating with the wrong fork or guzzling the soup or staining the cloth.

In a fit of rebellion Hanneh Breineh resolved never to go down to the public dining-room again, but to make use of the gas-stove in the kitchenette to cook her own meals. That very day she rode down to Delancey Street and purchased a new market-basket. For some time she walked among the haggling pushcart venders, relaxing and swimming in the warm waves of her old familiar past.

A fish-peddler held up a large carp in his black, hairy hand and waved it dramatically:

"Women! Women! Fourteen cents a pound!"

He ceased his raucous shouting as he saw Hanneh Breineh in her rich attire approach his cart.

"How much?" she asked, pointing to the fattest carp.

"Fifteen cents, lady," said the peddler, smirking as he raised his price.

"Swindler! Didn't I hear you call fourteen cents?" shrieked Hanneh Breineh, exultingly, the spirit of the penny chase surging in her blood. Diplomatically, Hanneh Breineh turned as if to go, and the fisherman seized her basket in frantic fear.

"I should live; I'm losing money on the fish, lady," whined the peddler. "I'll let it down to thirteen cents for you only."

"Two pounds for a quarter, and not a penny more," said Hanneh Breineh, thrilling again with the rare sport of bargaining, which had been her chief joy in the good old days of poverty.

"Nu, I want to make the first sale for good luck." The peddler threw the fish on the scale.

As he wrapped up the fish, Hanneh Breineh saw the driven look of worry in his haggard eyes, and when he counted out the change from her dollar, she waved it aside. "Keep it for your luck," she said, and hurried off to strike a new bargain at a pushcart of onions.

Hanneh Breineh returned triumphantly with her purchases. The basket under her arm gave forth the old, homelike odors of herring and garlic, while the scaly tail of a four-pound carp protruded from its newspaper wrapping. A gilded placard on the door of the apartment-house proclaimed that all merchandise must be delivered through the trade entrance in the rear; but Hanneh Breineh with her basket strode proudly through the marble-paneled hall and rang nonchalantly for the elevator.

The uniformed hall-man, erect, expressionless, frigid with dignity, stepped forward:

"Just a minute, madam. I'll call a boy to take up your basket for you."

Hanneh Breineh, glaring at him, jerked the basket savagely from his hands. "Mind your own business!" she retorted. "I'll take it up myself. Do you think you're a Russian policeman to boss me in my own house?"

Angry lines appeared on the countenance of the representative of social decorum.

"It is against the rules, madam," he said, stiffly.

"You should sink into the earth with all your rules and brass buttons. Ain't this America? Ain't this a free country? Can't I take up in my own house what I buy with my own money?" cried Hanneh Breineh, reveling in the opportunity to shower forth the volley of invectives that had been suppressed in her for the weeks of deadly dignity of Riverside Drive.

In the midst of this uproar Fanny came in with Mrs. Van Suyden. Hanneh Breineh rushed over to her, crying:

"This bossy policeman won't let me take up my basket in the elevator."

The daughter, unnerved with shame and confusion, took the basket in her white-gloved hand and ordered the hall-boy to take it around to the regular delivery entrance.

Hanneh Breineh was so hurt by her daughter's apparent defense of the hall-man's rules that she utterly ignored Mrs. Van Suyden's greeting and walked up the seven flights of stairs out of sheer spite.

"You see the tragedy of my life?" broke out Fanny, turning to Mrs. Van Suyden.

"You poor child! You go right up to your dear, old lady mother, and I'll come some other time."

Instantly Fanny regretted her words. Mrs. Van Suyden's pity only roused her wrath the more against her mother.

Breathless from climbing the stairs, Hanneh Breineh entered the apartment just as Fanny tore the faultless millinery creation from her head and threw it on the floor in a rage.

"Mother, you are the ruination of my life! You have driven away Mrs. Van Suyden, as you have driven away all my best friends. What do you think we got this apartment for but to get rid of your fish smells and your brawls with the servants? And here you come with a basket on your arm as if you just landed from steerage! And this afternoon, of all times, when Benny is bringing his leading man to tea. When will you ever stop disgracing us?"

"When I'm dead," said Hanneh Breineh, grimly. "When the earth will cover me up, then you'll be free to go your American way. I'm not going to make myself over for a lady on Riverside Drive. I hate you and all your swell friends. I'll not let myself be choked up here by you or by that hall-boss policeman that is higher in your eyes than your own mother."

"So that's your thanks for all we've done for you?" cried the daughter.

"All you've done for me!" shouted Hanneh Breineh. "What have you done for me? You hold me like a dog on a chain! It stands in the Talmud; some children give their mothers dry bread and water and go to heaven for it, and some give their mother roast duck and go to Gehenna because it's not given with love."

"You want me to love you yet?" raged the daughter. "You knocked every bit of love out of me when I was yet a kid. All the memories of childhood I have is your everlasting cursing and yelling that we were gluttons."

The bell rang sharply, and Hanneh Breineh flung open the door.

"Your groceries, ma'am," said the boy.

Hanneh Breineh seized the basket from him, and with a vicious fling sent it rolling across the room, strewing its contents over the Persian rugs and inlaid floor. Then seizing her hat and coat, she stormed out of the apartment and down the stairs.

Mr. and Mrs. Pelz sat crouched and shivering over their meager supper when the door opened, and Hanneh Breineh in fur coat and plumed hat charged into the room.

"I come to cry out to you my bitter heart," she sobbed. "Woe is me! It is so black for my eyes!"

"What is the matter with you, Hanneh Breineh?" cried Mrs. Pelz in bewildered alarm.

"I am turned out of my own house by the brass-buttoned policeman that bosses the elevator. Oi-i-i-i! Weh-h-h-h! What have I from my life?

The whole world rings with my son's play. Even the President came to see it, and I, his mother, have not seen it yet. My heart is dying in me like in a prison," she went on wailing. "I am starved out for a piece of real eating. In that swell restaurant is nothing but napkins and forks and lettuce-leaves. There are a dozen plates to every bite of food. And it looks so fancy on the plate, but it's nothing but straw in the mouth. I'm starving, but I can't swallow down their American eating."

"Hanneh Breineh," said Mrs. Pelz, "you are sinning before God. Look on your fur coat; it alone would feed a whole family for a year. I never had yet a piece of fur trimming on a coat, and you are in fur from the neck to the feet. I never had yet a piece of feather on a hat, and your hat is all feathers."

"What are you envying me?" protested Hanneh Breineh. "What have I from all my fine furs and feathers when my children are strangers to me? All the fur coats in the world can't warm up the loneliness inside my heart. All the grandest feathers can't hide the bitter shame in my face that my children shame themselves from me."

Hanneh Breineh suddenly loomed over them like some ancient, heroic figure of the Bible condemning unrighteousness.

"Why should my children shame themselves from me? From where did they get the stuff to work themselves up in the world? Did they get it from the air? How did they get all their smartness to rise over the people around them? Why don't the children of born American mothers write my Benny's plays? It is I, who never had a chance to be a person, who gave him the fire in his head. If I would have had a chance to go to school and learn the language, what couldn't I have been? It is I and my mother and my mother's mother and my father and father's father who had such a black life in Poland; it is our choked thoughts and feelings that are flaming up in my children and making them great in America. And yet they shame themselves from me!"

For a moment Mr. and Mrs. Pelz were hypnotized by the sweep of her words. Then Hanneh Breineh sank into a chair in utter exhaustion. She began to weep bitterly, her body shaking with sobs.

"Woe is me! For what did I suffer and hope on my children? A bitter old age—my end. I'm so lonely!"

All the dramatic fire seemed to have left her. The spell was broken. They saw the Hanneh Breineh of old, ever discontented, ever complaining even in the midst of riches and plenty.

"Hanneh Breineh," said Mrs. Pelz, "the only trouble with you is that you got it too good. People will tear the eyes out of your head because you're complaining yet. If I only had your fur coat! If I only had your diamonds! I have nothing. You have everything. You are living on the fat of the land. You go right back home and thank God that you don't have my bitter lot."

"You got to let me stay here with you," insisted Hanneh Breineh. "I'll not go back to my children except when they bury me. When they will see my dead face, they will understand how they killed me."

Mrs. Pelz glanced nervously at her husband. They barely had enough covering for their one bed; how could they possibly lodge a visitor?

"I don't want to take up your bed," said Hanneh Breineh. "I don't care if I have to sleep on the floor or on the chairs, but I'll stay here for the night."

Seeing that she was bent on staying, Mr. Pelz prepared to sleep by putting a few chairs next to the trunk, and Hanneh Breineh was invited to share the rickety bed with Mrs. Pelz.

The mattress was full of lumps and hollows. Hanneh Breineh lay cramped and miserable, unable to stretch out her limbs. For years she had been accustomed to hair mattresses and ample woolen blankets, so that though she covered herself with her fur coat, she was too cold to sleep. But worse than the cold were the creeping things on the wall. And as the lights were turned low, the mice came through the broken plaster and raced across the floor. The foul odors of the kitchen-sink added to the night of horrors.

"Are you going back home?" asked Mrs. Pelz, as Hanneh Breineh put on her hat and coat the next morning.

"I don't know where I'm going," she replied, as she put a bill into Mrs. Pelz's hand.

For hours Hanneh Breineh walked through the crowded ghetto streets. She realized that she no longer could endure the sordid ugliness of her past, and yet she could not go home to her children. She only felt that she must go on and on.

In the afternoon a cold, drizzling rain set in. She was worn out from the sleepless night and hours of tramping. With a piercing pain in her heart she at last turned back and boarded the subway for Riverside Drive. She had fled from the marble sepulcher of the Riverside apartment to her old home in the ghetto; but now she knew that she could not live there again. She had outgrown her past by the habits of years of physical comforts, and these material comforts that she could no longer do without choked and crushed the life within her.

A cold shudder went through Hanneh Breineh, as she approached the apartment-house. Peering through the plate glass of the door she saw the face of the uniformed hallman. For a hesitating moment she remained standing in the drizzling rain, unable to enter, and yet knowing full well that she would have to enter.

Then suddenly Hanneh Breineh began to laugh. She realized that it was the first time she had laughed since her children had become rich. But it was the hard laugh of bitter sorrow. Tears streamed down her furrowed cheeks as she walked slowly up the granite steps.

"The fat of the land!" muttered Hanneh Breineh, with a choking sob as the hall-man with immobile face deferentially swung open the door— "the fat of the land!"

My Own People

With the suitcase containing all her worldly possessions under her arm, Sophie Sapinsky elbowed her way through the noisy ghetto crowds. Pushcart peddlers and pullers-in shouted and gesticulated. Women with market-baskets pushed and shoved one another, eyes straining with the one thought—how to get the food a penny cheaper. With the same strained intentness, Sophie scanned each tenement, searching for a room cheap enough for her dwindling means.

In a dingy basement window a crooked sign, in straggling, penciled letters, caught Sophie's eye: "Room to let, a bargain, cheap."

The exuberant phrasing was quite in keeping with the extravagant dilapidation of the surroundings. "This is the very place," thought Sophie. "There couldn't be nothing cheaper in all New York."

At the foot of the basement steps she knocked.

"Come in!" a voice answered.

As she opened the door she saw an old man bending over a pot of potatoes on a shoemaker's bench. A group of children in all degrees of rags surrounded him, greedily snatching at the potatoes he handed out.

Sophie paused for an instant, but her absorption in her own problem was too great to halt the question: "Is there a room to let?"

"Hanneh Breineh, in the back, has a room." The old man was so preoccupied filling the hungry hands that he did not even look up.

Sophie groped her way to the rear hall. A gaunt-faced woman answered her inquiry with loquacious enthusiasm. "A grand room for the money. I'll let it down to you only for three dollars a month. In the whole block is no bigger bargain. I should live so."

As she talked, the woman led her through the dark hall into an airshaft room. A narrow window looked out into the bottom of a chimney-like pit, where lay the accumulated refuse from a score of crowded kitchens.

"Oi weh!" gasped Sophie, throwing open the sash. "No air and no light. Outside shines the sun and here it's so dark."

"It ain't so dark. It's only a little shady. Let me only turn up the gas for you and you'll quick see everything like with sunshine."

The claw-fingered flame revealed a rusty, iron cot, an inverted potato barrel that served for a table, and two soap-boxes for chairs.

Sophie felt of the cot. It sagged and flopped under her touch. "The bed has only three feet!" she exclaimed in dismay.

"You can't have Rockefeller's palace for three dollars a month," defended Hanneh Breineh, as she shoved one of the boxes under the legless corner of the cot. "If the bed ain't so steady, so you got good neighbors. Upstairs lives Shprintzeh Gittle, the herring-woman. You can buy by her the biggest bargains in fish, a few days older.... What she got left over from the Sabbath, she sells to the neighbors cheap.... In the front lives Shmendrik, the shoemaker. I'll tell you the truth, he ain't no real shoemaker. He never yet made a pair of whole shoes in his life. He's a learner from the old country—a tzadik, a saint; but every time he sees in the street a child with torn feet, he calls them in and patches them up. His own eating, the last bite from his mouth, he divides up with them."

"Three dollars," deliberated Sophie, scarcely hearing Hanneh Breineh's chatter. "I will never find anything cheaper. It has a door to lock and I can shut this woman out... I'll take it," she said, handing her the money.

Hanneh Breineh kissed the greasy bills gloatingly. "I'll treat you like a mother! You'll have it good by me like in your own home."

"Thanks—but I got no time to shmoos. I got to be alone to get my work done."

The rebuff could not penetrate Hanneh Breineh's joy over the sudden possession of three dollars.

"Long years on you! May we be to good luck to one another!" was Hanneh Breineh's blessing as she closed the door.

Alone in her room—*her* room, securely hers—yet with the flash of triumph, a stab of bitterness. All that was hers—so wretched and so ugly! Had her eager spirit, eager to give and give, no claim to a bit of beauty—a shred of comfort?

Perhaps her family was right in condemning her rashness. Was it worthwhile to give up the peace of home, the security of a regular job—suffer hunger, loneliness, and want—for what? For something she knew in her heart was beyond her reach. Would her writing ever amount to enough to vindicate the uprooting of her past? Would she ever become articulate enough to express beautifully what she saw and felt? What had she, after all, but a stifling, sweatshop experience, a meager, night-school education, and this wild, blind hunger to release the dumbness that choked her?

Sophie spread her papers on the cot beside her. Resting her elbows on the potato barrel, she clutched her pencil with tense fingers. In the notebook before her were a hundred beginnings, essays, abstractions, outbursts of chaotic moods. She glanced through the titles: "Believe in Yourself," "The Quest of the Ideal."

Meaningless tracings on the paper, her words seemed to her now—a restless spirit pawing at the air. The intensity of experience, the surge of emotion that had been hers when she wrote—where were they? The words had failed to catch the life-beat—had failed to register the passion she had poured into them.

Perhaps she was not a writer, after all. Had the years and years of night-study been in vain? Choked with discouragement, the cry broke from her, "O—God—God help me! I feel—I see, but it all dies in me—dumb!"

Tedious days passed into weeks. Again Sophie sat staring into her notebook. "There's nothing here that's alive. Not a word yet says what's in me . . .

"But it *is* in me!" With clenched fist she smote her bosom. "It must be in me! I believe in it! I got to get it out—even if it tears my flesh in pieces—even if it kills me! . . .

"But these words—these flat, dead words . . .

"Whether I can write or can't write—I can't stop writing. I can't rest. I can't breathe. There's no peace, no running away for me on earth except in the struggle to give out what's in me. The beat from my heart—the blood from my veins—must flow out into my words."

She returned to her unfinished essay, "Believe in Yourself." Her mind groping—clutching at the misty incoherence that clouded her thoughts—she wrote on.

"These sentences are yet only wood—lead; but I can't help it—I'll push on—on—I'll not eat—I'll not sleep—I'll not move from this spot till I get it to say on the paper what I got in my heart!"

Slowly the dead words seemed to begin to breathe. Her eyes brightened. Her cheeks flushed. Her very pencil trembled with the eager onrush of words.

Then a sharp rap sounded on her door. With a gesture of irritation Sophie put down her pencil and looked into the burning, sunken eyes of her neighbor, Hanneh Breineh.

"I got yourself a glass of tea, good friend. It ain't much I got to give away, but it's warm even if it's nothing."

Sophie scowled. "You mustn't bother yourself with me. I'm so busy—thanks."

"Don't thank me yet so quick. I got no sugar." Hanneh Breineh edged herself into the room confidingly. "At home, in Poland, I not only had sugar for tea—but even jelly—a jelly that would lift you up to heaven. I thought in America everything would be so plenty, I could drink the tea out from my sugar-bowl. But ach! Not in Poland did my children starve like in America!"

Hanneh Breineh, in a friendly manner, settled herself on the sound end of the bed, and began her jeremiad.

"Yosef, my man, ain't no bread-giver. Already he got consumption the second year. One week he works and nine weeks he lays sick."

In despair Sophie gathered her papers, wondering how to get the woman out of her room. She glanced through the page she had written, but Hanneh Breineh, unconscious of her indifference, went right on.

"How many times it is tearing the heart out from my body—should I take Yosef's milk to give to the baby, or the baby's milk to give to Yosef? If he was dead the pensions they give to widows would help feed my children. Now I got only the charities to help me. A black year on them! They should only have to feed their own children on what they give me."

Resolved not to listen to the intruder, Sophie debated within herself: "Should I call my essay 'Believe in Yourself,' or wouldn't it be stronger to say, 'Trust Yourself'? But if I say, 'Trust Yourself,' wouldn't they think that I got the words from Emerson?"

Hanneh Breineh's voice went on, but it sounded to Sophie like a faint buzzing from afar. "Gottuniu! How much did it cost me my life to go and swear myself that my little Fannie—only skin and bones—that she is already fourteen! How it chokes me the tears every morning when I got to wake her and push her out to the shop when her eyes are yet shutting themselves with sleep!"

Sophie glanced at her wrist-watch as it ticked away the precious minutes. She must get rid of the woman! Had she not left her own sister, sacrificed all comfort, all association, for solitude and its golden possibilities? For the first time in her life she had the chance to be by herself and think. And now, the thoughts which a moment ago had seemed like a flock of fluttering birds had come so close—and this woman with her sordid wailing had scattered them.

"I'm a savage, a beast, but I got to ask her to get out—this very minute," resolved Sophie. But before she could summon the courage to do what she wanted to do, there was a timid knock at the door, and the wizened little Fannie, her face streaked with tears, stumbled in.

"The inspector said it's a lie. I ain't yet fourteen," she whimpered.

Hanneh Breineh paled. "Woe is me! Sent back from the shop? God from the world—is there no end to my troubles? Why didn't you hide yourself when you saw the inspector come?"

"I was running to hide myself under the table, but she caught me and she said she'll take me to the Children's Society and arrest me and my mother for sending me to work too soon."

"Arrest me?" shrieked Hanneh Breineh, beating her breast. "Let them only come and arrest me! I'll show America who I am! Let them only begin themselves with me!... Black is for my eyes... the groceryman will not give us another bread till we pay him the bill!"

"The inspector said..." The child's brow puckered in an effort to recall the words.

"What did the inspector said? Gottuniu!" Hanneh Breineh wrung her hands in passionate entreaty. "Listen only once to my prayer! Send on the inspector only a quick death! I only wish her to have her own house with twenty-four rooms and each of the twenty-four rooms should be twenty-four beds and the chills and the fever should throw her from one bed to another!"

"Hanneh Breineh, still yourself a little," entreated Sophie.

"How can I still myself without Fannie's wages? Bitter is me! Why do I have to live so long?"

"The inspector said..."

"What did the inspector said? A thunder should strike the inspector! Ain't I as good a mother as other mothers? Wouldn't I better send my children to school? But who'll give us to eat? And who'll pay us the rent?"

Hanneh Breineh wiped her red-lidded eyes with the corner of her apron.

"The president from America should only come to my bitter heart. Let him go fighting himself with the pushcarts how to get the eating a penny cheaper. Let him try to feed his children on the money the charities give me and we'd see if he wouldn't better send his littlest ones to the shop better than to let them starve before his eyes. Woe is me! What for did I come to America? What's my life—nothing but one terrible, never-stopping fight with the grocer and the butcher and the landlord..."

Suddenly Sophie's resentment for her lost morning was forgotten. The crying waste of Hanneh Breineh's life lay open before her eyes like pictures in a book. She saw her own life in Hanneh Breineh's life. Her efforts to write were like Hanneh Breineh's efforts to feed her children. Behind her life and Hanneh Breineh's life she saw the massed ghosts of thousands upon thousands beating—beating out their hearts against rock barriers.

"The inspector said..." Fannie timidly attempted again to explain.

"The inspector!" shrieked Hanneh Breineh, as she seized hold of Fannie in a rage. "Hellfire should burn the inspector! Tell me again about the inspector and I'll choke the life out from you—"

Sophie sprang forward to protect the child from the mother. "She's only trying to tell you something."

"Why should she yet throw salt on my wounds? If there was enough bread in the house would I need an inspector to tell me to send her to school? If America is so interested in poor people's children, then why don't they give them to eat till they should go to work? What learning can come into a child's head when the stomach is empty?"

A clutter of feet down the creaking cellar steps, a scuffle of broken shoes, and a chorus of shrill voices, as the younger children rushed in from school.

"Mamma—what's to eat?"

"It smells potatoes!"

"Pfui! The pot is empty! It smells over from Cohen's."

"Jake grabbed all the bread!"

"Mamma—he kicked the piece out from my hands!"

"Mamma—it's so empty in my stomach! Ain't there nothing?"

"Gluttons—wolves—thieves!" Hanneh Breineh shrieked. 'I should only live to bury you all in one day!"

The children, regardless of Hanneh Breineh's invectives, swarmed around her like hungry bees, tearing at her apron, her skirt. Their voices rose in increased clamor, topped only by their mother's imprecations. "Gottuniu! Tear me away from these leeches on my neck! Send on them only a quick death!... Only a minute's peace before I die!"

"Hanneh Breineh—children! What's the matter?" Shmendrik stood at the door. The sweet quiet of the old man stilled the raucous voices as the coming of evening stills the noises of the day.

"There's no end to my troubles! Hear them hollering for bread, and the grocer stopped to give till the bill is paid. Woe is me! Fannie sent home by the inspector and not a crumb in the house!"

"I got something." The old man put his hands over the heads of the children in silent benedicton. "All come in by me. I got sent me a box of cake."

"Cake!" The children cried, catching at the kind hands and snuggling about the shabby coat.

"Yes. Cake and nuts and raisins and even a bottle of wine."

The children leaped and danced around him in their wild burst of joy.

"Cake and wine—a box—to you? Have the charities gone crazy?" Hanneh Breineh's eyes sparkled with light and laughter.

"No—no," Shmendrik explained hastily. "Not from the charities—from a friend—for the holidays."

Shmendrik nodded invitingly to Sophie, who was standing in the door of her room. "The roomerkeh will also give a taste with us our party?"

"Sure will she!" Hanneh Breineh took Sophie by the arm. "Who'll say no in this black life to cake and wine?"

Young throats burst into shrill cries: "Cake and wine—wine and cake—raisins and nuts—nuts and raisins!" The words rose in a triumphant chorus. The children leaped and danced in time to their chant, almost carrying the old man bodily into his room in the wildness of their joy.

The contagion of this sudden hilarity erased from Sophie's mind the last thought of work and she found herself seated with the others on the cobbler's bench.

From under his cot the old man drew forth a wooden box. Lifting the cover he held up before wondering eyes a large frosted cake embedded in raisins and nuts.

Amid the shouts of glee Shmendrik now waved aloft a large bottle of grape-juice.

The children could contain themselves no longer and dashed forward.

"Shah—shah! Wait only!" He gently halted their onrush and waved them back to their seats.

"The glasses for the wine!" Hanneh Breineh rushed about hither and thither in happy confusion. From the sink, the shelf, the windowsill, she gathered cracked glasses, cups without handles—anything that would hold even a few drops of the yellow wine.

Sacrificial solemnity filled the basement as the children breathlessly watched Shmendrik cut the precious cake. Mouths—even eyes—watered with the intensity of their emotion.

With almost religious fervor Hanneh Breineh poured the grape-juice into the glasses held in the trembling hands of the children. So overwhelming was the occasion that none dared to taste till the ritual was completed. The suspense was agonizing as one and all waited for Shmendrik's signal.

"Hanneh Breineh—you drink from my Sabbath wine-glass!"

Hanneh Breineh clinked glasses with Shmendrik. "Long years on you—long years on us all!" Then she turned to Sophie, clinked glasses once more. "May you yet marry yourself from our basement to a millionaire!" Then she lifted the glass to her lips.

The spell was broken. With a yell of triumph the children gobbled the cake in huge mouthfuls and sucked the golden liquid. All the traditions of wealth and joy that ever sparkled from the bubbles of champagne smiled at Hanneh Breineh from her glass of California grape-juice.

"Ach!" she sighed. "How good it is to forget your troubles, and only those that's got troubles have the chance to forget them!"

She sipped the grape-juice leisurely, thrilled into ecstasy with each lingering drop. "How it laughs yet in me, the life, the minute I turn my head from my worries!"

With growing wonder in her eyes, Sophie watched Hanneh Breineh. This ragged wreck of a woman—how passionately she clung to every atom of life! Hungrily, she burned through the depths of every experience. How she flared against wrongs—and how every tiny spark of pleasure blazed into joy!

Within a half-hour this woman had touched the whole range of human emotions, from bitterest agony to dancing joy. The terrible despair at the onrush of her starving children when she cried out, "O that I should only bury you all in one day!" And now the leaping light of the words: "How it laughs yet in me, the life, the minute I turn my head from my worries."

"Ach, if I could only write like Hanneh Breineh talks!" thought Sophie. "Her words dance with a thousand colors. Like a rainbow it flows from her lips." Sentences from her own essays marched before her, stiff and wooden. How clumsy, how unreal, were her most labored phrases compared to Hanneh Breineh's spontaneity. Fascinated, she listened to Hanneh Breineh, drinking her words as a thirst-perishing man drinks water. Every bubbling phrase filled her with a drunken rapture to create.

"Up till now I was only trying to write from my head. It wasn't real—it wasn't life. Hanneh Breineh is real. Hanneh Breineh is life."

"Ach! What do the rich people got but dried-up dollars? Pfui on them and their money!" Hanneh Breineh held up her glass to be refilled. "Let me only win a fortune on the lotteree and move myself in my own bought house. Let me only have my first hundred dollars in the bank and I'll lift up my head like a person and tell the charities to eat their own cornmeal. I'll get myself an automobile like the kind rich ladies and ride up to their houses on Fifth Avenue and feed them only once on the eating they like so good for me and my children."

With a smile of benediction Shmendrik refilled the glasses and cut for each of his guests another slice of cake. Then came the handful of nuts and raisins.

As the children were scurrying about for hammers and iron lasts with which to crack their nuts, the basement door creaked. Unannounced, a woman entered—the "friendly visitor" of the charities. Her look of awful amazement swept the groups of merrymakers.

"Mr. Shmendrik!—Hanneh Breineh!" Indignation seethed in her voice. "What's this! A feast—a birthday?"

Gasps—bewildered glances—a struggle for utterance!

"I came to make my monthly visit—evidently I'm not needed."

Shmendrik faced the accusing eyes of the "friendly visitor." "Holiday eating..."

"Oh—I'm glad you're so prosperous."

Before anyone had gained presence of mind enough to explain things, the door had clanked. The "friendly visitor" had vanished.

"Pfui!" Hanneh Breineh snatched up her glass and drained its contents. "What will she do now? Will we get no more dry bread from the charities because once we ate cake?"

"What for did she come?" asked Sophie.

"To see that we don't over-eat ourselves!" returned Hanneh Breineh. "She's a 'friendly visitor'! She learns us how to cook cornmeal. By pictures and lectures she shows us how the poor people should live without meat, without milk, without butter, and without eggs. Always it's on the end of my tongue to ask her, 'You learned us to do without so much, why can't you yet learn us how to eat without eating?'"

The children seized the last crumbs of cake that Shmendrik handed them and rushed for the street.

"What a killing look was on her face," said Sophie. "Couldn't she be a little glad for your gladness?"

"Charity ladies—gladness?" the joy of the grape-wine still rippled in Hanneh Breineh's laughter. "For poor people is only cornmeal. Ten cents a day—to feed my children!"

Still in her rollicking mood Hanneh Breineh picked up the baby and tossed it like a Bacchante. "Could you be happy a lot with ten cents in your stomach? Ten cents—half a can of condensed milk—then fill yourself the rest with water!... Maybe yet feed you with all water and save the ten-cent pieces to buy you a carriage like the Fifth Avenue babies!..."

The soft sound of a limousine purred through the area grating and two well-fed figures in seal-skin coats, led by the "friendly visitor," appeared at the door.

"Mr. Bernstein, you can see for yourself." The "friendly visitor" pointed to the table.

The merry group shrank back. It was as if a gust of icy wind had swept all the joy and laughter from the basement.

"You are charged with intent to deceive and obtain assistance by dishonest means," said Mr. Bernstein.

"Dishonest?" Shmendrik paled.

Sophie's throat strained with passionate protest, but no words came to her release.

"A friend—a friend"—stammered Shmendrik—"sent me the holiday eating."

The superintendent of the Social Betterment Society faced him accusingly. "You told us that you had no friends when you applied to us for assistance."

"My friend—he knew me in my better time." Shmendrik flushed painfully. "I was once a scholar—respected. I wanted by this one friend to hold myself like I was."

Mr. Bernstein had taken from the bookshelf a number of letters, glanced through them rapidly and handed them one by one to the deferential superintendent.

Shmendrik clutched at his heart in an agony of humiliation. Suddenly his bent body straightened. His eyes dilated. "My letters—my life—you dare?"

"Of course we dare!" The superintendent returned Shmendrik's livid gaze, made bold by the confidence that what he was doing was the only scientific method of administering philanthropy. "These dollars, so generously given, must go to those most worthy.... I find in these letters references to gifts of fruit and other luxuries you did not report at our office."

"He never kept nothing for himself!" Hanneh Breineh broke in defensively. "He gave it all for the children."

Ignoring the interruption Mr. Bernstein turned to the "friendly visitor." "I'm glad you brought my attention to this case. It's but one of the many impositions on our charity... Come ..."

"Kossacks! Pogromschiks!" Sophie's rage broke at last. "You call yourselves Americans? You dare call yourselves Jews? You bosses of the poor! This man Shmendrik, whose house you broke into, whom you made to shame like a beggar—he is the one Jew from whom the Jews can be proud! He gives all he is—all he has—as God gives. *He is* charity.

"But you—you are the greed—the shame of the Jews! *All-right-niks*— fat bellies in fur coats! What do you give from yourselves? You may eat and bust eating! Nothing you give till you've stuffed yourselves so full that your hearts are dead!"

The door closed in her face. Her wrath fell on indifferent backs as the visitors mounted the steps to the street.

Shmendrik groped blindly for the Bible. In a low, quavering voice, he began the chant of the oppressed—the wail of the downtrodden. "I am afraid, and a trembling taketh hold of my flesh. Wherefore do the wicked live, become old, yea, mighty in power?"

Hanneh Breineh and the children drew close around the old man. They were weeping—unconscious of their weeping—deep-buried memories roused by the music, the age-old music of the Hebrew race.

Through the grating Sophie saw the limousine pass. The chant flowed on: "Their houses are safe from fear; neither is the rod of God upon them."

Silently Sophie stole back to her room. She flung herself on the cot, pressed her fingers to her burning eyeballs. For a long time she lay rigid, clenched—listening to the drumming of her heart like the sea against rock barriers. Presently the barriers burst. Something in her began pouring itself out. She felt for her pencil—paper—and began to write. Whether she reached out to God or man she knew not, but she wrote on and on all through that night.

The gray light entering her grated window told her that beyond was dawn. Sophie looked up: "Ach! At last it writes itself in me!" she whispered triumphantly. "It's not me—it's their cries—my own people—crying in me! Hanneh Breineh, Shmendrik, they will not be stilled in me, till all America stops to listen."

How I Found America

Every breath I drew was a breath of fear, every shadow a stifling shock, every footfall struck on my heart like the heavy boot of the Cossack.

On a low stool in the middle of the only room in our mud hut sat my father—his red beard falling over the Book of Isaiah open before him. On the tile stove, on the benches that were our beds, even on the earthen floor, sat the neighbors' children, learning from him the ancient poetry of the Hebrew race.

As he chanted, the children repeated:

> *"The voice of him that crieth in the wilderness,*
> *Prepare ye the way of the Lord.*
> *Make straight in the desert a highway for our God*
>
> *"Every valley shall be exalted,*
> *And every mountain and hill shall be made low,*

And the crooked shall be made straight,
And the rough places plain.

"And the glory of the Lord shall be revealed,
And all flesh shall see it together."

Undisturbed by the swaying and chanting of teacher and pupils, old Kakah, our speckled hen, with her brood of chicks, strutted and pecked at the potato-peelings which fell from my mother's lap, as she prepared our noon meal.

I stood at the window watching the road, lest the Cossack come upon us unawares to enforce the ukaz of the Czar, which would tear the bread from our mouths: "No Chadir [Hebrew school] shall be held in a room used for cooking and sleeping."

With one eye I watched ravenously my mother cutting chunks of black bread. At last the potatoes were ready. She poured them out of the iron pot into a wooden bowl and placed them in the center of the table.

Instantly the swaying and chanting ceased, the children rushed forward. The fear of the Cossacks was swept away from my heart by the fear that the children would get my potato.

The sentry deserted his post. With a shout of joy I seized my portion and bit a huge mouthful of mealy delight.

At that moment the door was driven open by the blow of an iron heel. The Cossack's whip swished through the air. Screaming, we scattered.

The children ran out—our livelihood gone with them.

"Oi weh," wailed my mother, clutching her breast, "is there a God over us—and sees all this?"

With grief-glazed eyes my father muttered a broken prayer as the Cossack thundered the ukaz: "A thousand rubles fine or a year in prison if you are ever found again teaching children where you're eating and sleeping."

"Gottuniu!" pleaded my mother, "would you tear the last skin from our bones? Where else can we be eating and sleeping? Or should we keep Chadir in the middle of the road? Have we houses with separate rooms like the Czar?"

Ignoring my mother's entreaties the Cossack strode out of the hut. My father sank into a chair, his head bowed in the silent grief of the helpless.

"God from the world"—my mother wrung her hands—"is there no end to our troubles? When will the earth cover me and my woes?"

I watched the Cossack disappear down the road. All at once I saw the whole village running toward us. I dragged my mother to the window to see the approaching crowd.

"Gewalt! What more is falling over our heads?" she cried in alarm.

Masheh Mindel, the water-carrier's wife, headed a wild procession. The baker, the butcher, the shoemaker, the tailor, the goatherd, the workers of the fields, with their wives and children, pressed toward us through a cloud of dust.

Masheh Mindel, almost fainting, fell in front of the doorway. "A letter from America!" she gasped.

"A letter from America!" echoed the crowd, as they snatched the letter from her and thrust it into my father's hands.

"Read! Read!" they shouted tumultuously.

My father looked through the letter, his lips uttering no sound. In breathless suspense the crowd gazed at him. Their eyes shone with wonder and reverence for the only man in the village who could read.

Masheh Mindel crouched at his feet, her neck stretched toward him to catch each precious word of the letter.

"To my worthy wife, Masheh Mindel, and to my loving son, Susha Feifel, and to my precious darling daughter, the apple of my eye, the pride of my life, Tzipkeleh!

"Long years and good luck on you! May the blessings from heaven fall over your beloved heads and save you from all harm!

"First I come to tell you that I am well and in good health. May I hear the same from you.

"Secondly, I am telling you that my sun is beginning to shine in America. I am becoming a person—a business man.

"I have for myself a stand in the most crowded part of America, where people are as thick as flies and every day is like market-day by a fair. My business is from bananas and apples. The day begins with my pushcart full of fruit, and the day never ends before I count up at least $2.00 profit—that means four rubles. Stand before your eyes . . . I . . . Gedalyeh Mindel, four rubles a day, twenty-four rubles a week!"

"Gedalyeh Mindel, the water-carrier, twenty-four rubles a week . . ." The words leaped like fire in the air.

We gazed at his wife, Masheh Mindel—a dried-out bone of a woman.

"Masheh Mindel, with a husband in America—Masheh Mindel, the wife of a man earning twenty-four rubles a week!"

We looked at her with new reverence. Already she was a being from another world. The dead, sunken eyes became alive with light. The worry for bread that had tightened the skin of her cheek-bones was gone. The sudden surge of happiness filled out her features, flushing her face as with wine.

The two starved children clinging to her skirts, dazed with excitement, only dimly realized their good fortune by the envious glances of the others.

"Thirdly, I come to tell you," the letter went on, "white bread and meat I eat every day just like the millionaires.

"Fourthly, I have to tell you that I am no more Gedalyeh Mindel—*Mister* Mindel they call me in America.

"Fifthly, Masheh Mindel and my dear children, in America there are no mud huts where cows and chickens and people live all together. I have for myself a separate room with a closed door, and before anyone can come to me, I can give a say, 'Come in,' or 'Stay out,' like a king in a palace.

"Lastly, my darling family and people of the Village of Sukovoly, there is no Czar in America."

My father paused; the hush was stifling. No Czar—no Czar in America! Even the little babies repeated the chant: "No Czar in America!"

"In America they ask everybody who should be the President, and I, Gedalyeh Mindel, when I take out my Citizens papers, will have as much to say who shall be the next President in America, as Mr. Rockefeller the greatest millionaire.

"Fifty rubles I am sending you for your ship-ticket to America. And may all Jews who suffer in Goluth from ukazes and pogroms live yet to lift up their heads like me, Gedalyeh Mindel, in America."

Fifty rubles! A ship-ticket to America! That so much good luck should fall on one head! A savage envy bit me. Gloomy darts from narrowed eyes stabbed Masheh Mindel.

Why should not we too have a chance to get away from this dark land? Has not every heart the same hunger for America? The same longing to live and laugh and breathe like a free human being? America is for all. Why should only Masheh Mindel and her children have a chance to the new world?

Murmuring and gesticulating, the crowd dispersed.

Each one knew everyone else's thought: How to get to America. What could they pawn? From where could they borrow for a ship-ticket?

Silently we followed my father back into the hut from which the Cossack had driven us a while before.

We children looked from mother to father and from father to mother.

"Gottuniu! The Czar himself is pushing us to America by this last ukaz." My mother's face lighted up the hut like a lamp.

"Meshugeneh Yidini!" admonished my father. "Always your head in the air. What—where—America? With what money? Can dead people lift themselves up to dance?"

"Dance?" The samovar and the brass pots rang and reëchoed with my mother's laughter. "I could dance myself over the waves of the ocean to America."

In amazed delight at my mother's joy we children rippled and chuckled with her.

My father paced the room—his face dark with dread for the morrow.

"Empty hands—empty pockets—yet it dreams itself in you America."

"Who is poor who has hopes on America?" flaunted my mother.

"Sell my red quilted petticoat that grandmother left for my dowry," I urged in excitement.

"Sell the feather beds, sell the samovar," chorused the children.

"Sure we can sell everything—the goat and all the winter things," added my mother; "it must be always summer in America."

I flung my arms around my brother and he seized Bessie by the curls, and we danced about the room crazy with joy.

"Beggars!" laughed my mother, "why are you so happy with yourselves? How will you go to America without a shirt on your back—without shoes on your feet?"

But we ran out into the road, shouting and singing: "We'll sell everything we got—we'll go to America."

"White bread and meat we'll eat every day—in America! In America!"

That very evening we fetched Berel Zalman, the usurer, and showed him all our treasures, piled up in the middle of the hut.

"Look, all these fine feather beds, Berel Zalman," urged my mother; "this grand fur coat came from Nijny itself. My grandfather bought it at the fair."

I held up my red quilted petticoat, the supreme sacrifice of my ten-year-old life.

Even my father shyly pushed forward the samovar. "It can hold enough tea for the whole village."

"Only a hundred rubles for them all," pleaded my mother; "only enough to lift us to America. Only one hundred little rubles."

"A hundred rubles? Pfui!" sniffed the pawnbroker. "Forty is overpaid. Not even thirty is it worth."

But coaxing and cajoling my mother got a hundred rubles out of him.

Steerage—dirty bundles—foul odors—seasick humanity—but I saw and heard nothing of the foulness and ugliness around me. I floated in showers of sunshine; visions upon visions of the new world opened before me.

From lips to lips flowed the golden legend of the golden country:

"In America you can say what you feel—you can voice your thoughts in the open streets without fear of a Cossack."

"In America is a home for everybody. The land is your land. Not like in Russia where you feel yourself a stranger in the village where you were born and raised—the village in which your father and grandfather lie buried."

"Everybody is with everybody alike, in America. Christians and Jews are brothers together."

"An end to the worry for bread. An end to the fear of the bosses over you. Everybody can do what he wants with his life in America."

"There are no high or low in America. Even the President holds hands with Gedalyeh Mindel."

"Plenty for all. Learning flows free like milk and honey."

"Learning flows free."

The words painted pictures in my mind. I saw before me free schools, free colleges, free libraries, where I could learn and learn and keep on learning.

In our village was a school, but only for Christian children. In the schools of America I'd lift up my head and laugh and dance—a child with other children. Like a bird in the air, from sky to sky, from star to star, I'd soar and soar.

"Land! Land!" came the joyous shout.

"America! We're in America!" cried my mother, almost smothering us in her rapture.

All crowded and pushed on deck. They strained and stretched to get the first glimpse of the "golden country," lifting their children on their shoulders that they might see beyond them.

Men fell on their knees to pray. Women hugged their babies and wept. Children danced. Strangers embraced and kissed like old friends. Old men and women had in their eyes a look of young people in love.

Age-old visions sang themselves in me—songs of freedom of an oppressed people.

America!—America!

PART II

Between buildings that loomed like mountains, we struggled with our bundles, spreading around us the smell of the steerage. Up Broadway, under the bridge, and through the swarming streets of the ghetto, we followed Gedalyeh Mindel.

I looked about the narrow streets of squeezed-in stores and houses, ragged clothes, dirty bedding oozing out of the windows, ash-cans and garbage-cans cluttering the side-walks. A vague sadness pressed down my heart—the first doubt of America.

"Where are the green fields and open spaces in America?" cried my heart. "Where is the golden country of my dreams?"

A loneliness for the fragrant silence of the woods that lay beyond our mud hut welled up in my heart, a longing for the soft, responsive earth of our village streets. All about me was the hardness of brick and stone, the stinking smells of crowded poverty.

"Here's your house with separate rooms like in a palace." Gedalyeh Mindel flung open the door of a dingy, airless flat.

"Oi weh!" my mother cried in dismay. "Where's the sunshine in America?"

She went to the window and looked out at the blank wall of the next house. "Gottuniu! Like in a grave so dark..."

"It ain't so dark, it's only a little shady." Gedalyeh Mindel lighted the gas. "Look only"—he pointed with pride to the dim gaslight. "No candles, no kerosene lamps in America, you turn on a screw and put to it a match and you got it light like with sunshine."

Again the shadow fell over me, again the doubt of America!

In America were rooms without sunlight, rooms to sleep in, to eat in, to cook in, but without sunshine. And Gedalyeh Mindel was happy. Could I be satisfied with just a place to sleep and eat in, and a door to shut people out—to take the place of sunlight? Or would I always need the sunlight to be happy?

And where was there a place in America for me to play? I looked out into the alley below and saw pale-faced children scrambling in the gutter. "Where is America?" cried my heart.

My eyes were shutting themselves with sleep. Blindly, I felt for the buttons on my dress, and buttoning I sank back in sleep again—the deadweight sleep of utter exhaustion.

"Heart of mine!" my mother's voice moaned above me. "Father is already gone an hour. You know how they'll squeeze from you a nickel for every minute you're late. Quick only!"

I seized my bread and herring and tumbled down the stairs and out into the street. I ate running, blindly pressing through the hurrying throngs of workers—my haste and fear choking each mouthful.

I felt a strangling in my throat as I neared the sweatshop prison; all my nerves screwed together into iron hardness to endure the day's torture.

For an instant I hesitated as I faced the grated window of the old dilapidated building—dirt and decay cried out from every crumbling brick.

In the maw of the shop, raging around me the roar and the clatter, the clatter and the roar, the merciless grind of the pounding machines.

Half maddened, half deadened, I struggled to think, to feel, to remember—what am I—who am I—why was I here?

I struggled in vain—bewildered and lost in a whirlpool of noise.

"America—America—where was America?" it cried in my heart.

The factory whistle—the slowing-down of the machines—the shout of release hailing the noon hour.

I woke as from a tense nightmare—a weary waking to pain.

In the dark chaos of my brain reason began to dawn. In my stifled heart feelings began to pulse. The wound of my wasted life began to throb and ache. My childhood choked with drudgery—must my youth too die—unlived?

The odor of herring and garlic—the ravenous munching of food—laughter and loud, vulgar jokes. Was it only I who was so wretched? I looked at those around me. Were they happy or only insensible to their slavery? How could they laugh and joke? Why were they not torn with rebellion against this galling grind—the crushing, deadening movements of the body, where only hands live and hearts and brains must die?

A touch on my shoulder. I looked up. It was Yetta Solomon from the machine next to mine.

"Here's your tea."

I stared at her, half hearing.

"Ain't you going to eat nothing?"

"Oi weh! Yetta! I can't stand it!" The cry broke from me. "I didn't come to America to turn into a machine. I came to America to make from myself a person. Does America want only my hands—only the strength of my body—not my heart—not my feelings—my thoughts?"

"Our heads ain't smart enough," said Yetta, practically. "We ain't been to school like the American-born."

"What for did I come to America but to go to school—to learn—to think—to make something beautiful from my life..."

"Sh-sh! Sh-sh! The boss—the boss!" came the warning whisper.

A sudden hush fell over the shop as the boss entered. He raised his hand.

Breathless silence.

The hard, red face with pig's eyes held us under its sickening spell. Again I saw the Cossack and heard him thunder the ukaz.

Prepared for disaster, the girls paled as they cast at each other sidelong, frightened glances.

"Hands," he addressed us, fingering the gold watch-chain that spread across his fat belly, "it's slack in the other trades and I can get plenty girls begging themselves to work for half what you're getting—only I ain't a skinner. I always give my hands a show to earn their bread. From now on, I'll give you fifty cents a dozen shirts instead of seventy-five, but I'll give you night-work, so you needn't lose nothing." And he was gone.

The stillness of death filled the shop. Each one felt the heart of the other bleed with her own helplessness.

A sudden sound broke the silence. A woman sobbed chokingly. It was Balah Rifkin, a widow with three children.

"Oi weh!" She tore at her scrawny neck. "The blood-sucker—the thief! How will I give them to eat—my babies—my babies—my hungry little lambs!"

"Why do we let him choke us?"

"Twenty-five cents less on a dozen—how will we be able to live?"

"He tears the last skin from our bones!"

"Why didn't nobody speak up to him?"

"Tell him he couldn't crush us down to worse than we had in Russia?"

"Can we help ourselves? Our life lies in his hands."

Something in me forced me forward. Rage at the bitter greed tore me. Our desperate helplessness drove me to strength.

"I'll go to the boss!" I cried, my nerves quivering with fierce excitement. "I'll tell him Balah Rifkin has three hungry mouths to feed."

Pale, hungry faces thrust themselves toward me, thin, knotted hands reached out, starved bodies pressed close about me.

"Long years on you!" cried Balah Rifkin, drying her eyes with a corner of her shawl.

"Tell him about my old father and me, his only bread-giver," came from Bessie Sopolsky, a gaunt-faced girl with a hacking cough.

"And I got no father or mother and four of them younger than me hanging on my neck." Jennie Feist's beautiful young face was already scarred with the gray worries of age.

America, as the oppressed of all lands have dreamed America to be, and America *as it is,* flashed before me—a banner of fire! Behind me I felt masses pressing—thousands of immigrants—thousands upon thousands crushed by injustice, lifted me as on wings.

I entered the boss's office without a shadow of fear. I was not I—the wrongs of my people burned through me till I felt the very flesh of my body a living flame of rebellion.

I faced the boss

"We can't stand it!" I cried. "Even as it is we're hungry. Fifty cents a dozen would starve us. Can you, a Jew, tear the bread from another Jew's mouth?"

"You fresh mouth, you! Who are you to learn me my business?"

"Weren't you yourself once a machine slave—your life in the hands of your boss?"

"You—loaferin—money for nothing you want! The minute they begin to talk English they get flies in their nose.... A black year on you—trouble-maker! I'll have no smart heads in my shop! Such freshness! Out you get... out from my shop!"

Stunned and hopeless, the wings of my courage broken, I groped my way back to them—back to the eager, waiting faces—back to the crushed hearts aching with mine.

As I opened the door they read our defeat in my face.

"Girls!" I held out my hands. "He's fired me."

My voice died in the silence. Not a girl stirred. Their heads only bent closer over their machines.

"Here, you! Get yourself out of here!" The boss thundered at me. "Bessie Sopolsky and you, Balah Rifkin, take out her machine into the hall.... I want no big-mouthed Americanerins in my shop."

Bessie Sopolsky and Balah Rifkin, their eyes black with tragedy, carried out my machine.

Not a hand was held out to me, not a face met mine. I felt them shrink from me as I passed them on my way out.

In the street I found I was crying. The new hope that had flowed in me so strong bled out of my veins. A moment before, our togetherness had made me believe us so strong—and now I saw each alone—crushed—broken. What were they all but crawling worms, servile grubbers for bread?

I wept not so much because the girls had deserted me, but because I saw for the first time how mean, how vile, were the creatures with whom I had to work. How the fear for bread had dehumanized their last shred of humanity! I felt I had not been working among human beings, but in a jungle of savages who had to eat one another alive in order to survive.

And then, in the very bitterness of my resentment, the hardness broke in me. I saw the girls through their own eyes as if I were inside of them. What else could they have done? Was not an immediate crust of bread for Balah Rifkin's children more urgent than truth—more vital than honor?

Could it be that they ever had dreamed of America as I had dreamed? Had their faith in America wholly died in them? Could my faith be killed as theirs had been?

Gasping from running, Yetta Solomon flung her arms around me.

"You golden heart! I sneaked myself out from the shop—only to tell you I'll come to see you to-night. I'd give the blood from under my nails for you—only I got to run back—I got to hold my job—my mother—"

I hardly saw or heard her—my senses stunned with my defeat. I walked on in a blind daze—feeling that any moment I would drop in the middle of the street from sheer exhaustion.

Every hope I had clung to—every human stay—every reality was torn from under me. I sank in bottomless blackness. I had only one wish left—to die.

Was it then only a dream—a mirage of the hungry-hearted people in the desert lands of oppression—this age-old faith in America—the beloved, the prayed-for "golden country"?

Had the starved villagers of Sukovoly lifted above their sorrows a mere rainbow vision that led them—where—where? To the stifling submission of the sweatshop or the desperation of the streets!

"O God! What is there beyond this hell?" my soul cried in me. "Why can't I make a quick end to myself?"

A thousand voices within me and about me answered:

"My faith is dead, but in my blood their faith still clamors and aches for fulfillment—*dead generations whose faith though beaten back still presses on—a resistless, deathless force!*

"In this America that crushes and kills me, their spirit drives me on—to struggle—to suffer—but never to submit."

In my desperate darkness their lost lives loomed—a living flame of light. Again I saw the mob of dusty villagers crowding around my father as he read the letter from America—their eager faces thrust out—their eyes blazing with the same hope, the same age-old faith that drove me on—

A sudden crash against my back. Dizzy with pain I fell—then all was darkness and quiet.

I opened my eyes. A white-clad figure bent over me. Had I died? Was I in the heaven of the new world—in America?

My eyes closed again. A misty happiness filled my being.

"Learning flows free like milk and honey," it dreamed itself in me.

I was in my heaven—in the schools of America—in open, sunny fields—a child with other children. Our lesson-books were singing birds and whispering trees—chanting brooks and beckoning skies. We breathed in learning and wisdom as naturally as flowers breathe in sunlight.

After our lessons were over, we all joined hands skipping about like a picture of dancing fairies I had once seen in a shop-window.

I was so full of the joy of togetherness—the great wonder of the new world; it pressed on my heart like sorrow. Slowly, I stole away from the other children into silent solitude, wrestling and praying to give out what surged in me into some form of beauty. And out of my struggle to shape my thoughts beautifully, a great song filled the world.

"Soon she's all right to come back to the shop—yes, nurse?" The voice of Yetta Solomon broke into my dreaming.

Wearily I opened my eyes. I saw I was still on earth.

Yetta's broad, generous face smiled anxiously at me. "Lucky yet the car that run you over didn't break your hands or your feet. So long you got yet good hands you'll soon be back by the machine."

"Machine?" I shuddered. "I can't go back to the shop again. I got so used to sunlight and quiet in the hospital I'll not be able to stand the hell again."

"Shah!—Shah!" soothed Yetta. "Why don't you learn yourself to take life like it is? What's got to be, got to be. In Russia, you could hope to run away from your troubles to America. But from America where can you go?"

"Yes," I sighed. "In the blackest days of Russia, there was always the hope from America. In Russia we had only a mud hut; not enough to eat and always the fear from the Cossack, but still we managed to look up to the sky, to dream, to think of the new world where we'll have a chance to be people, not slaves."

"What's the use to think so much? It only eats up the flesh from your bones. Better rest..."

"How can I rest when my choked-in thoughts tear me to pieces? I need school more than a starving man needs bread."

Yetta's eyes brooded over me. Suddenly a light broke. "I got an idea. There's a new school for greenhorns where they learn them anything they want..."

"What—where?" I raised myself quickly, hot with eagerness. "How do you know from it—tell me only—quick—since when—"

"The girl next door by my house—she used to work by cigars—and now she learns there."

"What does she learn?"

"Don't get yourself so excited. Your eyes are jumping out from your head."

I fell back weakly: "Oi weh! Tell me!" I begged.

"All I know is that she likes what she learns better than rolling cigars. And it's called 'School for Immigrant Girls.'"

"Your time is up. Another visitor is waiting to come in," said the nurse.

As Yetta walked out, my mother, with the shawl over her head, rushed in and fell on my bed kissing me.

"Oi weh! Oi weh! Half my life is out from me from fright. How did all happen?"

"Don't worry yourself so. I'm nearly well already and will go back to work soon."

"Talk not work. Get only a little flesh on your bones. They say they send from the hospital people to the country. Maybe they'll send you."

"But how will you live without my wages?"

"Davy is already peddling with papers and Bessie is selling lolly-pops after school in the park. Yesterday she brought home already twenty-eight cents."

For all her efforts to be cheerful, I looked at her pinched face and wondered if she had eaten that day.

Released from the hospital, I started home. As I neared Allen Street, the terror of the dark rooms swept over me. "No—no—I can't yet go back to the darkness and the stinking smells," I said to myself. "So long they're getting along without my wages, let them think I went to the country and let me try out that school for immigrants that Yetta told me about."

So I went to the Immigrant School.

A tall, gracious woman received me, not an employee, but a benefactress.

The love that had rushed from my heart toward the Statue in the Bay rushed out to Mrs. Olney. She seemed to me the living spirit of America. All that I had ever dreamed America to be shone to me out of the kindness of her brown eyes. She would save me from the sordidness that was crushing me, I felt the moment I looked at her. Sympathy and understanding seemed to breathe from her serene presence.

I longed to open my heart to her, but I was so excited I didn't know where to begin.

"I'm crazy to learn!" I gasped breathlessly, and then the very pressure of the things I had to say choked me.

An encouraging smile warmed the fine features.

"What trade would you like to learn—sewing-machine operating?"

"Sewing-machine operating?" I cried. "Oi weh!" I shuddered. "Only the thought 'machine' kills me. Even when I only look on clothes, it weeps in me when I think how the seams from everything people wear is sweated in the shop."

"Well, then"—putting a kind hand on my shoulder—"how would you like to learn to cook? There's a great need for trained servants and you'd get good wages and a pleasant home."

"Me—a servant?" I flung back her hand. "Did I come to America to make from myself a cook?"

Mrs. Olney stood abashed a moment. "Well, my dear," she said deliberately, "what would you like to take up?"

"I got ideas how to make America better, only I don't know how to say it out. Ain't there a place I can learn?"

A startled woman stared at me. For a moment not a word came. Then she proceeded with the same kind smile. "It's nice of you to want to help

America, but I think the best way would be for you to learn a trade. That's what this school is for, to help girls find themselves, and the best way to do is to learn something useful."

"Ain't thoughts useful? Does America want only the work from my body, my hands? Ain't it thoughts that turn over the world?"

"Ah! But we don't want to turn over the world." Her voice cooled.

"But there's got to be a change in America!" I cried. "Us immigrants want to be people—not 'hands'—not slaves of the belly! And it's the chance to think out thoughts that makes people."

"My child, thought requires leisure. The time will come for that. First you must learn to earn a good living."

"Did I come to America for a living?"

"What did you come for?"

"I came to give out all the fine things that was choked in me in Russia. I came to help America make the new world. . . . They said, in America I could open up my heart and fly free in the air—to sing—to dance—to live—to love. . . . Here I got all those grand things in me, and America won't let me give nothing."

"Perhaps you made a mistake in coming to this country. Your own land might appreciate you more." A quick glance took me in from head to foot. "I'm afraid that you have come to the wrong place. We only teach trades here."

She turned to her papers and spoke over her shoulder. "I think you will have to go elsewhere if you want to set the world on fire."

PART III

Blind passion swayed me as I walked out of the Immigrant School, not knowing where I was going, not caring. One moment I was swept with the fury of indignation, the next moment bent under the burden of despair. But out of this surging conflict one thought—one truth gradually grew clearer and clearer to me: Without comprehension, the immigrant would forever remain shut out—a stranger in America. Until America can release the heart as well as train the hand of the immigrant, he would forever remain driven back upon himself, corroded by the very richness of the unused gifts within his soul.

I longed for a friend—a real American friend—someone different from Mrs. Olney, someone who would understand this vague, blind hunger for release that consumed me. But how, where could I find such a friend?

As I neared the house we lived in, I paused terror-stricken. On the sidewalk stood a jumbled pile of ragged house-furnishings that looked familiar—chairs, dishes, kitchen pans. Amidst bundles of bedding and broken furniture stood my mother. Oblivious of the curious crowd, she lit the Sabbath candles and prayed over them.

In a flash I understood it all. Because of the loss of my wages while I was in the hospital, we had been evicted for unpaid rent. It was Sabbath eve. My father was in the synagogue praying and my mother, defiant of disgrace, had gone on with the ceremony of the Sabbath.

All the romance of our race was in the light of those Sabbath candles. Homeless, abandoned by God and man, yet in the very desolation of the streets my mother's faith burned—a challenge to all America.

"Mammeh!" I cried, pushing through the crowd. Bessie and Dave darted forward. In a moment the four of us stood clinging to one another, amid the ruins of our broken home.

A neighbor invited us into her house for supper. No sooner had we sat down at the table than there was a knock at the door and a square-figured young woman entered, asking to see my mother.

"I am from the Social Betterment Society," she said. "I hear you've been dispossessed. What's the trouble here?"

"Oi weh! My bitter heart!" I yet see before me the anguish of my mother's face as she turned her head away from the charity lady.

My father's eyes sank to the floor. I could feel him shrink in upon himself like one condemned.

The bite of food turned to gall in my throat.

"How long have you been in America? Where were you born?" She questioned by rote, taking out pad and pencil.

The silence of the room was terrible. The woman who had invited us for supper slunk into the bedroom, unable to bear our shame.

"How long have you been in America?" repeated the charity lady.

Choked silence.

"Is there any one here who can speak?" She translated her question into Yiddish.

"A black year on Gedalyeh Mindel, the liar!" my mother burst out at last. "Why did we leave our home? We were among our own. We were people there. But what are we here? Nobodies—nobodies! Cats and dogs at home ain't thrown in the street. Such things could only happen in America—the land without a heart—the land without a God!"

"For goodness' sakes! Is there any one here intelligent enough to answer a straight question?" The charity lady turned with disgusted impatience from my mother to me. "Can you tell me how long you have been in this country? Where were you born?"

"None of your business!" I struck out blindly, not aware of what I was saying.

"Why so bold? We are only trying to help you and you are so resentful."

"To the Devil with your help! I'm sick no longer. I can take care of my mother—without your charity!"

The next day I went back to the shop—to the same long hours—to the same low wages—to the same pig-eyed, fat-bellied boss. But I was no longer the same. For the first time in my life I bent to the inevitable. I accepted my defeat. But something in me, stronger than I, rose triumphant even in my surrender.

"Yes, I must submit to the shop," I thought. "But the shop shall not crush me. Only my body I must sell into slavery—not my heart—not my soul.

"To anyone who sees me from without, I am only a dirt-eating worm, a grub in the ground, but I know that above this dark earthplace in which I am sunk is the green grass—and beyond the green grass, the sun and sky. Alone, unaided, I must dig my way up to the light!"

Lunch-hour at the factory. My book of Shelley's poems before me and I was soon millions of miles beyond the raucous voices of the hungry eaters.

"Did you already hear the last news?" Yetta tore my book from me in her excitement.

"What news?" I scowled at her for waking me from my dreams.

"We're going to have electricity by the machines. And the forelady says that the new boss will give us ten cents more on a dozen waists!"

"God from the world! How did it happen—electricity—better pay?" I asked in amazement. For that was the first I had heard of improved conditions of work.

But little by little, step by step, the sanitation improved. Open windows, swept floors, clean wash-rooms, individual drinking-cups introduced a new era of factory hygiene. Our shop was caught up in the general movement for social betterment that stirred the country.

It was not all done in a day. Weary years of struggle passed before the workers emerged from the each-for-himself existence into an organized togetherness for mutual improvement.

At last, with the shortened hours of work, I had enough vitality left at the end of the day to join the night-school. Again my dream flamed. Again America beckoned. In the school there would be education—air, life for my cramped-in spirit. I would learn to form the thoughts that surged formless in me. I would find the teacher that would make me articulate.

Shelley was English literature.

So I joined the literature class. The course began with the "De Coverley Papers." Filled with insatiate thirst, I drank in every line with the feeling that any minute I would get to the fountain-heart of revelation.

Night after night I read with tireless devotion. But of what? The manners and customs of the eighteenth century, of people two hundred years dead.

One evening after a month's attendance, when the class had dwindled from fifty to four and the teacher began scolding us who were left for those who were absent, my bitterness broke.

"Do you know why all the girls are dropping away from the class? It's because they have too much sense to waste themselves on the 'De Coverley Papers.' Us four girls are four fools. We could learn more in the streets. It's dirty and wrong, but it's life. What are the 'De Coverley Papers'? Dry dust fit for the ash can."

"Perhaps you had better tell the board of education your ideas of the standard classics," she scoffed, white with rage.

"Classics? If all the classics are as dead as the 'De Coverley Papers,' I'd rather read the ads in the papers. How can I learn from this old man that's dead two hundred years how to live my life?"

That was the first of many schools I had tried. And they were all the same. A dull course of study and the lifeless, tired teachers—no more interested in their pupils than in the wooden benches before them—chilled all my faith in the American schools.

More and more the all-consuming need for a friend possessed me. In the street, in the cars, in the subways, I was always seeking, ceaselessly seeking, for eyes, a face, the flash of a smile that would be light in my darkness.

I felt sometimes that I was only burning out my heart for a shadow, an echo, a wild dream. But I couldn't help it. Nothing was real to me but my hope of finding a friend.

One day my sister Bessie came home much excited over her new high-school teacher. "Miss Latham makes it so interesting!" she exclaimed. "She stops in the middle of the lesson and tells us things. She ain't like a teacher. She's like a real person."

At supper next evening, Bessie related more wonder stories of her beloved teacher. "She's so different! She's friends with us. . . . To-day, when she gave us out our composition, Mamie Cohen asked from what book we should read up and she said, 'Just take it out of your heart and say it.'"

"Just take it out of your heart and say it." The simple words lingered in my mind, stirring a whirl of hidden thoughts and feelings. It seemed as if they had been said directly to me.

A few days later Bessie ran in from school, her cheeks flushed, her eyes dancing with excitement. "Give a look at the new poem teacher gave me to learn!" It was a quotation from Kipling:

"Then only the Master shall praise us,
And only the Master shall blame,
And no one shall work for money,
And no one shall work for fame;
But each for the joy of the working,
And each in his separate Star,
Shall draw the thing as he sees it
For the God of things as they are."

Only a few brief lines, but in their music the pulses of my being leaped into life. And so it was from day to day. Miss Latham's sayings kept turning themselves in my mind like a lingering melody that could not be shaken off. Something irresistible seemed to draw me to her. She beckoned to me almost as strongly as America had on the way over in the boat.

I wondered, "Should I go to see her and talk myself out from my heart to her?

"Meshugeneh! Where—what? How come you to her? What will you say for your reason?

"What's the difference what I'll say! I only want to give a look on her . . ."

And so I kept on restlessly debating. Should I follow my heart and go to her, or should I have a little sense?

Finally the desire to see her became so strong that I could no longer reason about it. I left the factory in the middle of the day to seek her out.

All the way to her school I prayed: "God—God! If I could only find one human soul that cared . . ."

I found her bending over her desk. Her hair was gray, but she did not look tired like the other teachers. She was correcting papers and was absorbed in her task. I watched her, not daring to interrupt. Presently she threw back her head and gave a little laugh.

Then she saw me. "Why, how do you do?" She rose. "Come and sit down."

I felt she was as glad to see me as though she had expected me.

"I feel you can help me," I groped toward her.

"I hope I can." She grasped my outstretched hands and led me to a chair which seemed to be waiting for me.

A strange gladness filled me.

"Bessie showed me the poem you told her to learn . . ." I paused bewildered.

"Yes?" Her friendly eyes urged me to speak.

"From what Bessie told me I felt I could talk myself out to you what's bothering me." I stopped again.

She leaned forward with an inviting interest. "Go on! Tell me all."

"I'm an immigrant many years already here, but I'm still seeking America. My dream America is more far from me than it was in the old country. Always something comes between the immigrant and the American," I went on blindly. "They see only his skin, his outside—not what's in his heart. They don't care if he has a heart. . . . I wanted to find someone that would look on me—myself . . . I thought you'd know yourself on a person first off."

Abashed at my boldness I lowered my eyes to the floor.

"Do go on . . . I want to hear."

With renewed courage I continued my confessional.

"Life is too big for me. I'm lost in this each-for-himself world. I feel shut out from everything that's going on. . . . I'm always fighting—fighting—with myself and everything around me. . . . I hate when I want to love and I make people hate me when I want to make them love me."

She gave me a quick nod. "I know—I know what you mean. Go on."

"I don't know what is with me the matter. I'm so choked. . . . Sundays and holidays when the other girls go out to enjoy themselves, I walk around by myself—thinking—thinking. . . . My thoughts tear in me and I can't tell them to no one! I want to do something with my life and I don't know what."

"I'm glad you came," she said. And after a pause, "You can help me."

"Help you?" I cried. It was the first time that an American suggested that I could help her.

"Yes indeed! I have always wanted to know more of that mysterious vibrant life—the immigrant. You can help me know my girls."

The repression of centuries seemed to rush out of my heart. I told her everything—of the mud hut in Sukovoly where I was born, of the Czar's pogroms, of the constant fear of the Cossack, of Gedalyeh Mindel's letter and of our hopes in coming to America.

After I had talked myself out, I felt suddenly ashamed for having exposed so much, and I cried out to her: "Do you think like the others that I'm all wrapped up in self?"

For some minutes she studied me, and her serenity seemed to project itself into me. And then she said, as if she too were groping, "No—no—but too intense."

"I hate to be so all the time intense. But how can I help it? Everything always drives me back in myself. How can I get myself out into the free air?"

"Don't fight yourself." Her calm, gray eyes penetrated to the very soul in me. "You are burning up too much vitality. . . .

"You know some of us," she went on—"not many, unfortunately—have a sort of divine fire which if it does not find expression turns into smoke.

This egoism and self-centeredness which troubles you is only the smoke of repression."

She put her hand over mine. "You have had no one to talk to—no one to share your thoughts."

I marveled at the simplicity with which she explained me to myself. I couldn't speak. I just looked at her.

"But now," she said, gently, "you have someone. Come to me whenever you wish."

"I have a friend," it sang itself in me. "I have a friend."

"And you are a born American?" I asked. There was none of that sure, all-right look of the Americans about her.

"Yes, indeed! My mother, like so many mothers,"—and her eyebrows lifted humorously whimsical,—"claims we're descendants of the Pilgrim fathers. And that one of our lineal ancestors came over in the Mayflower."

"For all your mother's pride in the Pilgrim fathers, you yourself are as plain from the heart as an immigrant."

"Weren't the Pilgrim fathers immigrants two hundred years ago?"

She took from her desk a book called "Our America," by Waldo Frank, and read to me: "We go forth all to seek America. And in the seeking we create her. In the quality of our search shall be the nature of the America that we create."

"Ach, friend! Your words are life to me! You make it light for my eyes!"

She opened her arms to me and breathlessly I felt myself drawn to her. Bonds seemed to burst. A suffusion of light filled my being. Great choirings lifted me in space.

I walked out unseeingly.

All the way home the words she read flamed before me: "We go forth all to seek America. And in the seeking we create her. In the quality of our search shall be the nature of the America that we create."

So all those lonely years of seeking and praying were not in vain! How glad I was that I had not stopped at the husk—a good job—a good living—but pressed on, through the barriers of materialism.

Through my inarticulate groping and reaching-out I had found the soul—the spirit—of America!

II.
CHILDREN
OF
LONELINESS

Mostly About Myself

I feel like a starved man who is so bewildered by the first sight of food that he wants to grab and devour the ice-cream, the roast, and the entrée all in one gulp. For ages and ages, my people in Russia had no more voice than the broomstick in the corner. The poor had no more chance to say what they thought or felt than the dirt under their feet.

And here, in America, a miracle has happened to them. They can lift up their heads like real people. After centuries of suppression, they are allowed to speak. Is it a wonder that I am too excited to know where to begin?

All the starved, unlived years crowd into my throat and choke me. I don't know whether it is joy or sorrow that hurts me so. I only feel that my release is wrung with the pain of all those back of me who lived and died, their dumbness pressing down on them like stones on the heart.

My mother who dried out her days fighting at the pushcarts for another potato, another onion into the bag, wearing out her heart and soul and brain with the one unceasing worry—how to get food for the children a penny cheaper—and my father, a Hebrew scholar and dreamer who was always too much up in the air to come down to such sordid thoughts as bread and rent, and the lost and wasted lives of my brothers and sisters and my grandfather and grandmother, and all those dumb generations back of me, are crying in every breath of every word that itself is struggling out of me.

I am the mad mob at a mass meeting, shouting with their hands and stamping with their feet to their leader: "Speech! Speech!" And I am also the bewildered leader struggling to say something and make myself heard through the deafening noise of a thousand clamoring voices.

I envy the writers who can sit down at their desks in the clear calm security of their vision and begin their story at the beginning and work it up logically, step by step, until they get to the end. With me, the end and the middle and the beginning of my story whirl before me in a mad blurr. And I can not sit still inside myself till the vision becomes clear and whole and sane in my brain. I'm too much on fire to wait till I understand what I see and feel. My hands rush out to seize a word from the end, a phrase from the middle, or a sentence from the beginning. I jot down any fragment of a thought that I can get hold of. And then I gather these fragments, words, phrases, sentences, and I paste them together with my own blood.

Think of the toil it takes to wade through a dozen pages that you must cut down into one paragraph. Sometimes, the vivisection I must commit on myself to create one little living sentence leaves me spent for days.

I thought when the editor asked me to write mostly about myself, telling of my own life, it would be so simple the thing would write itself. And just look at me at my desk! Before me are reams of jumbled pages of madness and inspiration, and I am trying to make a little sense of it all.

What shall I keep, and what shall I throw away? Which is madness, and which is inspiration? I never know. I pick and choose things like a person feeling his way in the dark. I never know whether the thoughts I've discarded are not perhaps better than the thoughts I've kept. With all the physical anguish I put into my work, I am never sure of myself. But I am sure of this, that the utterance of the ignorant like me is something like the utterance of the dying. It's mixed up and incoherent, but it has in it the last breath of life and death.

I am learning to accept the torture of chaos and confusion and doubt through which my thoughts must pass, as a man learns to accept a hump on his back, or the loss of an arm, or any affliction which the fates thrust upon him.

I am learning, as I grow older, to be tolerant with my own inadequacy.

I am learning slowly to stop wasting myself in trying to make myself over on the pattern of some better organized, more educated person than I. I no longer waste precious time wishing for the brains of a George Eliot, or the fluency of a George Sand, or the marvelous gifts of words of a May Sinclair. Here I am as I am, and life is short and work is long. With this limited brain of my inadequate self, I must get the most work done. I can only do the best I can and leave the outcome in the hands of the Higher Power.

I am aware that there's a little too much of I-I-I, too much of self-analysis and introspection in my writing. But this is because I was forced to live alone so much. I spent most of my youth at work I hated, work which called only for the use of the hands, the strength of my body—not my heart, not my brain. So my thoughts, instead of going out naturally to the world around me, were turned in upon myself.

I look upon my self-analysis and introspection as so much dirt through which I have to dig before I can come into the light of objectivity and see the people of the worlds around me.

Writing is to me a confession—not a profession. I know a man, a literary hack, who calls himself a dealer in words. He can write to order on any subject he is hired to write about. I often marvel at the swift ease with which he can turn from literary criticism to politics, or psychoanalysis. A fatal fluency enables him to turn out thousands of words a day in the busy factory of his brain, without putting anything of himself into it.

But I can never touch the surfaces of things. I can write only from the depths. I feel myself always under the aching weight of my thoughts. And words are luring lights that beckon to me through the thick mist of vague dumb thoughts that hang over me and press down on me.

I am so in love with the changing lights and shades of words that I almost hate their power over me, as you hate the tyranny of the people you love too much. I almost hate writing, because I love so passionately to express the innermost and outermost of my thoughts and feelings. And the words I write are never what I started out to express, but what come out of my desire for expression.

Often, I read my own writing as though it were somebody else's. My own words mock at me with their glaring unreality. Where is that burning vividness of things that possessed me when I began? Why did I kill myself so for nothing? Are these stiff, stilted words me?

I stare at the pages that represent so many days and nights of labor more bitter, more violent, than childbirth. What has happened? Has my terrific passion for giving out my experiences only built a barrier of barren words against the experience that I held so close?

It's as if every kiss, every embrace of the lover and the beloved instead of fusing them into a closer oneness only drew them farther and farther apart. Every written word instead of bringing the vision nearer only pushes it farther and farther away.

Blind rage and despair sweep through me.

"It's so real in me," I cry. "Why is it so empty, so dead, the minute I try to say it?"

I stand beating at my own incapacity, as one beating out his last breath at an inanimate stone wall.

"Anzia Yezierska, get out of your own way," I cry. "You yourself are holding back your own light by wanting to seize the sun and stars in your clutching hand. Your grabbing greed for words has choked the life out of them. Tear up all those precious pages. Throw to the winds all your fine phrases, all your fancy language. You're not clever enough to say things that make an effect. You can only be real, or nothing."

Writing is ordinarily the least part of a man. It is all there is of me. I want to write with every pulse of my blood and every breath of my spirit. I want to write waking or dreaming, year in and year out. I burn up in this all-consuming desire my family, my friends, my loves, my clothes, my food, my very life.

And yet the minute my writing gets into print, I hate the sight of it. I have all the patience in the world to do over a page a thousand times. But the moment it gets out of my hand I can't bear to touch it with a pitchfork. The minute a manuscript gets into print it's all dead shells of the past to me.

I know some people who hate the books I write, and because they hate my books they hate me. I want to say to them now that I, too, hate the stuff I write. Can't we be friends and make the mutual hatred of my books a bond instead of a barrier? My books are not me.

Is this a contradiction of anything I said in the page above? I do not claim to be logical or consistent. I do not claim to think things out; I only feel out my feelings, and the only thing true about feelings is that they change and become different in the very process of utterance. The minute I say a thing with the absolute sincerity of my being, up rushes another thought that hits my most earnest sincerity in the face and shows it up for a lie.

I am alive and the only thing real in my aliveness is the vitality of unceasing change. Sometimes I wake up in the morning with a fresh new thought that sweeps out of the window all of the most precious thoughts of the day before.

Perhaps by the time I shall have reached the end of this little sketch, I shall have refuted every statement I tried to make at the beginning. I can not help it. I am not attempting to write a story to fit into the set mold of a magazine. I am trying to give you the changing, baffling, contradictory substance of which my life is made.

I remember my mother's ecstatic face when she burst into the house and announced proudly that though she never had had a chance to learn the alphabet, she could read the names of the streets and she could find her way to the free dispensary without having to be led by us.

"I'm no longer blind," she cried, tossing up her market basket in a gesture of triumph. "The signs of the streets are like pictures before my eyes. Delancey Street has the black hooks one way, and Essex Street has black hooks the other way." She tore off her blue-checked apron. "I can also be a lady and walk without having to beg people to show me the way."

Something of my mother's wonder was mine when, without knowing the first alphabet of literature, I had discovered that beauty was anywhere a person tries to think out his thoughts. Beauty was no less in the dark basement of a sweatshop than in the sunny, spacious halls of a palace. So that I, buried alive in the killing blackness of poverty, could wrest the beauty of reality out of my experiences no less than the princess who had the chance to live and love, and whose only worry was which of her adorers she should choose for a husband.

I did not at first think it as clearly as I write it now. In fact, I did not think then at all. I only felt. And it gave me a certain power over the things that weighed over me, merely saying out on paper what I felt about them.

My first alphabet of self-expression was hatred, wrath, and rebellion. Once, during lunch hour while the other girls in the shop were eating and talking and laughing, I wrote out on my greasy lunch bag the thoughts that were boiling in me for a long, long time.

"I hate beautiful things," I began. "All day long I handle beautiful clothes, but not for me—only for others to wear. The rich with nothing but cold cash can buy the beautiful things made with the sweat of my hands, while I choke in ugliness." Merely writing out the wildness running through my head enabled me to wear the rags I had to wear with a certain bitter defiance.

But after a while, raving at things in the air ceased to bring me relief. I felt a little like my mother yelling and cursing at the children and the worries around her without knowing what or where. I felt like a woman standing in the middle of her upset house in the morning—beds not made, dishes not washed, dirty clothes and rags hanging over the chairs, all the drawers pushed out in mixed-up disorder, the broom with the dirt in the middle of the floor—and she not knowing where to begin.

I wanted order, order in my head. But then I was too mixed up with too many thoughts to put anything in its place. In a blind sort of way, in groping for order I was groping for beauty. I felt no peace in what I wrote unless I could make my words laugh and cry with the life of the poor I was living. I was always digging—digging for the beauty that I sensed back of the dirt and the disorder. Until I could find a way to express the beauty of that reality there was no rest in me. Like the woman who makes the beds or sweeps the house and lets the rest go, so I took hold of one idea at a time and pushed all the other ideas out of my head. And day and night I burned up my body and brain with that one idea until it got light all around me—the light of an idea that shaped itself in a living picture of living people.

When I saw my first story in print, I felt bigger than Columbus who discovered the New World. I felt bigger than the man who built the Brooklyn Bridge or the highest skyscraper in New York. I walked the streets, holding the magazine tight in my hands, laughing and crying to myself: "I had an idea and I thought it out. I did it, I did it! I'm not a crazy, I'm not a crazy!"

But the next day all my fiery gladness turned cold. I saw how far from the whole round circle of the idea was my printed story. And I was burning to do the same thing over again from another side, to show it up more.

Critics have said that I have but one story to tell and that I tell that one story in different ways each time I write. That is true. My one story is hunger. Hunger driven by loneliness.

But is not all of human life the story of our hunger, our loneliness? What is at the root of economics, sociology, literature, and all art but man's bread hunger and man's love hunger?

When I first started to write, I could only write one thing—different phases of the one thing only—bread hunger. At last, I've written out my bread hunger. And now I can write only the different phases of the one thing—loneliness, love hunger, the hunger for people.

In the days of poverty I used to think there was no experience that tears through the bottom of the earth like the hunger for bread. But now I know, more terrible than the hunger for bread is the hunger for people.

I used to be more hungry after a meal than before. Years ago, the food I could afford to buy only whetted my appetite for more food. Sometimes after I had paid down my last precious pennies for a meal in one of those white-tiled restaurants, I'd get so mad with hunger I'd want to dash the empty dishes at the heads of the waiters and cry out like a lunatic: "Don't feed me with plates and forks and tablecloth. I want real food. I want to bite into huge chunks of meat. I want butter and quarts of milk and eggs—dozens of eggs. I want to fill up for once in my life."

This unacted madness used to be always flying through my brain, morning, noon, and night. Whenever I wanted to think my thoughts were swept away by the sight of thick, juicy steaks and mounds of butter and platters full of eggs.

Now I no longer live in a lonely hall-room in a tenement. I have won many friends. I am invited out to teas and dinners and social affairs. And, I wonder, is my insatiable hunger for people so great because for so many centuries my race has been isolated in Ghettos, shut out of contact with others? Here in America races, classes, and creeds are free to meet and mingle on planes as high and wide as all humanity and its problems. And I am aching to touch all the different races, classes, and creeds at all possible points of contact, and I never seem to have enough of people.

When I first came to America, the coldness of the Americans used to rouse in me the fury of a savage. Their impersonal, non-committal air was like a personal insult to me. I longed to shake them out of their aloofness, their frozen stolidity. But now when I meet an Anglo-Saxon, I want to cry out to him: "We're friends, we're friends, I tell you! We understand the same things, even though we seem to be so different on the outside."

Sometimes a man and a woman are so different that they hate each other at first sight. Their intense difference stabs a sharp sword of fear into each heart. But when this fear that froze each into separate opposite-ness ever has a chance for a little sun of understanding, then the very difference that drew them apart pulls them closer than those born alike. Perhaps that accounts for the devouring affinity between my race and the Anglo-Saxon race.

In my early childhood, my people hammered into me defeat, defeat, because that was the way they accepted the crushing weight of life. Life had crushed my mother, so without knowing it she fed defeat with the milk of her bosom into the blood and bone of her children. But this thing that stunted the courage, the initiative, of the other children roused the fighting devils in me.

When yet barely able to speak, I began to think and question the justice of the world around me and to assert my rights.

"Mamma," I asked out of a clear sky, "why does Masha Stein have butter on her bread every morning, and why is our bread always hard and dry, and nothing on it?"

"Butter wills itself in you," shrieked my mother, as she thrust the hash of potato peelings in front of me for my noonday meal. "Have you got a father a businessman, a butcher, or a grocer, a bread-giver, like Masha Stein's father? You don't own the dirt under Masha's doorstep. You got a father a scholar. He holds himself all day with God; he might as well hang the beggar's bag on his neck and be done with it."

At the time I had no answer. I was too young to voice my revolt against my mother's dark reasoning. But the fact that I did not forget this speech of so many years ago shows how her black pessimism cut against my grain.

I have a much clearer memory of my next rebellion against the thick gloom in which my young years were sunk.

"Mamma, what's a birthday?" I cried, bursting into the house in a whirl of excitement. "Becky, the pawnbroker's girl on the block, will have a birthday to-morrow. And she'll get presents for nothing, a cake with candles on it, and a whole lot of grand things from girls for nothing—and she said I must come. Could I have a birthday, too, like she?"

"Woe is to me!" cried my mother, glaring at me with wet, swollen eyes. "A birthday lays in your head? Enjoyments lays in your head?" she continued bitterly. "You want to be glad that you were born into the world? A whole lot you got to be glad about. Wouldn't it be better if you was never born already?"

At the harsh sound of my mother's voice, all my dreams took wing. In rebellion and disappointment, I thrust out my lips with a trembling between retort and tears. It was as if the devil himself urged my mother thus to avenge herself upon her helpless children for the aches and weariness of her own life. So she went on, like a horse bolting down hill, feeling the pressure of the load behind him.

"What is with you the great joy? That you ain't got a shirt on your back? That you ain't got no shoes on your feet? Why are you with yourself so happy? Is it because the landlord sent the moving bill, and you'll be lying in the street tomorrow, already?"

I had forgotten that we had received a notice of eviction, for unpaid rent, a few days before. A frenzy of fear had taken possession of my mother as she anticipated the horror of being thrown into the street. For hours at a time I would see her staring at the wall with a glassy stare of a madman.

"With what have you to be happy, I ask only?" she went on. "Have you got money lying in the bank? Let the rich people enjoy themselves. For them is the world like made to order. For them the music plays. They can have birthdays. But what's the world to the poor man? Only one terrible, never-stopping fight with the groceryman and the butcher and the landlord."

I gazed at my mother with old, solemn eyes, feeling helplessly sucked into her bitterness and gloom.

"What's a poor man but a living dead one?" she pursued, talking more to herself than to me. "You ought to light a black candle on your birthday. You ought to lie on your face and cry and curse the day you was born!"

Crushed by her tirade, I went out silently. The fairy dream of the approaching birthday had been rudely shattered. Blinded with tears, I sat down on the edge of the gutter in front of our tenement.

"Look, these are the pink candles for the birthday cake!" A poke in the back from Becky startled me. "Aren't they grand? And mamma will buy me a French doll, and papa said he'd give me a desk, and my aunt will give me a painting set, and every girl that comes will bring me something different."

"But what's the use?" I sobbed. "I ain't got nothing for no present, and I can't come—and my mother is so mean she got mad and hollered like hell because I only asked her about the birthday, and—." A passionate fit of sobbing drowned my words.

In an instant, Becky had her arms about me. "I want you to come without a present," she said. "I will have a lot of presents anyhow."

Assured of her welcome, I went the next day. But as I opened the door, fear seized me. I paused trembling, holding the knob in my hand, too dazed by the sight before me to make a step. More than the strangeness of the faces awed me. Ordinary home comforts, cushioned chairs, green ferns between white curtains, the bright rugs on the floor, were new and wonderful to me. Timorously, I edged my way into the room, so blinded by the shimmering colors of the cakes and fruits and candies that covered the table that I did not see Becky approaching me with outstretched arms.

"Mamma, this is that little immigrant girl who never had a birthday," she said, "so I wanted to show her mine."

Becky's father glanced at her all in white, with pink ribbons on her curls, as she stood beside me in my torn rags reeking with the grime of neglect. A shudder of revulsion went through him at the sight of me.

"See what Becky has to mix up with on the block," he whispered to his wife. "For God's sake, give her a nickel, give her some candy, give her anything, but let her run along."

Street child that I was, my instinct sensed the cold wave of his thought without hearing the exact words. Breaking away from Becky's detaining hand, I made for the door.

"I want to go home! I want to go home!" I sobbed, as I ran out of the room.

Whitman has said, "It is as lucky to die as it is to be born." And I put his thought into my own words, "It is as lucky not to have advantages as it is to have them." I mean that facing my disadvantages—the fears, the discouragements, the sense of inferiority—drove me to fight every inch of the way for things I demanded out of life. And, as a writer, the experience of forcing my way from the bottommost bottom gave me the knowledge of the poor that no well-born writer could possibly have.

I am thinking, for instance, of Victor Hugo and his immortal book, "Les Misérables." It's great literature, but it isn't the dirt and the blood of the poor that I saw and that forced me to write. Or take the American,

Jack London. When he wrote about tramps he roused the sense of reality in his readers, because he had been a tramp. But later, when he tried to make stories of the great unwashed of the cities—again this was only literature.

The clear realization that literature is beyond my reach, that I must either be real or nothing, enables me to accept my place as the cobbler who must stick to his last, and gives my work any merit it may have. I stand on solid ground when I write of the poor, the homeless, and the hungry.

Like many immigrants who expected to find America a realized Utopian dream, I had my disillusions. I quote here from an article which was published in "Good Housekeeping" in June, 1920.

> When the editor told me that he would give me the chance to speak to the Americans out of my heart and say freely, not what I ought to feel—not what the Americans want me to feel—but what I actually do feel—something broke loose in me—a tightness that had held me strained like one whose fists are clenched—resisting—resisting—
>
> Resisting what? Had I not come to America with open, outstretched arms, all my earthly possessions tied up in a handkerchief and all the hopes of humanity singing in my heart?
>
> Had I not come to join hands with all those thousands of dreamers who had gone before me in search of the Golden Land? As I rushed forward with hungry eagerness to meet the unexpected welcoming, the very earth danced under my feet. All that I was, all that I had, I held out in my bare hands to America, the beloved, the prayed-for land.
>
> But no hand was held out to meet mine. My eyes burned with longing—seeking—seeking for a comprehending glance. Where are the dreamers? cried my heart. My hands dropped down, my gifts unwanted.
>
> I found no dreamers in America. I found rich men, poor men, educated men, ignorant men—struggling—all struggling—for bread, for rent, for banks, for mines. Rich and poor, educated and ignorant—straining—straining—wearing out their bodies, their brains, for the possession of things—money, power, position—their dreams forgotten.
>
> I found in his rich land man still fighting man, as in the poorest part of the old country. Just as the starving Roumanian Jews, who had nothing to eat in their homeland but herring, when they became millionaires still ate herring from gold plates at banquets, so through-

out America, the dollar fight that grew up like a plague in times of poverty, killing the souls of men, still goes on in times of plenty.

I had expected to work in America, but work at the thing I loved—work with my mind, my heart, prepared for my work by education. I had dreamed of free schools, free colleges, where I could learn to give out my innermost thoughts and feelings to the world. But no sooner did I come off the ship than hunger drove me to the sweatshop, to become a "hand"—not a brain—not a soul—not a spirit—but just a "hand"—cramped, deadened into a part of a machine—a hand fit only to grasp, not to give.

Time came when I was able to earn my bread and rent. I earned what would have been wealth to me in Poland. My knotted nerves relaxed. I began to breathe like a free human being. Ach! Maybe I could yet make something of myself. My choked-in spirit revived. There was a new light in my eyes, new strength in my arms and fingers. New hopes, new dreams beckoned to me. Should I take a night course in college, or buy myself the much-longed-for books, or treat myself to a little vacation to have time to think?

Then the landlady came with the raise in rent. The loaf of bread that was five cents became ten. Milk that was eight cents a quart became eighteen. Shoes, clothes, everything doubled and tripled in price. I felt like one put on a rack—thumb-screws torturing my flesh—pay—pay—pay!

What had been enough to give me comfort yesterday became starvation to-day. Always the cost of living leaping over the rise in wages. Never free from poverty—even in America.

And then I clenched my hands and swore that I would hold my dream of America—and fight for it. I refuse to accept the America where men make other men poor—create poverty where God has poured out wealth. I refuse to accept the America that gives the landlord the right to keep on raising my rent and to drive me to the streets when I do not earn enough to meet his rapacious demands.

I cry out in this wilderness for America—my America—different from all other countries. In this America promised to the oppressed of all lands, there is enough so that man need not fight man for his bread, but work with man, building the beauty that for hundreds of years, in thousands of starved villages of Europe, men have dreamed was America—beautiful homes—beautiful cities—beautiful lives reaching up for higher, ever higher visions of beauty.

I know you will say what right have I to come here and make demands upon America. But are not my demands the breath, the very life of America? What, after all, is America, but the response to

the demands of immigrants like me, seeking new worlds in which
their spirits may be free to create beauty? Were not the Pilgrim
Fathers immigrants demanding a new world in which they could be
free to live higher lives?

Yes, I make demands—not in arrogance, but in all humility. I
demand—driven by my desire to give. I want to give not only that
which I am, but that which I might be if I only had the chance. I
want to give to America not the immigrant you see before you—
starved, stunted, resentful, on the verge of hysteria from repression.
I want to give a new kind of immigrant, full grown in mind and
body—loving, serving, upholding America.

By writing out my protests and disillusions, I aired and clarified them.
Slowly, I began to understand my unreasoning demands upon America
and what America had to offer. I saw that America was a new world in the
making, that anyone who has something real in him can find a way to
contribute himself in this new world. But I saw I had to fight for my
chance to give what I had to give, with the same life-and-death earnestness
with which a man fights for his bread.

What had I with my empty hands and my hungry heart to give to
America? I had my hunger, my homelessness, my dumbness, my blind
searchings and gropings for what I knew not. I had to give to America my
aching ignorance, my burning desire for knowledge. I had to give to
America the dirt and the ugliness of my black life of poverty and my
all-consuming passion for beauty.

As long as I kept stretching out my hands begging, begging for others
to understand me, for friendship, for help—as long as I kept begging them
to give me something—so long I was shut out from America. But the
moment I understood America well enough to tell her about herself as I
saw her—the moment I began to express myself—America accepted my
self-expression as a gift from me, and from everywhere hands reached out
to help me.

With the money I earned writing out stories of myself and my people,
I was enabled to go abroad and to take another look around the Old World.
I traveled from city to city. My special purpose was to talk to the poor
people in the different countries and see how their chance to live compared
with the chances of those in America.

I find that in no other country has the newcomer such a *direct* chance
to come to the front and become a partner in the making of the country.
Not where you come from, but what is in you and what you are, counts
in America.

In no other country is there such healthy rebellion, such vital discontent, as there is among the poor in America. And the rebellion and discontent of the poor is in proportion to how well off they are. The poor people demand more of America than they ever dared to demand of their homeland, because America is brimming over with riches enough for everybody.

Life in America is a swift, sharp adventure. In the old countries things are more or less settled. In America, the soil is young, and the people are young blossoming shoots of a new-grown civilization.

The writers of Europe can only be stylists, because life and traditions are fixed with them. In America life is yet unexplored, and lived new by each newcomer. And that is why America is such virgin stuff for the novelist.

Fiction is a mirror of life as it is being lived at the moment. And the moments are more static in Europe than in America. I admit that art is not so highly developed in America as in Europe, because art is a decoration, and America is a young country too turbulent with life to take time to decorate itself.

I, who used to be the most violent rebel of an immigrant, now find myself the most ardent defender of America. I see every flaw of America perhaps more clearly than ever before. I know the ruthless commercialism of our big cities, the grabbing greed of landlords since the war making the thought of home almost impossible to the poor. I know that the gospel of success which rules in America hurts itself, because failure and defeat have revelations for humanity's deeper growth, to which success is deaf and dumb and blind.

I know how often the artists, the makers of beauty in America, are driven to the wall by the merciless extortion of those who sell the means of existence. But I know, too, that those of the artists who survive are vitalized by the killing things which had failed to kill them. America has no place for the dawdling, soft-spined, make-believe artists that swarm the Paris cafés.

In the sunshine of the opportunities that have come to me, I am always aware of those around me and behind me who lacked the terrific vitality, the brutal self-absorption with which I had to fight for my chance or be blotted out. My eyes will always turn back with loneliness and longing for the old faces and old scenes that I loved more than my life. But though it tears my heart out of my body to go on, I must go on.

There's no going back to the Old World for anyone who has breathed the invigorating air of America. I return to America with the new realization that in no other country would a nobody from nowhere—one of the millions of lonely immigrants that pour through Ellis Island—a dumb thing with nothing but hunger and desire—get the chance to become articulate that America has given me.

America and I

As one of the dumb, voiceless ones I speak. One of the millions of immigrants beating, beating out their hearts at your gates for a breath of understanding.

Ach! America! From the other end of the earth from where I came, America was a land of living hope, woven of dreams, aflame with longing and desire.

Choked for ages in the airless oppression of Russia, the Promised Land rose up—wings for my stifled spirit—sunlight burning through my darkness—freedom singing to me in my prison—deathless songs tuning prison-bars into strings of a beautiful violin.

I arrived in America. My young, strong body, my heart and soul pregnant with the unlived lives of generations clamoring for expression.

What my mother and father and their mother and father never had a chance to give out in Russia, I would give out in America. The hidden sap of centuries would find release; colors that never saw light—songs that died unvoiced—romance that never had a chance to blossom in the black life of the Old World.

In the golden land of flowing opportunity I was to find my work that was denied me in the sterile village of my forefathers. Here I was to be free from the dead drudgery for bread that held me down in Russia. For the first time in America, I'd cease to be a slave of the belly. I'd be a creator, a giver, a human being! My work would be the living joy of fullest self-expression.

But from my high visions, my golden hopes, I had to put my feet down on earth. I had to have food and shelter. I had to have the money to pay for it.

I was in America, among the Americans, but not of them. No speech, no common language, no way to win a smile of understanding from them, only my young, strong body and my untried faith. Only my eager, empty hands, and my full heart shining from my eyes!

God from the world! Here I was with so much richness in me, but my mind was not wanted without the language. And my body, unskilled, untrained, was not even wanted in the factory. Only one of two chances was left open to me: the kitchen, or minding babies.

My first job was as a servant in an Americanized family. Once, long ago, they came from the same village from where I came. But they were so well-dressed, so well-fed, so successful in America, that they were ashamed to remember their mother tongue.

"What were to be my wages?" I ventured timidly, as I looked up to the well-fed, well-dressed "American" man and woman.

They looked at me with a sudden coldness. What have I said to draw away from me their warmth? Was it so low from me to talk of wages? I shrank back into myself like a low-down bargainer. Maybe they're so high up in well-being they can't any more understand my low thoughts for money.

From his rich height the man preached down to me that I must not be so grabbing for wages. Only just landed from the ship and already thinking about money when I should be thankful to associate with "Americans."

The woman, out of her smooth, smiling fatness assured me that this was my chance for a summer vacation in the country with her two lovely children. My great chance to learn to be a civilized being, to become an American by living with them.

So, made to feel that I was in the hands of American friends, invited to share with them their home, their plenty, their happiness, I pushed out from my head the worry for wages. Here was my first chance to begin my life in the sunshine, after my long darkness. My laugh was all over my face as I said to them: "I'll trust myself to you. What I'm worth you'll give me." And I entered their house like a child by the hand.

The best of me I gave them. Their house cares were my house cares. I got up early. I worked till late. All that my soul hungered to give I put into the passion with which I scrubbed floors, scoured pots, and washed clothes. I was so grateful to mingle with the American people, to hear the music of the American language, that I never knew tiredness.

There was such a freshness in my brains and such a willingness in my heart that I could go on and on—not only with the work of the house, but work with my head—learning new words from the children, the grocer, the butcher, the iceman. I was not even afraid to ask for words from the policeman on the street. And every new word made me see new American things with American eyes. I felt like a Columbus, finding new worlds through every new word.

But words alone were only for the inside of me. The outside of me still branded me for a steerage immigrant. I had to have clothes to forget myself that I'm a stranger yet. And so I had to have money to buy these clothes.

The month was up. I was so happy! Now I'd have money. *My own, earned* money. Money to buy a new shirt on my back—shoes on my feet. Maybe yet an American dress and hat!

Ach! How high rose my dreams! How plainly I saw all that I would do with my visionary wages shining like a light over my head!

In my imagination I already walked in my new American clothes. How beautiful I looked as I saw myself like a picture before my eyes! I saw how I would throw away my immigrant rags tied up in my immigrant shawl. With money to buy—free money in my hands—I'd show them that I could look like an American in a day.

Like a prisoner in his last night in prison, counting the seconds that will free him from his chains, I trembled breathlessly for the minute I'd get the wages in my hand.

Before dawn I rose.

I shined up the house like a jewel-box.

I prepared breakfast and waited with my heart in my mouth for my lady and gentleman to rise. At last I heard them stirring. My eyes were jumping out of my head to them when I saw them coming in and seating themselves by the table.

Like a hungry cat rubbing up to its boss for meat, so I edged and simpered around them as I passed them the food. Without my will, like a beggar, my hand reached out to them.

The breakfast was over. And no word yet from my wages.

"Gottuniu!" I thought to myself. "Maybe they're so busy with their

own things they forgot it's the day for my wages. Could they who have everything know what I was to do with my first American dollars? How could they, soaking in plenty, how could they feel the longing and the fierce hunger in me, pressing up through each visionary dollar? How could they know the gnawing ache of my avid fingers for the feel of my own, earned dollars? *My* dollars that I could spend like a free person. *My* dollars that would make me feel with everybody alike!

Breakfast was long past.

Lunch came. Lunch passed.

Oi-i weh! Not a word yet about my money.

It was near dinner. And not a word yet about my wages.

I began to set the table. But my head—it swam away from me. I broke a glass. The silver dropped from my nervous fingers. I couldn't stand it any longer. I dropped everything and rushed over to my American lady and gentleman.

"*Oi weh!* The money—my money—my wages!" I cried breathlessly.

Four cold eyes turned on me.

"Wages? Money? The four eyes turned into hard stone as they looked me up and down. "Haven't you a comfortable bed to sleep, and three good meals a day? You're only a month here. Just came to America. And you already think about money. Wait till you're worth any money. What use are you without knowing English? You should be glad we keep you here. It's like a vacation for you. Other girls pay money yet to be in the country."

It went black for my eyes. I was so choked no words came to my lips. Even the tears went dry in my throat.

I left. Not a dollar for all my work.

For a long, long time my heart ached and ached like a sore wound. If murderers would have robbed me and killed me it wouldn't have hurt me so much. I couldn't think through my pain. The minute I'd see before me how they looked at me, the words they said to me—then everything began to bleed in me. And I was helpless.

For a long, long time the thought of ever working in an "American" family made me tremble with fear, like the fear of wild wolves. No—never again would I trust myself to an "American" family, no matter how fine their language and how sweet their smile.

It was blotted out in me all trust in friendship from "Americans." But the life in me still burned to live. The hope in me still craved to hope. In darkness, in dirt, in hunger and want, but only to live on!

There had been no end to my day—working for the "American" family.

Now rejecting false friendships from higher-ups in America, I turned back to the Ghetto. I worked on a hard bench with my own kind on either side of me. I knew before I began what my wages were to be. I knew what my hours were to be. And I knew the feeling of the end of the day.

From the outside my second job seemed worse than the first. It was in a sweatshop of a Delancey Street basement, kept up by an old, wrinkled woman that looked like a black witch of greed. My work was sewing on buttons. While the morning was still dark I walked into a dark basement. And darkness met me when I turned out of the basement.

Day after day, week after week, all the contact I got with America was handling dead buttons. The money I earned was hardly enough to pay for bread and rent. I didn't have a room to myself. I didn't even have a bed. I slept on a mattress on the floor in a rat-hole of a room occupied by a dozen other immigrants. I was always hungry—oh, so hungry! The scant meals I could afford only sharpened my appetite for real food. But I felt myself better off than working in the "American" family, where I had three good meals a day and a bed to myself. With all the hunger and darkness of the sweatshop, I had at least the evening to myself. And all night was mine. When all were asleep, I used to creep up on the roof of the tenement and talk out my heart in silence to the stars in the sky.

"Who am I? What am I? What do I want with my life? Where is America? Is there an America? What is this wilderness in which I'm lost?"

I'd hurl my questions and then think and think. And I could not tear it out of me, the feeling that America must be somewhere, somehow—only I couldn't find it—*my America,* where I would work for love and not for a living. I was like a thing following blindly after something far off in the dark!

"Oi weh!" I'd stretch out my hand up in the air. "My head is so lost in America! What's the use of all my working if I'm not in it? Dead buttons is not me."

Then the busy season started in the shop. The mounds of buttons grew and grew. The long day stretched out longer. I had to begin with the buttons earlier and stay with them till later in the night. The old witch turned into a huge greedy maw for wanting more and more buttons.

For a glass of tea, for a slice of herring over black bread, she would buy us up to stay another and another hour, till there seemed no end to her demands.

One day, the light of self-assertion broke into my cellar darkness.

"I don't want the tea. I don't want your herring," I said with terrible boldness. "I only want to go home. I only want the evening to myself!"

"You fresh mouth, you!" cried the old witch. "You learned already too much in America. I want no clock-watchers in my shop. Out you go!"

I was driven out to cold and hunger. I could no longer pay for my mattress on the floor. I no longer could buy the bite in the mouth. I walked the streets. I knew what it is to be alone in a strange city, among strangers.

But I laughed through my tears. So I learned too much already in America because I wanted the whole evening to myself? Well America has yet to teach me still more: how to get not only the whole evening to myself, but a whole day a week like the American workers.

That sweatshop was a bitter memory but a good school. It fitted me for a regular factory. I could walk in boldly and say I could work at something, even if it was only sewing on buttons.

Gradually, I became a trained worker. I worked in a light, airy factory, only eight hours a day. My boss was no longer a sweater and a blood-squeezer. The first freshness of the morning was mine. And the whole evening was mine. All day Sunday was mine.

Now I had better food to eat. I slept on a better bed. Now, I even looked dressed up like the American-born. But inside of me I knew that I was not yet an American. I choked with longing when I met an American-born, and I could say nothing.

Something cried dumb in me. I couldn't help it. I didn't know what it was I wanted. I only knew I wanted. I wanted. Like the hunger in the heart that never gets food.

An English class for foreigners started in our factory. The teacher had such a good, friendly face, her eyes looked so understanding, as if she could see right into my heart. So I went to her one day for an advice:

"I don't know what is with me the matter," I began. "I have no rest in me. I never yet done what I want."

"What is it you want to do, child?" she asked me.

"I want to do something with my head, my feelings. All day long, only with my hands I work."

"First you must learn English." She patted me as if I was not yet grown up. "Put your mind on that, and then we'll see."

So for a time I learned the language. I could almost begin to think with English words in my head. But in my heart the emptiness still hurt. I burned to give, to give something, to do something, to be something. The dead work with my hands was killing me. My work left only hard stones on my heart.

Again I went to our factory teacher and cried out to her: "I know already to read and write the English language, but I can't put it into words what I want. What is it in me so different that can't come out?"

She smiled at me down from her calmness as if I were a little bit out of my head. "What *do you want* to do?"

"I feel. I see. I hear. And I want to think it out. But I'm like dumb in me. I only feel I'm different—different from everybody."

She looked at me close and said nothing for a minute. "You ought to join one of the social clubs of the Women's Association," she advised.

"What's the Women's Association?" I implored greedily.

"A group of American women who are trying to help the working-girl find herself. They have a special department for immigrant girls like you."

I joined the Women's Association. On my first evening there they announced a lecture: "The Happy Worker and His Work," by the Welfare director of the United Mills Corporation.

"Is there such a thing as a happy worker at his work?" I wondered. "Happiness is only by working at what you love. And what poor girl can ever find it to work at what she loves? My old dreams about my America rushed through my mind. Once I thought that in America everybody works for love. Nobody has to worry for a living. Maybe this welfare man came to show me the *real* America that till now I sought in vain.

With a lot of polite words the head lady of the Women's Association introduced a higher-up that looked like the king of kings of business. Never before in my life did I ever see a man with such a sureness in his step, such power in his face, such friendly positiveness in his eye as when he smiled upon us.

"Efficiency is the new religion of business," he began. "In big business houses, even in up-to-date factories, they no longer take the first comer and give him any job that happens to stand empty. Efficiency begins at the employment office. Experts are hired for the one purpose, to find out how best to fit the worker to his work. It's economy for the boss to make the worker happy." And then he talked a lot more on efficiency in educated language that was over my head.

I didn't know exactly what it meant—efficiency—but if it was to make the worker happy at his work, then that's what I had been looking for since I came to America. I only felt from watching him that he was happy by his job. And as I looked on this clean, well-dressed, successful one, who wasn't ashamed to say he rose from an office-boy, it made me feel that I, too, could lift myself up for a person.

He finished his lecture, telling us about the Vocational Guidance Center that the Women's Association started.

The very next evening I was at the Vocational Guidance Center. There I found a young, college-looking woman. Smartness and health shining from her eyes! She, too, looked as if she knew her way in America. I could tell at the first glance: here is a person that is happy by what she does.

"I feel you'll understand me," I said right away.

She leaned over with pleasure in her face: "I hope I can."

"I want to work by what's in me. Only, I don't know what's in me. I only feel I'm different."

She gave me a quick, puzzled look from the corner of her eyes. "What are you doing now?"

"I'm the quickest shirtwaist hand on the floor. But my heart wastes away by such work. I think and think, and my thoughts can't come out."

"Why don't you think out your thoughts in shirtwaists? You could learn to be a designer. Earn more money."

"I don't want to look on waists. If my hands are sick from waists, how could my head learn to put beauty into them?"

"But you must earn your living at what you know, and rise slowly from job to job."

I looked at her office sign: "Vocational Guidance." "What's your vocational guidance?" I asked. "How to rise from job to job—how to earn more money?"

The smile went out from her eyes. But she tried to be kind yet. "What *do* you want?" she asked, with a sigh of last patience.

"I want America to want me."

She fell back in her chair, thunderstruck with my boldness. But yet, in a low voice of educated self-control, she tried to reason with me:

"You have to *show* that you have something special for America before America has need of you."

"But I never had a chance to find out what's in me, because I always had to work for a living. Only, I feel it's efficiency for America to find out what's in me so different, so I could give it out by my work."

Her eyes half closed as they bored through me. Her mouth opened to speak, but no words came from her lips. So I flamed up with all that was choking in me like a house on fire:

"America gives free bread and rent to criminals in prison. They got grand houses with sunshine, fresh air, doctors and teachers, even for the crazy ones. Why don't they have free boarding-schools for immigrants— strong people—willing people? Here you see us burning up with something different, and America turns her head away from us."

Her brows lifted and dropped down. She shrugged her shoulders away from me with the look of pity we give to cripples and hopeless lunatics.

"America is no Utopia. First you must become efficient in earning a living before you can indulge in your poetic dreams."

I went away from the vocational guidance office with all the air out of my lungs. All the light out of my eyes. My feet dragged after me like dead wood.

Till now there had always lingered a rosy veil of hope over my emptiness, a hope that a miracle would happen. I would open up my eyes some day and suddenly find the America of my dreams. As a young girl hungry for love sees always before her eyes the picture of lover's arms around her, so I saw always in my heart the vision of Utopian America.

But now I felt that the America of my dreams never was and never could be. Reality had hit me on the head as with a club. I felt that the America that I sought was nothing but a shadow—an echo—a chimera of lunatics and crazy immigrants.

Stripped of all illusion, I looked about me. The long desert of wasting days of drudgery stared me in the face. The drudgery that I had lived through, and the endless drudgery still ahead of me rose over me like a withering wilderness of sand. In vain were all my cryings, in vain were all frantic efforts of my spirit to find the living waters of understanding for my perishing lips. Sand, sand was everywhere. With every seeking, every reaching out I only lost myself deeper and deeper in a vast sea of sand.

I knew now the American language. And I knew now, if I talked to the Americans from morning till night, they could not understand what the Russian soul of me wanted. They could not understand *me* any more than if I talked to them in Chinese. Between my soul and the American soul were worlds of difference that no words could bridge over. What was that difference? What made the Americans so far apart from me?

I began to read the American history. I found from the first pages that America started with a band of Courageous Pilgrims. They had left their native country as I had left mine. They had crossed an unknown ocean and landed in an unknown country, as I.

But the great difference between the first Pilgrims and me was that they expected to make America, build America, create their own world of liberty. I wanted to find it ready made.

I read on. I delved deeper down into the American history. I saw how the Pilgrim Fathers came to a rocky desert country, surrounded by Indian savages on all sides. But undaunted, they pressed on—through danger— through famine, pestilence, and want—they pressed on. They did not ask the Indians for sympathy, for understanding. They made no demands on anybody, but on their own indomitable spirit of persistence.

And I—I was forever begging a crumb of sympathy, a gleam of understanding from strangers who could not sympathize, who could not understand.

I, when I encountered a few savage Indian scalpers, like the old witch of the sweatshop, like my "Americanized" countryman, who cheated me of my wages—I, when I found myself on the lonely, untrodden path through which all seekers of the new world must pass, I lost heart and said: "There is no America!"

Then came a light—a great revelation! I saw America—a big idea—a deathless hope—a world still in the making. I saw that it was the glory of America that it was not yet finished. And I, the last comer, had her share to give, small or great, to the making of America, like those Pilgrims who came in the *Mayflower*.

Fired up by this revealing light, I began to build a bridge of understanding between the American-born and myself. Since their life was shut out from such as me, I began to open up my life and the lives of my people to them. And life draws life. In only writing about the Ghetto I found America.

Great chances have come to me. But in my heart is always a deep sadness. I feel like a man who is sitting down to a secret table of plenty, while his near ones and dear ones are perishing before his eyes. My very joy in doing the work I love hurts me like secret guilt, because all about me I see so many with my longings, my burning eagerness, to do and to be, wasting their days in drudgery they hate, merely to buy bread and pay rent. And America is losing all that richness of the soul.

The Americans of to-morrow, the America that is every day nearer coming to be, will be too wise, too open-hearted, too friendly-handed, to let the least last-comer at their gates knock in vain with his gifts unwanted.

An Immigrant Among the Editors

Ever since I began to read the American magazines one burning question has consumed me: Why is it that only the thoughts of educated people are written up? Why shouldn't sometimes a servant girl or a janitress or a coal-heaver give his thoughts to the world? We who are forced to do the drudgery of the world, and who are considered ignorant because we have no time for school, could say a lot of new and different things, if only we had a chance to get a hearing.

Very rarely I'd come across a story about a shop-girl or a washerwoman. But they weren't real stories. They were twisted pictures of the way the higher-ups see us people. They weren't as we are. They were as unreal as the knowledge of the rich about the poor. Often I'd read those smooth-flowing stories about nothing at all, and I'd ask myself, Why is it that so many of the educated, with nothing to say, know how to say that nothing with such an easy flow of words, while I, with something so aching to be said, can say nothing?

I was like a prison world full of choked-in voices, all beating in my brain to be heard. The minute I'd listen to one voice a million other voices would rush in crying for a hearing, till I'd get too excited and mixed up to know what or where.

Sometimes I'd see my brain as a sort of Hester Street junk-shop, where a million different things—rich uptown silks and velvets and the cheapest kind of rags—were thrown around in bunches. It seemed to me if I struggled from morning till night all my years I could never put order in my junk-shop brain.

Ach! If I only had an education, I used to think. It seemed to me that educated people were those who had their hearts and their heads so settled down in order that they could go on with quiet stillness to do anything they set out to do. They could take up one thought, one feeling at a time without getting the rest of themselves mixed up and excited over it. They had each thought, each feeling, laid out in separate shelves in their heads. So they could draw out one shelf of ideas while the rest of their ideas remained quiet and still in the orderly place inside of them.

With me my thoughts were not up in my head. They were in my hands and feet, in the thinnest nerves of my hair, in the flesh and blood of my whole body. Everything hurt in me when I tried to think; it was like struggling up toward something over me that I could never reach—like tearing myself out inch by inch from the roots of the earth—like suffering all pain of dying and being born.

And when I'd really work out a thought in words, I'd want to say it over and over a million times, for fear maybe I wasn't saying it strong enough. And I'd clutch at my few little words as a starving man clutches at crumbs. I could never sit back with the feeling that I had said what I wanted to say, like the educated people, who are sure of themselves when they say something. The real thing I meant remained inside of me for want of deeper, more burning words than I had yet found in the cold English language.

With all the confused unsureness of myself, I was absolutely sure I had great things in me. I felt that all I needed was the chance to reach the educated higher-ups, and all the big things in me would leap out quicker than lightning. But how was I to reach these American-born higher-ups when they were so much above me? I could never get into their colleges because I could never take the time to learn all the beginnings from schools to pass their entrance examinations. And even if I had the time to study, I wasn't interested in grammar and arithmetic and dry history and still drier and deader literature about Chaucer and Marlowe. I was too much on fire trying to think out my own thoughts to get interested in the dust and ashes of dead and gone ones. And yet I was so crazy to reach those who had all that book-learning from school in their heads that I was always dreaming of the wonderful educated world that was over me.

Sometimes I'd wake up in the middle of the night and stare through the darkness at an imaginary world of educated people that would invite me in to share with them their feast of learning. I saw them sitting around a table talking high thoughts, all the wisdom of the ages flowing from lip to lip like living light. I saw just how they talked and how they looked, because once I had worked as a waitress in a professor's house. Their words were over my head, but the sound of their low voices went through me like music of all that I longed and dreamed and desired to be.

I used to hold myself tight-in, like a wooden dummy, when I passed them the food. My lips were tight together, my eyes half-closed, like a Chinaman's, as though I didn't see or hear anything but my one business of waiting on them. But all the time something in the choked stillness of me was crying out to them: "I'm no dummy of a servant. I want to be like you. I could be like all of you if I only had a chance."

"If I only had a chance" kept going round and round in my head.

"Make your chance," a still voice goaded me.

"If I could only write out my wonderful thoughts that fly away in the air I'd get myself a first place in America."

"*Nu*, go ahead. Think connectedly for one minute. Catch your crazy wild birds and bring them down to earth."

And so I pushed myself on to begin the adventure of writing out my thoughts.

But who'll print what I write? was my next bother.

In my evenings off I used to go to the library and kept looking and looking through all the magazines to see where I could get a start. At last I picked out three magazines that stood out plainly for their special interest in working people. I will call them The Reformer, The People, and Free Mankind.

Free Mankind was a thin, white, educated-looking magazine, without covers, without pictures, without any advertising. It gave me the feeling when I looked through the pages that it was a head without a body. Most of the articles were high words in the air. I couldn't make out what they were talking about, but some of the editorials talked against paying rent. This at once got me on fire with interest, because all my life the people I knew were wearing out their years worrying for the rent. If this magazine was trying to put the landlords out of business, I was with it. So, fired by the inspiration of the moment, I rushed to see the editor of Free Mankind.

I don't remember how I ever pushed myself past the telephone girl and secretary, but I found myself talking face to face with a clean, cold, high-thinking head, Mr. Alfred Nott, editor-boss of Free Mankind. My burning enthusiasm turned into ice through all my bones as I looked into the terrible, clean face and cold eyes of this clean cold higher-up. But I heard my words rushing right on to him like the words of a soap-box speaker who is so on fire with his thoughts that even the cold ones from uptown are forced to listen to him.

"I can put a lot of new life into your magazine," I said. "I have in me great new ideas about life, and I'm crazy to give them out to you. Your magazine is too much up in the head and not enough down on earth. It's all words, words, long-winded empty words in emptiness. Your articles are something like those long sermons about nothing, that put people to sleep. I can wake up your readers like lightning. I can make your magazine mean living things to living people."

The man fell back in his chair as if frightened. His mouth opened to speak, but no words came from his lips.

"What you tell us about not paying rent is good enough," I went on. "But you should tell us how to put an end to all that. I know enough about not having a place to sleep in to write you something that will wake up the dead. You're not excited enough with feelings when you write, because you live in a soft steam-heated place with plenty of money to pay for it. But the poor like me, with little rent, and drying out their heads worrying for that little, they feel what it is to be under the foot of those Cossacks, the landlords. In my stories I'd write for you, I'd get the readers so mad, they'd rush out and do something."

Even while I was yet talking, Mr. Nott slipped out of the chair and disappeared like a frightened rabbit. I could see him vanishing through the door before I could stop my flow of words. I looked about me in the empty room. I felt as if I'd been slapped in the face.

I ran out of the office with tears in my eyes. And I couldn't stop my crying in the street. So this is his Free Mankind! When a person comes to him with something real he runs away as from a madman. Here was a paper that would reform the world, and its boss wouldn't even listen to one of the people he was setting out to save.

But there were other magazines in America, I told myself. The Reformer flashed before my eyes, because I remember it said on the back page, "It speaks for the average man."

I found myself again face to face with an editor—John Blair, the great liberal, the friend of an American President, the starter of a new school that was to gather all the minds of the new world. With this man I thought I'd begin by asking him a question instead of rushing myself out to him in all my hungry eagerness.

"Mr. Blair," I demanded in a voice of choked-in quietness, "do you think that the educated people know it all?"

He looked at me for a long minute. His lips closed together, his eyes cool like a judge. I felt he looked me over to decide in what shelf I belonged in the filing bureau of his college head.

"No, my dear young woman. I don't say that educated people have a monopoly of knowledge, but they are the only ones that know how to use it."

"Then it's only the thoughts of educated people for your magazine," I cried disappointedly. "How about people like me with a lot to say but can't put it in fancy language? Isn't your new school to be different from the old colleges in that you want to bring out the new thoughts of new people like me? Wouldn't you want to give a person like me a chance in your magazine?"

"But can you express yourself logically, reasonably—"

"Logic—reason! Reason—logic!" I jumped from the chair with excitement. "That's why your magazine is so dull, so dead, because all your living thoughts die down in the ashes of dead logic. Reason and logic aren't life. Hunger and desire is life. I know, because I'm burning up with it. With this hunger they paint pictures and write books and sing songs—"

"You Russians are full of interesting stuff. But you're so incoherent. You'd be no use to us unless you could learn to think clearly."

"I know my thoughts are all mixed up," I pleaded with educated quietness, "but it's only because I have so much to give and nobody wants it. Wouldn't it be better for your magazine to have my mixed-up aliveness instead of the cold logic from your college writers?"

He smiled down pityingly on me.

"I'm afraid that such a chaotic mind as yours would be useless to an intellectual journal. Good-day."

Not crushed, but bitter and hard and with head high, I walked out of The Reformer office. Were all the magazines that set themselves up to save the world headed by such narrow-thinking czars? Only to prove that all of them were run by the same clique of college professors, I went to the office of The People.

Here the editor didn't run from me like a frightened rabbit or sting me with logic like John Blair. He cut short the interview by going over to the shelf and taking down a book which he handed to me with pitying kindness. "This will help you to think and maybe to write."

Out in the street, I gave a look at the book. It was Genung's "Psychology of Madness." It grew black and red before my eyes. So it's madness to want to give out my thoughts to the world? They turn me down like a crazy beggar only because I come to give them new ideas.

I threw the book away in the nearest ash-can. But that word "madness" was to me like a red rag to a bull. I had to write now or go crazy with the wrath these reformers roused in me.

"What's my place in America?" I asked myself. "Must I remain a choked-in servant in somebody's kitchen or somebody's factory, or will I find a way to give out my thoughts to America?"

So what I wrote was the story of myself—myself lost in America.

It was like new air in my lungs to let myself loose on paper. But how could I get it to the American people? One thing I was sure of. I wasn't going to subject myself to another insult from those reform magazines. I don't know how it happened, but I picked out Wharton's Magazine, the most literary magazine of all those I looked over, simply because it looked so solidly high above the rest. My desperate need for a hearing made me bold. In my ragged coat and torn shoes I walked into that breath-taking rich office, like a millionaire landlord with pockets full of rent money.

"Do you want something new and different for your magazine?" I asked with the low voice and the high head of an American-born.

Friendly eyes turned on me. "We're always seeking something new and different. Have you got it?"

I looked right into the friendly eyes. This was Mr. Robert Reeves, the editor. He had the clean, well-dressed look of the born higher-up. But how different from those others! His face was human. And there was a shine in the eyes that warmed me.

"I'm an immigrant," I said. "I have worked in kitchens, factories, and sweatshops. I'm dying away with the loneliness of my thoughts, so I wrote myself out in a story."

He snatched up the papers and began to read. A quick light flashed into his eyes. Then he turned to me.

"I can see you have something original. But I can't decide just now. You'll hear from me as soon as I have read it through."

I could hardly walk the street for excitement. My life hung on this man's answer. And it came two days later in a small envelope. He offered me two hundred dollars for my story.

I couldn't believe it wasn't a dream. And I rushed with the letter to his office. "You could have given me a hundred dollars, fifty, twenty-five, and it would have been to me a fortune. But two hundred—do you mean really to give that much to me?"

He chuckled to himself, and I rushed right on. "I thought New York was a den of thieves. The landlord robbing you with the rent, and the restaurants cheating the strength out of every bite of food you buy. And I thought the college higher-ups were only educated cowards with dish-water in their veins—scared to death of hungry people like me—scared to look at the face of suffering. Their logic and their reason—only how to use their book-learning brains to shut out their hearts—to make themselves deaf, dumb, and blind to the cry of hunger and want knocking at their doors."

"Just because you felt all that so deeply, you were able to put fire in your words."

A thousand windows of light burst open in me as I listened to him. I was like something choked for ages in the tight chains of ignorance and fear, breathing the first breath of free air. For the first time my eyes began to see, my ears began to hear, my heart began to understand the world's wonder and the beauty.

A great pity welled up in my heart for the Alfred Notts and the John Blairs whom I had so mercilessly condemned. Poor little educated ones! Why did I fear them and envy them and hate them so for nothing? They were only little children putting on a long wooden face, playing teacher to the world. And I was a little scared child afraid of teacher—afraid they were grown-ups with the power to hurt me and shut me out from the fun of life.

Why wasn't I scared of Robert Reeves from the first minute? It was because he didn't frighten people with his highness. He didn't wear a wooden face of dignity. He was no reformer—no holy social worker—only a human being who loved people.

That one flash of understanding from Robert Reeves filled me with such enthusiasm for work that I shut myself off from the rest of the world and began turning out story after story.

Years passed. The only sign of success I became aware of was the increasing flood of mail that poured in on me. People who wanted to be writers asked me for literary help. People who imagined I was rolling in money sent me begging letters for aid. At the beginning I wanted to help them all. But I soon saw that I'd have to spend all my time answering the demands of foolish self-seekers who had nothing in common with me. And so I had to harden my heart against these time-wasting intruders.

One day, as I walked out of my house absorbed in one of the characters that I was writing about, some one stopped me. I looked up. A pale, thin, hungry-eyed young man asked timidly: "May I speak to you for a minute?" Then he told me that he had written a book, and that the publishers had turned it down, so he had printed it himself. "And I want your opinion," he pleaded, "because none of the critics would listen to me."

"I'm too busy," I said, irritably. "If you had to print the book yourself, it means it's no good."

"I thought you, who once had such a hard struggle, would remember— would understand."

"There's nothing to understand except that you killed yourself with the public." And I walked off.

I tried to resume the trend of my thoughts. But I could not think. The pale face, the hungry eyes followed me accusingly in the street. "You who once struggled would understand" rang in my ears. And suddenly I realized how brutal I had been.

"But it's the merciless truth," I defended. Nobody could help him till he finds himself. Nobody helped me till I had found myself.

"No—I'm all wrong," another voice cried. "Robert Reeves helped me. I could never have helped myself all alone. You can only help yourself half the way. The other half is some Hand of God in the shape of a human contact."

Something hurt so deep in me, I couldn't work that day. I couldn't sleep that night. The pale face and the hungry eyes kept staring at me through the darkness. I, who judged the Alfred Notts and the John Blairs—I saw myself condemned as one of them. I had let myself get so absorbed with the thoughts in my head that I ceased to have a heart for the people about me.

What would I not have given to see that young man and tell him how I suffered for my inhuman busy-busyness, which had shut my eyes to the hungry hands reaching up to me. But I never saw him again. And yet that man whom I had turned away like a beggar had brought me the life of a new awakening. He had made me aware that I could never contribute my deepest to America if I lost the friendly understanding of humanity that Robert Reeves had given me—if I lost the one precious thing that makes life real—the love for people—even if they are lost, wandering, crazy people.

To the Stars

"**There** are too many writers and too few cooks." The Dean laughed at her outright; his superior glance placed her: "The trouble with you is that you are a Russian Jewess. You want the impossible."

Sophie Sapinsky's mouth quivered at the corners, and her teeth bit into the lower lip to still its trembling.

"How can you tell what's possible in me before I had a chance," she said.

"My dear child,"—Dean Lawrence tried to be kind,—"the magazine world is overcrowded with native-born writers who do not earn their salt. What chance is there for you, with your immigrant English? You could never get rid of your foreign idiom. Quite frankly, I think you are too old to begin."

"I'm not so old like I look." Sophie heard a voice that seemed to come from somewhere within her speak for her. "I'm only old from the crushed-in things that burn me up. It dies in me, my heart, if I don't give out what's in me."

"My dear young woman,"—the Dean's broad tolerance broke forth into another laugh,—"you are only one of the many who think that they have something to say that the world is longing to hear." His easy facetiousness stung her into further vehemence.

"But I'm telling you I ain't everybody." With her fist she struck his desk, oblivious of what she was doing. "I'm smart from myself, not from books. I never had a chance when I was young, so I got to make my chance when I'm 'too old.' I feel I could yet be younger than youth if I could only catch on to the work I love."

"Take my advice. Retain the position that assures you a living. Apply yourself earnestly to it, and you will secure a measure of satisfaction."

The Dean turned to the mahogany clock on his desk. Sophie Sapinsky was quick to take the hint. She had taken up too much of his time, but she could not give up without another effort.

"I can't make good at work that chokes me."

"Well, then see the head of the English department," he said, with a gesture of dismissal.

The Professor of English greeted Sophie with a tired, lifeless smile that fell like ashes on her heart. A chill went through her as she looked at his bloodless face. But the courage of despair drove her to speak.

"I wasted all my youth slaving for bread, but now I got to do what I want to do. For me,—oh, you can't understand,—but for me, it's a case of life or death. I got to be a writer, and I want to take every course in English and literature from the beginning to the end."

The professor did not laugh at Sophie Sapinsky as the Dean had done. He had no life left for laughter. But his cold scrutiny condemned her.

"I know," she pleaded, "I ain't up to those who had a chance to learn from school, but inside me I'm always thinking from life, just like Emerson. I understand Emerson like he was my own brother. And he says: 'Trust yourself. Hold on to the thoughts that fly through your head, and the world has got to listen to you even if you're a nobody.' Ideas I got plenty. What I want to learn from the college is only the words, the quick language to give out what thinks itself in me—just like Emerson."

The preposterous assumption of this ignorant immigrant girl in likening herself to the revered sage of Concord staggered the professor. He coughed.

"Well,—er,"—he paused to get the exact phrase to set her right, "Emerson in his philosophy assumed a tolerant attitude that, unfortunately, the world does not emulate. Perhaps you remember the unhappy outcome of your English entrance examination."

Sophie Sapinsky reddened painfully. The wound of her failure was still fresh.

"In order to be eligible for our regular college courses, you would have to spend two or three years in preparation."

Blindly, Sophie turned to go. She reached for the door. The professor's prefunctory good-bye fell on deaf ears.

She swung the door open. The president of the college stood before her. She remembered it was he who had welcomed the extension students on the evening of her first attendance. He moved deferentially aside for her to pass. For one swift instant Sophie looked into kindly eyes. "Could he understand? Should I cry out to him to help me?" flashed through her mind. But before she could say a word he passed and the door had closed. Sophie stopped in the hall. Had she the courage to wait until he came out. "He's got feelings," her instincts urged her. "He's not an all-right-nik, a stone heart like the rest of them."

"Ach!" cried her shattered spirit, "What would he, the head of them all, have to do with me? He wouldn't even want to stop to listen."

Too crushed to endure another rebuff, she dragged her leaden feet down the stairs and out into the street. All the light went out of her eyes, the strength out of her arms and fingers. She could think or feel nothing but the choked sense of her defeat.

That night she lay awake staring into the darkness. Every nerve within her cried aloud with the gnawing ache of her unlived life. Out of the dim corners the dim specter of her stunted girlhood rose to mock her—the wasted poverty-stricken years smothered in the steaming pots of other people's kitchens. "Must I always remain buried alive in the black prison of my dumbness? Can't I never learn to give out what's in me? Must I choke myself in the smoke of my own fire?"

Centuries of suppression, generations of illiterates clamored in her: "Show them what's in you! If you can't write it in college English, write it 'immigrant English!'"

She flung from her the college catalog. About to trample on it, she stopped.

The catalog had fallen open at the photograph of the president. There looked up at her the one kind face in the heartless college world. The president's eyes gazed once more steadily into hers. Sophie hesitated; but not to be thwarted of her vengeance, she tore out his picture and laid it on the table, then she ripped the catalog, and stuffed the crumpled pages into the stove. It roared up the chimney like the song of the valkyrie. She threw back her head with triumph, and once more her eyes met the president's.

"Let them burn, these dead-heads. Who are they, the bosses of education? What are they that got the say over me if I'm fit to learn or not fit to learn? Dust and ashes, ashes and dust. But you," she picked up the picture, "you still got some life. But if you got life, don't their dry dust choke you?"

The wrestlings of her sleepless night only strengthened her resolve to do the impossible, just because it seemed impossible. "I can tear the stars out of heaven if it wills itself in me," her youth cried in her. "Whether I know how to write or don't know how to write, I'll be a writer."

She was at the steaming stove of the restaurant at the usual hour the next morning. She stewed the same *tzimmas*, fried the same *blintzes*, stuffed the same *miltz*. But she was no longer the same. Her head was in a whirl with golden dreams of her visionary future.

All at once a scream rent the air.

"*Koosh!* where in hell is your head?" thundered her employer. "The *blintzee* burning in front of her nose, and she stands there like a *yok* with her eyes in the air!"

"Excuse me," she mumbled in confusion, setting down the pan. "I was only thinking for a minute."

"Thinking?" His greasy face purpled with rage. "Do I pay you to think or to cook? For what do I give you such wages? What's the world coming to? *Pfui!* A cook, a greenhorn, a nothing—also me a thinker!"

Sophie's eyes flamed.

"Maybe in Smyrna, from where you come, a cook is a nothing. In America everybody is a person."

"Bolshevik!" he yelled. "Look only what fresh mouths the unions make from them! Y'understand me, in my restaurant one thing on a time: you cook or you think. If you wan' to think, you'll think outside."

"All right, then; give me my wages!" she retorted, flaring up. "The Czar is dead. In America cooks are also people."

Sophie tore off her apron and thrust it at the man.

To the cheapest part of the East Side she went in her search for a room. Through the back alleys and yards she sought for a place that promised to be within her means. And then a smeared square of cardboard held between the iron grating of a basement window caught her eye. "Room to let—a bargain—cheap!"

"Only three dollars a month," said the woman in answer to Sophie's inquiry.

The girl opened a grimy window that faced a blank wall.

"*Oi weh!* Not a bit of air!"

"What do you need yet air for the winter?" cried Hannah Breineh. "When the cold comes, the less air that blows into your room, the warmer you can keep yourself. And when it gets hot in summer you can take your mattress up on the roof. Everybody sleeps on the roof in summer."

"But there's so little light," said Sophie.

"What more light do you yet need? A room is only for to sleep by night. When you come home from work, it's dark, anyway. *Gottunui!* It's so dark on my heart with trouble, what difference does it make a little darkness in the room?"

"But I have to work in my room all day. I must have it light."

"*Nu*, I'll let you keep the gas lighted all day long," Hannah Breineh promised.

"Three dollars a month," deliberated Sophie. The cheapness would give her a sense of freedom that would make up for the lack of light and air. She paid down her first month's rent.

Her house, securely hers. Yet with the flash of triumph came a stab of bitterness. All that was hers was so wretched and so ugly! Had her eager spirit, eager to give, no claim to a bit of beauty, a shred of comfort?

Over the potato-barrel she flung a red shawl, once her mother's, and looked through her bag for something to cover an ugly break in the plaster. She could find nothing but the page torn from the college catalog.

"It's not so sunny and airy here as in your college office," she said, tacking the photograph on the wall; "but, maybe you'd be a realer man if once in your life you had to put up with a hole like this for a room."

Sophie spread her papers on the cot beside her. With tense fingers she wrote down the title of her story, then stopped, and stared wildly at the ceiling.

Where was the vision that had haunted her all these days? Where were the thoughts and feelings that surged like torrents through her soul? Merely the act of putting her pencil to paper, and her thoughts became a blur; her feelings, a dumb ache in her heart. Ach! Why must she kill herself to say what can never be said in words. But how did Emerson and Shakespeare seize hold of their vision? What was the source of their death-less power?

The rusty clock struck six.

"I ought to run out now for the stale bread, or it will be all sold out, and I will have to pay twice as much for the fresh," flashed through her mind.

"*Oi weh!*" she wailed, covering her eyes. "It's a stomach slave I am, not a writer. I forget my story, I forget everything, thinking only of saving a few pennies."

She dragged herself back to the page in front of her and resumed her task with renewed vigor.

"Sarah Lubin was sixteen years old when she came to America. She came to get an education, but she had to go to a factory for bread," she wrote laboriously, and then drew back to study her work. The sentences were wooden, dead, inanimate things. The words laughed up at her, mockingly.

Perhaps she was not a writer, after all. Writers never started stories in this way. Her eyes wandered over to the bed, a hard, meager cot. "I must remember to fix the leg, or it will tip to-night," she mused.

"Here I am," she cried despairingly, "thinking of my comforts again! And I thought I'd want nothing; I'd live only to write." Her head sank to the rough edge of the potato-barrel. "Perhaps I was a fool to give up all for this writing."

"Too many writers and too few cooks": the Dean's words closed like a noose around her anguished soul.

When she looked up, the kind face of the college president smiled down at her.

"Then what is it in me that's tearing and gnawing and won't let me rest?" she pleaded. The calm faith of the eyes leveled steadily at her seemed to rebuke her despair. The sure faith of that lofty face lifted her out of herself. She was humble before such unwavering power. "Ach!" she prayed, "How can I be so sure like you? Help me!"

Sophie became a creature possessed. She lived for one idea, was driven by one resistless passion, to write. As the weeks and months passed and her savings began to dwindle, her cheeks grew paler and thinner, the shadows under her restless eyes were black hollows of fear.

There came a day more deadly than death, when she had to face failure. She took out the thinning wad from her stocking and counted out her remaining cash: one, two, three dollars, and some nickels and dimes. How long before the final surrender? If she kept up her rigorous ration of dry bread and oatmeal, two or three weeks more at most. And then? An end to dreams. An end to ambition. Back to the cook-stove, back to the stifling smells of *tzimmas*, hash, and *miltz*.

No, she would never let herself sink back to the kitchen. But where could she run from the terror of starvation?

The bitterest barb of her agony was her inability to surrender. She was crushed, beaten, but she could not give up the battle. The unvoiced dream in her still clamored and ached and strained to find voice. A resistless something in her that transcended reason rose up in defiance of defeat.

"A black year on the landlord!" screamed Hannah Breineh through the partition. "The rent he raised, so what does he need to worry yet if the gas freezes? *Gottuniu!* Freeze should only the marrow from his bones!"

Sophie turned back to the little stove in an attempt to light the gas under the pan of oatmeal. The feeble flame flickered and with a faint protest went out. Hannah Breineh poked in her tousled head for sympathy.

"Woe is me! Woe on the poor what ain't yet sick enough for the hospital!"

As the chill of the gathering dusk intensified, Sophie seemed to see herself carried out on a stretcher to the hospital, numb, frozen.

"God from the world! Better a quick death than this slow freezing!" With the perpetual gnawing of hunger sapping her strength, Sophie had not the courage to face another night of torment. Drawing her shabby shawl more tightly around her, she hurried out. "Where now?" she asked as a wave of stinging snow blinded her. Hannah Breineh's words came back to her: "The hospital!" Why not? Surely they couldn't refuse to shelter her just over night in a storm like this.

But when she reached Beth Israel her heart sank. She looked in timidly at the warm, beckoning lights.

"Ach! How can I have the gall to ask them to take me in? They'll think I'm only a beggar from the street."

She paced the driveway of the building, back and forth and up and down, in envy of the sick who enjoyed the luxury of warmth.

"To the earth with my healthy body!" she cursed. "Why can't I only break a bone or something?"

With a sudden courage of despair she mounted the steps to the superintendent's office; but one glance of the man's well-fed face robbed her of her nerve.

She sank down on the bench of the waiting applicants, glancing stealthily at the others, feeling all the guilt of a condemned criminal.

When her turn came, the blood in her ears pounded from terror and humiliation. She could not lift her eyes from the floor to face this feelingless judge of the sick and suffering.

"I'm so killed with the cold," she stammered, twisting the fringes of her shawl. "If I could only warm myself up in a bed for the night—"

The man looked at her suspiciously.

"If we fill up our place with people like you, we'll have no room left for the sick. We have a flu epidemic."

"So much you're doing for the flu people, why can't you help me before I get it?" she spoke with that suppressed energy which was the keynote of her whole personality.

"Have you a fever?" he asked, his professional eye arrested by the unnatural flush on her face.

"Fever?" she mumbled. "A person has got to be already dead in his coffin before you'd lift a finger to help." She sped from the office into the dreary reception-hall.

On her way out her eye was caught by the black-faced type on the cover of a magazine that lay on the center-table.

SHORT-STORY COMPETITION

Five Hundred Dollar Prize
for the Best Love Story of a Working Girl

WRITE YOUR OWN LOVE STORY
If you have never lived Love, let it be your
dream of Love

As she read the magical words the color rushed to her cheeks. Forgotten was the humiliation of the superintendent's refusal to take her in; forgotten were the cold, the hunger. Her whole being leaped at the words:

"Write your own Love story. If you have never lived Love, let it be your dream of Love."

"Your dream of Love." The words were as wine in her blood. Was there ever a girl who hungered and dreamed of love as she? It was as though in the depths of her poverty and want the fates had challenged her to give substance to her dreams. She stumbled out of the huge building, her feet in the snow, her mind in the clouds.

"God from the world! The gas is burning again!" cried Hannah Breineh as she groped her way back into her cellar-room. "The children are dancing over the fire like for a holiday. All day they had nothing to warm in their bellies, and the coffee tastes like wine from heaven."

"Wine from heaven!" repeated the girl. "What wine but love from heaven?" and she clutched the magazine more tightly to her shrunken chest.

In the flicker of the gas-jet the photograph on the wall greeted her like a living thing. With the feel of the steady gaze upon her, she reread the message that was to her an invitation and a challenge; and as she read, the dingy little room became alive with light. The understanding eyes seemed to pour vision into her soul. What was the purpose of all the harsh experience that had been hers till now but to make her see just this—that love, and love only, was the one vital force of life? What was the purpose of all the privation and want she had endured but to make her see more poignantly this ethereal essence of love? The walls of her little room dissolved. The longing for love that lay dumb within her all her years took shape in human form. More real than life, closer than the beat within her heart, was this radiant, all-consuming vision that possessed her.

She groped for pencil and paper and wrote, unaware that she was writing. It was as if a hand stronger than her own was laid upon hers. Her power seemed to come from some vast, fathomless source. The starved passions of all the starved ages poured through her in rhythmic torrent of words—words that flashed and leaped with the resistless fire of youth burning through generations of suppression.

Not until daylight filtered through the grating of her window did the writing cease, nor was she aware of any fatigue. An ethereal lightness, a sense of having escaped from the trammels of her body, lifted her as on wings. Her radiant face met the responsive glow of understanding that shone down on her from the wall. "It's your light shining through me," she exulted. "It's your kind eyes looking into mine that made my dumbness speak."

For the moment the contest was forgotten. She was seized by an irresistible impulse to take her outpourings to the man who had inspired her. "Let him only see what music he made of me." Gathering tightly to her heart the scribbled sheets of paper, she hurried to the university.

A whole hour she waited at his office door. As she saw him coming, she could wait no longer, but ran toward him.

"Read it only," she said, thrusting the manuscript at the bewildered man. "I'll be back in an hour."

"What exotic creature was this, with her scattered pages of scrawling script and eager eyes?" President Irvine wondered. He concluded she was one of the immigrant group before which he had lectured.

She returned, to find the manuscript still in his hand.

"Tell me," he asked with an enthusiasm new to him, "where did you get all this?"

"From the hunger in me. I was born to beat out the meaning of things out of my own heart."

Puzzled, he studied her. She was thin, gaunt with a wasting power of frustrated passion in young flesh. There was the shadow of blank nights staring out of her eyes. Here was a personality, he thought, who might reveal to him those intangible qualities of the immigrant—qualities he could not grasp, which baffled, fascinated him.

He questioned her, and she poured out her story to him with unrestrained eagerness.

"I couldn't be an actress or a singer, because you got to be young and pretty for that; but for a writer nobody cares who or what you are so long as the thoughts you give out are beautiful."

He laughed, and it was an appreciative, genial laugh.

"You ain't at all like a professor, cold and hard like ice. You are a person so real," she naively said, interrupting the tale of her early struggles, her ambitions, and the repulse that had been hers in this very university of his. And then in sudden apprehension she cried out: "Maybe the Dean and the English Professor were right. Maybe only those with long education get a hearing in America. If you would only fix this up for me—change the immigrant English."

"Fix it up?" he protested. "There are things in life bigger than rules of grammar. The thing that makes art live and stand out throughout the ages is sincerity. Unfortunately, education robs many of us of the power to give spontaneously, as mother earth gives, as the child gives. You have poured out not a part, but the whole of yourself. That's why it can't be measured by any of the prescribed standards. It's uniquely you."

Her face lighted with joy at his understanding.

"I never knew why I hated to be Americanized. I was always burning to dig out the thoughts from my own mind."

"Yes, your power lies in that you are yourself. Your message is that of your people, and it is all the stronger because you are not a so-called assimilated immigrant."

Ach! Just to hear him talk! It was like the realization of a power in life itself to hold her up and carry her to the heights.

"Will you leave this manuscript here, so that I can have my secretary type it for you?" he asked as he took her to the door. "I can have it done easily. And I shall write to you as soon as I have time for another long talk about your work."

Only after she had left did she fully realize the wonder of this man's kindness.

"That's America," she whispered. "Where but in America could something so beautiful happen? A crazy, choked-in thing like me and him such a gentleman talking together about art and life like born equals. I poverty and he plenty; I ignorance and he knowledge; I from the bottom and he from the top. And yet he making me feel like we were from always friends."

A few days later the promised note came. How quick he was with his help, as if she were his only concern! Bare-headed, uncoated, she ran to him—this prince of kindness—repeating over and over again the words of the letter.

Her spirit crashed to the ground when she learned that he had been suddenly called to a conference at Washington. "He would return in a fortnight," said the model-mannered secretary who answered her feverish questions.

Wait a fortnight? She couldn't. Why, the contest would be over by that time. Then it struck her, the next best thing—the Professor of English. With a typewritten manuscript in her hand, he must listen to her. And just to be admitted to his short-story class for one criticism was all she would ask.

But small a favor as it seemed to her, it was greater than the Professor was in a position to grant.

"To concede to your request would establish a precedent that would be at variance with the university," he vouchsafed.

"University regulations, precedents? What are you talking?" And clutching at his sleeve, hysterically, she pleaded: "Just this once, my life hangs on getting this story perfect, and you can save me by this one criticism."

Her burning desire knew no barrier, recognized no higher authority. And the Professor, contrary to his reason, contrary to his experienced judgment, yielded without knowing why to the preposterous demands of this immigrant girl.

In the end of the last row of the lecture-hall Sophie waited breathlessly for the Professor to get to her story. After a lifetime of waiting it came. As from a great distance she heard him announce the title.

"This was not written by a member of the class," he went on, "but is the attempt of a very ambitious young person. Its lack of form demonstrates the importance of the fundamentals of technic in which we have drilled."

His reading aloud of the manuscript was followed by a chorus of criticism—criticism that echoed the professor's own sentiments: "It's not a story; it has no plot"; "feeling without form"; "erotic, over-emotional."

She could hardly wait for the hour to be over to get back this living thing of hers that they were killing. When she left the class all the air seemed to have gone out of her lungs. She dragged her leaden feet back to her room and sank on her cot a heap of despair.

All at once she jumped up.

"What do they know, they, with only their book-learning?" If the President had understood her story, there might be others who would understand. She must have faith enough in herself to send it forth for a judgment of a world free from rules of grammar. In a fury of defiance she mailed the story.

Weeks of torturous waiting for news of the contest followed—weeks when she dogged the postman's footsteps and paced the lonely streets in restless suspense. How could she ever have hoped to win the prize? Why was she so starving for the golden hills in the sky? If only for one day she could stop wasting her heart for the impossible!

Exhausted, spent, she lay on her cot when Hannah Breineh, more than usually disturbed by the girl's driven look, opened the door softly.

"Here you got it, a letter. I hope it's such good luck in it as the paper is fine."

"What's the matter?" cried Hannah Breineh in alarm at the girl's sudden pallor as the empty envelope fluttered from limp fingers.

For answer Sophie held up her check. "Five hundred dollars," she cried, "and the winner of the first prize!"

Hannah Breineh felt of the check. She read it. It was actually true. Five hundred dollars! In a flurry of excitement she called the neighbors in the hallways, and then hurried to the butcher, pushing through the babbling women who crowded around the counter. "People listen only! My *roomerkeh* got a five-hundred-dollar prize!"

"Five hundred dollars?" The words leaped from lips to lips like fire in the air. "Ach! only the little bit of luck! Did she win it on the lotteree?"

"Not from the lotteree. Just wrote something from her head. And you ought to see her only, a dried-up bone of a girl, and yet so smart."

In a few moments Sophie was mobbed in her cellar by the gesticulating crowd of women who hurried in to gaze upon the miracle of good luck. With breathless awe hands felt of her, and reverently of the check. Yes, even mouths watered with an envy that was almost worship! They fell on her neck and kissed her.

"May we all live to have such luck to get rich quick!" they chorused.

The following day Sophie's picture was in the Jewish evening paper. The Ghetto was drunk with pride because one of their number, and "only a dried-up bone of a girl," had written a story good enough to be printed in a magazine of America. Their dreams of romance had found expression in the overwhelming success of this greenhorn cook.

In one day Sophie was elevated to a position of social importance by her achievement. When she walked in the street, people pointed at her with their fingers. She was deluged with requests "to give a taste" of the neighbors' cooking.

When she went to the baker for her usual stale bread, the man picked out the finest loaf.

"Fresh bread for you in honor of your good luck. And here's yet an *Apfel Strudel* for good measure." Nor would he take the money she offered. "Only eat it with good health. I'm paid enough with the honor that somebody with such luck steps into my store."

"Of course," explained Hannah Breineh. "People will give you the last bite from their mouth when you're lucky, because you don't need their favors. But if you're poor, they're afraid to be good to you, so you should not hang on their necks for help."

But the greatest surprise that awaited Sophie was the letter from the professor congratulating her upon her success—

"The students have unanimously voted you to be their guest of honor at luncheon on Saturday," it read. "May we hope for the honor of your company for that occasion?"

The sky is falling to the earth—she a guest of honor of a well-fed, well-dressed world! She to break bread with those high up in rules of grammar! Sophie laughed aloud for the first time in months. Lunch at the hotel! A vision of snowy tablecloths, silver forks, delicate china, and sparkling glasses dazzled her. Yes, she would go, and go as she was. The clothes that had been good enough to starve and struggle in must be good enough to be feasted and congratulated in.

She was surprised at the sense of cold detachment with which she entered the hotel lobby.

"Maybe it's my excuse to myself for going that makes me feel that I'm so above it," she told herself. The grandeur, the lights, the luster, and glamour of a magnificent hotel—she took it all in, her nose in the air.

At the entrance of the banquet-hall stood the professor, smiling, smiling. And all these people in silks and furs and broadcloth wanted to shake hands with her. Again, without knowing why, she longed to laugh aloud.

Not until Professor———, smiling more graciously than ever, reached the close of his speech, not until he referred to her for the third time as having reached "the stars through difficulties," did she realize that she who had looked on, she who had listened, she who had wanted so to laugh, was a person quite different from the uncouth girl with the shabby sweater and broken shoes whom the higher-ups were toasting and flattering.

"I've never made a talk yet in my life," she said in answer to the calls for "Speech! Speech!" "But these are grand words from the professor, 'To the stars through difficulties.'" She looked around on these stars of the college world whom, after all her struggles, she had reached. "Yes, 'To the stars through difficulties!'" She nodded with a queer little smile, and sat down amidst a shower of applause.

In a daze Sophie left the heated banquet-hall. She walked blindly, struggling to get hold of herself, struggling in vain. Every reality, every human stay, seemed to slip from her. A stifled sense of emptiness weighed her down like a dead weight.

"What's the matter with me?" she cried. "Why do the higher-ups crush me so with nothing? Why is their smiling politeness only a hidden hurt in my heart?"

The flattering voices, the puppet-like smiles, the congratulations that sounded like mockery, were now so distant, so unreal as was the girl with her nose in the air. What cared these people wrapped in furs that the winter wind pierced through her shabby sweater? What cared they if her heart died in her from loneliness?

An aching need for human fellowship pressed upon her, a need for someone who cared for her regardless of failure or success. In a sudden dimming vision she saw the only real look of sympathy that had ever warmed her soul. Of them all, this man with the understanding eyes had known that what she wanted to say was worth saying before it got into print. If she could only see him—him *himself!*

If she could only pass the building where he was she would feel calm and serene again! All her bitterness and resentment would dissolve, all her doubts turn to faith. Who knows? Perhaps he had already come back. Her feet seemed winged as they flew without her will, almost without her consciousness, toward the place where she thought he might be.

As she ran up the steps she knew he was there without being told. Even as she sent her name in, the door opened, and he stood there, the living light of the late afternoon glow. He wasn't a bit startled by her sudden appearance. He merely greeted her, and led her in silence to his inner study. But there was a quality about the silence that made her feel at ease, as if he had been expecting her.

"I have things to say to you," she faltered. "Do you have time?"

For answer he pushed closer to the blazing logs an easy-chair, and motioned her into it. There no longer seemed any need to say what she had planned. His mere presence filled her with a healing peace.

"And it was so black for my eyes only a while before!" She spoke aloud her thought and paused, embarrassed.

"Black for your eyes?" he repeated, leaning toward her with an inviting interest.

"You know I was first on the table by the hotel?"

His eyebrows lifted whimsically.

"Tell me about it," he urged.

"All those higher-ups what didn't care a pinch of salt for me myself making such a fuss over a little accident of good luck!"

"Accident! You have won your way inch by inch grappling with life." His calm, compelling look seemed to flood her with strength. "You have what our colleges can not give, the courage to face yourself, the power to think. And now all your past experiences are so much capital to be utilized. Do you see the turning-point I mean?"

"The turning-point in my life is to know I got a friend. I owe it to the world to do something, to be something, after this miracle of your kindness." And at his deepening smile, "But you are not kind in a leaning-down sort of kindness. You got none of that what-can-I-do-for-you-my-poor-child-look in you."

Her effusiveness embarrassed him.

"You make too much out of nothing."

"Nothing?" Her eyes were misty with emotion. "I was something wild up in the air, and I couldn't get hold of myself all alone, and you—you made me for a person."

"I can not tell you how it affects me that in some way I do not understand I have been the means of bringing release to you. Of course," he added quickly, "I was only an instrument, not a cause. Just as a spade which digs the ground is not a cause of the fertility of the soil or of the lovely flowers which spring forth. I can not get away from the poetic, the religious experience which has so unexpectedly overtaken me."

She listened to him in silent wonder. How different he was from the college people she had met at luncheon that day!

"I can't put it in words," she said haltingly, "but I owe it to you, this confession. I can't help it. I used to hate so the educated! 'Why should they know everything, and me nothing,' it cried in me. 'Here I'm dying to learn, to be something, and they holding tight all the learning like misers hiding gold.'"

President Irvine did not answer. After a while he began talking in his calm voice of his dream of democracy in education, of the plans under way for the founding of the new school.

"I see it all!" She leaped to her feet under the inspiration of his words. "This new school is not to be only for the higher-ups by the higher-ups. It's to be for everybody—the tailor and the fish-peddler and the butcher. And the teachers are not to be professors, talking to us down from their heads, but living people talking out of their hearts. It's to be what there never yet was in this country—a school for the people."

President Irvine had the sensation of being swept out of himself upon strange, sunlit shores. The bleak land of merely intellectual perception lay behind him. Her ardor, her earnestness broke through the habitual restraint of the Anglo-Saxon.

"Let me read you a part of my lecture on the new school," he said, the contagion of her enthusiasm vibrant in his low voice. "Teachers, above all others, have occasion to be distressed when the earlier idealism of welcome to the oppressed is treated as a weak sentimentalism; when sympathy for the unfortunate and those who have not had a fair chance is regarded as a weak indulgence fatal to efficiency. The new school must aim to make up to the disinherited masses by conscious instruction, by the development of personal power for the loss of external opportunities consequent upon the passing of our pioneer days. Otherwise, power is likely to pass more and more into the hands of the wealthy, and we shall end with the same alliance between intellectual and artistic culture and economic power through wealth which has been the curse of every civilization in the past, and which our fathers in their democratic idealism thought this nation was to put to an end."

"Grand!" she cried, clapping her hands ecstatically. "Your language is a little too high over my head for me to understand what you're talking about, but I feel I know what you mean to say. You mean, in the new school, America is to be America, after all." Eyes tense, brilliant, held his. "I'll give you an advice," she went on. "Translate your lecture in plain words like they translate things from Russian into English or English into Russian. If you want your new school to be for the people, so you got to begin by talking in the plain words of the people. You got to feel out your thoughts from the heart and not from the head."

Her words were like bullets that shot through the static security of his traditional past.

"Perhaps I can learn from you how to be simple."

"Sure! I feel I can learn you how to put flesh and blood into your words so that everybody can feel your thoughts close to the heart." The gesticulating hands swayed before him like waves of living flame. "Stand before your eyes the people, the dumb, hungry people—hungry for knowledge. You got that knowledge. And when you talk in that high-headed lecture language, it's like you threw stones to those who are hungry for bread."

Then they were both silent, lost in their thoughts. There was a new light in her eyes, new strength in her arms and fingers, when she rose to go.

"I shall never see the America which is to be," he said as he took her hand in parting. "It will not come in my day. But I have seen its soul like a free wild bird, beating its wings not against bars but against the skies that the light might come through and reveal the earth to be."

She walked down the corridor and out of the building still under the spell of his presence. "Like a free wild bird! like a free wild bird!" sang in her heart.

She had nearly reached home when she became aware that tears were running down her cheeks, but they were tears of a soul filled to the brim—tears of vision and revelation. The glow of the setting sun illuminated the earth. She saw the soul beneath the starved, penny-pinched faces of the Ghetto. The raucous voices of the hucksters, the haggling women, the shrill cries of the children—all seemed to blend into one song of new dawn, of hope and of faith fulfilled.

"After all," she breathed in prayerful gratitude, "it is 'to the stars through difficulties.' A *meshugeneh* like me, a cook from Rosinsky's Restaurant burning her way up to the President for a friend!"

Children of Loneliness

"Oh, Mother, can't you use a fork?" exclaimed Rachel as Mrs. Ravinsky took the shell of the baked potato in her fingers and raised it to her watering mouth.

"Here, *Teacherin* mine, you want to learn me in my old age how to put the bite in my mouth?" The mother dropped the potato back into her plate, too wounded to eat. Wiping her hands on her blue-checked apron, she turned her glance to her husband, at the opposite side of the table.

"Yankev," she said bitterly, "stick your bone on a fork. Our *teacherin* said you dassn't touch no eatings with the hands."

"All my teachers died already in the old country," retorted the old man. "I ain't going to learn nothing new no more from my American daughter." He continued to suck the marrow out of the bone with that noisy relish that was so exasperating to Rachel.

"It's no use," stormed the girl, jumping up from the table in disgust; "I'll never be able to stand it here with you people."

"'You people'? What do you mean by 'you people'?" shouted the old man, lashed into fury by his daughter's words. "You think you got a different skin from us because you went to college?"

"It drives me wild to hear you crunching bones like savages. If you people won't change, I shall have to move and live by myself."

Yankev Ravinsky threw the half-gnawed bone upon the table with such vehemence that a plate broke into fragments.

"You witch, you!" he cried in a hoarse voice tense with rage. "Move by yourself! We lived without you while you was away in college, and we can get on without you further. God ain't going to turn his nose on us because we ain't got table manners from America. A hell she made from this house since she got home."

"*Shah!* Yankev *leben,*" pleaded the mother, "the neighbors are opening the windows to listen to our hollering. Let us have a little quiet for a while till the eating is over."

But the accumulated hurts and insults that the old man had borne in the one week since his daughter's return from college had reached the breaking-point. His face was convulsed, his eyes flashed, and his lips were flecked with froth as he burst out in a volley of scorn:

"You think you can put our necks in a chain and learn us new tricks? You think you can make us over for Americans? We got through till fifty years of our lives eating in our own old way—"

"Woe is me, Yankev *leben!*" entreated his wife. "Why can't we choke ourselves with our troubles? Why must the whole world know how we are tearing ourselves by the heads? In all Essex Street, in all New York, there ain't such fights like by us."

Her pleadings were in vain. There was no stopping Yankev Ravinsky once his wrath was roused. His daughter's insistence upon the use of a knife and fork spelled apostasy, Anti-Semitism, and the aping of the Gentiles.

Like a prophet of old condemning unrighteousness, he ran the gamut of denunciation, rising to heights of fury that were sublime and godlike, and sinking from sheer exhaustion to abusive bitterness.

"*Pfui* on all your American colleges! *Pfui* on the morals of America! No respect for old age. No fear for God. Stepping with your feet on all the laws of the holy Torah. A fire should burn out the whole new generation. They should sink into the earth, like Korah."

"Look at him cursing and burning! Just because I insist on their changing their terrible table manners. One would think I was killing them."

"Do you got to use a gun to kill?" cried the old man, little red threads darting out of the whites of his eyes.

"Who is doing the killing? Aren't you choking the life out of me? Aren't you dragging me by the hair to the darkness of past ages every minute of the day? I'd die of shame if one of my college friends should open the door while you people are eating."

"You—you—"

The old man was on the point of striking his daughter when his wife seized the hand he raised.

"*Mincha!* Yankev, you forgot *Mincha!*"

This reminder was a flash of inspiration on Mrs. Ravinsky's part, the only thing that could have ended the quarreling instantly. *Mincha* was the prayer just before sunset of the orthodox Jews. This religious rite was so automatic with the old man that at his wife's mention of *Mincha* everything was immediately shut out, and Yankev Ravinsky rushed off to a corner of the room to pray.

"*Ashrai Yoishwai Waisahuh!*"

"Happy are they who dwell in Thy house. Ever shall I praise Thee. *Selah!* Great is the Lord, and exceedingly to be praised; and His greatness is unsearchable. On the majesty and glory of Thy splendor, and on Thy marvelous deeds, will I meditate."

The shelter from the storms of life that the artist finds in his art, Yankev Ravinsky found in his prescribed communion with God. All the despair caused by his daughter's apostasy, the insults and disappointments he suffered, were in his sobbing voice. But as he entered into the spirit of his prayer, he felt the man of flesh drop away in the outflow of God around him. His voice mellowed, the rigid wrinkles of his face softened, the hard glitter of anger and condemnation in his eyes was transmuted into the light of love as he went on:

"The Lord is gracious and merciful; slow to anger and of great loving-kindness. To all that call upon Him in truth He will hear their cry and save them."

Oblivious to the passing and repassing of his wife as she warmed anew the unfinished dinner, he continued:

"Put not your trust in princes, in the son of man in whom there is no help." Here Reb Ravinsky paused long enough to make a silent confession for the sin of having placed his hope on his daughter instead of on God. His whole body bowed with the sense of guilt. Then in a moment his humility was transfigured into exaltation. Sorrow for sin dissolved in joy as he became more deeply aware of God's unfailing protection.

"Happy is he who hath the God of Jacob for his help, whose hope is in the Lord his God. He healeth the broken in heart, and bindeth up their wounds."

A healing balm filled his soul as he returned to the table, where the steaming hot food awaited him. Rachel sat near the window pretending to read a book. Her mother did not urge her to join them at the table, fearing another outbreak, and the meal continued in silence.

The girl's thoughts surged hotly as she glanced from her father to her mother. A chasm of four centuries could not have separated her more completely from them than her four years at Cornell.

"To think that I was born of these creatures! It's an insult to my soul. What kinship have I with these two lumps of ignorance and superstition? They're ugly and gross and stupid. I'm all sensitive nerves. They want to wallow in dirt."

She closed her eyes to shut out the sight of her parents as they silently ate together, unmindful of the dirt and confusion.

"How is it possible that I lived with them and like them only four years ago? What is it in me that so quickly gets accustomed to the best? Beauty and cleanliness are as natural to me as if I'd been born on Fifth Avenue instead of the dirt of Essex Street."

A vision of Frank Baker passed before her. Her last long talk with him out under the trees in college still lingered in her heart. She felt that she had only to be with him again to carry forward the beautiful friendship that had sprung up between them. He had promised to come shortly to New York. How could she possibly introduce such a born and bred American to her low, ignorant, dirty parents?

"I might as well tear the thought of Frank Baker out of my heart," she told herself. "If he just once sees the pigsty of a home I come from, if he just sees the table manners of my father and mother, he'll fly through the ceiling."

Timidly, Mrs. Ravinsky turned to her daughter.

"Ain't you going to give a taste the eating?"

No answer.

"I fried the *lotkes* special for you—"

"I can't stand your fried, greasy stuff."

"Ain't even my cooking good no more either?" Her gnarled, hard-worked hands clutched at her breast. "God from the world, for what do I need yet any more my life? Nothing I do for my child is no use no more."

Her head sank; her whole body seemed to shrivel and grow old with the sense of her own futility.

"How I was hurrying to run by the butcher before everybody else, so as to pick out the grandest, fattest piece of *brust!*" she wailed, tears streaming down her face. "And I put my hand away from my heart and put a whole fresh egg into the *lotkes,* and I stuffed the stove full of coal like a millionaire so as to get the *lotkes* fried so nice and brown; and now you give a kick on everything I done—"

"Fool woman," shouted her husband, "stop laying yourself on the ground for your daughter to step on you! What more can you expect from a child raised up in America? What more can you expect but that she should spit in your face and make dirt from you?" His eyes, hot and dry under their lids, flashed from his wife to his daughter. "The old Jewish eating is poison to her; she must have *trefa* ham—only forbidden food."

Bitter laughter shook him.

"Woman, how you patted yourself with pride before all the neighbors, boasting of our great American daughter coming home from college! This is our daughter, our pride, our hope, our pillow for our old age that we were dreaming about! This is our American *teacherin!* A Jew-hater, an Anti-Semite we brought into the world, a betrayer of our race who hates her own father and mother like the Russian Czar once hated a Jew. She makes herself so refined, she can't stand it when we use the knife or fork the wrong way; but her heart is that of a brutal Cossack, and she spills her own father's and mother's blood like water."

Every word he uttered seared Rachel's soul like burning acid. She felt herself becoming a witch, a she-devil, under the spell of his accusations.

"You want me to love you yet?" She turned upon her father like an avenging fury. "If there's any evil hatred in my soul, you have roused it with your cursed preaching."

"*Oi-i-i!* Highest One! Pity Yourself on us!" Mrs. Ravinsky wrung her hands. "Rachel, Yankev, let there be an end to this knife-stabbing! *Gottuniu!* My flesh is torn to pieces!"

Unheeding her mother's pleading, Rachel rushed to the closet where she kept her things.

"I was a crazy idiot to think that I could live with you people under one roof." She flung on her hat and coat and bolted for the door.

Mrs. Ravinsky seized Rachel's arm in passionate entreaty.

"My child, my heart, my life, what do you mean? Where are you going?"

"I mean to get out of this hell of a home this very minute," she said, tearing loose from her mother's clutching hands.

"Woe is me! My child! We'll be to shame and to laughter by the whole world. What will people say?"

"Let them say! My life is my own; I'll live as I please." She slammed the door in her mother's face.

"They want me to love them yet," ran the mad thoughts in Rachel's brain as she hurried through the streets, not knowing where she was going, not caring. "Vampires, bloodsuckers fastened on my flesh! Black shadow blighting every ray of light that ever came my way! Other parents scheme and plan and wear themselves out to give their child a chance, but they put dead stones in front of every chance I made for myself."

With the cruelty of youth to everything not youth, Rachel reasoned:

"They have no rights, no claims over me like other parents who do things for their children. It was my own brains, my own courage, my own iron will that forced my way out of the sweatshop to my present position in the public schools. I owe them nothing, nothing, nothing."

II

Two weeks already away from home. Rachel looked about her room. It was spotlessly clean. She had often said to herself while at home with her parents: "All I want is an empty room, with a bed, a table, and a chair. As long as it is clean and away from them, I'll be happy." But was she happy?

A distant door closed, followed by the retreating sound of descending footsteps. Then all was still, the stifling stillness of a rooming-house. The white, empty walls pressed in upon her, suffocated her. She listened acutely for any stir of life, but the continued silence was unbroken save for the insistent ticking of her watch.

"I ran away from home burning for life," she mused, "and all I've found is the loneliness that's death." A wave of self-pity weakened her almost to the point of tears. "I'm alone! I'm alone!" she moaned, crumpling into a heap.

"Must it always be with me like this," her soul cried in terror, "either to live among those who drag me down or in the awful isolation of a hall bedroom? Oh, I'll die of loneliness among these frozen, each-shut-in-himself Americans! It's one thing to break away, but, oh, the strength to go on alone! How can I ever do it? The love instinct is so strong in me; I can not live without love, without people."

The thought of a letter from Frank Baker suddenly lightened her spirits. That very evening she was to meet him for dinner. Here was hope—more than hope. Just seeing him again would surely bring the certainty.

This new rush of light upon her dark horizon so softened her heart that she could almost tolerate her superfluous parents.

"If I could only have love and my own life, I could almost forgive them for bringing me into the world. I don't really hate them; I only hate them when they stand between me and the new America that I'm to conquer."

Answering her impulse, her feet led her to the familiar Ghetto streets. On the corner of the block where her parents lived she paused, torn between the desire to see her people and the fear of their nagging reproaches. The old Jewish proverb came to her mind: "The wolf is not afraid of the dog, but he hates his bark." "I'm not afraid of their black curses for sin. It's nothing to me if they accuse me of being an Anti-Semite or a murderer, and yet why does it hurt me so?"

Rachel had prepared herself to face the usual hail-storm of reproaches and accusations, but as she entered the dark hallway of the tenement, she heard her father's voice chanting the old familiar Hebrew psalm of "The Race of Sorrows":

"Hear my prayer, O Lord, and let my cry come unto Thee.

For my days are consumed like smoke, and my bones are burned as an hearth.

I am like a pelican of the wilderness.

I am like an owl of the desert.

I have eaten ashes like bread and mingled my drink with weeping."

A faintness came over her. The sobbing strains of the lyric song melted into her veins like a magic sap, making her warm and human again. All her strength seemed to flow out of her in pity for her people. She longed to throw herself on the dirty, ill-smelling tenement stairs and weep: "Nothing is real but love—love. Nothing so false as ambition."

Since her early childhood she remembered often waking up in the middle of the night and hearing her father chant this age-old song of woe. There flashed before her a vivid picture of him, huddled in the corner beside the table piled high with Hebrew books, swaying to the rhythm of his Jeremiad, the sputtering light of the candle stuck in a bottle throwing uncanny shadows over his gaunt face. The skull-cap, the side-locks, and the long gray beard made him seem like some mystic stranger from a far-off world and not a father. The father of the daylight who ate with a knife, spat on the floor, and who was forever denouncing America and Americans was different from this mystic spirit stranger who could thrill with such impassioned rapture.

Thousands of years of exile, thousands of years of hunger, loneliness, and want swept over her as she listened to her father's voice. Something seemed to be crying out to her to run in and seize her father and mother in her arms and hold them close.

"Love, love—nothing is true between us but love," she thought.

But why couldn't she do what she longed to do? Why, with all her passionate sympathy for them, should any actual contact with her people seem so impossible? No, she couldn't go in just yet. Instead, she ran up on the roof, where she could be alone. She stationed herself at the air-shaft opposite their kitchen window, where for the first time since she had left in a rage she could see her old home.

Ach! What sickening disorder! In the sink were the dirty dishes stacked high, untouched, it looked, for days. The table still held the remains of the last meal. Clothes were strewn about the chairs. The bureau drawers were open, and their contents brimmed over in mad confusion.

"I couldn't endure it, this terrible dirt!" Her nails dug into her palms, shaking with the futility of her visit. "It would be worse than death to go back to them. It would mean giving up order, cleanliness, sanity, everything that I've striven all these years to attain. It would mean giving up the hope of my new world—the hope of Frank Baker."

The sound of the creaking door reached her where she crouched against the air-shaft. She looked again into the murky depths of the room. Her mother had entered. With arms full of paper bags of provisions, the old woman paused on the threshold, her eyes dwelling on the dim figure of her husband. A look of pathetic tenderness illumined her wrinkled features.

"I'll make something good to eat for you, yes?"

Reb Ravinsky only dropped his head on his breast. His eyes were red and dry, sandy with sorrow that could find no release in tears. Good God! Never had Rachel seen such profound despair. For the first time she noticed the grooved tracings of withering age knotted on his face and the growing hump on her mother's back.

"Already the shadow of death hangs over them," she thought as she watched them. "They're already with one foot in the grave. Why can't I be human to them before they're dead? Why can't I?"

Rachel blotted away the picture of the sordid room with both hands over her eyes.

"To death with my soul! I wish I were a plain human being with a heart instead of a monster of selfishness with a soul."

But the pity she felt for her parents began now to be swept away in a wave of pity for herself.

"How every step in advance costs me my heart's blood! My greatest tragedy in life is that I always see the two opposite sides at the same time. What seems to me right one day seems all wrong the next. Not only that, but many things seem right and wrong at the same time. I feel I have a right to my own life, and yet I feel just as strongly that I owe my father and mother something. Even if I don't love them, I have no right to step over them. I'm drawn to them by something more compelling than love. It is the cry of their dumb, wasted lives."

Again Rachel looked into the dimly lighted room below. Her mother placed food upon the table. With a self-effacing stoop of humility, she entreated, "Eat only while it is hot yet."

With his eyes fixed almost unknowingly, Reb Ravinsky sat down. Her mother took the chair opposite him, but she only pretended to eat the slender portion of the food she had given herself.

Rachel's heart swelled. Yes, it had always been like that. Her mother had taken the smallest portion of everything for herself. Complaints, reproaches, upbraidings, abuse, yes, all these had been heaped by her upon her mother; but always the juiciest piece of meat was placed on her plate, the thickest slice of bread; the warmest covering was given to her, while her mother shivered through the night.

"Ah, I don't want to abandon them!" she thought; "I only want to get to the place where I belong. I only want to get to the mountain-tops and view the world from the heights, and then I'll give them everything I've achieved."

Her thoughts were sharply broken in upon by the loud sound of her father's eating. Bent over the table, he chewed with noisy gulps a piece of herring, his temples working to the motion of his jaws. With each audible swallow and smacking of the lips, Rachel's heart tightened with loathing.

"Their dirty ways turn all my pity into hate." She felt her toes and her fingers curl inward with disgust. "I'll never amount to anything if I'm not strong enough to break away from them once and for all." Hypnotizing herself into her line of self-defense, her thoughts raced on: "I'm only cruel to be kind. If I went back to them now, it would not be out of love, but because of weakness—because of doubt and unfaith in myself."

Rachel bluntly turned her back. Her head lifted. There was iron will in her jaws.

"If I haven't the strength to tear free from the old, I can never conquer the new. Every new step a man makes is a tearing away from those clinging to him. I must get tight and hard as rock inside of me if I'm ever to do the things I set out to do. I must learn to suffer and suffer, walk through blood and fire, and not bend from my course."

For the last time she looked at her parents. The terrible loneliness of their abandoned old age, their sorrowful eyes, the wrung-dry weariness on their faces, the whole black picture of her ruined, desolate home, burned into her flesh. She knew all the pain of one unjustly condemned, and the guilt of one with the spilt blood of helpless lives upon his hands. Then came tears, blinding, wrenching tears that tore at her heart until it seemed that they would rend her body into shreds.

"God! God!" she sobbed as she turned her head away from them, "if all this suffering were at least for something worthwhile, for something outside myself. But to have to break them and crush them merely because I have a fastidious soul that can't stomach their table manners, merely because I can't strangle my aching ambitions to rise in the world!"

She could no longer sustain the conflict which raged within her higher and higher at every moment. With a sudden tension of all her nerves she pulled herself together and stumbled blindly down stairs and out of the house. And she felt as if she had torn away from the flesh and blood of her own body.

III

Out in the street she struggled to get hold of herself again. Despite the tumult and upheaval that racked her soul, an intoxicating lure still held her up—the hope of seeing Frank Baker that evening. She was indeed a storm-racked ship, but within sight of shore. She need but throw out the signal, and help was nigh. She need but confide to Frank Baker of her break with her people, and all the dormant sympathy between them would surge up. His understanding would widen and deepen because of her great need for his understanding. He would love her the more because of her great need for his love.

Forcing back her tears, stepping over her heart-break, she hurried to the hotel where she was to meet him. Her father's impassioned rapture when he chanted the Psalms of David lit up the visionary face of the young Jewess.

"After all, love is the beginning of the real life," she thought as Frank Baker's dark, handsome face flashed before her. "With him to hold on to, I'll begin my new world."

Borne higher and higher by the intoxicating illusion of her great destiny, she cried:

"A person all alone is but a futile cry in an unheeding wilderness. One alone is but a shadow, an echo of reality. It takes two together to create reality. Two together can pioneer a new world."

With a vision of herself and Frank Baker marching side by side to the conquest of her heart's desire, she added:

"No wonder a man's love means so little to the American woman. They belong to the world in which they are born. They belong to their fathers and mothers; they belong to their relatives and friends. They are human even without a man's love. I don't belong; I'm not human. Only a man's love can save me and make me human again."

It was the busy dinner-hour at the fashionable restaurant. Pausing at the doorway with searching eyes and lips eagerly parted, Rachel's swift glance circled the lobby. Those seated in the dining-room beyond who were not too absorbed in one another, noticed a slim, vivid figure of ardent youth, but with dark, age-old eyes that told of the restless seeking of her homeless race.

With nervous little movements of anxiety, Rachel sat down, got up, then started across the lobby. Half-way, she stopped, and her breath caught.

"Mr. Baker," she murmured, her hands fluttering toward him with famished eagerness. His smooth, athletic figure had a cock-sureness that to the girl's worshipping gaze seemed the perfection of male strength.

"You must be doing wonderful things," came from her admiringly, "you look so happy, so shining with life."

"Yes,"—he shook her hand vigorously,—"I've been living for the first time since I was a kid. I'm full of such interesting experiences. I'm actually working in an East Side settlement."

Dazed by his glamourous success, Rachel stammered soft phrases of congratulation as he led her to a table. But seated opposite him, the face of this untried youth, flushed with the health and happiness of another world than that of the poverty-crushed Ghetto, struck her almost as an insincerity.

"You in an East Side settlement?" she interrupted sharply. "What reality can there be in that work for you?"

"Oh," he cried, his shoulders squaring with the assurance of his master's degree in sociology, "it's great to get under the surface and see how the other half live. It's so picturesque! My conception of these people has greatly changed since I've been visiting their homes." He launched into a glowing account of the East Side as seen by a twenty-five-year-old college graduate.

"I thought them mostly immersed in hard labor, digging subways or slaving in sweatshops," he went on. "But think of the poetry which the immigrant is daily living!"

"But they're so sunk in the dirt of poverty, what poetry do you see there?"

"It's their beautiful home life, the poetic devotion between parents and children, the sacrifices they make for one another—"

"Beautiful home life? Sacrifices? Why, all I know of is the battle to the knife between parents and children. It's black tragedy that boils there, not the pretty sentiments that you imagine."

"My dear child,"—he waved aside her objection,—"you're too close to judge dispassionately. This very afternoon, on one of my friendly visits, I came upon a dear old man who peered up at me through horn-rimmed glasses behind his pile of Hebrew books. He was hardly able to speak English, but I found him a great scholar."

"Yes, a lazy old do-nothing, a blood-sucker on his wife and children."

Too shocked for remonstrance, Frank Baker stared at her.

"How else could he have time in the middle of the afternoon to pore over his books?" Rachel's voice was hard with bitterness. "Did you see his wife? I'll bet she was slaving for him in the kitchen. And his children slaving for him in the sweatshop."

"Even so, think of the fine devotion that the women and children show in making the lives of your Hebrew scholars possible. It's a fine contribution to America, where our tendency is to forget idealism."

"Give me better a plain American man who supports his wife and children and I'll give you all those dreamers of the Talmud."

He smiled tolerantly at her vehemence.

"Nevertheless," he insisted, "I've found wonderful material for my new book in all this. I think I've got a new angle on the social types of your East Side."

An icy band tightened about her heart. "Social types," her lips formed. How could she possibly confide to this man of the terrible tragedy that she had been through that very day? Instead of the understanding and sympathy that she had hoped to find, there were only smooth platitudes, the sightseer's surface interest in curious "social types."

Frank Baker talked on. Rachel seemed to be listening, but her eyes had a far-off, abstracted look. She was quiet as a spinning-top is quiet, her thoughts and emotions revolving within her at high speed.

"That man in love with me? Why, he doesn't see me or feel me. I don't exist to him. He's only stuck on himself, blowing his own horn. Will he never stop with his 'I,' 'I,' 'I'? Why, I was a crazy lunatic to think that just because we took the same courses in college, he would understand me out in the real world."

All the fire suddenly went out of her eyes. She looked a thousand years old as she sank back wearily in her chair.

"Oh, but I'm boring you with all my heavy talk on sociology." Frank Baker's words seemed to come to her from afar. "I have tickets for a fine musical comedy that will cheer you up, Miss Ravinsky—"

"Thanks, thanks," she cut in hurriedly. Spend a whole evening sitting beside him in a theater when her heart was breaking? No. All she wanted was to get away—away where she could be alone. "I have work to do," she heard herself say. "I've got to get home."

Frank Baker murmured words of polite disappointment and escorted her back to her door. She watched the sure swing of his athletic figure as he strode away down the street, then she rushed upstairs.

Back in her little room, stunned, bewildered, blinded with her disillusion, she sat staring at her four empty walls.

Hours passed, but she made no move, she uttered no sound. Doubled fists thrust between her knees, she sat there, staring blindly at her empty walls.

"I can't live with the old world, and I'm yet too green for the new. I don't belong to those who gave me birth or to those with whom I was educated."

Was this to be the end of all her struggles to rise in America, she asked herself, this crushing daze of loneliness? Her driving thirst for an education, her desperate battle for a little cleanliness, for a breath of beauty, the tearing away from her own flesh and blood to free herself from the yoke of her parents—what was it all worth now? Where did it lead to? Was loneliness to be the fruit of it all?

Night was melting away like a fog; through the open window the first lights of dawn were appearing. Rachel felt the sudden touch of the sun upon her face, which was bathed in tears. Overcome by her sorrow, she shuddered and put her hand over her eyes as though to shut out the unwelcome contact. But the light shone through her fingers.

Despite her weariness, the renewing breath of the fresh morning entered her heart like a sunbeam. A mad longing for life filled her veins.

"I want to live," her youth cried. "I want to live, even at the worst."

Live how? Live for what? She did not know. She only felt she must struggle against her loneliness and weariness as she had once struggled against dirt, against the squalor and ugliness of her Ghetto home.

Turning from the window, she concentrated her mind, her poor tired mind, on one idea.

"I have broken away from the old world; I'm through with it. It's already behind me. I must face this loneliness till I get to the new world. Frank Baker can't help me; I must hope for no help from the outside. I'm alone; I'm alone till I get there.

"But am I really alone in my seeking? I'm one of the millions of immigrant children, children of loneliness, wandering between worlds that are at once too old and too new to live in."

Brothers

$\mathcal{I}$ had just begun to unpack and arrange my things in my new quarters when Hanneh Breineh edged herself confidingly into my room and started to tell me the next chapter in the history of all her roomers.

"And this last one what sleeps in the kitchen," she finished, "he's such a stingy—Moisheh the Schnorrer they call him. He washes himself his own shirts and sews together the holes from his socks to save a penny. Think only! He cooks himself his own meat once a week for the Sabbath and the rest of the time it's cabbage and potatoes or bread and herring. And the herring what he buys are the squashed and smashed ones from the bottom of the barrel. And the bread he gets is so old and hard he's got to break it with a hammer. For why should such a stingy grouch live in this world if he don't allow himself the bite in the mouth?"

It was no surprise to me that Hanneh Breineh knew all this, for everybody in her household cooked and washed in the same kitchen, and everybody knew what everybody else ate and what everybody else wore down to the number of patches on their underwear.

"And by what do you work for a living?" she asked, as she settled herself on my cot.

"I study at college by day and I give English lessons and write letters for the people in the evening."

"Ach! So you are learning for a *teacherin?*" She rose, and looked at me up and down and down and up, her red-lidded eyes big with awe. "So that's why you wanted so particular a room to yourself? Nobody in my house has a room by herself alone just like you. They all got to squeeze themselves together to make it come out cheaper."

By the evening everybody in that house knew that I was a *teacherin,* and Moisheh the Schnorrer was among my first applicants for instruction.

"How much will you charge me for learning me English, a lesson?" he blurted, abrupt because of his painful bashfulness.

I looked up at the tall, ungainly creature with round, stooping shoulders, and massive, shaggy head—physically a veritable giant, yet so timid, so diffident, afraid almost of his own shadow.

"I wanna learn how to sign myself my name," he went on. "Only—you'll make it for me a little cheaper—yes?"

"Fifty cents an hour." I answered, drawn by the dumb, hunted look that cried to me out of his eyes.

Moisheh scratched his shaggy head and bit the nails of his huge, toil-worn hand. "Maybe—could you yet—perhaps—make it a little cheaper?" he fumbled.

"Aren't you working?"

His furrowed face colored with confusion. "Yes—but—but my family. I got to save myself together a penny to a penny for them."

"Oh! So you're already married?"

"No—not married. My family in Russia—*mein* old mother and Feivel, *mein* doctor brother, and Berel the baby, he was already learning for a bookkeeper before the war."

The coarse peasant features were transformed with tenderness as he started to tell me the story of his loved ones in Russia.

"Seven years ago I came to America. I thought only to make quick money to send the ship-tickets for them all, but I fell into the hands of a cockroach boss.

"You know a cockroach boss is a *landsmann* that comes to meet the greenhorns by the ship. He made out he wanted to help me, but he only wanted to sweat me into my grave. Then came the war and I began to earn big wages; but they were driven away from their village and my money didn't get to them at all. And for more than a year I didn't know if my people were yet alive in the world."

He took a much-fingered, greasy envelope from his pocket. "That's the first letter I got from them in months. The bookkeeper boarder read it for me already till he's sick from it. Only read it for me over again," he begged as he handed it to me upside down.

The letter was from Smirsk, Poland, where the two brothers and their old mother had fled for refuge. It was the cry of despair—food—clothes—shoes—the cry of hunger and nakedness. His eyes filled and unheeding tears fell on his rough, trembling hands as I read.

"That I should have bread three times a day and them starving!" he gulped. "By each bite it chokes me. And when I put myself on my warm coat, it shivers in me when I think how they're without a shirt on their backs. I already sent them a big package of things, but until I hear from them I'm like without air in my lungs."

I wondered how, in their great need and in his great anxiety to supply it, he could think of English lessons or spare the little money to pay for his tuition.

He divined my thoughts. "Already seven years I'm here and I didn't take for myself the time to go night-school," he explained. "Now they'll come soon and I don't want them to shame themselves from their *Amerikaner* brother what can't sign his own name, and they in Russia write me such smart letters in English."

"Didn't you go to school like your brothers?"

"Me—school?" He shrugged his toil-stooped shoulders. "I was the only bread-giver after my father he died. And with my nose in the earth on a farm how could I take myself the time to learn?"

His queer, bulging eyes with their yearning, passionate look seemed to cling to something beyond—out of reach. "But my brothers—ach! my brothers! They're so high educated! I worked the nails from off my fingers, but only they should learn—they should become people in the world."

And he deluged me with questions as to the rules of immigrant admission and how long it would take for him to learn to sign his name so that he would be a competent leader when his family would arrive.

"I ain't so dumb like I look on my face." He nudged me confidentially. "I already found out from myself which picture means where the train goes. If it's for Brooklyn Bridge, then the hooks go this way"—he clumsily drew in the air with his thick fingers—"And if it's for the South Ferry then the words twist the other way around."

I marveled at his frank revelation of himself.

"What is your work?" I asked, more and more drawn by some hidden power of this simple peasant.

"I'm a presser by pants."

Now I understood the cause of the stooped, rounded shoulders. It must have come from pounding away with a heavy iron at an ironing board, day after day, year after year. But for all the ravages of poverty, of mean, soul-crushing drudgery that marked this man, something big and indomitable in him fascinated me. His was the strength knitted and knotted from the hardiest roots of the earth. Filled with awe, I looked up at him. Here was a man submerged in the darkness of illiteracy—of pinch and scraping and want—yet untouched—unspoiled, with the same simplicity of spirit that was his as a wide-eyed, dreamy youth in the green fields of Russia.

We had our first lesson, and, though I needed every cent I could earn, I felt like a thief taking his precious pennies. But he would pay. "It's worth to me more than a quarter only to learn how to hold up the pencil," he exulted as he gripped the pencil upright in his thick fist. All the yearning, the intense desire for education were in the big, bulging eyes that he raised toward me. "No wonder I could never make those little black hooks for words; I was always grabbing my pencil like a fork for sticking up meat."

With what sublime absorption he studied me as I showed him how to shape the letters for his name! Eyes wide—mouth open—his huge, stoop-shouldered body leaning forward—quivering with hunger to grasp the secret turnings of "the little black hooks" that signified his name.

"M-o-i-s-h-e-h," he repeated after me as I guided his pencil.

"Now do it alone," I urged.

Moisheh rolled up his sleeve like one ready for a fray. The sweat dripped from his face as he struggled for the muscular control of his clumsy fingers.

Night after night he wrestled heroically with the "little black hooks." At last his efforts were rewarded. He learned how to shape the letters without any help.

"God from the world!" he cried with childishly pathetic joy as he wrote his name for the first time. "This is me—Moisheh!" He lifted the paper and held it off and then held it close, drunk with the wonder of the "little black hooks." They seemed so mysterious to him, and his eyes loomed large—transfigured with the miracle of seeing himself for the first time in script.

It was the week after that he asked me to write his letter, and this time it was from my eyes that the unheeding tears dropped as I wrote the words he dictated.

To my dear Loving Mother, and to my worthy Honorable Brother Feivel, the Doctor, and to my youngest brother, the joy from my life, the light from mine eyes, Berel, the Bookkeeper!

Long years and good luck to you all. Thanks the highest One in Heaven that you are alive. Don't worry for nothing. So long I have yet my two strong hands to work you will yet live to have from everything plenty. For all those starving days in Russia, you will live to have joy in America.

You, Feivel, will yet have a grand doctor's office, with an electric dentist sign over your door, and a gold tooth to pull in the richest customers. And you, Berel, my honorable bookkeeper, will yet live to wear a white starched collar like all the higher-ups in America. And you, my loving mother, will yet shine up the block with the joy from your children.

I am sending you another box of things, and so soon as I get from you the word, I'll send for you the ship-tickets, even if it costs the money from all the banks in America.

Luck and blessings on your dear heads. I am going around praying and counting the minutes till you are all with me together in America.

Our lessons had gone on steadily for some months and already he was able to write the letters of the alphabet. One morning before I was out of bed he knocked at my door.

"Quick only! A blue letter printed from Russia!" he shouted in an excited voice.

Through the crack of the door he shoved in the cablegram. "Send ship-tickets or we die—pogrom," I read aloud.

"Weh—weh!" A cry of a dumb wounded animal broke from the panic-stricken Moisheh.

The cup of coffee that Hanneh Breineh lifted to her lips dropped with a crash to the floor. "Where pogrom?" she demanded, rushing in.

I reread the cablegram.

"Money for ship-tickets!" stammered Moisheh. He drew forth a sweaty money-bag that lay hid beneath his torn gray shirt and with trembling hands began counting the greasy bills. "Only four hundred and thirty-three dollars! Woe is me!" He cracked the knuckles of his fingers in a paroxysm of grief. "It's six hundred I got to have!"

"*Gottuniu!* Listen to him only!" Hanneh Breineh shook Moisheh roughly. "You'd think he was living by wild Indians—not by people with hearts...."

"Boarders!" she called. "Moisheh's old mother and his two brothers are in Smirsk where there's a pogrom."

The word "pogrom" struck like a bombshell. From the sink, the stove, they gathered, in various stages of undress, around Moisheh, electrified into one bond of suffering brotherhood.

Hanneh Breineh, hand convulsively clutching her breast, began an impassioned appeal. "Which from us here needs me to tell what's a pogrom? It drips yet the blood from my heart when I only begin to remember. Only nine years old I was—the *pogromschiks* fell on our village.... Frightened!... You all know what's to be frightened from death—frightened from being burned alive or torn to pieces by wild wolves—but what's that compared to the cold shiverings that shook us by the hands and feet when we heard the drunken Cossacks coming nearer and nearer our hut. The last second my mother, like a crazy, pushed me and my little sister into the chimney. We heard the house tremble with shots—cries from my mother—father—then stillness. In the middle of the black night my little sister and I crawled ourselves out to see—" Hanneh Breineh covered her eyes as though to shut out the hideous vision.

A pause.... Everybody heard everybody's heart beating. Before our eyes burned the terrible memory which Hanneh Breineh had tried to shut out and tried in vain....

Again Hanneh Breineh's voice arose. "I got no more breath for words—only this—the last bite from our mouths, the last shirt from our backs we got to take away to help out Moisheh. It's not only Moisheh's old mother that's out there—it's our own old mother—our own flesh-and-blood brothers.... Even I—beggar that I am—even I will give my only feather bed to the pawn."

A hush, and then a tumult of suppressed emotions. The room seethed with wild longings of the people to give—to help—to ease their aching hearts sharing Moisheh's sorrow.

Shoolem, a gray, tottering rag-picker, brought forth a grimy cigar box full of change. "Here is all the pennies and nickels and dimes I was saving and saving myself for fifteen years. I was holding by life on one hope—the hope that some day I would yet die before the holy walls from Jerusalem." With the gesture of a Rothschild he waved it in the air as he handed it over. "But here you got it, Moisheh. May it help to bring your brothers in good luck to America!"

Sosheh, the finisher, turned aside as she dug into her stocking and drew forth a crisp five-dollar bill. "That all I got till my next pay. Only it should help them," she gulped. "I wish I had somebody left alive that I could send a ship-ticket to."

Zaretsky, the match-maker, snuffed noisily a pinch of tobacco and pulled from his overcoat pocket a book of War Savings stamps. "I got fourteen dollars of American Liberty. Only let them come in good luck and I'll fix them out yet with the two grandest girls in New York."

The ship bearing Moisheh's family was to dock the next morning at eleven o'clock. The night before Hanneh Breineh and all of us were busy decorating the house in honor of the arrivals. The sound of hammering and sweeping and raised, excited voices filled the air.

Sosheh, the finisher, standing on top of a soap-box, was garnishing the chandelier with red-paper flowers.

Hanneh Breineh tacked bright, checked oilcloth on top of the wash-tubs.

Zaretsky was nailing together the broken leg of the table.

"I should live so," laughed Sosheh, her sallow face flushed with holiday joy. "This kitchen almost shines like a parlor, but for only this—" pointing to the sagging lounge where the stained mattress protruded.

"Shah! I'll fix this up in a minute so it'll look like new from the store." And Hannah Breineh took out the red-flowered, Sabbath tablecloth from the bureau and tucked it around the lounge.

Meantime Moisheh, his eyes popping with excitement, raised clouds of dust as he swept dirt that had been gathering since Passover from the corners of the room.

Unable to wait any longer for the big moment, he had been secretly planning for weeks, zip! under the bed went the mountain of dirt, to be followed by the broom, which he kicked out of sight.

"Enough with the cleaning!" he commanded. "Come only around," and he pulled out from the corner his Russian steamer-basket.

"Oi—oi—oi—oi, and ai—ai!" the boarders shouted, hilariously. "Will you treat us to a holiday cake maybe?"

"Wait only!" He gesticulated grandly as he loosened the lock.

One by one he held up and displayed the treasured trousseau which little by little he had gathered together for his loved ones.

A set of red-woolen underwear for each of the brothers, and for his mother a thick, gray shirt. Heavy cotton socks, a blue-checked apron, and a red-velvet waist appeared next. And then—Moisheh was reduced to gutteral grunts of primitive joy as he unfolded a rainbow tie for Feivel, the doctor, and pink suspenders for his "baby" brother.

Moisheh did not remove his clothes—no sleep for him that night. It was still dark when the sound of his heavy shoes, clumping around the kitchen as he cooked his breakfast, woke the rest of us.

"You got to come with me—I can't hold myself together with so much joy," he implored. There was no evading his entreaties, so I promised to get away as soon as I could and meet him at the dock.

I arrived at Ellis Island to find Moisheh stamping up and down like a wild horse. "What are they holding them so long?" he cried, mad with anxiety to reach those for whom he had so long waited and hungered.

I had to shake him roughly before I could make him aware of my presence, and immediately he was again lost in his eager search of the mob that crowded the gates.

The faces of the immigrants, from the tiniest babe at its mother's breast to the most decrepit old gray-haired man, were all stamped with the same transfigured look—a look of those who gazed for the first time upon the radiance of the dawn. The bosoms of the women heaved with excitement. The men seemed to be expanding, growing with the surge of realized hopes, of dreams come true. They inhaled deeply, eager to fill their stifled bodies and souls with the first life-giving breath of free air. Their eyes were luminous with hope, bewildered joy and vague forebodings. A voice was heard above the shouted orders and shuffling feet—above the clamor of the pressing crowds—"*Gott sei dank!*" The pæan of thanksgiving was echoed and reechoed—a pæan of nations released—America.

I had to hold tight to the bars not to be trampled underfoot by the crowd that surged through the gates. Suddenly a wild animal cry tore from Moisheh's throat. "*Mammeniu! Mammeniu!*" And a pair of gorilla-like arms enfolded a gaunt, wasted little figure wrapped in a shawl.

"Moisheh! my heart!" she sobbed, devouring him with hunger-ravaged eyes.

"*Ach!*" she trembled—drawing back to survey her first-born. "From the bare feet and rags of Smirsk to leather shoes and a suit like a Rothschild!" she cried in Yiddish. "*Ach!*—I lived to see America!"

A dumb thing laughing and crying he stood there, a primitive figure, pathetic, yet sublime in the purity of his passionate love, his first love—his love for his mother.

The toil-worn little hand pulled at his neck as she whispered in Moisheh's ear, and as in a dream he turned with outstretched arms to greet his brothers.

"Feivel—*mein* doctor!" he cried.

"Yes, yes, we're here," said the high-browed young doctor in a tone that I thought was a little impatient. "Now let's divide up these bundles and get started." Moisheh's willing arms reached out for the heaviest sack.

"And here is my *teacherin!*" Moisheh's grin was that of a small boy displaying his most prized possession.

Berel, the baby, with the first down of young manhood still soft on his cheeks, shyly enveloped my hand in his long sensitive fingers. "How nice for you to come—a *teacherin*—an *Amerikanerin!*"

"Well—are we going?" came imperiously from the doctor.

"Yeh—yeh!" answered Moisheh. "I'm so out of my head from joy, my feet don't work." And, gathering the few remaining lighter packages together, we threaded our way through the crowded streets—the two newly arrived brothers walking silently together.

"Has Moisheh changed much?" I asked the doctor as I watched the big man help his mother tenderly across the car tracks.

"The same Moisheh," he said, with an amused, slightly superior air.

I looked at Berel to see if he was of the same cloth as the doctor, but he was lost in dreamy contemplation of the towering sky-scrapers.

"Like granite mountains—the tower of Babel," Berel mused aloud.

"How do they ever walk up to the top?" asked the bewildered old mother.

"Walk!" cried Moisheh, overjoyed at the chance to hand out information. "There are elevators in America. You push a button and up you fly like on wings."

Elated with this opportunity to show off his superior knowledge, he went on: "I learned myself to sign my name in America. Stop only and I'll read for you the sign from the lamp-post," and he spelled aloud, "W-a-l-l —Wall."

"And what street is this?" asked the doctor, as we came to another corner.

Moisheh colored with confusion, and the eyes he raised to his brother were like the eyes of a trapped deer pleading to be spared. "L-i-b—" He stopped. "Oh, *weh!*" he groaned, "the word is too long for me."

"Liberty," scorned the doctor. "You are an *Amerikaner* already and you don't know Liberty?"

His own humiliation forgot in pride of his brother's knowledge, Moisheh nodded his head humbly.

"Yeh—yeh! You are greener and yet you know Liberty. And I, an *Amerikaner,* is stuck by the word." He turned to me with a pride that brought tears to his eyes. "Didn't I tell you my brothers were high educated? Never mind—they won't shame me in America."

A look of adoration drank in the wonder of his beloved family. Overcome with a sense of his own unworthiness, he exclaimed, "Look only on me—a nothing and a nobody." He breathed in my ear, "And such brothers!" With a new, deeper tenderness, he pressed his mother's slight form more closely to him.

"More Bolsheviki!" scoffed a passerby.

"Trotzky's ambassadors," sneered another.

And the ridicule was taken up by a number of jeering voices.

"Poor devils!" came from a richly dressed Hebrew, resplendent in his fur collar and a diamond stud. There was in his eyes a wistful, reminiscent look. Perhaps the sight of these immigrants brought back to him the day he himself had landed, barefoot and in rags, with nothing but his dreams of America.

The street was thronged with hurrying lunch-seekers as we reached lower Broadway. I glanced at Moisheh's brothers, and I could not help noticing how different was the calm and care-free expression of their faces from the furtive, frantic acquisitive look of the men in the financial district.

But the moment we reached our block the people from the stoops and windows waved their welcome. Hanneh Breineh and all the boarders, dressed up in their best, ran to meet us.

"Home!" cried the glowing Moisheh. "*Mazeltuff.* Good luck!" answered Hanneh Breineh.

Instantly we were surrounded by the excited neighbors whose voices of welcome rose above the familiar cries of the hucksters and pedlers that lined the street.

"Give a help!" commanded Hanneh Breineh as she seized the bundles from Moisheh's numbed arms and divided them among the boarders. Then she led the procession triumphantly into her kitchen.

The table, with a profusion of festive dishes, sang aloud its welcome.

"Rockefeller's only daughter couldn't wish herself grander eatings by her own wedding," bragged the hostess as she waved the travelers to the feast. A brass pot filled with *gefüllte fisch* was under the festooned chandelier. A tin platter heaped high with chopped liver and onions sent forth its inviting aroma. *Tzimmes—blintzes—*a golden roasted goose swimming in its own fat ravished the senses. Eyes and mouths watered at sight of such luscious plenty.

"White bread!—*Ach!*—white bread!" gasped the hunger-ravaged old mother. Reaching across the table, she seized the loaf in her trembling hands. "All those starving years—all those years!" she moaned, kissing its flaky whiteness as though it were a living thing.

"Sit yourself down—*mutterel!*" Hanneh Breineh soothed the old woman and helped her into the chair of honor. "White bread—even white bread is nothing in America. Even the charities—a black year on them— even the charities give white bread to the beggars."

Moisheh, beaming with joy of his loved ones' nearness, was so busy passing and repassing the various dishes to his folks that he forgot his own meal.

"*Nu*—ain't it time for you also to sit yourself down like a person?" urged Hanneh Breineh.

"*Takeh—takeh!*" added his mother. "Take something to your mouth."

Thereupon Moisheh rolled up his sleeves and with the zest of a hungry cave-man attacked the leg of a goose. He no sooner finished than he bent ravenously over the meat-platter, his forehead working with rhythm to his jaws.

"Excuse me," stammered Moisheh, wiping his lips with the end of his shirt-sleeve and sticking the meat on a fork.

"What's the difference how you eat so long you got what to eat?" broke in Zaretsky, grabbing the breast of the goose and holding it up to his thick lips.

His sensibilities recoiling at this cannibalistic devouring of food, Berel rose and walked to the air-shaft window. His arms shot out as though to break down the darkening wall which blotted out the daylight from the little room. "Plenty of food for the body, but no light for the soul," he murmured, not intending to be heard.

Feivel, the doctor, lit a cigarette and walked up and down the room restlessly. He stopped and faced his younger brother with a cynical smile. "I guess America is like the rest of the world—you get what you take—sunlight as well as other things—"

"How take sunlight? What do you mean?"

"I mean America is like a dish of cheese *blintzes* at a poor-house. The beggars who are the head of the table and get their hands in first, they live and laugh—"

Hanneh Breineh wiped her lips with the corner of her apron and faced him indignantly. "You ain't yet finished with your first meal in America and already you're blowing from yourself like it's coming to you yet better."

"But why come to America?" defended Berel, the poet, "unless it give you what's lacking in other lands? Even in the darkest days in Russia the peasants had light and air."

"Hey, Mr. Greenhorn Doctor—and you, young feller," broke in Zaretsky, the block politician, "if you don't like it here then the President from America will give you a free ride back on the same ship on which you came from."

Silenced by Zaretsky's biting retort, the doctor lit a cigarette and sent leisurely clouds of smoke ceilingward.

Moisheh, who had been too absorbed in his food to follow the talk, suddenly looked up from his plate. Though unable to grasp the trend of the conversation, he intuitively sensed the hostile feeling in the room.

"Why so much high language," he asked, "when there's yet the nuts and raisins and the almonds to eat?"

A few months later Hanneh Breineh came into my room while peeling potatoes in her apron. "Greenhorns ain't what greenhorns use to be," she said, as she sat down on the edge of my cot. "Once when greenhorns came, a bone from a herring, a slice from an onion, was to them milk and honey; and now pour golden chicken-fat into their necks, and they turn up their nose like it's coming to them yet better."

"What is it now?" I laughed.

Hanneh Breineh rose. "Listen only to what is going on," she whispered, as she noiselessly pushed open the door and winked to me to come over and hear.

"I'm yet in debt over my neck. In God's name, how could you spend out so much money for only a little pleasure," remonstrated Moisheh.

"Do you think I'm a *schnorrer* like you? I'm a man, and I have to live," retorted the doctor.

"But two dollars for one evening in the opera only, when for ten cents you could have seen the grandest show in the movies!"

The doctor's contemptuous glance softened into a look of condescending pity. "After all, my presser of pants, what a waste the opera would be on you. Your America's the movies."

"Two dollars!" cried the little old mother, wringing her hands despairingly. "Moisheh didn't yet pay out for the ship-tickets."

"Ship-tickets—bah!—I wish he had never brought us to this golden country—dirt, darkness, houses like stalls for cattle!" And in a fury of disgust, not unmitigated with shame at his loss of temper, he slammed the door behind him.

"*Oi weh!*" wailed the care-worn old mother. "Two dollars for an opera, and in such bad times!"

"*Ach! Mammeniu,*" Moisheh defended, "maybe Feivel ain't like us. Remember he's high-educated. He needs the opera like I need the bite of bread. Maybe even more yet. I can live through without even the bite of bread, but Feivel must have what wills itself in him."

Hanneh Breineh closed the door and turned to me accusingly. "What's the use from all your education, if that's what kind of people it makes?"

"Yes," I agreed with Hanneh Breineh, "Education without heart is a curse."

Hanneh Breineh bristled. "I wish I should only be cursed with an education. It's only by the American education is nothing. It used to be an honor in Russia to shine a doctor's shoes for him."

"So you're for education, after all?" I ventured, trying the impossible—to pin Hanneh Breineh down.

"Blood-suckers!" Hanneh Breineh hissed. "Moisheh dries out the marrow from his head worrying for the dollar, and these high-educated brothers sit themselves on top of his neck like leeches. Greenhorns—opera—the world is coming to an end!"

•

Work with the Immigration Department took me to Washington for almost a year. As soon as I returned to New York I went to the only home I knew—Hanneh Breineh's lodging-house.

My old friend, Moisheh, greeted me at the door. *"Teacherin!"* he cried, with a shout of welcome, and then called to his mother. "Come quick. See only who is here!"

Sleeves rolled up and hands full of dough, the little soul hurried in. "The sky is falling to the earth!" she cried. "You here? And are you going to stay?"

"Sure will she stay," said Moisheh, helping me remove my things.

"And where are Hanneh Breineh and the boarders?" I questioned.

"Out on a picnic by Coney Island."

"And why didn't you and your mother go?"

"I got to cook Feivel's dinner," she gesticulated with doughy palms.

"And I got my Coney Island here," said Moisheh.

To my great delight I saw he had been reading the life of Lincoln—the book I had left him the day I went away.

"My head is on fire thinking and dreaming from Lincoln. It shines before my face so real, I feel myself almost talking to him."

Moisheh's eyes were alive with light, and as I looked at him I felt for the first time a strange psychic resemblance between Moisheh and Lincoln. Could it be that the love for his hero had so transformed him as to make him almost resemble him?

"Lincoln started life as a nothing and a nobody," Moisheh went on, dreamily, "and he made himself for the President from America—maybe there's yet a chance for me to make something from myself!"

"Sure there is. Show only what's in you and all America reaches out to help you."

"I used to think that I'd die a presser by pants. But since I read from Lincoln, something happened in me. I feel I got something for America— only I don't know how to give it out. I'm yet too much of a dummox—"

"What's in us must come out. I feel America needs you and me as much as she needs her Rockefellers and Morgans. Rockefellers and Morgans only pile up mountains of money; we bring to America the dreams and desires of ages—the youth that never had a chance to be young—the choked lives that never had a chance to live."

A shadow filmed Moisheh's brooding eyes. "I can't begin yet to think from myself for a few years. First comes my brothers. If only Feivel would work for himself up for a big doctor and Berel for a big writer then I'll feel myself free to do something...."

"Shah! I got great news for you," Moisheh announced. "Feivel has already his doctor's office."

"Where did he get all the money?"

"On the installment plan I got him the chair and the office things. Now he's beginning to earn already enough to pay almost half his rent."

"Soon he'll be for dinner." The old lady jumped up. "I got to get his eating ready before he comes." And she hastened back to the kitchen-stove.

"And Berel—what does he do?" I inquired.

"Berel ain't working yet. He's still writing from his head," explained Moisheh. "Wait only and I'll call him. He's locked himself up in his bedroom; nobody should bother him."

"Berel!" he called, tapping respectfully at the door.

"*Yuk!*" came in a voice of nervous irritation. "What is it?"

"The *teacherin* is here," replied Moisheh. "Only a minute."

"It's me," I added. "I'd like to see you."

Berel came out, hair disheveled, with dreamy, absent look, holding pencil and paper in his hand. "I was just finishing a poem," he said in greeting to me.

"I have been looking for your name in the magazines. Have you published anything yet?"

"I—publish in the American magazines?" he flung, hurt beyond words. "I wouldn't mix my art with their empty drivel."

"But, surely, there are some better magazines," I protested.

"Pshah! Their best magazines—the pink-and-white jingles that they call poetry are not worth the paper they're printed on. America don't want poets. She wants plumbers."

"But what will you do with the poetry you write?"

"I'll publish it myself. Art should be free, like sunlight and beauty. The only compensation for the artist is the chance to feed hungry hearts. If only Moisheh could give me the hundred dollars I'd have my volume printed at once."

"But how can I raise all the money when I'm not yet paid out with Feivel's doctor's office?" remonstrated Moisheh. "Don't you think if— maybe you'd get a little job?"

An expression of abstraction came over Berel's face, and he snapped, impatiently: "Yes—yes—I told you that I would look for a job. But I must write this while I have the inspiration."

"Can't you write your inspiration out in the evening?" faltered Moisheh. "If you could only bring in a few dollars a week to help pay ourselves out to the installment man."

Berel looked at his brother with compassionate tolerance. "What are to you the things of the soul? All you care for is money—money—money!

You'd want me to sell my soul, my poetry, my creative fire—to hand you a few dirty dollars."

The postman's whistle and the cry, "Berel Pinski!"

Moisheh hurried downstairs and brought back a large return envelope.

"Another one of those letters back," deplored the mother, untactfully. "You're only making the post-office rich with the stamps from Moisheh's blood money."

"Dammit!" Defeat enraged the young poet to the point of brutality. "Stop nagging me and mixing in with things you don't understand!" He struck the rude table with his clenched fist. "It's impossible to live with you thickheads—numskulls—money-grubbing worms."

He threw on his hat and coat and paused for a moment glowering in the doorway. "Moisheh," he demanded, "give me a quarter for carfare. I have to go uptown to the library." Silently the big brother handed him the money, and Berel flung himself out of the room.

The door had no sooner closed on the poet than the doctor sauntered into the room. After a hasty "Hello," he turned to Moisheh. "I have a wonderful chance—but I can't take advantage of it."

"What!" cried Moisheh, his face brightening.

"My landlord invited me to his house to-night, to meet his only daughter."

"Why not go?" demanded Moisheh.

"Sure you got to go," urged the mother, as she placed the food before him. "The landlord only got to see how smart you are and he'll pull you in the richest customers from uptown."

Feivel looked at his clothes with resigned contempt. "H—m," he smiled bitterly. "Go in this shabby suit? I have too much respect for myself."

There was troubled silence. Both brother and mother were miserable that their dear one should be so deprived.

Moisheh moved over to the window, a worried look on his face. Presently he turned to his brother. "I'd give you the blood from under my nails for you but I'm yet so behind with the installment man."

The doctor stamped his foot impatiently. "I simply have to have a suit! It's a question of life and death.... Think of the chance! The landlord took a liking to me—rich as Rockefeller—and an only daughter. If he gives me a start in an uptown office I could *coin* money. All I need is a chance—the right location. Ten—twenty—fifty dollars an hour. There's no limit to a dentist's fee. If he sets me up on Riverside Drive I could charge a hundred dollars for work I get five for in Rutgers Street!"

"Can I tear myself in pieces? Squeeze the money from my flesh?"

"But do you realize that, once I get uptown, I could earn more in an hour that you could in a month? I'll pay you back every penny a hundred times over."

"*Nu*—tell me only—what can I do? Anything you'll say—"

"Why—you have your gold watch."

Moisheh's hand leaped to the watch in his vest pocket. "My gold watch! My prize from the night-school?" he pleaded. "It ain't just a watch—it's given me by the principal for never being absent for a whole year."

"Oh, rot!—you, with your sentimentality! Try to understand something once." The doctor waved his objections aside. "Once I get my start in an uptown office I can buy you a dozen watches. I'm telling you my whole future depends on the front I put up at the landlord's house, and still you hesitate!"

Moisheh looked at his watch, fingering it tenderly. "*Oi weh!*" he groaned "It's like a piece from my heart. My prize from the night-school," he mumbled, brokenly; "but take it if you got to have it."

"You'll get it back," confidently promised the doctor, "get it back a hundred times over." And as he slipped the watch into his pocket, Moisheh's eyes followed it doggedly. "So long, *mammeniu;* no dinner for me to-day." Feivel bestowed a hasty good-bye caress upon his old mother.

The doctor was now living in an uptown boarding house, having moved some weeks before, giving the excuse that for his business it was necessary to cultivate an uptown acquaintance. But he still kept up his office in Rutgers Street.

One morning after he had finished treating my teeth, he took up a cigarette, nervously lit it, attempted to smoke, and then threw it away. I had never seen the suave, complacent man so unnerved and fidgety. Abruptly he stopped in front of me and smiled almost affectionately.

"You are the very person I want to speak to this morning—you are the only person I want to speak to," he repeated.

I was a little startled, for this manner was most unlike him. Seldom did he even notice me, just as he did not notice most of Moisheh's friends. But his exuberant joyousness called out my instinctive response, and before I knew it I was saying, "If there's anything I can do for you I'll be only too happy."

He took a bill from his pocket, placed it in my hand, and said, with repressed excitement: "I want you to take my mother and Moisheh to see 'Welcome Stranger.' It's a great show. It's going to be a big night with me, and I want them to be happy, too."

I must have looked puzzled, for he narrowed his eyes and studied me, twice starting to speak, and both times stopping himself.

"You must have thought me a selfish brute all this time," he began.

"But I've only been biding my time. I must make the most of myself, and now is my only chance—to rise in the world."

He stopped again, paced the floor several times, placed a chair before me, and said: "Please sit down. I want to talk to you."

There was a wistful pleading in his voice that none could resist, and for the first time I was aware of the compelling humanness of this arrogant intellectual.

"I'll tell you everything just as it is," he started. And then he stopped again. "*Ach!*" he groaned. "There's something I would like to talk over with you—but I just can't. You wouldn't understand.... A great thing is happening in my life to-night—but I can't confide it to anyone—none can understand. But—I ask of you just this: Will you give Moisheh and my mother a good time? Let the poor devils enjoy themselves for once!"

As I walked out of the office, the bill still crumpled in my hand, I reproached myself for my former harsh condemnation of the doctor. Perhaps all those months, when I had thought him so brutally selfish, he had been building for the future.

But what was this mysterious good fortune that he could not confide to anyone—and that none could understand?

"Doctor Feivel gave me money to take you to the theater," I announced as I entered the house.

"Theater!" chorused Moisheh and his mother, excitedly.

"Yes," I said. "Feivel seemed so happy to-day, and he wanted you to share his happiness."

"Feivel, the golden heart!" The old mother's eyes were misty with emotion.

"*Ach!* Didn't I tell you even if my brother is high-educated, he won't shame himself from us?" Moisheh faced me triumphantly. "I was so afraid since he moved himself into an uptown boarding-house that maybe we are losing him, even though he still kept up his office on Rutgers Street." Moisheh's eyes shone with delight.

"I'll tell you a little secret," said he, leaning forward confidentially. "I'm planning to give a surprise to Feivel. In another month I'll pay myself out for the last of Feivel's office things. And for days and nights I'm going around thinking and dreaming about buying him an electric sign. Already I made the price with the installment man for it." By this time his recital was ecstatic. "And think only—what *mein* doctor will say, when he'll come one morning from his uptown boarding-house and find my grand surprise waiting for him over his office-door!"

All the way to the theater Moisheh and his mother drank in the glamour and the glitter of the electric signs of Broadway.

"*Gottuniu!* If I only had the money for such a sign for Feivel," Moisheh sighed, pointing to the chewing-gum advertisement on the roof of a building near the Astor. "If I only had Rockefeller's money. I'd light up America with Feivel's doctor-sign!"

When we reached the theater, we found we had come almost an hour too early.

"Never mind—*mammeniu!*" Moisheh took his mother's arm tenderly. "We'll have time now to walk ourselves along and see the riches and lights from America."

"I should live so," he said, surveying his mother affectionately. "That red velvet waist and this new shawl over your head makes your face so shine, everybody stops to give a look on you."

"Yeh—yeh! You're always saying love words to every woman you see."

"But this time it's my mother, so I mean it from my heart."

Moisheh nudged me confidentially. "*Teacherin!* See only how a little holiday lifts up my *mammeniu!* Don't it dance from her eyes the joy like from a young girl?"

"Stop already making fun from your old mother."

"You old?" Moisheh put his strong arm around his mother's waist. "Why, people think we're a young couple on our honeymoon."

"Honeymoon—*ach!*" The faded face shone with inward visioning. "My only wish is to see for my eyes my sons marry themselves in good luck. What's my life—but only the little hope from my children? To dance with the bride on my son's wedding will make me the happiest mother from America."

"Feivel will soon give you that happiness," responded Moisheh. "You know how the richest American-born girls are trying to catch on to him. And no matter how grand the girl he'll marry himself to, you'll have the first place of honor by the wedding."

As we turned in at Forty-Fifth Street a curious crowd blocked our path. A row of sleek limousines stood before the arched entrance of the Van Suydden Hotel.

"Look only—a wedding! Let's give a look on the bride!" exclaimed Moisheh's mother, eagerly. A wedding was, in her religion, the most significant ceremony in life. And for her sake we elbowed our way toward the front.

A procession of bridesmaids in shimmering chiffons, bedecked with flowers, were the first to tread the carpeted steps.

Then we saw the bride...And then—Good God!—was it possible?

Moisheh clutched his mother's hand convulsively. Could it really be their Feivel?

The two stood gaping blindly, paralyzed by the scene before them.

Suddenly—roused by the terrible betrayal—the mother uttered a distorted sob of grief. "Feivel—son *mein!* What have you done to me?"

Moisheh grasped the old woman more firmly as the bride tossed her head and turned possessive eyes on her husband—their son and brother.

The onlookers murmured appreciatively, thrilled by the pretty romance.

Enraged by the stupid joy of the crowd which mocked her misery, the old mother broke from Moisheh's hold with wiry strength and clawed wildly at the people around her.

"Feivel—black curses—!" she hissed—and then she crumpled, fainting, into Moisheh's arms.

Unaware of the disturbance outside, the happy couple passed into the festive reception-hall.

With quick self-control, Moisheh motioned to a taxicab out of which had just emerged another wedding-guest. Then he gently lifted the fainting form of the little mother in beside him.

And all through the night the bitter tears of betrayed motherhood poured over the shrunken bosom where Feivel, as a suckling infant, had once helped himself to life.

A Bed for the Night

A drizzling rain had begun to fall. I was wet and chilled to the bone. I had just left the free ward of a hospital where I had been taken when ill with the flu. It was good to be home again! Even though what I called home were but the dim, narrow halls of a rooming-house. With a sigh of relief I dropped my suit-case in the vestibule.

As the door swung open, the landlady met me with: "Your room is taken. Your things are in the cellar."

"My room?" I stammered, white with fear. "Oh no—please Mrs. Pelz!"

"I got a chance to rent your room at such a good price, I couldn't afford to hold it."

"But you promised to keep it for me while I was away. And I paid you for it—"

"The landlord raised me my rent and I got to get it out from the roomers," she defended. "I got four hungry mouths to feed—"

"But maybe I would have paid you a little more," I pleaded, "if you had only told me. I have to go back to work to-day. How can I get another room at a moment's notice?"

"We all got to look out for ourselves. I am getting more than twice as much as you paid me from this new lodger," she finished triumphantly. "And no housekeeping privileges."

"You must give me time!" My voice rose into a shriek. "You can't put a girl out into the street at a moment's notice. There are laws in America—"

"There are no laws for roomers."

"No law for roomers?" All my weakness and helplessness rushed out of me in a fury of rebellion. *"No law for roomers?"*

"I could have put your things out in the street when your week was up. But being you were sick, I was kind enough to keep them in the cellar. But your room is taken." She said with finality. "I got to let my rooms to them as pay the most. I got to feed my own children first. I can't carry the whole world on my back."

I tried to speak. But no voice came to my lips. I felt struck with a club on the head. I could only stare at her. And I must have been staring for some time without seeing her for I had not noticed she had gone till I heard a voice from the upper stairs, "Are you still there?"

"Oh—yes—yes—I—I—am—going—going." I tried to rouse my stunned senses which seemed struck to the earth.

"There's no money in letting rooms to girls," my landlady continued, as she came down to open the door for me. "They're always cooking, or washing, or ironing and using out my gas. This new roomer I never hear nor see except in the morning when he goes to work and at night when he comes to sleep."

I staggered out in a bewildered daze. I leaned against the cold iron lamp-post. It seemed so kind, so warm. Even the chill, drizzling rain beating on my face was almost human. Slowly, my numbed brain began to recollect where I was. Where should I turn? To whom? I faced an endless maze of endless streets. All about me strangers—seas of jostling strangers. I was alone—shelterless!

All that I had suffered in rooming-houses, rushed over me. I had never really lived or breathed like a free, human being. My closed door assured me no privacy. I lived in constant dread of any moment being pounced upon by my landlady for daring to be alive. I dared not hang out my clothes on a line in the fresh air. I was forced to wash and dry them stealthily at night, over chairs and on my trunk. I was under the same restraint when I did my simple cooking although I paid dearly for the gas I used.

This ceaseless strain of don't move here and don't step there, was far from my idea of home. But still it was shelter from the streets. I had become almost used to it. I had almost learned not to be crushed by it. Now, I was shut out—kicked out like a homeless dog.

All thoughts of reporting at my office left my mind. I walked and walked, driven by despair. Tears pressed in my throat, but my eyes were dry as sand.

I tried to struggle out of my depression. I looked through the furnished-room sections of the city. There were no cheap rooms to be had. The prices asked for the few left, were ten, twelve, and fifteen dollars a week.

I earn twenty-five dollars a week as a stenographer. I am compelled to dress neatly to hold down my job. And with clothes and food so high, how could I possibly pay more than one third of my salary for rent?

In my darkness I saw a light—a vision of the Settlement. As an immigrant I had joined one of the social clubs there and I remembered there was a residence somewhere in that building for the workers. Surely they would take me in till I had found a place where I could live.

"I'm in such trouble!" I stammered, as I entered the office of the head resident. "My landlady put me out because I couldn't pay the raise in rent."

"The housing problem is appalling," Miss Ward agreed, with her usual professional friendliness. "I wish I could let you stay with us, my child, but our place is only for social workers."

"Where should I go?" I struggled to keep back my tears. "I'm so terribly alone."

"Now—now, dear child," Miss Ward patted my shoulder encouragingly. "You mustn't give way like that. Of course I'll give you the addresses of mothers of our neighborhood."

One swift glance at the calm, well-fed face and I felt instantly that Miss Ward had never known the terror of homelessness.

"You know, dear, I want to help you all I can," smiled Miss Ward, trying to be kind, "and I'm always glad when my girls come to me."

"What was the use of my coming to you?" I was in no mood for her make-believe Settlement smile. "If you don't take me in, aren't you pushing me in the street—joining hands with my landlady?"

"Why—my dear!" The mask of smiling kindness dropped from Miss Ward's face. Her voice cooled. "Surely you will find a room in this long list of addresses I am giving you."

I went to a dozen places. It was the same everywhere. No rooms were to be had at the price I could afford.

Crushed again and again, the habit of hope still asserted itself. I suddenly remembered there was one person from whom I was almost sure of getting help—an American woman who had befriended me while still an immigrant in the factory. Her money had made it possible for me to take up the stenographic course. Full of renewed hope I sped along the streets. My buoyant faith ever expectant could think of one outcome only.

Mrs. Olney had just finished dictating to her secretary, when the maid ushered me into the luxurious library.

"How good it is to see you! What can I do for you?" The touch of Mrs. Olney's fine hand, the sound of her lovely voice was like the warming breath of sunshine to a frozen thing. A choking came in my throat. Tears blinded me.

"If it wasn't a case of life and death, I wouldn't have bothered you so early in the morning."

"What's the trouble, my child?" Mrs. Olney was all concern.

"I can't stand it any longer! Get me a place where I can live!" And I told her of my experiences with my landlady and my hopeless room-hunting.

"I have many young friends who are in just your plight," Mrs. Olney consoled, "And I'm sending them all to the Better Housing Bureau."

I felt as though a powerful lamp went out suddenly within my soul. A sharp chill seized me. The chasm that divides those who have and those who have not yawned between us. The face I had loved and worshiped receded and grew dim under my searching gaze.

Here was a childless woman with a house full of rooms to herself. Here was a philanthropist who gave thousands of dollars to help the poor. And here I tried to tell her that I was driven out into the street—shelterless. And her answer to my aching need was "The Better Housing Bureau."

Again I turned to the unfeeling glare of the streets. A terrible loneliness bled in my heart. Such tearing, grinding pain was dragging me to the earth! I could barely hold myself up on my feet. "Ach! Only for a room to rest!" And I staggered like a dizzy drunkard to the Better Housing Bureau.

At the waiting-room I paused in breathless admiration. The soft grays and blues of the walls and hangings, the deep-seated divans, the flowers scattered in effective profusion, soothed and rested me like silent music. Even the smoothly fitting gown of the housing specialist seemed almost part of the color scheme.

As I approached the mahogany desk, I felt shabby—uncomfortable in this flawless atmosphere, but I managed somehow to tell of my need. I had no sooner explained the kind of room I could afford than the lady requested the twenty-five cents registration fee.

"I want to see the room first," I demanded.

"All our applicants pay in advance."

"I have only a two dollar bill and I don't get my pay till Monday."

"Oh, that's all right. I'll change it," she offered obligingly. And she took my one remaining bill.

"Where were you born? What is your religion?"

"I came for a room and not to be inquisitioned," I retorted.

"We are compelled to keep statistics of all our applicants."

Resentfully, I gave her the desired information and with the addresses she had given me, I recommenced my search. At the end of another futile hour of room-hunting there was added to the twenty-five cents registration fee, an expense of fifteen cents for carfare. And I was still homeless.

I had been expecting to hear from my sister who had married a prosperous merchant and whom I hadn't seen for years. In my agitation, I had forgotten to ask for my mail and I went back to see about it. A telegram had come, stating that my sister was staying at the Astor and I was to meet her there for lunch.

I hastened to her. For, although she was now rich and comfortable, I felt that after all she was my sister and she would help me out.

"How shabby you look!" She cast a disapproving glance at me from head to foot. "Couldn't you dress decently to meet me, when you knew I was staying at this fashionable hotel?"

I told her of my plight.

"Why not go to a hotel till you find a suitable room?" she blandly advised.

My laughter sounded unreal so loud it was, as I reminded her, "Before the French Revolution, when starving people came to the queen's palace clamoring for bread, the queen innocently exclaimed, 'Why don't they eat cake?'"

"How disagreeable you are! You think of no one but yourself. I've come here for a little change, to get away from my own troubles and here you come with your hatefulness."

I hadn't known the relief of laughter, but now that I was started I couldn't stop, no more than I could stop staring at her. I tried to associate this new being of silks and jewels with the woman who had worked side by side with me in the factory.

"How you act! I think you're crazy," she admonished and glanced at her wrist-watch. "I'm late for my appointment with the manicurist. I have to have my nails done after this dusty railway trip."

And I had been surprised at the insensate settlement worker, at my uncomprehending American friend who knew not the meaning of want. Yet here was my own sister, my own flesh and blood, reared in the same ghetto, nurtured in the same poverty, ground in the same sweatshop treadmill, and because she had a few years of prosperity, because she ate well and dressed well and was secure, she was deaf to my cry.

Where I could hope for understanding, where I could turn for shelter, where I was to lay my head that very night, I knew not. But this much suddenly came to me, I was due to report for work that day. I was shut out on every side, but there in my office at least, awaited me the warmth and sunshine of an assured welcome. My employer would understand and let me take off the remainder of the day to continue my search.

I found him out and instead, awaiting me, was a pile of mail which he had left word I should attend to. The next hour was torture. My power of concentration had deserted me. I tapped the keys of my typewriter with my fingers, but my brain was torn with worry, my nerves ready to snap. The day was nearly spent. Night was coming on and I had no place to lay my head.

I was finishing the last of the letters when he came. After a friendly greeting, he turned to the letters. I dared not interrupt until the mail was signed.

"Girl! What's wrong? That's not like you!" He stared at me. "There are a dozen mistakes in each letter."

A blur. Everything seemed to twist and turn around me. Red and black spots blinded me. A clenched hand pounded his desk and I heard a voice, that seemed to come from me, screaming like a lunatic. "I have no home—no home—not even a bed for the night!"

Then all I remember is the man's kindly tone as he handed me a glass of water. "Are you feeling better?" he asked.

"My landlady put me out," I said between labored breaths. "Oh-h I'm so lonely! Not a place to lay my head!"

I saw him fumble for his pocketbook and look at me strangely. His burning gaze seemed to strip me naked—pierce me through and through from head to foot. Something hurt so deep I choked with shame. I seized my hat and coat and ran out.

It was getting dark when I reached the entrance of Central Park. Exhausted, I dropped to the nearest bench. I didn't even know I was crying.

"Are you lonely, little one?" A hand slipped around my waist and a dapper, young chap moved closer. "Are you lonely?" he repeated.

I let him talk. I knew he had nothing real to offer, but I was so tired, so ready to drop the burden of my weary body that I had no resistance in me. "There's no place for me," I thought to myself. "Everyone shuts me out. What difference what becomes of me? Who cares?"

My head dropped to his shoulder. And the cry broke from me, "I have no place to sleep in to-night."

"Sleep?" I could feel him draw in his breath and a bloodshot gleam leaped into his eyes. "You should worry. I'll take care of that."

He flashed a roll of bills tauntingly. "How about it, kiddo? Can you change me a twenty-dollar bill?"

As his other hand reached for me, I wrenched loose from him as from the cloying touch of pitch. "I wish I were that kind! I wish I were your kind! But I'm not!"

His hands dropped from the touch of me as though his flesh was scorched and I found I was alone.

I walked again. At the nearest telephone pay station I called up the women's hotels. None had a room left for less than two dollars. My remaining cash was forty cents short. The Better Housing Bureau had robbed me of my last hope of shelter.

I passed Fifth Avenue and Park Avenue mansions. Many were closed, standing empty. I began counting the windows, the rooms. Hundreds and hundreds of empty rooms, hundreds and hundreds of luxuriously furnished homes, and I homeless—shut-out. I felt I was abandoned by God and man and no one cared if I perished or went mad. I had a fresh sense of why the spirit of revolution was abroad in the land.

Blindly I retraced my steps to the park bench. I saw and felt nothing but a devouring sense of fear. It suddenly came over me that I was not living in a world of human beings, but in a jungle of savages who gorged themselves with food, gorged themselves with rooms, while I implored only a bed for the night. And I implored in vain.

I felt the chaos and destruction of the good and the beautiful within me and around me. The sight of people who lived in homes and ate three meals a day filled me with the fury of hate. The wrongs and injustices of the hungry and the homeless of all past ages burst from my soul like the smouldering lava of a blazing volcano. Earthquakes of rebellion raced through my body and brain. I fell prone against the bench and wept not tears, but blood.

"Move along! No loitering here!" The policeman's club tapped me on the shoulder. Then a woman stopped and bent over me.

I couldn't move. I couldn't lift my head.

"Tell your friend to cut out the sob-stuff," the officer continued, flourishing his club authoritatively. "On your way both of youse. Y'know better than to loaf around here, Mag."

The woman put her hand on mine in a friendly, little gesture of protection. "Leave her alone! Can't you see she's all in? I'll take care of her."

Her touch filled me with the warmth of shelter. I didn't know who or what she was but I trusted her.

"Poor kid!—What ails her? It's a rough world all alone."

There was no pity in her tone, but comprehension, fellowship. From childhood I'd had my friendships and many were dear to me. But this woman without a word, without a greeting, had sounded the depths of understanding that I never knew existed. Even as I looked up at her she lifted me from the bench and almost carried me through the arbor of trees to the park entrance. My own mother couldn't have been more gentle. For a moment it seemed to me as if the spirit of my dead mother had risen from her grave in the guise of this unknown friend.

Only once the silence between us was broken. "Down on your luck, kid?" Her grip tightened on my arm. "I've been there myself. I know all about it."

She knew so well, what need had she of answer? The refrain came back to me: "Only themselves understand themselves and the likes of themselves, as souls only understand souls."

In a darkened side street we paused in front of a brownstone house with shutters drawn.

"Here we are! Now for some grub! I'll bet a nickel you ain't ate all day." She vaulted the rickety stairs two at a time and led the way into her little room. With a gay assertiveness she planted me into her one comfortable chair attempting no apology for her poverty—a poverty that winked from every corner and could not be concealed. Flinging off her street clothes she donned a crimson kimona and rummaged through the soap box in which her cooking things were kept. She wrung her hands with despair as if she suffered because she couldn't change herself into food.

Ah! The magic of love! It was only tea and toast and an outer crust of cheese she offered—but she offered it with the bounty of a princess. Only the kind look in her face and the smell of the steaming tray as she handed it to me—and I was filled before I touched the food to my lips. Somehow this woman who had so little had fed me as people with stuffed larders never could.

Under the spell of a hospitality so real that it hurt as divine, beautiful things hurt, I felt ashamed of my hysterical worries. I looked up at her and marveled. She was so full of God-like grace—and so unconscious of it!

Not until she had tucked the covers warmly around me did I realize that I was occupying the only couch she had.

"But where will you sleep?" I questioned.

A funny little laugh broke from her. "I should worry where I sleep."

"It's so snug and comfy," I yawned, my eyes heavy with fatigue. "It's good to take from you—"

"Take? Aw, dry up kid! You ain't taking nothing," she protested, embarrassed. "Tear off some sleep and forget it."

"I'll get close to the wall, and make room for you," I murmured as I dropped off to sleep.

When I woke up I found, to my surprise, the woman was sleeping in a chair with a shawl wrapped around her like a huge statue. The half of the bed which I had left for her had remained untouched.

"You were sleeping so sound, I didn't want to wake you," she said as she hurried to prepare the breakfast.

I rose refreshed, restored—sane. It was more than gratitude that rushed out of my heart to her. I felt I belonged to someone, I had found home at last.

As I was ready to leave for work, I turned to her. "I am coming back to-night," I said.

She fell back of a sudden as if I had struck her. From the quick pain that shone in her face, I knew I had hurt something deep within her. Her eyes met mine in a fixed gaze but she did not see me, but stared through me into the vacancy of space. She seemed to have forgotten my presence and when she spoke her voice was like that of one in a trance. "You don't know what you're asking. I—ain't—no—good."

"You no good? God from the world! Where would I have been without you? Even my own sister shut me out—Of them all, you alone opened the door and spread for me all you had."

"I ain't so stuck on myself as the *good* people, although I was as good as any of them at the start. But the first time I got into trouble, instead of helping me, they gave me the marble stare and the frozen heart and drove me to the bad."

I looked closely at her, at the dyed hair, the rouged lips, the defiant look of the woman driven by the Pharisees from the steps of the temple. Then I saw beneath. It was as though her body dropped away from her and there stood revealed her soul—the sorrows that gave her understanding—the shame and the heart-break that she turned into love.

"What is good or bad?" I challenged. "All I know is that I was hungry and you fed me. Shelterless and you sheltered me. Broken in spirit and you made me whole—"

"That stuff's all right, but you're better off out of here—"

I started toward her in mute protest.

"Don't touch me," she cried. "Can't you see—the smut all over me? Ain't it in my face?"

Her voice broke. And like one possessed of sudden fury, she seized me by the shoulder and shoved me out.

As the door slammed, I heard sobbing—loosened torrents of woe. I sank to my knees. A light not of this earth poured through the door that had shut on me. A holiness enveloped me.

This woman had changed the world for me. I could love the people I had hated yesterday. There was that something new in me, a light that the dingiest rooming-house could not dim, nor all the tyranny of the landlady shut out.

Vague, half-remembered words flashed before me in letters of fire. "Despised and rejected of men"—a woman of sorrows and acquainted with grief.

Dreams and Dollars

Spring was in the air. But such radiant, joyous spring as one coming out of the dark shadows of the Ghetto never could dream. Earth and sky seemed to sing with the joy of an unceasing holiday. Rebecca Yudelson felt as if she had suddenly stepped into fairyland where the shadow of sorrow or sickness, where the black blight of poverty had never been.

An ecstasy of wonder and longing shone from her hungry, young eyes as she gazed at the luxurious dwellings. Such radiance of color! Fruits, flowers, and real orange trees! Beauty and plenty! Each house outshone the other in beauty and plenty.

Fresh from the East Side tenements, worn from the nerve-racking grind of selling ribbons at the Five- and Ten-Cent Store, the residential section of Los Angeles was like a magic world of romance too perfect to be real. She had often seen the Fifth Avenue palaces of the New York millionaires when she had treated herself to a bus ride on a holiday, but nothing she had ever seen before compared with this glowing splendor.

"And in one of these mansions of sunshine and roses my own sister lives!" she breathed. "How could Minnie get used to so much free space and sunshine for every day?"

Ten years since Minnie had left Delancey Street. Ten years' freedom from the black worry for bread. There must have come a new sureness in her step, and new joy in life in her every movement. And to think that Abe Shmukler from cloaks and suits had bought her and brought her to this new world!

Rebecca wondered if her sister ever thought back to Felix Weinberg, the poet, who had loved her and whom she had given up to marry this bank-account man.

With the passionate ardor of adolescence Rebecca had woven an idyl for herself out of her sister's love affair. Felix Weinberg had become for her the symbol of beauty and romance. His voice, his face, the lines he had written to Minnie colored Rebecca's longings and dreams. With the love cadence of the poet's voice still stirring in her heart, she put her finger mechanically on the door-bell.

The door was opened by a trim maid in black whose superior scrutiny left Rebecca speechless.

Her own sister Minnie with a stiff lady for a servant.

"My sister, is she in? I just came from New York."

"Rebecca!" cried a familiar voice, as she was smothered in hungry arms. "*Oi weh!* How many years! You were yet so little then. Now you're a grown-up person." And overcome by the memories of their Ghetto-days together, they sobbed in one another's arms.

Rebecca had been prepared for a change in Minnie. Ten years of plenty. But to think that Abe Shmukler with his cloaks and suits could have blotted out the fine sensitiveness of the sister she had loved and left in its place his own gross imprint! Minnie's thin long fingers were now heavy and weighted with diamonds. The slender lines of her figure had grown bulky with fat.

"And to think that you who used to shine up the street like a princess in your homemades are such a fashion-plate now?" Rebecca laughed reproachfully.

They drew apart and gazed achingly at one another. Rebecca's soul grew faint within her as though her own flesh and blood had grown alien to her. Why couldn't Minnie have lifted Abe to her high thoughts? Why did she let him drag her down to his cloaks and suits—make her a thing of store-bought style?

"Minnie—Minnie!" the younger sister wept, bewildered. "Where have you gone? What have you done with yourself?"

Minnie brushed away her tears and laughed away her sister's reproach. "Did you want me to remain always an East Side *yenteh?*"

Then she hugged the young sister with a fresh burst of affection. "Rebecca, you little witch! All you need is a little style. I'll take you to the best stores, and when I get through with you, no one will guess that you came from Delancey Street."

"You have the same old heart, Minnie, although you shine like a born Mrs. Vanderbilt."

"No wonder you have no luck for a man with those clothes," Minnie harped back to the thing uppermost in her mind.

"But you weren't fixed up in style when Felix Weinberg was so crazy about you."

"Do you ever see him?" came eagerly.

"Yes, I meet him every once in a while, but his thoughts are far away when he talks to me." She paused overcome by a rush of feeling. "Sometimes, in my dreams, I feel myself crying out to him, 'Look at me! Can't you see I'm here?'"

"Don't be a little fool and let yourself fall in love with a poet. He's all right for poetry, but to get married you need a man who can make a living. I sent for you not only because I was lonesome and wanted you near but because I have a man who'll be a great catch for you. He's full of money and crazy to marry himself."

"Aren't there plenty of girls in California for him?"

"But he's like Abe. He wants the plain, settled-down kind."

"Am I the plain, settled-down kind like my sister?" thought Rebecca.

And so the whole afternoon sped by in reminiscence of the past and golden plans for the future. Minnie told with pride that her children were sent to a swell camp where they rubbed sleeves with the millionaire children of California. Abe had sold out the greater share of his cloaks-and-suits business to Moe Mirsky—this very man whom Minnie had picked out for Rebecca.

"And if we have the luck to land him, I'll charge you nothing for the match-making. My commission will be to have you live near me."

Before Rebecca could answer there was a footstep in the outer hall and a hearty voice called, "So your sister has come! No wonder you're not standing by the door waiting to kiss your husband."

Abe Shmukler, fatter and more prosperous than ten years ago, filled the doorway with his bulk. "Now there'll be peace in the house," he exploded, genially. "I've had nothing from my wife but cryings from lonesomeness since I brought her here. You'll have to keep my wife company till we get you a man."

Instinctively Rebecca responded to the fulsomeness of Abe's greeting. His sincerity, his simple joy in welcoming her touched her. She wondered if her sister had been quite fair to this big, happy-hearted man.

And even as she wondered, the vision of Felix Weinberg stood before her. This man of fire and romance and dreams, against Abe Shmukler, was like sunrise and moonrise and song against cloaks and suits. How could any woman who had known the fiery wonder of the poet be content with this tame ox-like husband?

"I've already picked out a man for you, so you can settle near us for good," said Abe giving Rebecca another affectionate hug.

Again her heart warmed to him. He was so well-intentioned, so lovable. The world needed those plain, bread-and-butter men. Their affection-craving natures, their generous instincts kept the home-fire burning.

Abe fulfilled the great essentials of life. He was a good provider, a good husband, a good father, and a genial host. But though he could feed her sister with the fat of the land, what nourishment could this stolid bread-giver provide for the heart, the soul, the mind?

Rebecca's reverie was interrupted by the jangle of the telephone.

"I'll bet it's already that man asking if you arrived." Abe winked at his wife and twitted his sister-in-law under the chin as he picked up the receiver.

"Yes, she's here," Rebecca heard Abe say. And turning to his wife, "Minnie, our friend Moe is coming for dinner."

"Coming right for dinner," cried Minnie. "Quickly we must fix you up. I can't have that man see you looking like a greenhorn just off the ship."

Rebecca surveyed herself critically in the gilt mirror. The excitement of the arrival had brought a faint flush to her cheeks. Her hair had become softer, wavier in the moist California air.

"Why can't I see your Rockefeller prince as I am?" Rebecca was not aware that her charm was enhanced by the very simplicity of her attire. "Is he so high-toned that plain me is not good enough for him?"

Her sister cut short her objections and hurried her upstairs where she tried on one gown after another. But they were all too big.

Then on a sudden thought she snatched a long, filet scarf which she draped loosely around Rebecca's neck.

"Why, you look like a picture for a painter." Even Minnie, accustomed now to the last word in style recognized that the little sister had a charm of personality that needed no store-bought clothes to set it off.

Awaiting them at the foot of the stairs was the smiling Abe. Behind him with one hand grasping the banisters, stood a short, stocky young man. Under his arm he held tightly to his side a heart-shaped box of candy tied with a flowing red ribbon.

"*Nu,* look him over, kid! Ain't he the swellest feller you ever set your eyes on? Ain't you glad you left your ribbon-counter for your California prince?"

Abe's color outshone the red ribbon which tied his box of candy. With a clumsy flourish, he bowed and offered it to the girl. In a panic of confusion, Rebecca let the box slip from her nervous fingers. And Moe stooped jerkily to recover it.

Abe burst into loud laughter.

"Oh! *Shlemiel!*" Minnie cried, shaking him by the arm. "You're a grand brother-in-law." And led the way to the dining-room.

Never had Rebecca seen such a rich spread of luxuries. Roast squabs, a silver platter of *gefüllte fisch,* shimmering cut glass containing chopped chicken livers and spiced jellies. The under-nourished girl saw for the first time a feast of plenty fit for millionaires.

"What's this—a holiday?" she asked, recovering her voice.

"Don't think you're yet in Delancey Street," admonished the host. "In California, the fat of the land is for every day."

As they fell to the food, Rebecca understood the over-fed look of those about her. She wondered if she would have sufficient self-control not to make a pig of herself with such delicious plenty, making the eyes glisten, the mouth water, and the heart glad as with song.

Rebecca, watching Moe as he smacked his lips in enjoyment of every mouthful, understood why he wanted the plain, settled-down kind of girl. A home, a wife, and fat dimpled babies belonged to him as flowers and all green-growing things belong to the earth.

"*Nu,* could you tell on my sister-in-law that she never had meat except on a holiday, the way she eats like a bird?" Abe began anew his raillery. And it was not until after dinner when Minnie dragged her Abe away to a neighbor that Moe and Rebecca had a chance to talk together.

"I got something grand to show you," Moe burst out once the road was clear. Why waste time and words in the slow love-making of cheap-skates who haven't the shekels to show? His money could talk. And he led her out proudly to see his red-lacquered limousine. "Swellest car in the market, and I got it the minute your sister said you were coming."

Rebecca was thrilled with this obvious flattery. It was the first time she had had a man so on his knees to her.

"To-morrow I take you for a ride," he said with the sure tone that came into his voice when he concluded a good sale of cloaks and suits.

She nodded happily as they walked back to the parlor. Moe continued his eager questions: Was she crazy for the movies? Did they have good vaudeville out there on the East Side? Why did she not come sooner to California? His eyes traveled over the girl with thick satisfaction. "How becoming it would be to you, diamonds on your neck!" And he rubbed his palms ecstatically.

It was good to be made love to even though the man was not a poet. Till now she had only eaten out her heart for a look, a word, from Felix Weinberg. What a fool she was not to have come to California a year ago as Minnie had begged her.

"I was so scared I'd be lonesome here, so far away from what I'm used to," she said, with a look that told him that a woman's home is where love is. "Now I wonder how I'll ever be able to go back," she finished softly.

"Go back! You got to stay!" he commanded masterfully.

"And I'll see that you shouldn't be so skinny. You got to eat more," and suiting his action to his word, he forced more candy upon the already over-filled girl.

Then he offered to teach her how to play cards. "Minnie and Abe are such grand poker players," he explained.

"My sister Minnie playing cards?"

"*Shah!* Little Queen, you'll have to learn cards too. There ain't no other pleasure for women here, except cards or the movies or vaudeville, and the bills don't change more than once a week." And he told her that it was the custom in their group to play every night in a different house.

A sudden pity gripped him. He longed to brighten the lonely look of this little greenhorn, put roses into her pale thin cheeks.

"Tell me what is your best pleasure," he asked with the sweeping manner of a Rothschild.

"Ach! How I love music!" The glow of an inner sun lit up her face. "I can't afford a seat in the opera, but even if I have to stand all evening and save the pennies from my mouth, music I've got to have."

"Haw—ha!" He laughed in advance of his own humor. "My sweetest music is the click of the cash-register. The ring of the dollars I make is grander to me than the best songs on the phonograph."

His face became suddenly alive. For the first time she saw Moe galvanized into a man of action, a man of power. The light that burned throughout the ages in the eyes of poets and prophets burned also in the eyes of the traders of her race.

"When I was a little hungry boy in the gutters of the Ghetto, the only songs I heard were the bargaining cries over pennies. Even when I worked myself up to a clothing store in Division Street, they were still tearing my flesh in pieces, squeezing out cheaper, another dime, another nickel from a suit." But the eloquent story of his rise in the world till now, here he was King of Clothing, fell upon deaf ears. Rebecca had ceased to listen.

She saw again their kitchen on Sunday night. Felix Weinberg's pale face under the sputtering gas-jet—her sister leaning eagerly forward, her hand instinctively reaching toward him across the table,—her face alight with the inner radiance that glowed from him like a burning sun. She, Rebecca, close to him, at his feet, all atremble with the nearness of him. The children on his knees, clutching at his neck, peering from behind his shoulder. The eternal cadences of Keats and Shelley, the surging rhythm of their song playing upon their hearts, holding them enthralled with a music that they felt all the more deeply because they did not understand.

Even mother, puttering busily with the pots at the stove, would pause in her work, drawn by the magic of the enraptured group.

"*Nu*, with a clean apron I'm also a person to listen," she said as she tore from her the soiled rag which she wore while working around the stove and reached for a clean blue-checked apron that she wore only for holidays.

"Ah, *Mammeniu!*" Felix would respond. "In honor of this shining beautifulness, I'll read something special for you," and he would open his Browning. At the words Rabbi Ben Ezra, *mammeniu's* sigh was the joy of a child in fairyland.

> "*Grow old along with me. The best of life is yet to be,*
> *The last of life for which the first was made.*"

Then, like a child repeating its well-loved lesson for the hundredth time, "*Nu*, I didn't yet live out my years," she would breathe happily. "It will only begin my real life when my children work themselves up in America."

What matter if they had only potato-soup for supper—only the flavor of fried onions in a little suet to take the place of meat? What matter if the two chairs were patched with boards and the rickety table had for its support a potato barrel? Wonder and beauty filled the room. Voices of poets and prophets of all time were singing in their hearts.

And all that, Minnie had given up. For what? For silver platters with *gefüllte fisch*. For roast squabs. For spiced jellies. And the dollar music from cash-registers.

Yes, Minnie, like this blustering Moe, had worked herself up in America. She had a rich house, a Rolls-Royce car,—a lady servant to wait on her body. But what had happened to her spirit, her soul—the soul that had once been watered and flowered with the love-songs of a poet?

"You see, in California nobody worries for bread," broke in the heavy gutteral voice of Moe Mirsky. "People's only troubles is how to enjoy themselves."

Excited, high-pitched voices from the hallway and Minnie and Abe entered. "So much your sister is crazy for you that she tore herself away from the cards to be with you the first night," said Abe with an inquisitive, quizzical look at the young couple.

"And I was winning at the first shot, too," Minnie added.

"My wife is the best poker player in the bunch," Abe asserted.

"Wait, you'll see Friday night when they come around." And turning back to Moe, "You've got to teach her quick the cards, so she can join the company."

"Cards don't go in her head at all," Moe looked with unconcealed proprietorship at his future wife. "I guess she ain't yet used to a little pleasure. Let's only introduce her to our society and she'll soon learn what it is a good time."

The next few days were spent in a wild orgy of shopping. Not only was Rebecca to be made presentable to the higher society in which generous Abe was anxious she should shine, but Minnie was also preparing herself for a month's vacation in Catalina Islands with some of Abe's new real-estate friends. As Abe's wife it was a matter of business that she should be more richly dressed than the wives of his prosperous competitors.

For the first time in her life Rebecca saw things bought not because they were needed but because they appealed to her sister's insatiate eye.

"When will you ever have enough things," Rebecca remonstrated. "Why are we going from store to store like a couple of drunkards from bar to bar. The more you buy, the more drunk you get to buy more."

"Just only this one dress. That's the newest thing in style and so becoming."

"But you have so much already. Your closet is so stacked full."

"I saw Mrs. Rosenbaum wear something like it. And Abe wouldn't want she should come dressed better than I."

At last Rebecca was to meet her sister's society friends. Although Minnie and Abe despaired of making little Rebecca stylish, they were satisfied by Friday night that at least she could be introduced without her Delancey Street background too evident.

The dining-room table covered with green baize was piled high with pyramids of poker chips. Packs of cards were on the table. A mahogany cellarette laden with Scotch, cognac, bottles of White Rock, and high-ball glasses stood nearby.

Minnie was radiant in a black-and-gold-spangled dress. The shine of Abe's cheeks outdid the diamond that glistened from his shirt front. Moe, who had arrived before the rest of the guests, had brought Rebecca another heart-shaped gift, containing "the most smelly perfume in the whole drug store."

Before the guests arrived, Moe devoted himself to showing Rebecca the sequence of the cards; but, try as she would, she could make no sense out of it.

"It's such a waste of time. It's so foolish, so brainless..."

"Is it foolish, brainless to win five hundred, a thousand in one little night?" cried Moe, the ring of the cash-register in his voice.

"It's not only to win money," broke in Minnie. "Cards are life to me. When I play I get so excited I forget about everything. There's no past—no future—only the now—the life of the game."

"Just the same," put in Abe doggedly, "when you win you're crazy to grab in more, and when you lose, you're crazy to stake it all to win again."

Dimly, Rebecca began to see the lure of gambling. It was as contagious as smallpox. Minnie had caught the poison from Abe and his friends. In a world where there was no music, no books, no spiritual stimulus, where people had nothing but money, what else was there to fill the eternal emptiness but excitement?

The guests arrived. Mrs. Rosenbaum and her husband, the biggest department-store owner of Los Angeles. Mr. and Mrs. Soikolsky, real-estate owners of half of Hollywood. Mr. Einstein, the Tecla of California, whose wife and children had just sailed for the Orient.

As Rebecca was introduced to one solid citizen after another, she was unable to distinguish between them. The repellently prosperous look of the "all-rightnik" stamped them all. The vulgar boastfulness of the man who had forced his way up in the world only to look down with smug superiority upon his own people.

"Always with your thoughts in the air," chuckled Moe, a stubby hand tenderly reaching toward her.

The sad eyes of the little greenhorn stirred vague memories in his heart, warming things welled up in him to say to her, but Abe interrupted by calling the guests to their places. A wave of expectancy swept over the gathering as they elbowed themselves about the table. Eyes sharp. Measuring glances shot from one to the other. A business-like air settled upon the group.

Abe poured a generous drink of whisky for each. "*Nu*, my friends, only get yourself drunk enough, so I can have a chance to win once from you."

A fresh pack of cards was opened. The deal fell to the tight-laced, high-bosomed Mrs. Rosenbaum whose fat fingers flashed with diamonds as she dealt.

"You got to sit here, by me, all evening to bring me luck," Moe whispered in Rebecca's ear, and drew a chair for her alongside of him.

An audible silence pervaded the room. The serious business of the game began. Unconsciously, Rebecca was caught by the contagion of their excitement. She even began to hope that Minnie would win; that she would bring luck to the well-meaning Moe.

"Usual limit, five dollars," Abe declared.

Moe explained that the white chips represented one dollar, the blue two and the red five and the yellow ten.

Slowly the air became filled with smoke and the smell of alcohol. The betting rose higher and higher. Rebecca could stand it no longer and rushed from the room, to the parlor. She looked with sharp distaste at the gaudy furnishings. Till now she had been taken in by the glamour of her sister's wealth. But now, the crowded riches of the place choked her. Who had chosen all this? Her sister or her sister's husband? Here and there was a beautiful pillow or finely woven rug; but its beauty was killed by the loud clash of color, the harsh glare of cheap gilt. Cheapness and showiness stuck like varnish over the costly fabrics of the room. It was a sort of furniture display Rebecca had often seen in department stores. It smelled Cloaks and Suits.

The vivid pale face of the poet with eyes that burned with the fire of beauty gazed accusingly at the rich velvet hangings and over-stuffed furniture that had won Minnie away from him.

How different Minnie's home would have been if she had married the poet! A small room in a tenement. A bare floor. A bare table. A room that lacked beautiful things but was filled with beautiful thoughts. Felix Weinberg's flaming presence, the books he read, the dreams he dreamed, the high thoughts that lit up his face would have filled the poorest room with sunshine. The shrill voices of the dining-room startled her.

"Ach! What's the matter?" Rebecca gasped in a panic. "Are they killing themselves?" and hurried in.

She could hardly distinguish the faces, so thick was the air with smoke and whisky-fumes. The look of wild animals distorted their features. Mrs. Rosenbaum's hair had slipped from its net. Her own sister was flushed, disheveled. Moe's face was set in sullen, bitter lines as he called for more money. A scoffing devil of greed seemed to possess them all. It was bedlam let loose.

"No use showing that you come from Division Street, even if you did lose a couple of hundred," Minnie shrilled savagely at Moe.

"You're worse than that pushcart kike," leered the half-drunken Abe. "What a wife! What a wife! She'd steal the whites out from my eyes. She'd grab the gold out of my teeth."

There followed an avalanche of abuse between her sister, her husband, and the sodden Moe. Rebecca had never heard such language used.

"They're only drunk. They don't know what they're saying," she apologized for them to herself.

Thank God, her mother, her father couldn't see what Cloaks and Suits had made of Minnie! Her own sister a common card-player! Where was that gentle bud of a girl whom Felix had loved? How was that fine spirit of hers lost in this wild lust for excitement? And these people whom she called friends, this very Moe whom she had picked out for her to marry,—what were they? All-rightniks—the curse of their people, the shame of their race, Jews dehumanized, destroyed by their riches. Glutted stomachs—starved souls, escaped from the prison of poverty only to smother themselves in the fleshpots of plenty.

It was toward noon the next day that Minnie with dull, puffy eyes and aching head stumbled into Rebecca's room. The half-filled valise was on the bed, clothes were piled on chairs, and the trunk open as if ready for packing.

"What's this? Are you eloping with Moe?" Minnie was too spent from the night of excitement to be surprised at anything, but a closer look at Rebecca's tear-stained face aroused her from her apathy. "Yok! Can't you speak?" she demanded irritably.

"My God! How can you stand it here—this life of the flesh! What have you here, in this land of plenty, but overeating, oversleeping—"

"Why shouldn't I overeat?" Minnie hurled back. "I was starved enough all my youth. Never knew the taste of meat or milk till I came here. I slaved long enough in the sweatshop. The world owes me a little rest." Her face grew hard with bitter memories. "I don't know how I stood it there, in the dirt of Delancey Street, ten people in three rooms, like herring in a barrel, without a bathtub, without—"

"Marble bathtubs—bathing yourself morning and night don't yet keep your soul alive. How could you have sunk yourself into such drunken card-playing."

"If not for cards I'd be dead from loneliness. Are there any people to talk to here?" She threw out bediamond hands in a gesture of helplessness. "I hate Abe like poison when he's home so much of the time. Cards and clothes help me run away from myself—help me forget my terrible emptiness." Minnie reached out imploringly to her sister. "Here you see how I'm dying before your eyes, and yet you want to leave me."

Rebecca felt herself growing hard and inhuman. Didn't she love her sister enough to respond to her cry of loneliness? But the next moment she knew that though it tore the heart out of her body she could never stand this bloated ease of the flesh into which Minnie was trying to beguile her.

"Would you want me to marry Moe and bury myself alive in cloaks and suits like you? I'd rather starve on dry crusts where life is real, where there's still hope for higher things. It would kill me to stay here another day. Your fine food, your fresh air, your velvet limousine smothers me.... It's all a desert of emptiness painted over with money. Nothing is real. The sky is too blue. The grass is too green. This beauty is all false paint, hiding dry rot. There's only one hope for you. Leave your killing comforts and come with me."

"And what about the children?" Minnie leaped to her feet in quick defense. "I want them to have a chance in life. I couldn't bear to have them go through the misery and dirt that nearly killed me. You're not a mother. You don't know a mother's heart."

"Your mother's heart—it's only selfishness! You're only trying to save yourself the pain of seeing your children go through the struggle that made you what you are. No—" she corrected, "that made you what you once were."

Rebecca towered over her sister like the living spirit of struggle revolting against the deadening inertia of ease.

"What is this chance that you are giving your children? To rub sleeves with millionaire children? Will that feed their hungry young hearts? Fire their spirits for higher things? Children's hands reach out for struggle. Their youth is hungry for hardships, for danger, for the rough fight with life even more than their bodies are hungry for bread."

Minnie looked at her little sister. From where came that fire, that passion? She saw again Felix Weinberg's flaming eyes. She heard again his biting truths, the very cadence of his voice.

Minnie buried her throbbing head in the pillows. As surely as Rebecca sold ribbons over the counter at ten cents a yard, so surely Minnie knew that she had sold her own soul for the luxuries which Abe's money had bought. And now it was out of her power to call this real part of her back. The virus of luxury had eaten into her body and soul till she could no longer exist without it.

"If I could only go back with you," she sobbed impotently, "if I could only go back."

Love and hate tore at Rebecca's heart—love of Minnie and hatred of the fleshpots that were destroying her sister. The days and nights of the journey home were spent in tortured groping for the light. Ach—Sisters! Flesh of one flesh, blood of one blood, aching to help one another in the loneliness of life, yet doomed like strangers to meet only to part again. If she could only talk out her confusion to some one. Felix Weinberg! Now he could make her clear! And suddenly she knew—knew with burning certainty that after ten years of worshiping him at a distance she must come to him face to face. Truth itself was driving her to him.

As she got off the train, her feet instinctively led her to the cellar café on East Broadway, where far into the morning hours Felix Weinberg and his high-thinking friends were to be found. Even before she caught sight of him at a corner table surrounded by his followers, she felt a vast relief. She looked in through the grated window. How different these—her own people—from the dollar-chasers she had just left! The dirt, the very squalor of the place was life to her, as the arrogant cleanliness, the strutting shirt-fronts of Cloaks and Suits had deadened her. Here rags talked high thoughts and world philosophies, like princes at a royal court. Here, only what was in your heart and head counted, not your bank account or the shine of your diamonds.

Even the torn wallpaper in this palace of dreams had a magic all its own. The pictures, the poems, the fragmentary bits of self-expression that were scribbled everywhere were marks of the vivid life that surged about— clamoring to be heard.

She never knew how she got inside, but as in a dream she heard herself talking to him—looking straight into Felix's eyes in a miraculously natural way as if her whole life was but leading up to this grand moment.

The youth who used to light up their little kitchen with his flaming presence was gone. In his place had come a man grown strong with suffering. Fine as silk and strong as steel shone every feature. He was scarred with all the hurts of the world—hurts that lay like whip lashes on the furrows of his face. She felt that nothing would be too small or too big for him to understand.

"Years ago when I was only that big at your feet," Rebecca measured the table height with her hand, "your words were life to me. Now I come three thousand miles to talk my heart out with you." And she told him everything, her doubt of herself, her hard intolerance of the plain bread-and-butter people, her revolt against her own flesh and blood.

His face lit with quick comprehension. He stopped sipping his glass of tea and leaned toward her across the table. With every word, with every gesture, she revealed herself as one of his own kind! This girl of whose existence he had scarcely been aware, all these years, seemed suddenly to have grown up under his very eyes, and he had not seen her till now.

"Don't you see, little heart," he responded warmly, "the dollars are their dreams. They eat the fleshpots with the same passionate intensity that they once fasted in faith on the Day of Atonement. They've been hungry for so many centuries. Let them eat! Give them only a chance for a few generations. They'll find their souls again. The deeper down under the surface you get, the more you see that the dollar-chasers are also pursuing a dream, but their dream is different than ours, that is all."

"Where did you get to feel and know so much?" she breathed adoringly.

He did not answer. But his eyes dwelt on her in ardent reverie, marveling at the gift of the gods that she was. Through unceasing frustration of the things for which he had striven, he had come to a point of understanding the materialists no less than the dreamers. He had learned to forgive even Minnie who had turned from his love for the security of wealth. But here was the glowing innocence of a girl with the heart and brain of a woman—a woman in his own poet's world, one who had rejected the fleshpots of her own free will. It was as if after years of parching thirst, life had suddenly brought him a draught of wine, a heady vintage of youth, of living poetry, of love, perhaps. Straining closer to her, he abandoned himself to the exaltation that swept him and passionately kissed her hand.

"No—no! It was Minnie you always loved," Rebecca gasped, frightened at his ardor.

"Minnie I loved as a dreaming youth, a half-fledged poet," he flashed back at her. "But you—you—!"

She knew now why she had come back home again—back to the naked struggle for bread—back to the crooked, narrow streets filled with shouting children, the haggling pushcarts and bargaining housewives—back to the relentless, penny-pinched poverty—but a poverty rich in romance, in dreams,—rich in its very hunger of unuttered, unsung beauty.

The Lord Giveth

I

One glance at his wife's tight-drawn mouth warned Reb Ravinsky of the torrent of wrath about to burst over his head.

"*Nu*, my bread-giver? Did you bring me the rent?" she hurled at him between clenched teeth.

Reb Ravinsky had promised to borrow money that morning to ward off their impending eviction for unpaid rent, but no sooner had he stepped out of his house than all thought of it fled from his mind. Instinctively, he turned to the synagogue where he had remained all day absorbed in the sacred script. It was easier to pray and soar the heights with the prophets of his race than to wrestle with sordid, earthly cares.

"Holy Jew! Why didn't you stay away a little longer?" She tore at her wig in her fury. "Are you a man like other men? Does your wife or your child lay in your head at all? I got to worry for rent. I got to worry for bread. If you got to eat you eat. If you ain't got to eat you ain't hungry. You fill yourself only with high thoughts. You hold yourself only with God.

Your wife and your child can be thrown in the street to shame and to laughter. But what do you care? You live only for the next world. You got heaven in your head. The rest of your family can rot in hell."

Reb Ravinsky stood mute and helpless under the lash of her tongue. But when she had exhausted her store of abuse, he cast upon her a look of scorn and condemnation.

"*Ishah Rah! Evil woman!*" he turned upon her like an ancient prophet denouncing ungodliness.

"*Ishah Rah!*" he repeated. His voice of icy passion sent shivers up and down her spine.

"*Ishah Rah!*" came for the third time with the mystic solemnity that subdued her instantly into worshipful subjection. "Tear away your man from God! Tear him away from the holy Torah! Lose the one precious thing in life, the one thing that makes a Jew stand out over all other nations of the world, the one thing that the Czar's *pogroms* and all the sufferings and murders of the Jews could not kill in the Jew—the hope for the next world!"

Like a towering spirit of righteousness afire with the word of God he loomed over her.

"I ask you by your conscience, should I give up the real life, the true life, for good eating, good sleeping, for a life in the body like the *Amoratzim* here in America? Should I make from the Torah a pick with which to dig for you the rent?"

Adjusting his velvet skull-cap, the last relic of his rabbinical days, he caught the woman's adoring look. Memories of his past splendor in Russia surged over him. He saw his people coming to him from far and near to learn wisdom from his lips. Drawing himself to his full height, he strode across the room and faced her.

"Why didn't you marry yourself to a tailor, a shoemaker, a thick-head, a money-maker—to a man of the flesh—a rabbi who can sell his religion over the counter as a butcher sells meat?"

Mrs. Ravinsky gazed with fear and contrition at her husband's God-kindled face. She loved him because he was *not* a man of this world. Her darkest moments were lit up with pride in him, with the hope that in the next world the reflected glory of his piety might exalt her.

It wrung her heart to realize that against her will she was dragging him down with her ceaseless demands for bread and rent. *Ach!* Why was there such an evil thing as money in this world? Why did she have to torture her husband with earthly needs when all she longed for was to help him win a higher place in heaven?

Tears fell from her faded eyes. He could have wept with her—it hurt him so to make her suffer. But once and for all he must put a stop to her nagging. He must cast out the evil spirit of worry that possessed her lest it turn and rend him.

"Why are you killing yourself so for this life? *Ut!* See, death is already standing over you. One foot is already in the grave. Do you know what you'll get for making nothing from the Torah! The fires of hell are waiting for you! Wait—wait! I warn you!"

And as if to ward off the evil that threatened his house, he rushed to his shrine of sacred books and pulled from its niche a volume of his beloved Talmud. With reverence he caressed its worn and yellowed pages as he drank in hungrily the inspired words. For a few blessed moments he took refuge from all earthly storms.

II

In Schnipishock, Reb Ravinsky had been a Porush, a pensioned scholar. The Jews of the village so deeply appreciated his learning and piety that they granted him an allowance, so as to free the man of God from all earthly cares.

Arrived in the new world, he soon learned that there was no honored pension forthcoming to free him from the world of the flesh. For a time he eked out a bare living by teaching Hebrew to private scholars. But the opening of the Free Hebrew Schools resulted in the loss of most of his pupils.

He had been chosen by God to spread the light of the Torah—and a living must come to him, somehow, somewhere, if he only served faithfully.

In the meantime, how glorious it was to suffer hunger and want, even shame and derision, yet rise through it all as Job had risen and proclaim to the world: "I know that my Redeemer liveth!"

Reb Ravinsky was roused from his ecstasy by his wife's loud sobbing. Thrust out from the haven of his Torah, he closed the book and began to pace the floor.

"Can fire and water go together? Neither can godliness and an easy life. If you have eyes of flesh and are blind, should I fall into your blindness? You care only for what you can put in your mouth or wear on your back; I struggle for the life that is together with God!"

"My rent—have you my rent? I warned you!" The landlord pushed through the half-open door flaunting his final dispossess notice under Reb Ravinsky's nose. "I got orders to put you out," he gloated, as he motioned to his men to proceed with the eviction.

Reb Ravinsky gripped the back of a chair for support.

"*Oi-i-i!* Black is me! Bitter is me!" groaned his wife, leaning limply against the wall.

For weeks she had been living in momentary dread of this catastrophe. Now, when the burly moving-men actually broke into her home, she surrendered herself to the anguish of utter defeat. She watched them disconnect the rusty stove and carry it into the street. They took the bed, the Passover dishes prayerfully wrapped to avoid the soil of leavened bread. They took the brass samovar and the Sabbath candlesticks. And she stood mutely by—defenseless—impotent!

"What did I sin?" The cry broke from her. "God! God! Is there a God over us and sees all this?"

The men and the things they touched were to Reb Ravinsky's far-seeing eyes as shadows of the substanceless dream of life in the flesh. With vision focussed on the next world, he saw in dim blurs the drama enacted in this world.

Smash to the floor went the sacred Sabbath wine-glass! Reb Ravinsky turned sharply, in time to see a man tumble ruthlessly the sacred Hebrew books to the floor.

A flame of holy wrath leaped from the old man's eyes. His breath came in convulsive gasps as he clutched with emaciated fingers at his heart. The sacrilege of the ruffians! He rushed to pick up the books, kissing each volume with pious reverence. As he gathered them in his trembling arms, he looked about confusedly for a safe hiding-place. In his anxiety for the safety of his holy treasure, he forgot the existence of his wife and ran with his books to the synagogue as one runs from a house on fire. So overwrought was he that he nearly fell over his little daughter running up the stairs.

"Murderer!" screamed Mrs. Ravinsky, after him. "Run, run to the synagogue! Holy Jew! See where your religion has brought us. Run—ask God to pay your rent!"

She turned to her little Rachel who burst into the room terrified.

"See, my heart! See what they've done to us! And your father ran to hide himself in the synagogue. You got no father—nobody to give you bread. A lost orphan you are."

"Will the charity lady have to bring us eating again?" asked Rachel, her eyes dilated with dread. "Wait only till I get old enough to go to the shop and earn money." And she reached up little helpless arms protectingly.

The child's sympathy was as salt on the mother's wounds.

"For what did we come to America?"

The four walls of her broken home stared back their answer.

Only the bundles of bedding remained, which Rachel guarded with fierce defiance as though she would save it from the wreckage.

Pushing the child roughly aside, the man slung it over his shoulder.

Mrs. Ravinsky, with Rachel holding on to her skirts, felt her way after him, down the dark stairway.

"My life! My blood! My featherbed!.. she cried, as he tossed the family heirloom into the gutter. *Gewalt!*" prostrate, she fell on it. "How many winters it took my mother to pick together the feathers! My mother's wedding present...."

III

From the stoops, the alleys, and the doorways, the neighbors gathered. Hanneh Breineh, followed by her clinging brood, pushed through the throng, her red-lidded eyes big with compassion. "Come the while in by me."

She helped the grief-stricken woman to her feet. "We're packed like herring in a barrel, but there's always room for a push-in of a few more."

Lifting the featherbed under her arm she led the way to her house.

"In a few more years your Rachel will be old enough to get her working-papers and all your worries for bread will be over," she encouraged, as she opened the door of her stuffy little rooms.

The commotion on the street corner broke in upon the babble of gossiping women in the butcher shop. Mr. Sopkin paused in cutting the meat.

"Who did they make to move?" he asked, joining the gesticulating mob at the doorway.

"*Oi weh!* Reb Ravinsky?"

"God from the sky! Such a good Jew! Such a light for the world!"

"Home, in Russia, they kissed the ground on which he walked, and in America, they throw him in the street."

"Who cares in America for religion? In America, everybody has his head in his belly."

"Poor little Rachel! Such a smart child! Writes letters for everybody on the block."

"Such a lazy do-nothing! All day in the synagogue!" flung the pawnbroker's wife, a big-bosomed woman, her thick fingers covered with diamonds. "Why don't he go to work in a shop?"

A neighbor turned upon her. "Here! Hear her only! Such a pig-eater! Such a fat-head! She dares take Reb Ravinsky's name in her mouth."

"Who was she from home? A water-carrier's wife, a cook! And in America she makes herself for a person—shines up the street with her diamonds."

"Then leave somebody let know the charities." With a gesture of self-defense, the pawnbroker's wife fingered her gold beads. "I'm a lady-member from the charities."

"The charities? A black year on them!" Came a chorus of angry voices.

"All my enemies should have to go to the charities for help."

"Woe to anyone who falls into the charities' hands!"

"One poor man with a heart can help more than the charities with all their money."

Mr. Sopkin hammered on his chopping-block, his face purple with excitement. "*Weiber!* With talk alone you can't fill up the pot."

"*Takeh! Takeh!*" Eager faces strained forward. "Let's put ourselves together for a collection."

"I'm not yet making Rockefeller's millions from the butcher business, but still, here's my beginning for good luck." And Mr. Sokin tossed a dollar bill into the basket on the counter.

A woman, a ragged shawl over her head, clutched a quarter in her gaunt hand. "God is my witness! To tear out this from my pocket is like tearing off my right hand. I need every cent to keep the breath in the bodies of my *Kinder*, but how can we let such a holy Jew fall in the street?"

"My enemies should have to slave with such bitter sweat for every penny as me." Hanneh Hayyeh flung out her arms still wet with soap-suds and kissed the ten-cent piece she dropped into the collection.

Mr. Sopkin walked to the sidewalk and shook the basket in front of the passers-by. "Take your hand out from your pocket! Take your bite away from your mouth! Who will help the poor if not the poor?"

A shower of coins came pouring in. It seemed not money—but the flesh and blood of the people—each coin a part of a living heart.

The pawnbroker's wife, shamed by the surging generosity of the crowd, grudgingly peeled a dollar from the roll of bills in her stocking and started to put it into the collection.

A dozen hands lifted in protest.

"No—no! Your money and our money can't mix together!"

"Our money is us—our bodies! Yours is the profits from the pawnshop! Hold your *trefah* dollar for the charities!"

IV

Only when the Shammes, the caretaker of the synagogue, rattling his keys, shook Reb Ravinsky gently and reminded him that it was past closing time did he remember that somewhere waiting for him—perhaps in the street— were his wife and child.

The happening of the day had only deepened the intensity with which he clung to God and His Torah. His lips still moved in habitual prayer as with the guidance of neighbors he sought the new flat which had been rented for a month with the collection money.

Bread, butter, milk, and eggs greeted his gaze as he opened the door.

"*Nu,* my wife? Is there a God over us?" His face kindled with guileless faith. "The God that feeds the little fishes in the sea and the birds in the air, has he not fed us? You see, the Highest One takes care of our earthly needs. Our only business here is to pray for holiness to see His light!"

A cloud of gloom stared up at him out of his wife's darkening eyes. "Why are you still so black with worry?" he admonished. "If you would only trust yourself on God, all good would come to us yet."

"On my enemies should fall the good that has come to us," groaned Mrs. Ravinsky. "Better already death than to be helped again by the pity from kind people."

"What difference how the help comes, so long we can keep up our souls to praise God for His mercy on us?"

Despair was in the look she fixed upon her husband's lofty brow—a brow untouched by time or care—smooth, calm, and seamless as a child's. "No wonder people think that I'm your mother. The years make you younger. You got no blood in your body—no feelings in your heart. I got to close my eyes with shame to pass in the street the people who helped me, while you—you—shame can not shame you—poverty can not crush you—"

"Poverty? It stands in the Talmud that poverty is an ornament on a Jew like a red ribbon on a white horse. Those whom God chooses for His next world can't have it good here."

"Stop feeding me with the next world!" she flung at him in her exasperation. "Give me something on this world."

"Wait only till our American daughter will grow up. That child has my head on her," he boasted with a father's pride. "Wait only, you'll see the world will ring from her yet. With the Hebrew learning I gave her, she'll shine out from all other American children."

"But how will she be able to lift her head with other people alike if you depend yourself on the charities?"

"Woman! Worry yourself not for our Rachel! It stands in the Holy Book, the world is a wheel, always turning. Those who are rich get poor; if not they, then their children or children's children. And those who are poor like us, go up higher and higher. Our daughter will yet be so rich, she'll give away money to the charities that helped us. Isaiah said—"

"Enough—enough!" broke in Mrs. Ravinsky, thrilled in spite of herself by the prophecies of her holy man. "I know already all your smartness. Go, go, sit yourself down and eat something. You fasted all day."

V

Mrs. Ravinsky hoarded for her husband and child the groceries the neighbors had donated. For herself, she allowed only the left-overs, the crumbs, and crusts.

The following noon, after finishing her meager meal, she still felt the habitual gnawing of her undernourished body, so she took a sour pickle and cut off another slice of bread from the dwindling loaf. But this morsel only sharpened her craving for more food.

The lingering savor of the butter and eggs which she had saved for her family tantalized her starved nerves. Faint and weak from the struggle to repress her hunger, she grew reckless and for once in her life abandoned herself to the gluttonous indulgence of the best in her scant larder.

With shaking hand, she stealthily opened the cupboard, pilfered a knife-load of butter and spread it thickly on a second slice of bread. Cramming the whole into her mouth, she snatched two eggs and broke them into the frying pan. The smell of the sizzling eggs filled the air with the sweet fragrance of the Sabbath. "*Ach!* How the sun would shine in my heart if I could only allow myself the bite in my mouth!"

Memories of *gefüllte fisch* and the odor of freshly-baked *Apfel Strudel* dilated her nostrils. She saw herself back in Russia setting the Sabbath table when he was the honored wife of Reb Ravinsky.

The sudden holiday feeling that thrilled her senses smote her conscience. "*Oi weh!* Sinner that I am! Why should it will itself in me to eat like a person when my man don't earn enough for dry bread? What will we do when this is used up? Suppose the charities should catch me feasting myself with such a full hand?"

Bent ravenously over the eggs—one eye on the door—she lifted the first spoonful to her watering mouth as Rachel flew in, eyes wide with excitement.

"Mamma! The charity lady is coming! She's asking the fish-peddler on the stoop where we live now."

"Quick! Hide the frying-pan in the oven. Woe is me! The house not swept—dishes not washed—everything thrown around! Rachel! Quick only—sweep together the dirt in a corner. Throw those rags under the bed! *Oi weh*—quick—hide all those dirty things behind the trunk!"

In her haste to tidy up, she remembered the food in the cupboard. She stuffed it—broken egg-shells and all—into the bureau drawer. "*Oi weh!* The charity lady should only not catch us with all these holiday eatings. . . ."

VI

Footsteps in the hallway and Miss Naughton's cheery voice: "Here I am, Mrs. Ravinsky! What can I do to help now?"

With the trained eye of the investigator, she took in the wretched furniture, scant bedding, the undernourished mother and child.

"What seems to be wrong?" Miss Naughton drew up a three-legged stool. "Won't you tell me so we can get at the root of the trouble? She put her hand on the woman's apron with a friendly little gesture.

Mrs. Ravinsky bit her lips to force back the choking pressure of tears. The life, the buoyancy, the very kindness of the "charity lady" stabbed deeper the barb of her wretchedness.

"Woe is me! On all my enemies my black heart! So many babies and young people die every day, but no death comes to hide me from my shame."

"Don't give way like that," pleaded Miss Naughton, pained by the bitterness that she tried in vain to understand. "If you will only tell me a few things so I may the better know how to help you."

"Again tear me in pieces with questions?" Mrs. Ravinsky pulled at the shrunken skin of her neck.

"I don't like to pry into your personal affairs, but if you only knew how often we're imposed upon. Last week we had a case of a woman who asked us to pay her rent. When I called to investigate, I found her cooking chicken for dinner!"

The cot on which Mrs. Ravinsky sat creaked under her swaying body.

"You see, we have only a small amount of money," went on the unconscious inquisitor, "and it is but fair it should go to the most deserving cases."

Entering a few preliminary notes, Miss Naughton looked up inquiringly. "Where is Mr. Ravinsky?"

"In the synagogue."

"Has he no work?"

"He can't do no work. His head is on the next world."

Miss Naughton frowned. She was accustomed to this kind of excuse. "People who are not lazy can always find employment."

Seeing Mrs. Ravinsky' sudden pallor, she added kindly: "You have not eaten to-day. Is there no food in the house?"

Mrs. Ravinsky staggered blindly to her feet. "No—nothing—I didn't yet eat nothing."

The brooding gray of Rachel's eyes darkened with shame as she clutched protectingly at her mother's apron. The uncanny, old look of the solemn little face seemed to brush against Miss Naughton's very heartstrings—to reproach the rich vigor of her own glowing youth.

"Have you had any lunch, dear?" The "charity lady's" hand rested softly on the tangled mat of hair.

"No—nothing—nothing," the child echoed her mother's words.

Miss Naughton rose abruptly. She dared not let her feelings get the best of her. "I am going to get some groceries." She sought for an excuse to get away for a moment from the misery that overwhelmed her. "I'll be back soon."

"Bitter is me!" wailed Mrs. Ravinsky, as the "charity lady" left the room. "I can never lift up my head with other people alike. I feel myself lower than a thief, just because I got a husband who holds himself with God all day."

She cracked the knuckles of her bony fingers. "*Gottuniu!* Listen better to my prayer! Send on him only a quick death. Maybe if I was a widow, people would take pity on me and save me from this gehenna of charity."

VII

Ten minutes later, Miss Naughton returned with a bag of supplies. "I am going to fix some lunch for you." She measured cocoa into a battered saucepan. "And soon the boy will come with enough groceries for the whole week."

"Please, please," begged Mrs. Ravinsky. "I can't eat now—I can't—."

"But the child? She needs nutritious food at once."

Rachel's sunken little chest rose and fell with her frightened heart-beat, as she hid her face in her mother's lap.

"Small as she is, she already feels how it hurts to swallow charity eating," defended Mrs. Ravinsky.

Miss Naughton could understand the woman's dislike of accepting charity. She had coped with this pride of the poor before. But she had no sympathy with this mother who fostered resentment in her child toward the help that was so urgently needed. Miss Naughton's long-suffering patience broke. She turned from the stove and resolutely continued her questioning.

"Has your husband tried our employment bureau?"

"No."

"Then send him to our office to-morrow at nine. He can be a janitor—or a porter—"

"My man? My man a janitor or a porter?" Her eyes flamed. "Do you know who was my man in Russia? The fat of the land they brought him just for the pleasure to listen to his learning. Barrels full of meat, pots full of chicken-fat stood packed in my cellar. I used to make boilers of jelly at a time. The *gefüllte fisch* only I gave away is more than the charities give out to the poor in a month."

Miss Naughton could not suppress a smile. "Why did you leave it then, if it was all so perfect?"

"My *gefüllte fisch!* Oi-i-i! Oi-i!! My *Apfel Strudel*—my beautiful *Apfel Strudel!*" she kept repeating, unable to tear herself away from the dream of the past.

"Can you live on the *Apfel Strudel* you had in Russia? In America, a man must work to support his family—"

"All thick-heads support their families," defended Reb Ravinsky's wife. "Any fat-belly can make money. My man is a light for the world. He works for God who feeds even the worms under the stone."

"You send your husband to my office. I want to have a talk with him."

"To your office? *Gottuniu!* He won't go. In Schnipishock they came to him from the four ends of the world. The whole town blessed itself with his religiousness."

"The first principle of religion is for a man to provide for his family. You must do exactly as we say—or we can not help you."

"Please, please." Mrs. Ravinsky entreated, cringing and begging. "We got no help from nobody now but you. I'll bring him to your office to-morrow."

The investigator now proceeded with the irksome duty of her more formal questions. "How much rent do you pay? Do you keep any boarders? Does your husband belong to any society or lodge? Have you relatives who are able to help you?"

"*Oi-i-i!* What more do you want from me?" shrieked the distracted woman.

Having completed her questions, Miss Naughton looked about the room. "I am sorry to speak of it, but why is your flat in such disorder?"

"I only moved in yesterday. I didn't get yet time to fix it up."

"But it was just as bad in the last place. If you want our help you must do your part. Soap and water are cheap. Anyone can be clean."

The woman's knees gave way under her, as Miss Naughton lifted the lids from the pots on the stove.

And then—*gewalt!* It grew black before Mrs. Ravinsky's eyes. She collapsed into a pathetic heap to the floor. The "charity lady" opened the oven door and exposed the tell-tale frying pan and the two eggs!

Eyes of silent condemnation scorched through the terror-stricken creature whose teeth chattered in a vain struggle to defend herself. But no voice came from her tortured throat. She could only clutch at her child in a panic of helplessness.

Without a word, the investigator began to search through every nook and corner and at last she came to the bureau drawer and found butter, eggs, cheese, bread, and even a jar of jelly.

"For shame!" broke from the wounded heart of the betrayed Miss Naughton. "You—you ask for charity!"

VIII

In the hall below, Reb Ravinsky, returning from the synagogue, encountered a delivery boy.

"Where live the Ravinskys?" the lad questioned.

"I'm Reb Ravinsky," he said, leading the way, as he saw the box of groceries.

Followed by the boy, Reb Ravinsky flung open the door and strode joyfully into the room. "Look only! How the manna is falling from the sky!"

Ignoring Reb Ravinsky, Miss Naughton motioned to the box. "Take those things right back," she commanded the boy.

"How you took me in with your hungry look!" There was more of sorrow than scorn in her voice. "Even teaching your child to lie—and your husband a rabbi!—a religious man—too holy to work! What would be left for deserving cases, if we allowed such as you to defraud legitimate charity?"

With bowed head, Reb Ravinsky closed the door after the departing visitor. The upbraidings of the woman were like a whip-lash on his naked flesh. His heart ached for his helpless family. Darkness suffocated him.

"My hungry little lamb," wailed his wife, clinging to Rachel. "Where now can we turn for bread?"

Compassionate hands reached out in prayer over the grief-stricken mother and child. Reb Ravinsky stood again as he did before his flight to America, facing his sorrowing people. His wife's wailing for their lost store of bread brought back to him the bereaved survivors of the *pogrom*—the *pogrom* that snatched away their sons and daughters. Afire with the faith of his race, he chanted the age-old consolation. "The Lord giveth; the Lord taketh away. Blessed be the name of the Lord."

The Song Triumphant

I

"**W**here went your week's wages?" demanded Hanneh Breineh, her bony back humping like an angry cat's as she bent over the wash-tub.

Terrified, Moisheh gazed wildly at the ceiling, then dropped his eyes to the floor.

"Your whole week's wages—where went it?" insisted Hanneh.

She turned from the tub and shook her hands in his face.

"The shoes—Berel's shoes," Moisheh stumblingly explained. "I—I had to buy him shoes for his feet—not new shoes—only second-hand."

"Shoes yet for such a loafer? I'd drive him out naked—barefoot. Let him get the chills—the fever—only to get rid from him quick!"

None of the roomers of Hanneh Breineh's lodging-house could escape her tyrannous inquisition. Had she not been a second mother to Moisheh, the pants-presser, and to Berel, his younger brother? Did she not cook their supper for them every night, without any extra charge? In return for this motherly service she demanded a precise account of their expenditures of money or time, and of every little personal detail of their lives.

Red glints shot from Hanneh Breineh's sunken eyes.

"And for what more did you waste out my rent-money?"

"Books—he got to have 'em—more'n eating—more'n life!"

"Got to have books?" she shrieked. "Beggars—*Schnorrers*—their rent not paid—their clothes falling from them in rags—and yet they buy themselves books!" Viciously slapping the board with the shirt she had been rubbing, she straightened and faced Moisheh menacingly. "I been too good to you. I cooked and washed for you, and killed myself away to help you for nothing. So that's my thanks!"

The door opened. A lean youth with shining eyes and a disheveled mass of black hair rushed in.

"*Ach*, Moisheh! Already back from the shop? My good luck—I'm choking to tell you!"

The two drab figures huddled in the dim kitchen between the wash-tub and the stove gazed speechless at the boy. Even Hanneh Breineh was galvanized for the moment by the ecstatic, guileless face, the erect, live figure poised birdlike with desire.

"*Oi*, golden heart!" The boy grasped Moisheh's arm impetuously. "A typewriter! It's worth fifty dollars—maybe more yet—and I can get it for ten, if I grab it quick for cash!"

Moisheh glanced from the glowering landlady to his ardent brother. His gentle heart sank as he looked into Berel's face, with its undoubting confidence that so reasonable a want would not be denied him.

"Don't you think—maybe—ain't there something you could do to earn the money?"

"What more can I do than I'm already doing? You think only pressing pants is work?"

"Berel," said Moisheh, with frank downrightness, "you got your education. Why don't you take up a night-school? They're looking for teachers."

"Me a teacher? Me in that treadmill of deadness? Why, the dullest hand in a shop got more chance to use his brains than a teacher in their schools!"

"Well, then, go to work in a shop—only half days—the rest of the time give yourself over to your dreams in the air."

"Brother, are you gone crazy?" Berel gesticulated wildly. "I should go into that terrible sweat and grind of the machines? All the fire that creates in me would die in a day!"

The poet looked at the toil-scarred face of his peasant brother. For all his crude attempts at sympathy, how could he, with the stink of steam soaked into his clothes, with his poverty-crushed, sweatshop mind—how could he understand the anguish of thwarted creation, of high-hearted hopes that died unvoiced?

"But everybody got to work," Moisheh went on. "All your poetry is grand, but it don't pay nothing."

"Is my heart cry nothing, then? Nothing to struggle by day and by night for the right word in this strange English, till I bleed away from the torture of thoughts that can't come out?"

Berel stopped, and his eyes seemed transfigured with an inner light. His voice grew low and tense. Each word came deliberately, with the precision he used when swayed by poetic feeling.

"*Ach*, if I could only tell you of the visions that come to me! They flash like burning rockets over the city by night. Lips, eyes, a smile—they whisper to me a thousand secrets. The feelings that leap in my heart are like rainbow-colored playthings. I toss them and wrestle with them; and yet I must harness them. Only then can they utter the truth, when they are clear and simple so that a child could understand."

Turning swiftly, the words hissed from the poet's lips.

"Why do I have to bite the dirt for every little crumb you give me? I, who give my life, the beat of my heart, the blood of my veins, to bring beauty into the world—why do I have to beg—beg!"

He buried his face in his hands, utterly overcome.

Moisheh, with an accusing glance at Hanneh Breineh, as if she was in some measure to blame for this painful outburst, soothed the trembling Berel as one would a child.

"*Shah!*" He took from his pocket all his money. "Two dollars is all I yet got left, and on this I must stick out till my wages next Monday. But here, Berel, take half."

Shamed by Moisheh's generosity, and embittered by the inadequacy of the sum, Berel's mood of passionate pleading gave way to sullenness.

"Keep it!" he flung over his shoulder, and left the room.

II

Berel's thoughts surged wildly as he raced through the streets.

"Why am I damned and despised by them all? What is my crime? That I can't compromise? That I fight with the last breath to do my work—the work for which I was born?"

Instinctively his feet led him to the public library, his one sanctuary of escape from the sordidness of the world. But now there seemed no peace for him even here.

"Money—money!" kept pounding and hammering in his ears. "Get money or be blotted out!"

A tap on his shoulder. Berel turned and looked into a genial face, sleeked and barbered into the latest mold of fashion.

"Jake Shapiro!" cried the poet.

Five years ago these two had met on the ship bound for America. What dreams they had dreamed together on that voyage—Berel Pinsky, the poet, and Shapiro, the musician!

"What are you doing for a living? Still writing poetry?" asked Shapiro, as he glanced appraisingly at the haggard-eyed youth. In one swift look he took in the shabby garments that covered the thin body, the pride and the eagerness of the pale, hungry face. "I guess," added the musician, "your poetry ain't a very paying proposition!"

Incensed at the unconscious gibe, Berel turned with a supercilious curl of his lips.

"What's a sport like you doing here in the library?"

Shapiro pointed to a big pile of books from the copyright office.

"Chasing song titles," he said. "I'm a melody writer. I got some wonderful tunes, and I thought I'd get a suggestion for a theme from these catalogs."

"*Oi weh*, if for ideas you have to go to copyright catalogs!"

"Man, you should see the bunch of lyric plumbers I have to work with. They give me jingles and rimes, but nothing with a real heart thrill." He turned on Berel with sudden interest. "Show us some of your soul stuff."

Berel handed several pages to the composer. One after another, Shapiro read.

"High-brow—over the heads of the crowd," was his invariable comment.

Suddenly he stopped.

"By heck, there's a good idea for a sob song! What a title—'Aching Hearts'!" He grasped Berel's hand with genuine friendliness. "Your lines have the swing I've been looking for. Only a little more zip, a change here and there, and—"

"Change this?" Berel snatched the verses and put them back in his pocket. "There's my heart's blood in every letter of it!"

"Yes, it's heart stuff all right," placated the composer, realizing a good thing, and impatient as a hound on the scent. "Come along!" He took Berel by the arm. "I want to read your sob stuff to a little friend."

Flattered, but vaguely apprehensive, Berel followed Shapiro to the delectable locality known as Tin Pan Alley, and into the inner shrine of one of the many song houses to be found there.

"Maizie!" cried Shapiro to a vaudeville star who had been waiting none too patiently for his return. "I've found an honest-to-God poet!"

He introduced Berel, who blushed like a shy young girl.

"So you're a poet?" said Maizie.

Her eyes were pools of dancing lights as she laughed, aware of her effect on the transfixed youth. Berel stared in dazzled wonder at the sudden apparition of loveliness, of joy, of life. Soft, feminine perfume enveloped his senses. Like a narcotic, it stole over him. It was the first time he had ever been touched by the seductive lure of woman.

Shapiro sat down at a piano, and his hands brought from the tortured instrument a smashing medley of syncopated tunes.

"This needs lyric stuff with a heartbeat in it," he flung over his shoulder; "and you have just the dope."

His eyes met Maizie's significantly, and then veered almost imperceptibly in the direction of Berel.

"Go ahead, kid—vamp him! We've got to have him," was the message they conveyed to her.

Maizie put her hand prettily on the youth's arm.

"With an air like that, and the right lines—oh, boy, I'd flood Broadway with tears!"

Berel stood bewildered under the spell of her showy beauty. Unconsciously his hand went to his pocket, where lay his precious verses.

"I—I can't change my lines for the mob," he stammered.

But Maizie's little hand crept down his arm until it, too reached his pocket, while her face was raised alluringly to his.

"Let's see it, Mr. Poet—do, please!"

Suddenly, with a triumphant ripple of laughter, she snatched the pages and glanced rapidly through the song. Then, with her highly manicured fingers, she grasped the lapels of Berel's coat, her eyes dancing with a coquettish little twinkle.

"It's wonderful!" she flattered. "Just give me the chance to put it over, and all the skirts from here to Denver will be singing it!"

Shapiro placed himself in front of Berel and said with businesslike directness:

"I'll advance you two hundred bucks on this song, if you'll put a kick in it."

Two hundred dollars! The suddenness of the overwhelming offer left Berel stunned and speechless.

"Money—*ach*, money! To get a breath of release from want!" he thought. "Just a few weeks away from Hanneh Breineh's cursing and swearing! A chance to be quiet and alone—a place where I can have a little beauty!"

Shapiro, through narrowed lids, watched the struggle that was going on in the boy. He called for his secretary.

"Write out a contract," he ordered. "Words by Berel Pinsky—my melody."

Then he turned to the poet, who stood nervously biting his lips.

"If this song goes over, it'll mean a big piece of change for you. You get a cent and a half on every copy. A hit sometimes goes a million copies. Figure it out for yourself. I'm not counting the mechanical end of it— phonograph records—pianola rolls—hurdy-gurdies."

At the word "hurdy-gurdy" an aching fear shot through the poet's heart. His pale face grew paler as he met the smooth smile of the composer.

"Only to get a start," he told himself, strengthening his resolve to sell his poem with an equal resolve never to do so again.

"Well?" chuckled Shapiro.

He drew out a thick wallet from his pocket, and began counting out the fresh, green bills.

"I'll do it this once," said Berel, in a scarcely audible voice, as he pocketed the money.

"Gassed with gold!" exulted Shapiro to Maizie, after Berel left. "He's ours body and soul—bought and paid for!"

III

Hanneh Breineh's lodging house was in a hub-bub of excitement. A limousine had stopped before the dingy tenement, and Berel—a Berel from another world—stepped into the crowded kitchen.

How he was dressed! His suit was of the latest cut. The very quality of his necktie told of the last word in grooming. The ebony cane hanging on his arm raised him in the eyes of the admiring boarders to undreamed of heights of wealth.

There was a new look in his eyes—the look of the man who has arrived, and who knows that he has. Gone was the gloom of the insulted and the injured. Success had blotted out the ethereal, longing gaze of the hungry Ghetto youth. Nevertheless, to a discerning eye, a lurking discontent, like a ghost at a feast, still cast its shadow on Berel's face.

"He's not happy. He's only putting on," thought Moisheh, casting sidelong glances at his brother.

"You got enough to eat, and it shows on you so quick," purred Hanneh Breineh, awed into ingratiating gentleness by Berel's new prosperity.

With a large-hearted gesture, Berel threw a handful of change into the air for the children. There was a wild scramble of tangled legs and arms, and then a rush to the street for the nearest pushcart.

"*Oi weh!*" Hanneh Breineh touched Berel with reverent gratitude. "Give a look only how he throws himself around with his money!"

Berel laughed gleefully, a warm glow coming to his heart at this bubbling appreciation of his generosity.

"Hanneh Breineh," he said, with an impressive note in his voice, "did you ever have a twenty-dollar gold piece in your hand?"

An intake of breath was the only answer.

"Here it is."

Berel took from his pocket a little satin case, and handed it to her, his face beaming with the lavishness of the gift.

Hanneh Breineh gazed at the gold piece, which glistened with unbelievable solidity before her enraptured eyes. Then she fell on Berel's neck.

"You diamond prince!" she gushed. "Always I stood for your part when they all said you was crazy!"

The lean, hungry-faced boarders drank him in, envious worship in their eyes.

"Rockefeller—Vanderbilt!"

Exclamations of wonder and awe leaped from lip to lip, as they gazed at this Midas who was once a *schnorrer* in their midst.

Basking in their adulation like a bright lizard in the sun, Berel, with feigned indifference, lighted a thick cigar. He began to hum airily one of his latest successes.

"Ten thousand dollars for my last song!" he announced casually, as he puffed big rings of smoke to the ceiling.

"Riches rains on you!" Hanneh Breineh threw up her hands in an abandon of amazement. "Sing to me only that millionaires' song!"

Lifting her ragged skirts, she began to step in time to the tune that Berel hummed.

Out of all the acclaimers, Moisheh remained the only unresponsive figure in the room.

"Why your long face?" Hanneh Breineh shrieked. "What thunder fell on you?"

Moisheh shifted uncomfortably.

"I don't know what is with me the matter. I don't get no feelings from the words. It's only boom—boom—nothing!"

"Is ten thousand dollars nothing!" demanded the outraged Hanneh Breineh. "Are a million people crazy? All America sings his songs, and you turn up your nose on them. What do you know from life? You sweat from morning till night pressing out your heart's blood on your ironing board, and what do you get from it? A crooked back—a dried out herring face!"

" 'The prosperity of fools slayeth them,' " quoted Moisheh in Hebrew.

Berel turned swiftly on his brother.

"It's the poets who are slain and the fools who are exalted. Before, I used to spend three months polishing one little cry from the heart. Sometimes I sold it for five dollars, but most of the time I didn't. Now I shoot out a song in a day, and it nets me a fortune!"

"But I would better give you the blood from under my nails than you should sell yourself for dollars," replied Moisheh.

"Would you want me to come back to this hell of dirt and beg from you again for every galling bite of bread?" cried Berel, flaring into rage. "Your gall should burst, you dirt-eating muzhik!" he shouted with unreasoning fury, and fled headlong from the room.

This unaccountable anger from the new millionaire left all but Hanneh Breineh in a stupor of bewilderment.

"Muzhik! Are we all muzhiks, then?" she cried. A biting doubt of the generosity of her diamond prince rushed through her. "Twenty dollars only from so many thousands? What if he did dress out his stingy present in a satin box?"

She passed the gold piece around disdainfully.

"After all, I can't live on the shine from it. What'll it buy me—only twenty dollars? I done enough for him when he was a starving beggar that he shouldn't be such a piker to me!"

IV

A night of carousing had just ended. Berel Pinsky looked about his studio. Wine-glasses were strewn about. Hairpins and cigarette ashes littered the floor. A woman's rainbow-colored scarf, reeking with tobacco smoke and perfume, lay wantonly across the piano keys.

He strode to the window and raised the shade, but quickly pulled it down again. The sunlight hurt him. The innocent freshness of the morning blew accusingly against his hot brow.

He threw himself on the couch, but he could not rest. Like a distorted mirror, his mind reflected the happenings of the night before.

A table decked with flowers and glittering with silver and glass swam in vinous streaks of purple and amber. Berel saw white shoulders and sinuous arms—women's soft flesh against the black background of men's dress coats.

One mocking moment rose out of the reeling picture. A bright head pressed against his breast. His arms encircled a slender silken body. Pinnacled high above the devouring faces of his guests, hectic verses sputtered from his lips with automatic fluency.

It was this scene, spurting out of his blurred vision, that stabbed him like a hidden enemy within his soul. He had prostituted the divine in him for the swinish applause of the mob!

"God help me! God help me!" His body swayed back and forth in dumb, driven helplessness. "My sin!" he moaned, and sank to his knees.

Unconsciously he recalled the ritual chant of the Hebrews on the Day of Atonement—a chant he had not heard since he was a little child in Russia.

"'My sin—the sin I committed willfully and the sin without will. Behold, I am like a vessel filled with shame and confusion!'"

As he repeated the chant, beating his breast, his heart began to swell and heave with the old racial hunger for purging, for cleanness.

"My sin!" he cried. "I took my virgin gift of song and dragged it through the mud of Broadway!"

His turbulent penance burst into sobs—broke through the parched waste within him. From afar off a phrase fragrant as dew, but vague and formless, trembled before him. With a surge of joy, he seized pencil and paper. Only to catch and voice the first gush of his returning spirit!

"Wake up, you nut!"

Shapiro had come in unobserved, and stood before him like a grinning Mephistopheles. Berel look up, startled. The air boiled before him.

"See here—we got the chance of our life!" Shapiro, in his enthusiasm, did not notice Berel's grim mood. He shook the poet by the shoulder. "Ten thousand bucks, and not a worry in your bean! Just sign your name to this."

With a shudder of shame, Berel glanced at the manuscript and flung it from him.

"Sign my name to this trash?"

"Huh! You're mighty squeamish all of a sudden!"

"I can't choke no more my conscience."

"Conscience, hell! If we can't get the dope from you, I tell you, we got to get it from somebody else till you get back on the job!"

A cloud seemed to thicken Berel's glance.

"Here," he said, taking from his desk his last typewritten songs. "I've done my level best to grind this out."

Shapiro grasped the sheets with quickening interest. He read, and then shook his head with grieved finality.

"It's no use. It's not in you anymore. You've lost the punch."

"You mean to tell me that my verses wouldn't go?"

Berel's eyes shone like hot coals out of his blanched face.

"Look here, old pal," replied Shapiro, with patronizing pity. "You've just gone dry."

"You bloody ghoul!" Berel lifted his fist threateningly. "It's you who worked me dry—made of my name nothing but a trademark!"

"So that's what I get for all I done for you!" Revulsion at the boy's ingratitude swept through Shapiro like a fury. "What do you think I am? Business is business. If you ain't got the dope no more, why, you ain't better than the bunch of plumbers that I chucked!"

With a gutteral cry, Berel hurled himself forward like a tiger.

"You bloodsucker, you!"

A shriek from Maizie standing in the doorway. A whirling figure in chiffon and furs thrust itself between them, the impact pushing Shapiro back.

"Baby darling, you're killing me!" Soft arms clung about Berel's neck. "You don't want to hurt nobody—you know you don't—and you make me cry!"

Savagely Berel thrust the girl's head back and looked into her eyes. His face flashed with the shame of the betrayed manhood in him.

"I was a poet before you smothered my fire with your jazz!"

For an instant Maizie's features froze, terrified by an anger that she could not comprehend. Then she threw herself on his shoulder again.

"But it's in rehearsal—booked to the Coast. It's all up with me unless you sign!"

He felt her sobs pounding away his anger. A hated tenderness slowly displaced his fury. Unwillingly, his arms clasped her closer.

"This once, but never again," he breathed in her ear, as he crushed her to him.

Gently Maizie extricated herself, with a smile shining through her tear-daubed face.

"You darling old pet! I'll be grateful till I die," she said, thrusting the pen into Berel's hand.

With tragic acceptance of his weakness, Berel scrawled his well-known signature on one sheet after another. With a beaten look of hatred he handed them to Shapiro, now pacified and smiling.

Long after they had gone, Berel still sat in the same chair. He made no move. He uttered no sound. With doubled fists thrust between his knees, he sat there, his head sunken on his breast.

In the depths of his anguish a sudden light flashed. He picked up the rejected songs and read them with regained understanding. All the cheap triteness, the jazz vulgarity of the lines leaped at him and hit him in the face.

"*Pfui!*" he laughed with bitter loathing, as he flung the tawdry verses from him.

Like a prisoner unbound, he sprang to his feet. He would shake himself free from the shackles of his riches! All this clutter of things about him—this huge, stuffy house with its useless rooms—the servants—his limousine—each added luxury was only another bar shutting him out from the light.

For an instant he pondered how to get rid of his stifling wealth. Should he leave it to Moisheh or Hanneh Breineh? No—they should not be choked under this mantle of treasure that had nearly choked the life in him.

A flash of inspiration—Maizie! Gold help her, poor life-loving Maizie! He would give it to her outright—everything, down to the last kitchen pot—only to be a free man again!

As quick as thought Berel scribbled a note to his lawyer, directing him to carry out this reckless whim. Then he went to the closet where, out of some strange, whimsical sentiment, he still kept his shabby old coat and hat. In a moment he was the old Berel again. Still in his frenzy, he strode toward the door.

"Back—back to Hanneh Breineh—to Moisheh—back to my own people! Free—free!"

He waved his hands exultantly. The walls resounded with his triumphant laughter. Grasping his shabby old cap in his hand, he raised it high over his head and slammed the gold-paneled door behind him with a thundering crash.

V

"Last lot cheap! Apples sweet like honey!"

"Fresh, live fish!"

"Shoe laces, matches, pins!"

The raucous orchestra of voices rose and fell in whining, blatant discord. Into the myriad sounds the rumbling Elevated bored its roaring thunder. Dirty, multicolored rags—the pinions of poverty—fluttered from the crowded windows. Streams of human atoms surged up and down the sidewalk littered with filth. Horses and humans pounded and scuttled through the middle of the street.

Berel's face shone exultant out of the crowd. In the quickening warmth of this old, familiar poverty his being expanded and breathed in huge drafts of air. The jostling mass of humanity that pressed about him was like the close embrace of countless friends.

Ach, here in this elemental struggle for existence was the reality he was seeking. It cried to him out of the dirty, driven faces. Here was the life that has never yet been fully lived. Here were the songs that have not yet been adequately sung.

"A black year on you, robber, swindler! If I go to buy rotten apples, should you charge me for fruit from heaven?"

The familiar voice shot like a bolt to his awakening heart. He looked up to see Hanneh Breineh's ragged figure wedged in between two push-carts, her face ecstatic with the zest of bargaining.

"Hanneh Breineh!" he cried, seizing her market basket, and almost throwing himself on her neck in a rush of exuberant affection. "I've come back to you and Moisheh!"

"God from the world! What's this—you in rags?" A quick look of suspicion crept into her face. "Did you lose your money? Did you maybe play cards?"

"I left it all to her—you know—every cent of the ill-gotten money."

"Left your money to that doll's face?"

Hanneh clutched her head and peered at him out of her red-lidded eyes.

"Where's Moisheh?" Berel asked.

He came closer to her, his whole face expressing the most childlike faith in her acceptance of his helplessness, in the assurance of her welcome.

"Don't you yet know the pants-pressers was on a strike, and he owed me the rent for so long he went away from shame?"

"But where is he—my brother?" cried Berel, in despair.

"The devil knows, not me. I only know he owes me the rent!"

"Moisheh gone?" He felt the earth slipping from under him. He seized Hanneh Breineh's hand imploringly. "You can squeeze me in with the other boarders—put me up on chairs—over the wash-tub—anywhere. I got no one but you!"

"No one but me?" Thrusting him down to his knees, she towered above him like some serpent-headed fury. "What did you ever done for me when you had it good, that I should take pity on you now? Why was you such a stingy to me when you were rolling yourself in riches?"

Her voice came in thick gusts of passion, as the smoldering feeling of past neglect burst from her in volcanic wrath. "You black-hearted *schnorrer,* you!"

A crowd of neighbors and passers-by, who had gathered at her first cursing screams, now surged closer. With her passion for harangue, she was lifted to sublime heights of vituperative eloquence by her sensation-hungry audience.

"People! Give a look only! This dirty bum throws away all his money on a doll's face, and then wants me to take the bread from the mouths of my own children to feed him!" She shook her fist in Berel's face. "Loafer—liar! I was always telling you your bad end!"

A hoarse voice rose from the crowd.

"*Pfui,* the rotten rich one!"

"He used to blow from himself like a Vanderbilt!"

"Came riding around in automobiles!"

All the pent-up envy that they never dared express while he was in power suddenly found voice.

"He's crazy—*meshugeh!*"

The mob took up the abuse and began to press closer. A thick piece of mud from an unknown hand flattened itself on the ashen cheek of the shaken poet. Instantly the lust for persecution swept the crowd. Mud rained on the crouching figure in their midst. Hoarse invectives, shrieks, infamous laughter rose from the mob, now losing all control.

With the look of a hunted beast, Berel drove his way through the merciless crowd. His clothing swirled in streaming rags behind him as he fled on, driven by the one instinct to escape alive.

When he had outdistanced those who pursued, he dropped in a dark hallway of an alley. Utter exhaustion drained him of all thought, all feeling.

Dawn came. Still Berel slept. From the nearby street the clattering of a morning milk-wagon roused him slightly. He stirred painfully, then sank back into a dream which grew as vivid as life.

He saw himself a tiny, black ant in an ant-hill. While plodding toilfully with the teeming mass, he suddenly ventured on a path of his own. Then a huge, destroying force overwhelmed and crushed him, to the applause of the other ants, slaves of their traditional routine.

The pounding of a hammer rang above his head. He opened his eyes. A man was nailing a sign to the doorway into which he had sunk the night before. Berel rubbed his heavy-lidded eyes, and blinking, read the words:

MACHINE-HANDS WANTED

"Food! *Oi weh,* a bite to eat! A job should I take?"

The disjointed thoughts of his tired brain urged him to move. He tried to rise, but he ached in every limb. The pain in his stiff body brought back to him the terror through which he had lived the day before. More than starvation, he feared the abyss of madness that yawned before him.

"Machine-hand—anything," he told himself. "Only to be sane—only to be like the rest—only to have peace!"

This new humility gave him strength. He mounted the stairs of the factory and took his place in the waiting line of applicants for work.

VI

For weeks Berel Pinsky worked, dull and inanimate as the machines he had learned to drive. Work, eat, sleep—eat, sleep, work. Day after day he went to and from his hall-bedroom, day after day to and from the shop.

He had ceased to struggle. He had ceased to be an individual, a soul apart. He was a piece of a mass, a cog of a machine, an ant of an ant-hill. Individually he was nothing—they were nothing. Together, they made up the shop.

So he went on. Inert, dumb as a beast in a yoke, he brushed against his neighbors. He never talked. As if in a dream, he heard the shrill babble of the other shop hands rise above the roaring noises of the machines.

One day, while eating his scanty lunch, lost in a dull, wandering day-dream, he felt a movement at his elbow. Looking up, he saw Sosheh, the finisher, furtively reaching for a crust that had dropped from his thick slice of bread.

"You don't want it yet?" she questioned, her face coloring with confusion.

"No," he answered, surprised out of his silence. "But didn't you have any lunch?"

"I'm saving myself from my lunches to buy me a red feather on my new spring hat."

He looked at Sosheh curiously, and noticed for the first time the pinched look of the pale young face.

"Red over that olive paleness!" he mused. "How bright and singing that color would be!"

Moved by an impulse of friendliness, he pushed an apple toward her.

"Take it," he said. "I had one for my lunch already."

He watched her with smiling interest as she bit hungrily into the juicy fruit.

"Will your feather be as red as this apple?" he asked.

"Ach!" she said, with her mouth full. "If you could only give a look how that feather is to me becoming! The redness waves over my black hair like waves from red wine!"

"Why, that girl is a poet!" he thought, thrilled by the way her mind leaped in her dumb yearning for beauty.

The next noon she appeared with a paper bag in her hand. Reverently she drew forth a bright red cock's feather.

"Nu, ain't it grand? For two weeks my lunch money it is."

"How they want to shine, the driven things, even in the shop!" he mused. "Starving for a bit of bright color—denying themselves food for the shimmering touch of a little beauty!"

One morning, when he had risen to go to work in the gray dawn, he found his landlady bending over an ironing board in the dim gas-light, pressing a child's white dress. She put down the iron to give Berel his breakfast.

"My little Gittel is going to speak a piece to-day." Her face glowed as she showed him the frock. "Give a look only on those flowers I stitched out myself on the sash. Don't they smell almost the fields to you?"

He gazed in wonder at the mother's face beaming down at him. How could Tzipeh Yenteh still sense the perfume of the fields in this dead grind of work? How could his care-crushed landlady, with seven hungry mouths to feed—how could she still reach out for the beautiful? His path to work was lit up by Tzipeh Yenteh's face as she showed him her Gittel's dress in all its freshness.

Little by little he found himself becoming interested in the people about him. Each had his own hidden craving. Each one longed for something beautiful that was his and no one else's.

Beauty—beauty! *Ach,* the lure of it, the tender hope of it! How it filled every heart with its quickening breath! It made no difference what form it took—whether it was the craving for a bright feather, a passion for an ideal, or the love of man for woman. Behind it all was the same flaming hope, the same deathless upreaching for the higher life!

God, what a song to sing! The unperishable glamour of beauty, painting the darkest sweatshop in rainbow colors of heaven, splashing the gloom of the human ant-hill with the golden pigments of sunrise and sunset!

Lifted to winged heights by the onrush of this new vision, Berel swept home with the other toilers pouring from shops and factories.

How thankful he was for the joy of his bleak little room! He shut the door, secure in his solitude. Voices began to speak to him. Faces began to shine for him—the dumb, the oppressed, the toil-driven multitudes who lived and breathed unconscious of the cryings-out in them. All the thwarted longings of their lives, all the baffled feelings of their hearts, all the aching dumbness of their lips, rose to his sympathetic lips, singing the song of the imperishable soul in them.

Berel thought how Beethoven lay prone on the ground, his deaf ears hearing the beat of insects' wings, the rustle of grass, the bloom of buds, all the myriad voices of the pregnant earth. For the first time since the loss of his gift in the jazz pit of Tin Pan Alley, the young poet heard the rhythm of divine creation.

He drew a sheet of white paper before his eyes. From his trembling fingers flowed a poem that wrote its own music—every line a song—the whole a symphony of his regeneration.

"To think that I once despised them—my own people!" he mused. "*Ach,* I was too dense with young pride to see them then!"

His thoughts digging down into the soil of his awakened spirit, he cried aloud:

"Beauty is everywhere, but I can sing it only of my own people. Some one will find it even in Tin Pan Alley—among Maizie's life-loving crowd; but I, in this life, must be the poet of the factories—of my own East Side!"

VII

"It's me—Hanneh Breineh!"

A loud thumping at the door and a shrill chatter of voices broke in upon Berel's meditations.

"Me—Moisheh!"

"Come in!" he cried, welcoming this human inbreak after his long vigil.

"Here we got him!" Berel was smothered in Hanneh Breineh's gushing embrace. "Where did you run away that time, you crazy? Don't you yet know my bitter heart? I never mean nothing when I curse."

"For months it dried out our eyes from our heads looking for you," gulped Moisheh, tearing him from Hanneh's greedy arms.

Berel fell on his brother's neck, weeping out the whole rush and tide of his new-born humility.

"Mine own brother, with the old shine from his eyes!"

Moisheh held Berel off, then crushed him in another long hug. Hanneh Breineh, with ostentatious importance, held up her capacious market basket and drew forth a greasy bundle.

"Let's make from it a holiday, for good luck. It's only a bargain, this *Apfel Strudel*," she said apologetically, breaking it in pieces and giving one to each.

Berel's tears rang out in laughter.

"My own hearts—my own people!"

"*Mazeltuf!* Good luck!" chanted Hanneh Breineh, sipping hungrily the last drops of luscious juice that oozed from the *Apfel Strudel.*

Raising his piece on high, Moisheh chimed in:

"Good luck and the new life!"

III.
UNCOLLECTED
STORIES

This Is What $10,000 Did to Me

I was very poor. And when I was poor, I hated the rich. Now that I too have some means, I no longer hate them. I have found that the rich are as human as any of us.

When I lived in Hester Street, I could feel life only through the hurts and privations of Hester Street. Why were we cramped into the crowded darkness of dingy tenements? Because the heartless rich had such sunny palaces on Fifth Avenue. Why were we starving and wasting with want? Because the rich gorged themselves with the fat of the land.

And then it happened. I who thought myself doomed to Hester Street had the chance to move myself up to Fifth Avenue. And now where are the horns and hoofs that I always seemed to see at the sight of the well-fed, the well-dressed? Where's the righteous indignation that flared up in my breast when I saw people ride around in limousines? Where the hot sureness with which I condemned as criminals those who dared to have the things we longed to have but never could hope of having—furs and jewels and houses?

It began five years ago, just a few days before Christmas. shivering with cold, I walked up and down the shopping district of Fifth Avenue. I caught a glimpse of myself in the mirror of a passing shop window. What a pinched, starved thing! Worried, haunted eyes under a crumpled hat. Faded, ragged old coat. Over-patched shoes, pulling apart at the patches.

All about me fine ladies, sleek and warm in fur coats, stepping in and out of their cars. All about me shop windows glittering with ball gowns and gorgeous wraps. Riches and luxury everywhere, and I so crazed with want!

In one window a dazzling Christmas tree blinded me with rage. Why should there be Christmas in the world? Why this holiday spirit on Fifth Avenue when there's no holiday for Hester Street? Why these expectant, smiling faces of the shoppers buying useless presents for each other, when we didn't know from where would come our next meal?

I had been writing and starving for years. My stories, which appeared in the magazines from time to time, had been gathered together and published in a book called *Hungry Hearts*. Although reviewers praised it, my royalties were so small that it brought me little money and almost no recognition. People who read a book little know what small reward there is for the writer while he is still unknown—of his often solitary, starved existence. A book read in one evening may have taken the author years and years of the most agonizing toil to create.

On and on I walked through the gay street, shoved and elbowed by the hurrying crowd. Wild thoughts raced in the corner of my brain. If I could only throw a bomb right there in the middle of Fifth Avenue and shatter into a thousand bits all this heartlessness of buying and buying! The slush of the sidewalk creeping into the cracks of my shoes made me feel so wretchedly uncomfortable. Exhausted with the bitterness and hatred of my thoughts, my futile rebellion gradually settled into a dull melancholy. If I could only kill myself as a protest against the wrongs and injustices I had suffered! I did not really want to die. But I did so much want to shock the world out of its indifference.

Almost a sense of exaltation stole over me as I went on imagining the details of my death. I could see the beautiful limousine wrenched to a sudden stop. The pale chauffeur lifting my crushed, bleeding body in his arms. The whole world crowding around me, dumb, horrified. Then a voice breaking the hush of the crowd:

"This was the author of *Hungry Hearts*, and we left her to anguish and die in want!"

Already I saw the throngs mobbing the bookstores for my book. My last letter and my picture in the front page of every newspaper in the country. Everywhere people reading and taking *Hungry Hearts*. The whole world shaken with guilty sorrow for my tragic death—but too late!

Yes, on that dark day there seemed no way to take revenge for the cruel neglect of a heartless world but to blow out my brains or plunge under the wheels of the crowded traffic. My last letter was already shaping itself in my head as I hastened back to my room to write it.

How I dreaded to meet the landlady on the stairs! I could not bear to hear her nagging for the rent in my last tragic hour. Trembling with fear, I sneaked into my room.

There on the table lay a little yellow telegram!

I stared at it. Who in the world would send me a telegram?

I tore it open and read uncomprehendingly. It was from a well-known moving picture agent, saying that he could get for the film rights of my book the unheard sum of ten thousand dollars.

In a flash the whole world changed! And I was changed. It changed still more when, after negotiations for the book had been made, they offered to send me to California to collaborate on the screen version of *Hungry Hearts*.

There followed a wonderful trip across the continent, in a private compartment. I had to pinch myself to make sure that I was not dreaming when I entered the diner and ordered roast duck, asparagus, endive salad and strawberries with cream. I could treat myself with a full hand because a millionaire corporation was paying the bills.

"And this is no accident of good fortune, no matter of luck," I kept telling myself. "*Hungry Hearts* has earned it for me."

Arrived in Los Angeles, I was greeted with overwhelming friendliness by a representative of the company. In a gorgeous limousine, one of those limousines that I always condemned as a criminal luxury of the hated rich—in one of these limousines I was driven to a hotel.

Flowers filled my room. Flowers for me! I looked around, dazzled out of my senses. Luxurious comfort beyond dream all about me. I felt dizzy drunk with this sudden plunge into the world of wealth.

For the first day I stayed in my room struggling to pull together my bewildered wits. I wanted to let go and be happy. But I could not let go, nor be happy. All my Hester Street past rose up in arms against me. "Betrayer! Deserter!" my soul that once was cried accusingly.

The following morning a limousine called to take me to the studio in Culver City. A private office and a secretary were assigned to me. And that secretary! I wondered, would I have to get myself new clothes to match up to her style?

I suddenly became aware of my frumpy, old-fashioned dress against her youthful grace and up-to-dateness. I had heard of newly rich people who were always scared that their servants would look down on them out of the corners of their eyes. And I wondered, would I too let myself get shamed out of being what I am by the proud condescension of my grand secretary? Before I could finish my thought, Julian Josephson, that great scenario man, came in. One look of his eyes, the smile on his face, and I felt at home, among my own. Then other members of the scenario department joined us to discuss the plot for *Hungry Hearts*.

The minute we got busy, I was myself again. Happy for the first time since my good luck. *Ach,* what a heart-filling thing is work! In poverty or wealth, work has been to me the one escape from the storms of the soul within or the struggles with the world without.

At luncheon time I met the "eminent authors" that were working about the lot—Rupert Hughes, Gertrude Atherton, Leroy Scott, Alice Duer Miller, Gouverneur Morris and many others. What a thrilling experience it was to see them for the first time face to face, to talk to them as they were eating luncheon, just as if they were plain human beings!

One of the "eminent authors" invited me to dinner at his house that evening. Such things as dinner clothes or evening clothes never came into my mind. It seemed to me even if I had such fancy things I'd never know how to wear them. I stayed around the lot that afternoon, visiting the different sets. Before I knew it, it was time to go.

Again the company's limousine drove me to the place. A grave, dignified butler opened the door for me. Through the hall beyond I saw ladies almost half naked, in what seemed to me dressy, gay-colored night-gowns, and all the men in wedding suits.

"So these are evening clothes!" I pondered.

I wanted to rush back to my hotel, but my host saw me as he passed the hall and hastened over to welcome me.

"I might as well stay and see how 'eminent authors' dine," I thought. "How do they behave themselves at a party, these shining lights of the world?"

Upstairs, a fancy maid in a black uniform helped me take off my things. She gave me one look that said as plain as words, "From where do you come? You here—among 'eminent authors'?"

But the "eminent authors" themselves were such lively, plain people. They greeted me with such natural friendliness that I almost forgot I was different.

Cocktails were served. And then we seated ourselves about the table. Such a millionaire wedding feast! And that's what "eminent authors" called just dinner.

Four butlers were busy waiting on a dozen guests. Champagne—it would be impossible to count the bottles. As one rich dish after another was served, I thought of the people in Hester Street, starving, thrown in the street for unpaid rent. The cost of the champagne for that one dinner would be enough to feed a whole tenement house full of people . . . I remembered the picture of Nero fiddling before the fall of Rome. I had touched the two extremes of life—Hester Street—Hollywood.

At first there was a lot of educated talk about literature, art, Freud and other high things over my head. Then, warmed by the champagne, they began to talk about other authors. I felt happy just as if I were among my own people in Hester Street. Of course they didn't yell and holler or get excited like the people in Hester Street. They sat quite still in their chairs—ladies and gentlemen. But by the tones in their voices, the looks in their eyes, I saw again the tenants sitting on the stoop, tearing their neighbors to pieces behind their backs. These two "eminent" evening gowns were like those two girls with uncombed hair and flashing eyes fighting over some man. And that grand author lady, so proud of her best-selling books, made me think of that frowzy herring woman with a shawl over her head, nodding and talking behind her hand what was cooking in the neighbors' pots.

In the morning, still elated with the gay party of the night before, I awoke to the delicious feel of my soft, smooth bed. Such fresh, clean-smelling sheets! Warm, wool blankets finer than silk. Fresh air and sunshine flooded my room.

How far away was that dark hole in the tenements whence I came—six lodgers on one hard mattress on the floor, and the landlady with all her children in that narrow bed!

At the push of a button, a Japanese maid brought me my breakfast on a silver tray. Hot-house grapes—great purple ones, big as plums they looked to me. And the smell of that coffee in that silver pitcher and the fresh, buttered toast!

I laughed aloud at myself—crazy from Hester Street! You playing lady? You breakfasting in bed? You served on a silver tray? . . . Well, I'm only finding out how it feels. I'm only doing it for experience.

The limousine called to take me to my office. I felt so fine, so in love with the whole world as I relaxed against the cushions of the car. How much more comfortable than the crowded trolley! Would I ever be able to stand the elevated or subway after this?

My secretary was waiting for me as usual. I greeted her gaily.

"Don't you love it out here?" I laughed.

"Love it! When they don't pay me enough to live?" Then she poured out to me her bitter story. "In my home town in Iowa I got thirty-five a week. But I was crazy to work with the movies. I left a good job to come here. And all they pay is twenty-five dollars a week. I asked for a raise of five dollars. They refused it. It's impossible to get along on my wages. But a lot they care. It's take it or leave it with them. A dozen girls are ready to step into my job."

At every word my spirits sank. The joy over my good luck was over. In the next few days I met other stenographers, clerks, readers, stage hands. So many were horribly underpaid. The "eminent authors," the screen stars, the directors got fortunes for their work; the others drudged from morning till night for less than their bread.

Like a ghost at a feast, my secretary, and behind her the whole army of under-dogs at the studio, rose up before me every time I stepped into the limousine. There was no peace for me at my hotel.

I could stand it no longer. At the end of the week I went to the president of the company. "I'm so miserable in this grand hotel," I said.

"What? Aren't you comfortable?"

"I'm too comfortable—so comfortable—it makes me nervous. I've got to live plain like I'm used to. How much does it cost the company to keep me here?"

"About two hundred a week."

"Good heavens!" I cried. "Seven families with a dozen children each could live on that sum. Give me that money. I can live like a queen on fifty a week."

I left Hollywood a few months later, a tortured soul with a bank account. I had the money now to live securely for a few years. Security buys peace of mind to develop a soul. And here I was losing the very soul that my security was giving me. For now I was a capitalist—one of the class that I hated.

The moving picture company saw in my sudden fortune a good human interest story for the papers, to advertise *Hungry Hearts* throughout the country without cost. And I, new to the game of publicity, gave out one interview after another. And every interview was twisted and distorted. Soon the ten thousand dollars for the picture rights of *Hungry Hearts* grew to twenty-five thousand. The two hundred a week I was paid while assisting on the scenario became two thousand. And then from lips to lips it leaped to ten thousand a week. Such were some of the headlines in the ghetto papers—"From Want to Wealth—From Hester Street to Hollywood."

People who have been always comfortable can't know what it means to come into sudden wealth. My mail was full of begging letters. Poor relatives besieged me for money. And my conscience told me that if I were true to my soul I'd give all. I had hated the rich because they kept their wealth and refused to share it with the rest of the world. But how was I to begin to share?

Ten thousand dollars seemed a fairy tale when I was starving poor, but a few months at Hollywood had so changed me that it did not seem much now. Just about enough to keep me till I wrote my next book.

As the demands for money became more insistent, I grew resentful. "I've slaved and starved and risked all to write something real. I've earned what I've got. What right have they to it? Let them produce *Hungry Hearts*. Let them suffer and agonize for every little word as I suffered and agonized."

The more I tried to make myself feel right, the more uneasy I was. My self-defense turned in upon me like an accusation. I knew the pain of the unjustly condemned and the guilt of those who had committed a crime.

To end the turmoil and confusion of my soul, I took a trip to Europe. As I traveled from city to city and saw the crooked little alleys where the poor huddled on top of each other worse than in Hester Street, I wanted to atone for the luxury of my trip by going back steerage.

I had come steerage to America twenty years ago. Why should I not be able to return the same way? I felt that only by going back to my own people could I hope to regain my lost soul—my soul that I had lost with my sudden good luck.

I stood it one day only, in the steerage. The dingy, crowded, smelly berths, the coarse food, the thick, ugly dishes and the lack of table service that had become a necessity to me.

I realized that you can't be an immigrant twice.

When I returned to New York, I moved boldly into a hotel on Fifth Avenue.

I didn't have time now to hate the rich. I had to use my energies to make myself a better writer, to keep up with the cost of my new standards of living. Here I came in contact with other capitalists, other conspirators of wealth. I discovered they were not ogres, heartless oppressors of the poor. They were as human as other folks.

Now, as I sit alone in my room, watching the wonder of the sunset, I look back and see how happy I ought to have been when I was starving poor, but one of my own people. Now I am cut off by my own for acquiring the few things I have. And those new people with whom I dine and to whom I talk, I do not belong to them. I am alone because I left my own world.

Wild Winter Love

This is a story with an unhappy ending. And I too have become Americanized enough to be terrified of unhappy endings. Yet I have to drop all my work to write it.

Ever since I read in the papers about Ruth Raefsky, I've gone around without a head. I can't pull myself together somehow. Her story won't let me rest. It tears me out of my sleep at night. It leaps up at me out of every corner where I try to hide.

And it's dumb. Dumb. Words only push back the spirit of what I feel about her. The facts that I know so well dwindle into nothing. Only a piece of her life here, and a piece there—the end, the middle, and the beginning rush together in broken confusion.

The first thing that flashes to my mind is her outburst of impatience with the monotonous theme of love in American magazines. "You pick up one magazine after another, and it's all love-stories. Life isn't all sex. Why are they writing only about love, as if there was nothing else real to write about?"

How much she had learned of the realness and unrealness of love before she was through!

It was in the Bronx, the uptown ghetto, that I first met her. Even before we met, her neighbor's whisperings excited my interest.

"Imagine only—such a woman—a wife of a poor tailor—a house and a baby to take care of—and such a madness in her head—goes to night-school—wants to write herself a book of her life."

Her neighbor's voice was high-pitched with indignation. "The husband sweats from early morning till late at night, stitching his life away for every penny he earns. And she is such a lady, when she goes to the market, she don't bargain herself to get things cheaper like the rest of us. She takes it wrapped up, don't even look at the change. Just like a Gentile."

I had just moved in. It was one of those newly built five-story tenements with four three-room flats on each floor. She lived in the front and I in the rear. But it was weeks before I got on friendly terms with her.

All the other women sat around together with their baby-carriages in the sun, darning and mending, discussing what was cooking in the neighbors' pots. But she and her baby carriage were always off by themselves.

She seemed wrapped up inside herself. Not seeing, not hearing anything around her.

Sometimes she'd take up some pages and pencil from under the baby's pillow, jot down something. Then sit back very still, as if she were all alone, looking far out at the top of the world.

But when I met her in the store, or on the stairs, she looked like a neat, efficient, business-like person with a busy concentrated expression on her face. She answered my "good morning" and "good evening" with a nod and a smile, but no more.

Gradually her life pieced itself together out of the fragments of conversation we had.

She had met Dave, her husband, in the same shop where she had worked. He was a tailor, she a finisher.

The sudden urge to write did not begin till after she was married.

"We were so happy in our little flat, all to ourselves. At first Dave wanted me to fix up a 'parlor like by other people.' But I wanted a plain living room like in the settlement.

"'And why not?' he humored me. But I could see it wasn't because he thought the plain things I liked beautiful, but that he wanted me to have what I wanted.

"And so it was when I told him I had to write the story of my life. He hadn't much use for books. He only read the 'Vorwarts' and the 'Socialist Call.' He looked a little doubtful. But he loved me so, and he was so good and kind. He shrugged away his doubt. 'If you'll have from it pleasure, go ahead.'

"And so I began to go to night-school to learn how to write my life. But in a class of fifty, how much time can the teacher give to me?

"I didn't realize when I began how long it would take, how I'd have to tear my flesh in pieces for every little word. I am only just feeling out the beginning of my story. But now I can't stop myself."

I glanced up at her. Under that look of neat businesslike efficiency, a consuming passion flared up in her eyes. Her baby two years already. Writing every day since her marriage, and only just at the beginning.

"If I could only do it by myself! It's having to go to these teachers for help that kills me. Every evening this week they were reading in my class how Washington crossed the Delaware. Here I'm burning up with the crossing of my own Delaware. And I have to choke down my living story for a George Washington, dead a hundred years. All that waste, only to get the teacher's help for a few minutes after the class."

Her tightly clenched hands trembled with nervousness. I've seen the dumb who wanted to say something, but were too confused to know what they wanted to say. Here were brains and intelligence. Here was a woman who knew what she wanted to say, but was lost in the mazes of the new language. And more than the confusion of the new language was the realization that she was talking to strangers, to whom she always felt herself saying too much, yet not enough. To cold hard-headed Americans she was trying to make clear the feverish turmoil of the suppressed desire-driven ghetto.

One evening, several months later, I heard through the open air-shaft window loud quarreling in the Raefsky flat.

"Come to bed already. I waited up for you long enough. It's time to sleep."

"Oh, Dave! Stop bothering me. I only just got started. Why can't you go to sleep without me?"

No sound for a while.

"*Nu?* Not yet finished?"

"Let me alone, can't you? I've scrubbed and cooked and washed all day long. Only when the baby is asleep that I take to myself."

"*Gewalt!*" Dave's voice, raw with hurt, rose into a shriek. "There's an end to a man's patience. My gall is bursting. You're not a woman. I married myself to a *meshugeneh* with a book for her heart."

"God! What does that man want of me?"

"You know what I want. I want a home. I want a wife."

"Don't you have the things you like to eat? Was there ever a time that you did not have your clean shirt, your darned socks?"

"Oi-i-i! If you had flesh and blood in you, you wouldn't talk that way. What for did you marry me? So you could have a fool of a slave to give you everything, while you go on with your craziness?"

They drifted further and further apart. Whenever I entered their flat, I felt the cold chill that comes to you when you enter a house where the man and woman live under one roof yet live apart. It was only the love for their child that held them together in spite of the growing chasm between them.

As she became more and more consumed with her story, she grew impatient with the little special help she could get out of the night-school. She sought the club-leader of the settlement, a college student, the druggist on the corner, the doctor on the block. Anyone she met with a gleam of intelligence in their eyes, she would stop and make them listen to some little scene in her story that she happened to be working on. Their comments somehow helped her get a truer word, a deeper stroke in her picture.

And so the book built itself up piece by piece through the years.

I lost track of her for a long while when they moved away.

One day the club-leader of the settlement told me the exciting news that Ruth Raefsky had come through with her book, *Out of the Ghetto*.

Breathlessly I read the enthusiastic reviews of great critics who hailed Ruth Raefsky as the New Voice of the East Side.

So she got there at last! What a titanic struggle! With all her dumbness, her fearful unsureness of herself—to have pressed on and on—beaten out a voice in so much that was dumb.... The steerage ship on its way to America—Cherry Street. The sweatshop. The boss. The "hands." The landlord. The rag peddler. The pawnshop. The art theater. Dreams and the brutal battle for bread. Greed and self-sacrifice. The dirt and the beauty seething in the crowded ghetto—to have caught it all—framed it between the covers of a book!

How will she look released from that terrible burden? Would having reached her goal wipe away the tortured driven look on her face? What will she do with herself now? Can she pick up again the relationships she broke to pursue her dream?

I went to see her. I found her already famous. People whose names I read in the magazines were now among her guests for tea.

Success had not yet worked any miracles in her appearance. Though she was excited and elated, the tired strained expression was still on her face. Sleepless nights and tortured days still cried out of her eyes.

"How does it feel to be a famous living author?" I whispered.

"Will I ever be able to do my next thing? This is my worry now."

I wondered why she did not rejoice more in her good luck. Then Dave, grimy from his work in the shop, came in.

He tried to slip away. But Ruth pulled him forward. "Come, Dave. I want you to meet some of my friends."

He bowed awkwardly, hiding his dirty hands in his pockets. Everyone in the room felt the pain of his self-consciousness. As soon as he could, he shrank into a corner and didn't say a word till they had left.

Then he burst out: "My home is no more mine. I come tired from the shop. All I want is peace—and my house is crowded with strangers. Why didn't you tell me you'd have them here?"

"Why hide yourself from people?"

"They're not my people. But what's the difference? What do I count in his house? To a writer, what is a husband?"

"Oh, Dave!" Her voice was sharp with jangled nerves. "Don't let's go over all that again. My writing is no crime."

"Sure it's a crime," he cried, his eyes blazing. "The pleasure of writing is for millionaires. What right has a poor man's wife to give in to herself? Suppose it willed itself in me to write a book, who'd give you bread? I have to be a tailor, so you could shine in the world for a writer. Somebody's got to work for the rent."

I went away. I thought of an evening years ago, when I first knew them. Dave had come in from work, with eager shining eyes and a package in his hand. It was his wife's birthday. He had saved for months to surprise her with a Hungarian peasant shawl that he had seen her admire in a shop window. How he drank in pleasure out of his wife's delight as he wrapped the shawl around her! And now—the cold looks, the harsh voices with which they pushed one another away.

Some months later we made an appointment to meet for lunch. When the day came, I received word that she was ill. I went to see her. I found her prostrate with a headache.

She looked frightfully old. Her features stood out sharply. Her eyes seemed to have gone deep down into her head. She sat up in bed with a little jerk. Bright red spots burned on her cheeks. She barely stopped to greet me. She began talking at once, as though carrying on a conversation with herself.

"I'm a woman without a country. I'm up-rooted from where I started; and I can't find roots anywhere. I've lost the religion of my fathers. I've lost the human ties that hold other women. I can only live in the world I create out of my brain. I've got so that I can't live unless I write. And I can't write. The works have stopped in me. What will be my end?"

Her reserve had unloosed through exhaustion. I never heard her talk so much. It was a torrent of high-pitched nervous words.

"My writing began with my love for Dave. But I've gone on only in my brain. I've gone too far away from life. I don't know how to get back.

"I have so much more to give out than ever before. But something has stifled this giving-out power. My terrible inadequacy is killing me. What is the agony of death to this agony I now suffer—to feel, to see, to know—and to wither in sight of it all—stifled—dumb."

Soon after this, a nervous breakdown forced her to give her daughter to board, and she went away for the first vacation in her life.

I was seeing Dave, off and on, whenever I needed my clothes to be repaired.

"How's Ruth?" I asked toward the end of the summer.

"Now she's come back with a new craziness in her head. She's got to live alone. Such selfishness—" He stopped suddenly.

I was too embarrassed to press him for details. I hurried to see her at her new address. I expected her to be in a worse mental state, now that she was living the hermit. But she was radiant. Her face, her figure, her eyes, had a verve, a sparkle, a magnetism, that I never saw in her before.

"What has happened to you?" I cried. "You look a million years younger."

A light from away inside flashed up in her face. "I'm seeing for the first time how glorious it is just to be alive. Beauty is all about us—only I was too blind to see it till now. What is that verse in the Bible—'all things work together for good to them that love God'?"

I listened in amazement. I couldn't take my eyes away from her shining face.

"Solitude has done you good."

"Solitude is only an empty cup. I have rich red wine to fill my solitude."

Now I knew what had happened to her. "Who? Who is it? You—at forty-seven, in love?"

"Yes. And with a man even older than I. What does youth know about love? What can youth bring to love, but the inexperience, the unripeness of youth?"

For a moment I looked beneath the radiance of her face into the battle-scarred, life-worn lines that the years had dug into her throat and about her eyes. In that moment she was all of her forty-seven years old. But it was only for a moment. I was caught up again by the rich warmth of her voice, the inexhaustible energy that poured out of her as she talked.

"Outwardly, my lover is one of those cold reasonable Anglo-Saxons. A lawyer. A respectable citizen. Devoted to his wife. Adores his children. We're drawn to each other by something even more compelling than the love of man for woman, and woman for man. It's that irresistible force as terrible as birth and death that sometimes flares up between Jew and Gentile."

The resonance of her own voice was like fire that fed her. She looked far out—stern forehead, exultant eyes—seeing prophecies.

"These centuries of antagonism between his race and mine have burst out in us into this transcendent love. A love that burns through the barriers of race and class and creed.... Since Christ was crucified, a black chasm of hate yawned between his people and mine. But now and then threads of gold have spun through the darkness—links of understanding woven by fearless souls—Gentiles and Jews—men and women who were not afraid to trust their love."

"Mad-woman—poetess!" In a kind of envy I laughed aloud. But she was too inspired to hear me.

"It's because he and I are of a different race that we can understand one another so profoundly, touch the innermost reaches of the soul, beyond the reach of those who think they know us.

"When I talk to him, it's like traveling in foreign countries. He excites my imagination and releases my imagination....

"My writing is but a rushing fountain of song to him. I pour myself out at his feet, in poems of my people, their hopes, their dreams. He listens to me with the wonder of a child listening to adventure. It's all so fresh and new to him, my world, that it becomes fresh and new to me....

"In some way I do not understand I've been the means of bringing release to him too. I've awakened in him a new worship of life and beauty that none of the women of his class can ever dream is in him."

She threw back her head gloriously. Her laughter was a chant of triumph. "The wonderful way that man looks at me! It's like bathing in sunshine.... Dave has driven into me all these years that I'm a criminal. That fire in me, that makes me what I am—a crime. And this man washes away, as in healing oil, the guilt and self-defense with which my flesh and spirit is scarred. To him I can be just as I am. He wants me as I am."

The starved tailor's wife! How it had gone to her head, the little bit of love! But what wonder? For the first time in her life, she found a lover, an inspirer, and an audience all in one—a man of brains who understood the warm rich muddle of her experience.

I was all curiosity to see the man who had so changed this lonely ghetto woman. I got to watching for them. Walking the streets where they were likely to pass. At last I saw them. It was like seeing black and white, so intense, so startling was the contrast between them. His calm Anglo-Saxon face was like a background of rock for her volatile, tempestuous, Slavic temperament.

They lit up the street with their happiness. The world seemed to sweep away before their completeness in each other. And yet, he seemed quite an old man. No different from hundreds of other plain lawyers. She, for all the fire and vivacity that lighted up her face was unmistakably middle-aged. How could they let themselves be so wrapped up in each other? How shameless, at their age, to get so lost in their love!

But a rich power for work was that love. It put a new appeal, deeper humanity, into her writing. Her stories became the fad of the hour. Her stepping up into the world of success, while I was still low down in the struggle, gradually cut us off one from the other.

It was over three years that I had not seen her. By degrees I became aware that she appeared less and less in the public eye. I began to wonder what she was doing.

A sudden desire to see her swept me. But I pushed back the impulse.... What can we talk about now, when she's so happy?...

One morning I opened the newspaper as I sat down to breakfast. Ruth Raefsky's picture! Under it, in big letters—Suicide! I read on. But I was too shaken to take in anything. My brain was paralyzed by that one word—suicide.

Ruth Raefsky! So rich with life! So eager to live! She—of all people! I had to know the truth of what had happened. Suicide. That word meant nothing. What led to it, was her story.

I called on her relatives, her friends—on anyone who might know.

"Well, what can you expect? Left her husband, her child, for an affair with a married man," said her next-door neighbor.

And each one had something different to say.

"Such a haunted face as she had the last time I saw her! Poor thing! She looked so unhappy."

"You can't blame the man. The wife and daughters got wind of the affair. He wouldn't let them be hurt. Why should the innocent family suffer? So Ruth Raefsky had to go."

"He had a sense of duty to the community, if she didn't. I admire him for being strong enough, in the end, to do the right thing."

"How she must have suffered! She shut herself away from all of us. She wouldn't let any of us try to help her."

So their words fell about her—smug or compassionate.

How could they know the real Ruth Raefsky? Those years of toil by day and night, tearing up by the roots her starved childhood, her starved youth, trying to tell, in her personal story, the story of her people. How could they understand the all-consuming urge that drove her to voice her way across the chasm between the ghetto and America?

A lonely losing fight it was from the very beginning. Only for a moment, a hand of love stretched a magic bridge across the chasm. Inevitably the hand drew back. Inevitably the man went back to the safety of his own world.

In the fading of this dazzling mirage of friendship and love, vanished her courage, her dreams, her last illusion. And she leaped into the gulf that she could not bridge.

One Thousand Pages
of Research

Every time I walked along Upper Broadway, I saw them. Old men and old women, in their seventies, like me, seated side by side on the park benches set up by a benevolent city on the traffic islands dissecting the main roadway. Every time I passed those benches, stationary amidst the moving cars, I thought about how many more old people there must be all over the city, killing time, waiting for death.

Then one day it came to me. Right here in New York handicapped veterans were being trained for a new life; the blind were being taught skills; why couldn't the old be rehabilitated? After all, we still had much to give. We all had experience and many of us had professional training. Why was all this going to waste?

The idea took hold of me, and I decided to do something about it. I went to the university nearby. I talked. They listened—patiently, but helplessly. I was passed from one department to another. The Rehabilitation Department was only for young veterans. The Adult Education Department was mildly interested, but saw no way of adopting my idea. I persisted. At last I was directed to a psychologist—let us call him Professor Sidney Stone—who specialized in the "learning abilities of adults." I made my speech:

"We want to be of use. There are recreation centers for 'senior citizens' to keep them off the streets, to keep them from going mad in their lonely rooms. But I speak for the old who have brains and intelligence. We are not interested in finger painting and other childish hobbies. We don't want to kill time; we want to use it."

Professor Stone gave me a long, reflective look and said that he was trying to develop an intelligence test for older people. He suggested that if I could get together a group of women around my own age, we might start a "workshop on aging."

It takes six simpletons and one zealot to start a movement. I began recruiting among my friends and fellow has-beens, acquaintances from the reading room of the Public Library, from the cafeterias and the park benches—wherever lonely old people begin talking to one another without introductions. Some had pensions, annuities, social security; one had a family inheritance; a few existed on dwindling savings and others on public welfare. Their enthusiasm was almost unanimous.

We gathered for our first seminar with name tags pinned to our shoulders, looking up at the professor like children on their first day of school. "You are an unusual group of women," he began. "You have the intelligence to voice your own problems and to help us understand the old who cannot speak for themselves. You can throw light on one of the major dilemmas before us today—how to use the potentialities of the old." He was a plump, middle-aged man with a fringe of graying hair around his bald spot, but to us he represented youth, charm, the opportunity to work and live again.

He leaned back in his chair, stroking his lapels. "Many approaches have been made to the problem of aging, but this discussion group is unique. It is to be a study of the old by the old. It is something new to meet a new need of our time. Science has salvaged scrap metal and even found vitamins and valuable oils in refuse, but old people are extravagantly wasted."

Charlotte Hicks, the ex-schoolteacher among us and the only one who had a notebook, was writing down everything the professor said. The rest of us could only look at him, devouring his words. They were like a bell, calling us to prayer; his genial smile made us feel he saw something special in each one of us. "We cannot tell in advance whether we can solve your personal problems right now," he concluded. "We cannot promise you anything except the satisfaction of working together for something that concerns us all."

The professor rose and the first seminar was concluded. We followed him from the room like a dutiful congregation after an inspiring sermon. Things were indeed looking up. I flung my arms around dour Mrs. Monahan.

Our second session began with questionnaires—age, family history, former occupation, education, how do you feel about growing old? I sat with the blank forms in front of me, thinking about the past. I grew up at the turn of the century, before child labor laws or compulsory schooling. Brief night-school courses in English had only sharpened my hunger for education. Then (could it have been forty years ago?) I stumbled into writing—novels about my experiences in the sweatshops of the Lower East Side. A brief, incredible success in Hollywood was followed by long years of groping, trial and error, and finally silence. Suddenly, shocked, I found that old age was upon me. Editors who had encouraged me were dead. My stories had faded into period pieces. A new generation of writers was creating a new literature.

We handed in our questionnaires. Professor Stone turned on the tape recorder and leaned back in his chair. He talked into a tiny microphone: "When does old age begin?"

Charlotte Hicks, sixty-nine and the youngest of the group, was the first to speak. She hadn't felt old, she explained, until she applied for a tutoring job at a teacher's agency and was told to say she was fifty instead of sixty-five. Charlotte snatched off her glasses. She was in a rage. "That man told me to lie!"

Kathleen Monahan, who had the worries of the world in her wrinkled face, was incredulous. "Holy Mother! What's a few lies? I tell 'em every day. Is there anyone in this room who doesn't? When my social worker comes snooping around, asking how I spend my money, can I tell her everything?"

The professor did his best to restore order and bring the ladies back to the subject. I said that feeling old was not a matter of years and Rose agreed by defining old age as the time where there is nothing left to look forward to.

Kathleen Monahan eyed Rose's blue cashmere sweater and expressed the view that those who had gone through the hell of home relief probably had less time to feel sorry for themselves.

Alice, the oldest, intervened as peacemaker. She had outlived the doctors with whom she had worked, outlived what the Depression had left of her family fortune. Nearly eighty, she had been forced to go on relief.

"I wasn't aware of age," she said with a slight smile, "until I was seventy-nine and walked up the stone stairs of the Welfare Office to apply for Old Age Assistance. I worked for the poor all my life. But not until I was one of them did I see what goes on under the name of charity."

We did not look at one another. The only sound was the mechanical purr of the tape recorder. Professor Stone watched us in silence.

Alice turned to Kathleen. "You know that Old Age Assistance provides hardly enough for food and rent. The morning paper, news of what's going on in the world, is as necessary to me as coffee for breakfast. I made ten dollars knitting a sweater and was so proud of it I showed the case worker the money I earned. The next month ten dollars was deducted from my check."

Derisive laughter at Alice's innocence was followed by a storm of indignation. We all began to talk, outshouting each other.

"Ladies! Please!" Professor Stone called us to order. "Pensions are not the subject here. We're wasting time." He paused. "Instead of dwelling on your grievances, have you ever thought of volunteering your services to your neighborhood community center, church, or hospital? In helping others we touch something greater than ourselves."

Anger and disappointment were in every face but Alice's. No one spoke. The closing bell put an end to the embarrassing silence.

In the street I burst out. Was our work then worth nothing? Why should we volunteer? Just because we're old? The very thing we needed was the self-respect that comes with getting paid for working.

At our next session, Professor Stone picked up a glass, partially filled it at the water tap and opined that there were negative and positive ways of looking at everything. The glass, for example, could be considered either as half empty or as half full. It was up to us. Even if this country abolished forced retirement and prejudice against the old, what would each of us then be able to do?

Alice was the first to see what he meant. "I could be a clinic receptionist as long as I didn't have to stand. Or I could work in a doctors' telephoning service."

The other ladies took up the cry. Kathleen could still "cook in six different languages," and even the usually silent Rose Broder debated her chances of becoming a chaperone or housekeeper.

"When you think of your positive assets, you conquer your prejudices against old age," Professor Stone continued. He turned to Charlotte, whose face had grown fixed and still while the others were talking. "Miss Hicks! What are your positive assets?"

"My thirty-five years of teaching," Charlotte retorted in her clipped schoolteacher's voice. "Methods of teaching change, of course, and my eyesight isn't as good as it used to be. But what made me a good teacher is still in me. My age is the one unpardonable sin."

Minerva Neilson stood up and sorrowfully took the floor. "I was a columnist for thirty years. My column in our hometown paper was the first thing anybody read. When the editor died, his grandson took over. 'We need a change,' he said. 'We want something new.'" She wiped her eyes with her knuckles like a child. "The young have overrun the world."

"All that you ladies have said only accentuates the importance of thinking positively," the professor concluded. "The body weakens with the years, hearing, sight and speed lessen, but the power to serve is ageless...."

And so we went from week to week. Professor Stone would open every session with a smile, greeting us approvingly, secure in the confidence that our project was the opening wedge in an entirely new approach to the problems of old age. He reassured us that as a result of the facts that were being recorded, a revolution against compulsory retirement would be initiated. Facts, the professor said, "have a power and vitality of their own." By way of reply, Minerva Neilson stood up one day in class, her scarf as usual thrown with studied artlessness over her shoulders, and told the professor that if she did succeed in getting a book published, she'd dedicate it to him. Grateful and embarrassed, the professor seized his briefcase and dismissed us five minutes early.

The tape recorder never stopped purring. What is "intelligence in the old"? What is "creative maturity"? How can we learn to "think constructively"? Our discussion trailed off into abstractions and the professor's words sailed higher and higher over our heads. If we could only stop talking, I thought sometimes, and meet in silence as the Quakers do, then maybe he would finally understand.

The dreaded last day of the seminar came. Professor Stone walked in, smiling as always. "Are old people too close to death to be able to talk about it freely?" he began. "A social worker told me to avoid the subject when speaking to the aged. But your attitude toward death is an important aspect of our inquiry, so I deferred the question until we had the broadest possible orientation."

As usual, Charlotte Hicks, the youngest, was the first to speak. "I could die tomorrow. It wouldn't matter. Nobody needs me; nobody would care." She was suddenly on her feet. "I just can't stand the sight of old people! Why don't they just finish us off quickly, instead of prolonging our uselessness!"

The professor's pencil point broke with a loud snap. It was out at last! An odd, reckless excitement possessed the room. At last, after all those months of talking, somebody had said what we all felt. (Were we jealous of Charlotte's comparative youth? Were we glad to discover that she was in the same boat with the rest of us? Perhaps—but there was more to it than that.) Charlotte snapped off her glasses and tapped them lightly against her hand. "From childhood on I was taught to save—to save for a rainy day, to save for the future. Well, now I've got my pension—but what's the use of living without being able to work?"

Kathleen Monahan had the final say. "I can't quite imagine myself under the sod, not yet. There's an old saying: the young may die, the old must die—but not me." Why are we wasting time talking about death, I wondered. *How are we going to live until we die?*

Professor Stone fumbled with his papers, his face gray and tired as if all the old women in the room had inflicted their impotence on him. There was, regrettably, no time to answer these questions, he said. The fact that we could still ask them, though, was encouraging. He glanced at his watch, took a deep breath, and offered us his concluding remarks. We had started something that, developed and expanded, might lead to great changes in ways of dealing with the problem of old age. Our discussions and case histories were only the first of a series, and these already comprised over a thousand pages of data. When these were analyzed and collated, a report would be drawn up that would no doubt be of great benefit to future students of gerontology. This was only the beginning. He thanked us for the insights he had gained from our seminar and expressed the hope that it had been "a profitable year for us all." One by one we bade the professor good-bye, and filed out.

Unwilling, or afraid, to disperse, we made our way as a group to the school cafeteria. We sat around a table, mute as mourners, sipping tea. "We talked our heads off—for what?" asked Kathleen Monahan.

"For a thousand pages of research," I replied.

"He had a job to do and he did it," said Alice, calmly.

"So our seminar was only a job to him?"

"We were only statistics to him," said Charlotte Hicks. "Dots on a graph." Methodically she began tearing the pages from her notebook, watching them flutter to the ground.

"His heart," said Minerva Neilson, "is wired to a tape recorder."

Kathleen Monahan stood up and took hold of her shopping bag. "What dopes we were. A whole year wasted, only to find out the professor don't know nothing."

"What did you want him to do?" Alice asked. "Be God? Make us young again?"

"Where do we go from here?" I asked.

A Chair in Heaven

I met Sara Rosalsky's daughter, Mrs. Hyman, at the home of a friend where I was baby-sitting. One day she asked me to work for her.

"I need someone to sit with my mother. She is seventy-nine, has nothing to do all day, and she has to have someone to talk to. My brothers don't have time for her, so it's up to me."

Mrs. Hyman hesitated a moment. She gave me a long reflective look before she went on. "You're almost my mother's age, you'd be wonderful company for her, and I'd pay well. I'm a nervous wreck, and I must have a rest. I need someone to sit with her a few times a week. Would you do it?"

She offered to pay five dollars a visit, and I needed those few extra dollars. I agreed to visit her mother Monday and Wednesday afternoons.

Mr. and Mrs. Hyman called for me in their car the next afternoon.

"We'll introduce you as a friend," Mrs. Hyman said on our way to her mother's house. "Mamma loves to talk about herself. All you have to do is listen—"

"But for heaven's sake," Mr. Hyman added apprehensively, "don't let on that you're being paid." He took a ten-dollar bill from his wallet and handed it to me. "This covers today and next Wednesday."

The old lady met us at the door. She gave her daughter a swift, disapproving glance. "Another new suit?" She fingered the cloth of the sleeve appraisingly as her daughter jerked away. "Well, it's good stuff, but the style ain't for you. It makes you look like a barrel of potatoes." Then she saw me. Her gray eyes, oddly young in her deep-wrinkled face, lighted in glad surprise.

"Who is this? Come in! Come in! Don't stand there at the door!" Limping on her cane, one leg stiff with arthritis, she led the way to the living room.

Alongside Sara Rosalsky's tall, wiry figure, Mrs. Hyman looked short and dumpy, over-shadowed by her mother's extraordinary vitality.

"How's my big girl today?" Mr. Hyman kissed his mother-in-law on both cheeks with resounding smacks. Mrs. Hyman retreated into a corner as far away from her mother as possible, took her knitting out of the bag and began clicking her needles.

"This is a friend of ours, a writer," Mr. Hyman waved toward me, proudly. "She heard about your charities for widows and orphans. So she wanted to meet you."

Sara Rosalsky's rapacious gray eyes took swift inventory of the lines in my face, the shabbiness of my hat, the darned patches at the elbows of my sweater. "So you're a writer?" I felt her looking me over with the same intensity with which she had appraised the cloth of her daughter's suit. "If you are really a writer, then I got for you a story! My own story!" She reached for a leather-bound scrapbook and handed it to me. "Read! Read only who I am!"

Yellowed clippings were pasted down with scotch tape. "Sara Rosalsky, President of the United Sisters"... "Sara Rosalsky Donates $5,000"... "Sara Rosalsky"... "Sara Rosalsky." I closed the book and looked at her.

"Now you see who I was! And I'm still not yet dead!" Her voice grew shrill, as if she were still fighting at the pushcarts. "Education I never had. I scrubbed floors, cleaned toilets, and collected garbage from a six-story tenement so my children should have college, so they shouldn't be, God forbid, tailors, janitors, or pushcart peddlers. I made one son a doctor, one a lawyer. And my daughter a schoolteacher—but not an old maid schoolteacher. That's why I cry to heaven, after all I did for them why should they leave me so alone?"

Mrs. Hyman's knitting fell to the floor. Her hands were clenched in her lap. "You're not alone now. We brought a friend. And you still complain. What more do you want?"

"How long since you were here? You leave your mother to die alone, like a dog in the street!"

"Shah! Shah!" Mr. Hyman put his arms around Mrs. Rosalsky. "You know Rose thinks the world of you. Why did she bring you her best friend? Come now! Let's have some tea with your wonderful apple strudel. Nobody can make apple strudel like you."

He got up from the overstuffed red velvet ottoman on which he had perched precariously, his short legs in hand-stitched gabardine slacks scarcely reaching the floor. Presently he reappeared with a big tray of steaming glasses of tea and a plate of apple strudel. The semblance of peace was restored.

As I drank my tea, I looked around. Fringes on the window shades, ruffles on the curtains. Shirred chiffon and lace adorned the lamp shades. Peacock feathers formed an arch over the huge gilt clock. All the rococo of the Bronx of fifty years before rioted here, in this room.

I glanced from the figurines and vases on the mantelpiece to the colorful scatter-rugs jostling one another on the red-carpeted floor.

"I see you like my things!" Mrs. Rosalsky nodded, pride of possession shining in her eyes. "I love color, beautiful things make me happy. Those are genuine peacock feathers," pointing with her cane. "And that clock comes from the palace of a Russian prince. It's worth a fortune! I got it at an auction for forty-nine fifty."

She leaned back in her chair, her eyes distantly focused, seeing past triumphs. "Ah-h! When I was young and had my health, I knew how to get bargains!"

"At whose expense, your bargains?" Savagely Mrs. Hyman pushed away her plate and threw open the window, as if choking for air.

Ignoring her daughter, Mrs. Rosalsky refilled my cup, and after insisting that I eat a second helping of strudel, she put the remaining piece in a napkin and smilingly handed it to me. "Here's something for you. Take it home—"

"Oh, no. Thank you—"

"Never mind thanking me, take it. Come soon again and I'll give you more."

As I was being driven home, I said to Mrs. Hyman, "Your mother is so alive for her age—"

"Yes. So alive that she wears us all out." Mrs. Hyman gave a long sigh. "That's why we need you."

The hoarded hurts of a lifetime rankled in her low, tight voice. "Mamma despises me because she neglected me. The days she went bargain-hunting at auction sales, I had to look after my brothers. But if a day passes and she has no one to talk to but the cleaning woman, she phones the neighbors that she's dying, abandoned by her children. She'll never die, she'll outlive us all—"

"No need to get hysterical," her husband laughed. "You know what the doctor said."

Mrs. Hyman turned to me. "She doesn't get under his skin the way she does with me. He can be nice to her."

"It's not everybody can do what she did with nothing," Mr. Hyman said with almost religious conviction. "In the Depression, when millionaires were jumping out of windows, she turned the hard times into a gold mine."

"But how did she do it?" Mrs. Hyman struck out angrily. "Painters, plumbers, carpenters were begging for work. God! How she wheedled and badgered them to rebuild that old rat-trap tenement! Labor and materials, everything—on credit—"

"Sure! She rode over people. She got what she wanted. And that's something not everybody can do. Not every janitress ends up owning five apartment houses."

Mrs. Hyman stared gloomily in front of her. "Just the same, when people say I resemble Mamma, I get frightened. I'd hate to be like her, even with all her money—not that I know how much she has."

Both mother and daughter had left a bad taste in my mouth, and I made up my mind not to take the job. But I had accepted advance payment for my next visit. I decided that it would be my last. However, the following Wednesday afternoon, when I walked in, Sara Rosalsky was so overjoyed to see me that my resolution faltered.

"Are you really here or am I dreaming?" The pleading tone of her voice was like a dog's licking of your hand, panting for affection. "How glad I am to see you! Did you maybe come for more apple strudel?"

"I came because I wanted to see you," I said.

"What a friend! What a pleasure is a friend when alone as I am alone."

She pointed to a red velvet armchair and sat down opposite in her rocker. Her white hair had a natural wave which set off her deeply lined but still handsome face. There was about her an ageless, elemental force hard to define. For a long moment she looked at me in silence. In that silence I saw myself in her eyes.

"Everybody is out to get something. But you're really a friend. You come to see me for myself. Even my own daughter comes only when she wants more money. But one good thing she did yet in her life—she brought you to me. The minute I saw you I felt I could talk myself out to you from under my heart."

The next morning Mrs. Hyman telephoned me. "You made a big hit with Mamma and you did a wonderful job for me. She says you're the only person who understands who she is. She is so proud to have a writer for a friend. Your check for next week is in the mail already."

I needed that check as desperately as Sara Rosalsky needed someone to talk to.

Weeks later, the daughter invited me to dinner. "It's a godsend to have you with Mamma," she said. "I used to be a nervous wreck when I had to see her. Now that she has you to talk to, she lets me alone. And I'm not a bit jealous." She laughed mirthlessly, but jealousy edged her voice as she went on. "I could never figure out Mamma's secret for making money. Even now, old as she is, and without lifting a finger, her real estate is going up. And the richer she gets, the more secretive she is. We know nothing about her will, yet her end might come any day."

But Sara Rosalsky, now that she had someone to talk to, instead of thinking of her end, reverted to her beginnings. "If you only could have seen me when I was young! It burned in me to do something, to work myself up in the world! My aunt who raised me, she hated me. To get away from her I married a man who could not even make a living. . . . I didn't know I was beautiful till the roomer next door asked to paint my picture. He looked like a prince. And I was afraid . . . you know men. They don't know when to stop. . . ."

She looked into the mirror. Her fingers caressed her withered cheek. "He said my skin was pure roses. . . . What a shape I had! Not like the skinny things these days! My bust! My hips!" Her hands rounded out her vanished curves. "And my husband was so jealous when men laid eyes on me! But I know God sees everything. And I was pure as an angel."

A smile, a furtive sense of humor glimmered in the corners of her eyes. "My daughter, poor thing, she isn't like me at all. I even had to get her a husband. My son Danny, the doctor, resembles me only in looks. But when it comes to brains, my son the lawyer has it. He's smarter than the others, but smart only for himself. If I'd trust him with my houses, I'd be in the street. God forbid I should have to ask him for a dollar."

Her torrent of emotion never abated. At every visit she bombarded me with another tale of herself. Together with the clippings and photographs in her scrapbook, her words made her seem less and less real, more and more like a record going around and around. . . . Often, against my will, I would doze off.

Sometimes pride in her achievements gave way to dark memories of her childhood in Poland. "I'd be better off to go begging by strangers than to be a *nebich*—a poor nobody—by my rich aunt. Never once a pair of shoes that fitted me! Everything a hand-me-down!"

The memory was an unbearable one. She opened the scrapbook.

"Look!" she cried exultantly, pointing to a faded photograph. "The United Sisters of the Fordham Temple, at a hundred-dollar-a-plate dinner, in honor of my birthday. Me! I gave it all to charity!" Prominent in the photograph was a huge banner, stretched above the speakers' table: "HAPPY BIRTHDAY! GOD BLESS OUR PRESIDENT SARA ROSALSKY!"

"Is there a joy on earth like the joy of taking your hand away from your heart to help the poor?" She beamed. "When I sent my birthday present, five thousand dollars, to the Federation, I felt like I bought myself a chair in heaven! And that's when I made my will."

She clasped her hands, gazing at her picture. "Where are they all? They used to come to me from everywhere, like to Mrs. Roosevelt, for my speeches, for my picture in the papers. I was a queen. Everybody smiled up to me. I had a million friends. And now, from all my friends I got only you."

She looked me over with affectionate tolerance.

"If I dressed you up you wouldn't know yourself."

With an effort, she pulled herself up on the cane, limped to the bureau, opened a drawer stuffed with scarves and shawls. She held up one shawl, then another, eyes gleaming. "You never ask for anything. And I like you so much I want to give you something." She wrapped a plaid silk shawl around me. "Why do you dress so plain, like a schoolteacher? This puts color in your face."

I looked in the mirror. The colors were so lovely. "Is it really for me?" I asked.

She felt the shawl with greedy fingers and snatched it off, whisking it into the drawer. "Oh no—this is handmade imported, from France—Paris! But I'll find you something you'll like." She rummaged in her crowded closet and pulled out a faded purple velvet hat with a rhinestone buckle and insisted that I try it on. It was no use attempting to convince her that I could never wear that hat. It was easier to accept than to argue her out of her benevolence. To reassure herself of her generosity, she insisted that I come to lunch the next day.

"You look like you don't eat enough. I'd like to feed you up."

I found the table set as for a feast.

"Is it a holiday?" I asked, surprised at the display.

"Your company is my holiday," she responded gaily. "You make me feel I'm still a person. You know how I can't sleep. But when you come, I forget all my worries and sleep like a child." She leaned over and took my hand in hers. "Tell me, dear friend! How would you like to live here with me?"

I looked at the nightmare around me. The peacock feathers, the gilt clock.

"Why should you pay rent for a hole in the wall when you can stay in my beautiful home and eat by me the best for nothing?" She piled more chicken on my plate. "I love company. If I could finish out my years with you, my friend, always near...."

She had a way of looking at me, seeing only herself. "Did I ever tell you how I started up in real estate with nothing but my two hands?" For the hundredth time she recited her rise from janitress to landlady. "Me, president of the United Sisters! And once I nearly starved to death! Such a story could go into the movies. You could make a fortune from writing my life—"

"Let me think it over," I said, slipping into my coat. She fingered the threadbare elbow of my sleeve. "Here! Let me give you carfare!"

Heretofore when she thought of carfare, she counted out the exact amount of change. Now she pushed a dollar bill into my hand. "Go in good health!"

I left, disgusted with myself for having accepted the dollar. At that moment I could understand the hate that Sara Rosalsky roused in her daughter, so that she had to hire me to substitute for her.

Waiting for the bus to take me home, I watched the branches of the trees against the autumn sky. "Nothing to do but listen," her daughter had said. Good God! The torture of listening to someone who cannot stop talking! By the time I got to my room the telephone was ringing. Mrs. Rosalsky in her imperious voice demanded, "Well, my good friend? How soon will you move over to me?"

My hand tightened into a fist as she went on. "You know me. What I want I want when I want it. And I want you by my side, the sooner the better."

"I'm sorry. No. No. I can't move—"

"Why?" she gasped, shocked into silence for a moment. Then she rushed on. "I can give you everything. I helped other people. I'd like to help you. I even got a cot all ready to put into my bedroom. In my beautiful home you'll have the best for nothing—"

"Thank you, but I have to live my own life in my own place," I said with finality.

At the usual time I went to get paid. Sara Rosalsky's daughter lived in a residence hotel on upper Broadway. Well-groomed people went in and out of the lobby. I picked up the house phone, asked for Mrs. Hyman. A moment later I heard her friendly, flustered voice.

"My brothers are here. You're just in time to join us for coffee and meet the rest of the family."

I was glad of her welcome, but in no mood to be scrutinized by her brothers. Though I could not live under one roof with Sara Rosalsky, I needed the money my two visits a week brought me. But knowing the daughter and son-in-law was enough. I did not want to get involved with the rest of the family.

They had finished eating and were sitting around smoking and drinking coffee when I walked in.

Mrs. Hyman drew up a chair for me. "Here's the friend that goes to see Mamma." She handed me a dish of plum pudding. "I knew you were coming, so I saved some dessert for you."

"And give our friend plenty of wine sauce," Mr. Hyman added.

The doctor, a slender, refined edition of his mother, smiled at me. "So you're the lady that Mother has taken such a fancy to?"

The lawyer held out a plump, manicured hand. "Sis has told us about you," he said in a mellow, cultivated voice. "I can easily understand Mother's liking you." Then turning to his sister, "Wasn't it wonderful that we found such a good friend for Mother?" As his appraising glance swept over me, I noticed his short, thickset figure smoothly draped in dark blue, and the fringe of graying hair about his baldness. I recalled his mother's words, "smarter than the others, but smart for himself."

Looking around, I was struck by the contrast between the color and clutter of Sara Rosalsky's over-crowded home and the fashionable austerity of the Hyman's apartment. Here an interior decorator had achieved something bloodless and impersonal. There was a deeper contrast in the faces. The children had their mother's sharp, strong features, but they were only pallid replicas of the mother's extraordinary vitality. The passion of desire which drove Sara Rosalsky had bled out between generations.

To my surprise they knew that their mother wanted me to live with her, and they tried to persuade me to do so.

"Just *like* Mamma to want you all to herself," Mrs. Hyman said. "But in a way it would be a relief if you could do it. The doctor said she may die in her sleep, or drop dead, any day. It would be a godsend for us all if someone like you were there to keep an eye on her all the time—"

"But—" I protested.

"We'd pay you for a full-time job, so you could afford to keep your own little place," Mr. Hyman urged.

I felt the full force of their solicitude mobilized, closing in on me. But I was determined not to be pressed into giving up my entire time to Sara Rosalsky, and so I told them I could only continue the usual two afternoons a week.

It was not until weeks later, when I had stopped in at Mrs. Hyman's for my check, that their real motives emerged.

Mrs. Hyman was serving me tea and cake when she leaned over confidentially. "I feel close enough to you now, after all these months, to be quite frank with you." She smiled nervously, imploring sympathy. "You know how secretive Mamma is. What we've never been able to find out is what she's worth. And yet her end may come any day."

It was all I could do to conceal my embarrassment at what her words implied.

"We all look upon you now not only as Mamma's friend, but as a friend of the family." She pushed her chair closer and clutched my hand with some of her mother's urgency. "You could help us enormously if you could get Mamma to talk to you about her will."

Something in my expression must have communicated itself to her. She suddenly stopped talking. But after a pause, she added desperately, "It's only reasonable! If we knew where we stood, we could plan a little better. Don't you see?"

I saw only too well. But by now I was so deeply implicated, so enmeshed in guilt, that I saw no way out. If I gave up the job suddenly because I hated the hypocrisy of posing as Sara Rosalsky's friend, she would be very much hurt. If I got the courage to tell her the truth, that I was being paid for every visit she thought to be the visit of a friend, wouldn't that shatter her? But if I remained on the job, I could never do what the daughter was really paying me to do. Now I realized how that first advance payment to pose as a friend had drawn me into Sara Rosalsky's struggle with her children. Anxiety over my involvement grew with my curiosity as to how it would end. With each succeeding visit I found myself caught more and more in a strange double role—employed by the daughter, but wanting to shield the mother from the very thing for which the daughter had hired me.

Mrs. Hyman had always been prompt in mailing the advance payments the times she made no arrangements for me to come to her apartment for a chat. Suddenly, one Monday morning, the check that I had been counting on failed to come. It was inconvenient, but I did not allow it to worry me. But when a week had passed and there was still no check, I was so disturbed that I stopped at Mrs. Hyman's before going to Sara Rosalsky. Over the house phone she sounded harassed and preoccupied. "Oh, it's you? I have your check. I'm on my way down. Please wait there for me."

A few minutes later she came out of the elevator and greeted me with a fixed smile which belied the anxiety in her eyes.

"I've been planning to talk to you," she said, opening her purse and handing me a check. "I might as well tell you right off—it won't be possible to keep you on with Mamma any longer."

I was too startled to say anything.

"You've done Mamma a lot of good. I know she'll miss you. But to carry you any longer is a luxury we can't afford. I've already told Mamma that you've been called to Boston, so she shouldn't pester you with telephones. I'm in a hurry to go to her right now."

I scarcely heard her. I thought only of getting away. I walked the streets hardly knowing where I was going. An hour later, entering the subway, I discovered the check still clenched in my hand.

By the time I got back to my room I had recovered sufficiently to feel vastly relieved. I had been magically freed from an exhausting hell of a job. And I had been paid. I told myself it was for the best.

But as the days passed, I could not get Sara Rosalsky out of my mind. I tried to reason with myself—you were hired, now you're fired, and that's that. But I could not reason myself out of my need to know what was happening to her. She is so alone, a voice within me pleaded. Her children are only waiting for her to die. She has no one but me. I have to go to her. Why so hot on the trail? another voice demanded. What's in it for you? If I abandon her, I abandon myself, my conscience cried.

What had started out as a casual job had become, despite all my resistance, a deeper commitment. You can be fired from a job, but not from a relationship. Yet when I tried to define for myself the relation that existed between Sara Rosalsky and me, I was plunged into a deeper muddle of confusion than on my first visit more than a year before.

I'd wake up in the middle of the night and, in a sudden burst of clarity, hear Sara Rosalsky's voice: "Take a good look at yourself!" As in a dream I saw that Sara Rosalsky was myself, the shadow I had left behind me, the shadow of father, mother, brothers and sisters—the relationships I had uprooted in my search for the life I had never found.

When I went to Sara Rosalsky, after a week's absence, my chief concern was to protect her from the knowledge that my friendship had been hired.

The cleaning woman answered my knock and showed me in. Sara Rosalsky sat in her high-backed chair by the window, staring into space, as if she had lost all contact with her surroundings. The shade was down. Even in the near-darkness I noticed how she had suddenly shrunken. Her nose, her cheekbones stood out sharply. Her eyes were sunk deep in her head.

I glanced quickly at the large, garish portrait of her that I had been called upon many times to admire. The artist had caught something ruthless and indomitable in the young eyes, and in the resolute mouth the fierce obsession of a will to possess—the hunger for love which strives only to conquer. I looked at the face of the dying old woman. Youth, beauty, ambition had come to this.

She mumbled to herself. "With what did I sin? I wanted my children should be smarter than me. College I gave them. Now, my enemies. Why is God punishing me?"

Suddenly she looked up at me.

"Now you come! Now!" she lashed out accusingly. "How could you go away to Boston without telling me? I thought you were my friend, I told you everything! But it didn't touch you! I was talking to a stone." Her outburst gave way to an anguished wail of helplessness.

Peering at me suspiciously, she said, "Did I just talk myself into it that you were my friend?"

Before I could frame my reply, she began fumbling at a tissue-wrapped parcel on the table. "I didn't think you'd come any more. And yet I still hoped. I wanted to give you this." And she thrust at me the shawl with which she had been unable to part a few weeks before.

"There is a God, isn't there?" She fixed the searching sharpness of her eyes on me. "Who makes life? Who makes death? Everything that lives must die. My time has come. I want to die."

She waved a hand at the bottles on the table. "There's enough there to finish me." The ghost of a smile turned into a look of despair. "In God's name! Save me from my children! Please, my friend, help me get into an old people's home! I want to die near people!"

Mrs. Hyman flared up like a maniac when I told her what her mother wanted. "A home for Mamma? She's insane! After all we did for her! Why should a home get the money?" It was as though I had put a match to gunpowder and the resentments of a lifetime exploded. "Senile! Mamma has been senile for the last ten years. Only her terror of dying keeps her alive. She's due for a stroke any day. She keeps going to spite us!"

Early next morning I was roused from sleep by the ringing of the telephone.

"My friend! My only friend! Come!" Sara Rosalsky implored. "Don't wait till I'm dead. They did it. They doped me. They moved me to a hotel where lives my son the doctor."

The door was partly open when I got there. She was in bed, propped on pillows. Her face was gray; sweat gathered in the deep furrows of her forehead. She looked uprooted in the alien hotel room. A terrible sadness was in her eyes. It came from long ago. The unloved, unwanted child persisted to the end—naked, alone, facing death.

She motioned to the nurse at her bedside to leave. I sat down beside her, put my hand on hers.

"Look on the walls! Empty, cold as the grave!" Her voice cracked into a sob. "They tore me away from my things before I'm yet dead—my pictures, my clock, my peacock feathers. I lived with them so long, they were company."

A choking spell seized her. When she regained her breath she dozed off for a few minutes. Suddenly, her bosom began to heave like a bellows. She sat up in a fury of indignation.

"They think they got me in their hands, but even from the grave, I'll show them yet!" She paused for breath, then hurried on. "Nothing I left them! Nothing! Everything I have, more than a million, will go to an old people's home."

Her head sank on the pillow. Anger, resentment, her life-blood ebbed away. In the wide-open eyes, no longer demanding, no longer commanding, I saw the peace that had never been there before. I realized that I was still holding her hand. Little by little, the warmth was receding from her fingers.

The nurse came in, touched her forehead, lifted her wrist. "Dead," she whispered, pulling down the lids over Sara Rosalsky's eyes.

For years after her death, the children fought in the courts for their mother's millions. I could not care who won—the children or the charity with which Sara Rosalsky had hoped to buy for herself a chair in heaven.

A Window Full of Sky

A few blocks away from the roominghouse where I live is an old people's home. "Isle of the Dead," I used to call it. But one day, after a severe attack of neuritis, I took a taxi to that house of doom from which I had fled with uncontrollable aversion for years. Cripples in wheelchairs and old men and women on benches stared into vacancy—joyless and griefless, dead to rapture and despair. With averted eyes I swept past these old people, sunning themselves like the timbers of some unmourned shipwreck.

The hallman pointed out a door marked "Miss Adcock, Admissions." I rapped impatiently. Almost as though someone had been waiting, the door opened, and there was Miss Adcock trimly tailored with not a hair out of place. Just looking at her made me conscious of my shabbiness, my unbrushed hair escaping from under my crumpled hat, the frayed elbows of my old coat. She pulled out a chair near her desk. Even her posture made me acutely aware of my bent old age.

The conflict, days and nights, whether to seek admission to the home or to die alone in my room, choked speech. A thin thread of saliva ran down from the corner of my mouth. I tried to wipe it away with my fingers. Miss Adcock handed me a Kleenex with a smile that helped me start talking.

"I've been old for a long, long time," I began, "but I never felt old before. I think I've come to the end of myself."

"How old are you?"

"Old enough to come here."

"When were you born?"

It's such a long time ago. I don't remember dates."

Miss Adcock looked at me without speaking. After a short pause she resumed her probing.

"Where do you live?"

"I live in a roominghouse. Can anyone be more alone than a roomer in a roominghouse?" I tried to look into her eyes, but she looked through me and somehow above me.

"How do you support yourself?"

"I have a hundred dollars a month, in Social Security."

"You know our minimum rate is $280 a month."

"I've been paying taxes all my life. I understood that my Social Security would be enough to get me in here...."

"It can be processed through Welfare."

I stood up, insulted and injured: "Welfare is charity. Why surrender self-respect to end up on charity?"

"Welfare is government assistance, and government assistance is not charity," Miss Adcock calmly replied. "I would like to explain this more fully when I have more time. But right now I have another appointment. May I come to see you tomorrow?"

I looked at Miss Adcock and it seemed to me that her offer to visit me was the handclasp of a friend. I was hungry for hope. Hope even made me forget my neuritis. I dismissed the thought of a taxi back to the roominghouse. I now had courage to attempt hobbling back with the aid of my cane. I had to pause to get my breath and rest on the stoops here and there, but in a way hope had cured me.

The prospect of Miss Adcock's visit gave me the strength to clean my room. Twenty years ago, when I began to feel the pinch of forced retirement, I had found this top-floor room. It was in need of paint and plumbing repairs. But the afternoon sun that flooded the room and the view across the wide expanse of tenement roofs to the Hudson and the Palisades beyond made me blind to the dirty walls and dilapidated furniture. Year after year the landlord had refused to make any repairs, and so the room grew dingier and more than ever in need of paint.

During my illness I had been too depressed to look at the view. But now I returned to it as one turns back to cherished music or poetry. The sky above the river, my nourishment in solitude, filled the room with such a great sense of space and light that my spirits soared in anticipation of sharing it with Miss Adcock.

When Miss Adcock walked into my room, she exclaimed: "What a nice place you have!" She made me feel that she saw something special in my room that no one else had ever seen. She walked to the window. "What a wonderful view you have here. I wonder if it will be hard for you to adjust to group living—eating, sleeping, and always being with others."

"I can no longer function alone," I told her. "At my age people need people. I know I have a lot to learn, but I am still capable of learning. And I feel the Home is what I need."

As if to dispel my anxiety, she said, "If you feel you can adjust to living with others, then of course the Home is the place for you. We must complete your application and arrange for a medical examination as soon as possible. By the way, wouldn't you like to see the room we have available right now? There are many applicants waiting for it."

"I don't have to see the room," I said in a rush.

She pressed my hand and was gone.

About two weeks later, Miss Adcock telephoned that I had passed the medical examination and the psychiatrist's interview. "And now," she said, "all that is necessary is to establish your eligibility for Welfare."

"Oh, thank you," I mumbled, unable to conceal my fright. "But what do you mean by eligibility? I thought I was eligible. Didn't you say . . . ?"

In her calm voice, she interrupted: "We have our own Welfare man. He comes to the Home every day. I'll send him to see you next Monday morning. As soon as I can receive his report, we can go ahead."

The Welfare man arrived at the appointed time.

"I'm Mr. Rader," he announced. "I am here to find out a few things to complete your application for the Home." The light seemed to go out of the room as he took possession of the chair. He was a thin little man, but puffed up, it seemed to me, with his power to give or withhold "eligibility." He put his attaché case reverently on the table, opened it, and spread out one closely printed sheet. "Everything you say," he cautioned, "will of course be checked by the authorities." He had two fountain pens in his breast pocket, one red and one black. He selected the black one. "How long have you lived here?"

"Twenty years."

"Show me the receipts." He leaned back in his chair and looked around the room with prying eyes. He watched me ruffling through my papers.

"I must have last month's receipt somewhere. But I don't bother with receipts. I pay the rent...they know me," I stammered. I saw him make rapid, decisive notations on his form.

"What are your assets?" he continued.

My lips moved but no words came out.

"Have you any stocks or bonds? Any insurance? Do you have any valuable jewelry?"

I tried to laugh away my panic. "If I had valuable jewelry, would I apply to get into the Home?"

"What are your savings? Let me see your bankbook." I stopped looking for the rent receipts and ransacked the top of my bureau. I handed him the bankbook. "Is that all your savings?" he asked. "Have you any more tucked away somewhere?" He looked intently at me. "This is only for the last few years. You must have had a bank account before this."

"I don't remember."

"You don't remember?"

Guilt and confusion made me feel like a doddering idiot. "I never remember where I put my glasses. And when I go to the store, I have to write a list or I forget what I came to buy."

"Have you any family or friends who can help you?" He glanced at his watch, wound it a little, and lit a cigarette, puffing impatiently. "Have you any professional diplomas? Do you go to a church or synagogue?"

I saw him making quick notes of my answers. His eyes took in every corner of the room and fixed on the telephone. He tapped it accusingly.

"That's quite an expense, isn't it?"

"I know it's a luxury," I said, "but for me it's a necessity."

He leaned forward. "You say you have no friends and no relatives. Who pays for it? Can you afford it?"

"I use some of my savings to pay for it. But I have to have it."

"Why do you have to have it?"

"I do have a few friends," I said impulsively, "but I'm terribly economical. Usually my friends call me."

I could feel my heart pounding. My "eligibility," my last stand for shelter, was at stake. It was a fight for life.

"Mr. Rader," I demanded, "haven't people on Social Security a burial allowance of $250? I don't want a funeral. I have already donated my body to a hospital for research. I claim the right to use that $250 while I am alive. The telephone keeps me alive."

He stood up and stared out the window. Then he turned to me, his forehead wrinkling: "I never handled a case like this before. I'll have to consult my superiors."

He wrote hastily for a few minutes, then closed the attaché case. "Please don't phone me. The decision rests in the hands of my superiors."

When the door closed, there was neither thought nor feeling left in me. How could Miss Adcock have sent this unseeing, unfeeling creature? But why blame Miss Adcock? Was she responsible for Welfare? She had given me all she had to give.

To calm the waiting time, I decided to visit the Home. The woman in charge took great pride in showing me the spacious reception hall, used on social occasions for the residents. But the room I was to live in was a narrow coffin, with a little light coming from a small window.

"I do not merely sleep in my room," I blurted out. "I have to live in it. How could I live without my things?"

She smiled and told me, "We have plenty of storage room in the house, and I'll assign space for all your things in one of the closets."

"In one of the closets! What earthly good will they do me there?" I suddenly realized that it would be hopeless to go on. Perhaps the coffin-like room and the darkness were part of the preparation I needed.

Back in my own place, the sky burst in upon me from the window and I was reminded of a long-forgotten passage in *War and Peace*. Napoleon, walking through the battlefield, sees a dying soldier and, holding up the flag of France, declaims: "Do you know, my noble hero, that you have given your life for your country?"

"Please! Please!" the soldier cries. "You are blotting out the sky."

Take Up Your Bed and Walk

For weeks, months, day in and day out, night in and night out, I had wrestled with the tangle of contradictions in my story, "A Window Full of Sky"—whether to die alone in my room in the roominghouse or seek help in an old people's home.

By the time the story was published, I no longer cared where or when I would die. Readers sent me letters. I could not answer any of them. Their praises seemed like flowers on a grave, lovingly tendered but powerless to rekindle the spark of life.

Then came a letter that called for an answer:

In my first year in high school our English class studied one of your short stories in an anthology of literature. I presumed you long dead and was quite pleased to read your recent piece.

I am now at New York Theological Seminary, in charge of the

Student Speaker's Bureau. I would like to have you speak to us about growing old in New York.

Our students have a long history of involvement in social problems of our city, although admittedly more often in the area of race and youth, but I think we could all profit from your visit.

The day before I had been hopeless, I could not see well enough to use my typewriter, but this sudden chance to speak to the young was so exciting—I seized pencil and paper and wrote:

My dear young friend,

I was deader than death and your letter called me back to life. Although I'm eighty-nine years old, weighted down with centuries of fears and worries, I feel myself not fully born. An opportunity to speak to young people about growing old makes me feel there is still something for me to do before I die.

Since I'm not an experienced speaker, I'll begin by reading my story and go on to answer questions.

The date of my talk was arranged, and I was so happy I did not know myself. But soon the old fear and doubt began to shadow my light heart. What a fool I was to grab at the chance to speak when I knew how scared I was to face an audience. Worse than my oncoming blindness was my failing memory. I'd forget a word, or a name; a paralysis of language would block my thoughts.

Distraught, I reached for the phone and called my young friend. But by the time I heard his "Hello" I was too confused to know why I was calling. I managed to stammer, "My magnifying glasses will enable me to read my story. If I only knew the kind of questions they might ask, I wouldn't be so nervous."

"May I come to see you? We could talk it over."

"You mean you want to see me? Thank you! Thank you! Come tomorrow, come any time—" and I hung up without setting a definite time for his coming.

When a few days had passed and he did not come, I told myself he had only been polite; he would not come. Why would he want to see an old has-been whom he thought already dead? The fear in my voice must have driven him away.

I sat at my window, consoling myself with my bit of sky while drinking tea. "When you're old, it's no use wishing for anything else than what happens. He won't come, and I'm glad he's not coming. I no longer exist.

Man is but a thing of naught. His day passes away like a shadow. . . ."

The bell rang. I went on sipping tea. Another ring. I did not want to see anyone. The bell rang louder and longer. I refused to budge.

Before I knew how it happened, Youth appeared in the doorway. Eyes filled with light, eyes that possessed the sky, walked in ahead of him.

"Mrs. Yezierska?" came in a loud voice, leaning toward me as if I were hard of hearing.

He was so radiant I could only gape at him like a deaf-mute, gulping swallows of tea.

To ease his embarrassment and perhaps my own, he asked, "Would you let me have a cup of tea with you?"

I pointed to the sink. Instantly he was there. A cup was washed, a saucepan scoured, filled with water, and on the stove. He found the box of tea, fixed himself a cup, refilled mine, and sat down confidently on the hassock at the foot of my chair.

He drank his tea with such gusto that it made my own taste like wine. I laughed and talked without knowing what I was laughing and talking about. All at once he brought me back to earth.

"Would it be possible for you to speak a week earlier?" he asked. "The man who was to speak on the 23rd of November cancelled. Can you help us out by coming sooner?"

"I-I don't see why not," I stammered, too scared to show my delight. He had seen me—talked to me, and he did not reject me. He wanted me a week earlier!

When the door closed behind him, I walked over to the gas plate and picked up the pot. It looked brighter than it had ever been before. The elan of his youth was still in the air where he had stood. He had scoured the dinginess out of my room and left behind his joy of being alive.

All at once I felt so enriched, so bewitched by the pure loving-kindness of my young friend that the story I had planned to read at the seminary—the story of a frightened old woman begging for a place to die in an old people's home—was no longer me. I wanted to live again. I wanted to be born again. But where was there a place in the world for an old woman to make a new start?

If only I could talk this over with him, I thought. Hadn't he as much as said to me: "Old woman! Wake up and live! Take up your bed and walk! You have work to do before you die!"

The next morning, when the phone rang, I felt him at the other end of the wire, as if in answer to my need.

"Hello," I quavered in a low voice.

"May I bring my girl to see you?"

I managed to say only, "I would be delighted."

I glanced at the pail of suds and rags by the window. I wanted to clean my room and dress up in my best. But before I could do anything, I heard their young voices outside.

I forgot my crippling neuritis and rushed to open the door, too excited to care that my old face was still in my old clothes.

"Come, come in!" I greeted them with outstretched arms and pointed to the one easy chair in my small room. "You're the guest of honor—" I told the girl.

"But you're the hostess." With a quick pat she eased me into the chair and then they alighted on the hassock, arms around each other, looking up at me as if I were a person—somebody special.

"Shall we celebrate with a cup of tea?" Jeff asked.

Swifter than lightning they were at the sink. They were not aware that the gas plate was rusty and caked with grease, that the battered tea kettle was stained with soot. Nor did they see the wornout wreck of a human being whom they had beguiled with the magic of their youth.

"Look at us," I said. "Here we are drinking tea together like a happy family."

I put down my cup and stood up without my cane. "This feast of communication, this flow of soul which you youngsters have steeped into my tea, I'll remember as long as I live."

In spite of their embarrassed smiles, I rushed on. "Your first visit," I told the boy, "might have been out of curiosity. At best, it was a business visit to settle the date of my talk. But bringing your girl to meet me—" I clutched her arm. "God on earth!" I cried. "With the whole world before you, how did you have time to visit me?"

"Come, come, honey," she said, gently releasing my hand from her arm. "This is the first time Jeff and I had the chance to visit a real live author."

"A chronicler of the Jewish immigrant in America," Jeff added, quoting his high school essay.

As in a dream they had suddenly appeared, and as in a dream I heard myself say, "Ever since I got your invitation, I've been worrying about what part of old age would interest young people."

"Stop worrying," he said. "Anything you tell us about yourself will be great. It seems incredible that an immigrant could come here, not knowing a word of English, and in a few years become a successful writer." His eyes were aglow. "We native Americans haven't the guts to plunge blindly into the unknown and achieve the impossible as you did."

Oi-i weh! I thought ruefully. He admires my do-or-die bravado. A beggar on horseback who drove his horse to death.

"You've been to Hollywood, haven't you?" the girl broke in. "My grandmother was president of the Theta Sigma Phi sorority the year that you were voted the Most Successful Woman of the Year."

Suddenly their fairytale visit plunged me into the nightmare I had wrestled with the night before, the dream in which I relived the day I faced the Theta Sigma Phi sorority at Ohio State University. Even in my dream I felt the self-importance, the pride born of fear as the applause mounted. There was something to being famous, after all. Success was worth all it cost to achieve. If I were a nobody, they would never have listened to me. But because I had become somebody, I was able to give them something to think about.

I was handed a telegram which I put underneath the others. More congratulations. More good wishes. Another invitation to be the guest of honor at a charity drive. A cocktail party for a celebrity from England. I opened the last telegram casually and glanced at the words, "Mother is dying..."

I do not recall how I took the train to New York, how I found the ward of the Presbyterian hospital. Memory has cut away everything until I was face to face with Mother's dying eyes. Those eyes holding the depths of a soul that I had never before taken time to see.

My earliest dream of becoming a writer flashed before me. My obsession that I must have a room with a door I could shut. To achieve this I left home. And so I cut myself off not only from my family, but from friends, from people. The door that I felt I must shut to become a writer had shut out compassion, feeling for pain and sorrow, love and joy of friends and neighbors. Father, Mother, sisters, brothers became alien to me, and I became an alien to myself.

I was so lost in memories that I was not aware of the silence that had fallen between us.

"You look so thoughtful," the girl's voice came to me from miles away. "Are you thinking of another story you'll write?"

"When you're as old as I am, it takes more time and more labor to get less and less written."

The girl turned smiling to the boy, "Who says you're old? Oscar Wilde said, 'There is no such thing as old age.'"

"Oscar Wilde died at forty," I retorted. "I'm eighty-nine. When I was young, I was the world within myself. Writing was the life of my life. It was my way of being born again."

I paused, afraid to let myself go, fearing that I might drive them away. But once I had started talking, everything in me rushed out to them.

"Last night I could not sleep. I could not rest. And when I read what I had written the last years, I was horrified at the lifelessness of so much labor which ended in nothing. A new generation of writers has risen. They have no more need of me than I had need of the old when I was young."

In the turmoil of emotion that overwhelmed me, my false teeth loosened and threatened to fall out of my mouth. With both fists I pushed them back into place.

They looked at one another, trying not to see me. But in my panic I felt as if my false teeth had exposed the naked skeleton of my dying body.

The girl glanced at her watch. "We really had a lovely time, but we must be going. We've been here most of the afternoon."

"Gewalt!" I implored. "Must you go so soon?"

"We would like to stay longer but we don't want to get you tired," Jeff explained.

"Tired? I've never been more alive," I said. "He who saves but a single life saves humanity. The humanity you saved today was me."

"To be honest with you, we really have to go." The girl patted my hand gently. "I have to turn in a paper by tomorrow morning, and Jeff promised to go over it with me."

"Why... we've just started to be friends," I cried.

"Yes, yes," he said, hurrying her out the door. "But we really must go."

As the door closed behind them, I felt guilt and the pain of the unjustly condemned. A few days later, I received a handsomely wrapped gift box containing eight samples of imported English tea, with a brief note from his girl:

In hopes that others will enjoy tea with you as we did.

The Open Cage

I live in a massive, outmoded apartment house, converted for roomers—a once fashionable residence now swarming with six times as many people as it was built for. Three hundred of us cook our solitary meals on two-burner gas stoves in our dingy furnished rooms. We slide past each other in the narrow hallways on our way to the community bathrooms, or up and down the stairs, without speaking.

But in our rooms, with doors closed, we are never really alone. We are invaded by the sounds of living around us; water gurgling in the sinks of neighboring rooms, the harsh slamming of a door, a shrill voice on the hall telephone, the radio from upstairs colliding with the television set next door. Worse than the racket of the radios are the smells—the smells of cooking mixing with the odors of dusty carpets and the unventilated accumulation left by the roomers who preceded us—these stale layers of smells seep under the closed door. I keep the window open in the coldest weather, to escape the smells.

Sometimes, after a long wait for the bathroom you get inside only to find that the last person left the bathtub dirty. And sometimes the man whose room is right next to the bath and who works nights, gets so angry with the people who wake him up taking their morning baths that he hides the bathtub stopper.

One morning I hurried to take my bath while the tub was still clean—only to find that the stopper was missing. I rushed angrily back to my room and discovered I had locked myself out. The duplicate key was downstairs in the office, and I was still in my bathrobe with a towel around my neck. I closed my eyes like an ostrich, not to be seen by anyone, and started down the stairway.

While getting the key, I found a letter in my mailbox. As soon as I was inside my room, I reached for my glasses on the desk. They weren't there. I searched the desk drawers, the bureau drawers, the shelf by the sink. Finally, in despair, I searched the pockets of my clothes. All at once I realized that I had lost my letter, too.

In that moment of fury I felt like kicking and screaming at my failing memory—the outrage of being old! Old and feeble-minded in a house where the man down the hall revenges himself on his neighbors, where roomer hates roomer because each one hates himself for being trapped in this house that's not a home, but a prison where the soul dies long before the body is dead.

My glance, striking the mirror, fixed in a frightened stare at the absurd old face looking at me. I tore off the eyeshade and saw the narrowing slits where eyes had been. Damn the man who hid the bathtub stopper. Damn them all!

There was a tap at the door and I ignored it. The tapping went on. I kicked open the door at the intruder, but no one was there. I took my ready-made printed sign—Busy, Please do not disturb!—and hung it on the door.

The tapping began again—no, no, no one at the door. It was something stirring in the farthest corner of the molding. I moved toward it. A tiny bird, wings hunched together, fluttered helplessly.

I jumped back at the terrible fear of something alive and wild in my room. My God, I told myself, it's only a little bird! Why am I so scared? With a whirring of wings, the bird landed on the window frame. I wanted to push it out to freedom, but I was too afraid to touch it.

For a moment I couldn't move, but I couldn't bear to be in the same room with that frightened little bird. I rushed out to Sadie Williams.

A few times, when her door was open, I had seen parakeets flying freely about the room. I had often overheard her love-talk to her birds who responded to her like happy children to their mother.

"Mamma loves baby; baby loves mamma; come honey-bunch, come darling tweedle-dee-tweedle-dum! Bonny-boy dearest, come for your bath."

Her room was only a few doors away, and yet she had never invited me in. But now I banged on her door, begging for help.

"Who is it?" she shouted.

"For God's sake!" I cried, "A bird flew into my room, it's stuck by the window, it can't fly out!"

In an instant she had brushed past me into my room.

"Where's the bird?" she demanded.

"My God," I cried, "Where is it? Where is it? It must have flown out."

Sadie moved to the open window. "Poor darling," she said. "It must have fallen out. Why didn't you call me sooner!"

Before I could tell her anything, she was gone. I sat down, hurt by her unfriendliness. The vanished bird left a strange silence in my room. Why was I so terrified of the helpless little thing? I might have given it a drink of water, a few crumbs of bread. I might have known what to do if only I had not lost my glasses, if that brute of a man hadn't hid the bathtub stopper.

A sudden whirring of wings crashed into my thoughts. The bird peered at me from the molding. I fled to Sadie Williams, "Come quick," I begged, "the bird—the bird!"

Sadie burst into my room ahead of me. There it was peering at us from the farthest corner of the molding. "Chickadee, chickadee, dee, dee, dee!" Sadie crooned, cupping her hands toward the bird. "Come, fee, fee, darling! Come, honey." On tiptoes she inched closer, closer, closer, cooing in that same bird-voice—until at last, in one quick, deft movement, she cupped the frightened bird in her hands. "Fee, fee, darling!" Sadie caressed it with a finger, holding it to her large breast. "I'll put you into the guest cage. It's just been cleaned for you."

Without consulting me, she carried the bird to her room. A little cage with fresh water was ready. Shooing away her parakeets, she gently placed the bird on the swing and closed the cage. "Take a little water, fee, fee dear," she coaxed. "I'll get some seed you'll like."

With a nimble leap the bird alighted on the floor of the cage and dipped its tiny beak into the water.

"It drinks! It drinks!" I cried joyfully. "Oh, Sadie, you've saved my baby bird!"

"Shhh!" she admonished, but I went on gratefully. "You're wonderful! Wonderful!"

"Shut up! You're scaring the bird!"

"Forgive me," I implored in a lower voice. "So much has happened to me this morning. And the bird scared me—poor thing! I'll—But I'm not dressed. May I leave my baby with you for a while longer? You know so well how to handle it."

Back in my room, I dressed hurriedly. Why did I never dream that anything so wonderful as this bird would come to me? Is it because I never had a pet as a child that this bird meant so much to me in the loneliness of old age? This morning I did not know of its existence. And now it had become my only kin on earth. I shared its frightened helplessness away from its kind.

Suddenly I felt jealous of Sadie caring for my bird, lest it get fonder of her than of me. But I was afraid to annoy her by coming back too soon. So I set to work to give my room a thorough cleaning to insure a happy home for my bird. I swept the floor, and before I could gather up the sweepings in the dustpan, another shower of loose plaster came raining down. How could I clean up the dinginess, the dirt in the stained walls?

An overwhelming need to be near my bird made me drop my cleaning and go to Sadie. I knocked at the door. There was no answer, so I barged in. Sadie was holding the tiny thing in her cupped hands, breathing into it, moaning anxiously. "Fee, fee, darling!"

Stunned with apprehension I watched her slowly surrendering the bird into the cage.

"What's the matter?" I clutched her arm.

"It won't eat. It only took a sip of water. It's starving, but it's too frightened to eat. We'll have to let it go—"

"It's my bird!" I pleaded. "It came to me. I won't let it go—"

"It's dying. Do you want it to die?"

"Why is it dying?" I cried, bewildered.

"It's a wild bird. It has to be free."

I was too stunned to argue.

"Go get your hat and coat, we're going to Riverside Drive."

My bird in her cage, I had no choice but to follow her out into the park. In a grove full of trees, Sadie stopped and rested the cage on a thick bush. As she moved her hand, I grabbed the cage and had it in my arms before either of us knew what I had done.

"It's so small," I pleaded, tightening my arms around the cage. "It'll only get lost again. Who'll take care of it?"

"Don't be a child," she said, coldly. "Birds are smarter than you." Then in afterthought she added, "You know what you need? You need to buy yourself a parakeet. Afterwards I'll go with you to the pet store and help you pick a bird that'll talk to you and love you."

"A bought bird?" I was shocked. A bird bought to love me? She knew so much about birds and so little about my feelings. "My bird came to me from the sky," I told her. "It came to my window of all the windows of the neighborhood."

Sadie lifted the cage out of my arms and put it back on the bush. "Now, watch and see," she said. She opened the cage door and very gently took the bird out, holding it in her hand and looking down at it.

"You mustn't let it go!" I said, "You mustn't . . ."

She didn't pay any attention to me, just opened her fingers slowly. I wanted to stop her, but instead I watched. For a moment, the little bird stayed where it was, then Sadie said something softly, lovingly, and lifted her hand with the bird on it.

There was a flutter, a spread of wings, and then the sudden strong freedom of a bird returning to its sky.

I cried out, "Look, it's flying!" My frightened baby bird soaring so sure of itself lifted me out of my body. I felt myself flying with it, and I stood there staring, watching it go higher and higher. I lifted my arms, flying with it. I saw it now, not only with sharpened eyesight, but with sharpened senses of love. Even as it vanished into the sky, I rejoiced in its power to go beyond me.

I said aloud, exulting. "It's free."

I looked at Sadie. Whatever I had thought of her, she was the one who had known what the little bird needed. All the other times I had seen her, she had remembered only herself, but with the bird she forgot.

Now, with the empty cage in her hand, she turned to go back to the apartment house we had left. I followed her. We were leaving the bird behind us, and we were going back into our own cage.

Preface to the 1985 Edition of
Hungry Hearts and Other Stories

The original edition of *Hungry Hearts,* the first book Anzia Yezierska wrote, is republished here sixty-five years after its initial appearance. Added to it in this new volume are three unusual, uncharacteristic stories of hers, never reprinted or collected in a book before, which reflect on the beginning and end of Yezierska's career.

Houghton Mifflin first published *Hungry Hearts* in 1920, after one of its stories, " 'The Fat of the Land,' " appearing in a magazine the year before, was named the Best Short Story of 1919 by Edward J. O'Brien. *Hungry Hearts* earned for Anzia, who was my mother, an overnight fortune (more than $10,000, a dazzling sum in those days) when it brought her to Hollywood to work on the silent film Samuel Goldwyn's company made from her book. Her second book, *Salome of the Tenements,* also sold to the movies—for a larger sum, $15,000.

For the next ten years, during which she wrote four more books, Anzia was a celebrity. Newspapers frequently retold the fairy tale of how my mother rose from New York's Lower East Side ghetto to literary stardom. But with the Depression of the 1930s, she lost her audience and her money as well. In 1950 her seventh book, *Red Ribbon on a White Horse,* restored to her a small measure of literary recognition; and thereafter she wrote a striking group of stories and essays about old age—among them, the last story in this book, "One Thousand Pages of Research." They were not much noticed then; they are getting more attention today along with the rest of her writing.

Anzia has been rediscovered by feminists and social historians during the past ten years. As her daughter, I regret that this began to happen only after her death in 1970, but I experience a continuing and pleased surprise that she is turning out to be so contemporary. This first book of hers went out of print in the original edition about fifty years ago. Although some of its short stories (for instance, "How I Found America" and " 'The Fat of the Land' ") have been reprinted in new anthologies throughout the succeeding years—so many times as to become classics—and although a few libraries preserved the original edition with rebinding, it has been virtually unknown to most readers for half a century. The three stories added here show what happened to Anzia after the publication of *Hungry Hearts*.

"This is What $10,000 Did to Me" was published in the October 1925 issue of *Cosmopolitan* magazine five years after *Hungry Hearts* appeared, three years after its movie. Anzia tells in that story the consequences of making so much money from the book. She never overcame her guilt for having become rich by writing about the poor, nor her tragic sense of loneliness because she had changed her circumstances so drastically:

> Now...I look back and see how happy I ought to have been when I was starving poor but one of my own people. Now I am cut off by my own for acquiring the few things I have. And those new people with whom I dine and to whom I talk, I do not belong to them. I am alone because I left my own world.

"Wild Winter Love," which Anzia wrote at the height of her own success, about an author whose love and work had failed, appeared in the February 1927 issue of *The Century Magazine*. It is written with the intensity of emotion which had attracted the readers of *Hungry Hearts*, but also, I think, with a superior, confident craftsmanship which Anzia had gained in six years' time. She was by then an experienced writer, much in demand. The real-life model for this story, with whom Anzia felt a close connection, was Rose Cohen, the author of *Out of the Shadows*. That book about the hardships of Cohen's life in the New York ghetto was published two years before *Hungry Hearts*, arousing Anzia's admiration and envy. (In 1918, she was collecting only rejection slips.) But *Out of the Shadows*, Cohen's only book, did not receive the acclaim that *Hungry Hearts* received. Four years after her book was published, Rose Cohen attempted suicide by jumping into the East River. She was rescued and disappeared from public notice thereafter.

"One Thousand Pages of Research," published by *Commentary* in July 1963, shows the difference of thirty-five years in its tone. Anzia was about eighty-two years old in 1963, still writing social protests—in this case, against society's exclusion of the old—but the story is almost drained of emotion, detached. It is a report on a project she initiated at Columbia University: she persuaded a psychology professor and a group of elderly women to join in a seminar about old age. Narrating the results, she became, for the first time in her writing career, a cynic.

She continued, in her eighties, to write stories in this dispassionate vein. In 1962 and 1965 the National Institute of Arts and Letters presented her with awards of $500 each, stating: "This is given you in recognition of your distinction as a writer." These tributes from other writers, a few years before her death, briefly pierced the obscurity to which she had long since returned.

Louise Levitas Henriksen